«СПИ СПОКОЙНО, ДОРОГОЙ ТОВАРИЩ!»

(Фантастическая повесть)

MOSCOW NIGHTS

(*Sleep Soundly, Dear Comrade*)

A Fantastic Tale
by
VLAS TENIN

translated by
MICHEL LE MASQUE
from the Russian

THE OLYMPIA PRESS

Published by The Olympia Press, Inc.

For catalogs, mail order service,
and all inquiries, write:
220 Park Avenue South,
New York, N.Y. 10003

PRINTED IN THE UNITED STATES OF AMERICA

MOSCOW NIGHTS

«СПИ СПОКОЙНО, ДОРОГОЙ ТОВАРИЩ!»

(Фантастическая повесть)

“. . . in an age when mighty states are collapsing in ruins, when the old forms of rule are falling apart, when our whole social world is about to expire, in this age the sensibilities of the individual are swiftly being transformed. The overwhelming urge for variety and pleasure is acquiring irresistible force. The forms of marriage and sexual relations in the bourgeois sense no longer satisfy us. A revolution is coming in the realm of marriage and sexual relations that is in harmony with the proletarian revolution.”

LENIN

(From a conversation with Klara Tsetkin.)

Contents

1. Farewell to the Dear Departed

The funeral was marked with appropriate solemnity.

Who among the friends and relatives of Afanasy Leontyevich Kondratyev could have foreseen that his earthly travels would end so abruptly in a Moscow cemetery? Having, in the face of all the odds, climbed high up the ladder of an internal trade organization that had recently expanded abroad—which meant frequent trips to international fairs—Kondratyev (R.I.P.) had looked to the future with such bright expectations! The great advantages of his position, which promised only to grow greater with time, had already benefited both his family and those intimate friends who had gathered to make some return payment through this last homage.

It was blatantly obvious that Soviet trade had been kind to Afanasy Leontyevich, obvious in the elegance of the clothes worn by his young widow and most of the others present, obvious in the air of untouchable superiority that set these fortunate beings apart from the common herd. All this, of course, only added to the sense of loss the mourners felt, and the poignancy was heightened by a Moscow spring sky, so distant and delicately azure, in which a scattering of the downiest of clouds, light and high, delicately unfurled themselves.

The sun burned down more hotly. Feeling its radiance, fresh grass, new leaves and vines gathered strength, insinuated themselves into every corner of the graveyard to soften with their glowing greens the stark whites and grays of the tombstones.

Everywhere the plants were thrusting themselves through the iron fence. This was a remote, seldom used corner of the cemetery, where the poorly-tended graves were being overrun by springy bushes, where the trees crowded together almost hiding the paths. It was thanks to the friendly intervention of Esper Ozirisovich Tsanatovsky—head of the Moscow Funeral Bureau—that the family of the departed had managed to get a private plot where a small but tasteful monument might be erected to commemorate the achievements and to honor the memory of Kondratyev, taken so cruelly before his time by a heart attack.

Tsanatovsky's efforts had not been entirely due to friendship, of course. In order to come up with sufficient inducement, the widow had had to cancel an order for a coat that was to be made by a furrier friend from some excellent silver fox pelts her husband had obtained. (Let's not examine here how Kondratyev had come by the furs; let us merely note that he had been justified in doing so. They had been reserved for export, but he had been outraged that our fair consumers were being unjustly deprived of such beauteous items by trade organizations pandering to the corrupt bourgeois tastes of the West.)

As a further demonstration of his esteem, Tsanatovsky had asked for a token that would, as he put it, preserve "an evergreen memory of the departed" in his heart, namely Kondratyev's electronic watch, a priceless item rather discreetly brought back by its deceased owner from his last fair abroad. It had never been worn; Kondratyev had kept it in a safe place, considering it not only an excellent ego-builder but a valuable investment should he decide to place it on the domestic market. (It wouldn't do to dwell on the methods by which Kondratyev derived such benefits from his job, interesting as they might be as illustrations of the adroitness and keen wit of mankind; pale imitators might be tempted to reap the fruits of his inventive mind. Such secrets should remain the property of those who have earned them—the deserving servants of the Soviet import-export trade.)

With Kondratyev's grave almost completely filled in, everyone present had lapsed into respectful silence. The rumble of the city was muted in the presence of eternity. Only the compelling, vibrantly living beauty of the young widow—framed by somber faces, lilacs and graves—challenged the brooding atmosphere.

She stood somewhat apart from the others, her severe dress, despite the rigidity with which she held herself, only serving to emphasize the sensuousness of her delicate figure. Gazing in frozen disbelief at the pile of fresh earth, she appeared very young and fragile. Her dark, deep-set eyes, her sober, withdrawn countenance, were filled with a longing that might have been mistaken by a superficial observer for carnal lust—rather than the grief she felt. Suffering could not mask her beauty, endowing it instead, by some strange law of emotional compensation, with an incongruous, almost sacrilegious radiance.

A whisper ran through the group and, hesitantly, one of the men approached her. He was a gray, balding citizen who exuded an air of officious pompous authority. After speaking with her briefly in a low voice, he walked to the opposite end of the rectangle cut into the earth. This was Ivan Ivanovich, one of her husband's colleagues, who was to deliver the eulogy. He slowly raised his head and, fixing his gaze on some imaginary point in space, engulfed them in the rolling waves of his hoarse, somewhat grating voice.

"Dear comrades and friends, Afanasy Leontyevich Kondratyev has left us, abandoning his earthly concerns in too untimely a fashion. He is with us no longer. He has gone, leaving behind him a young, inconsolable widow, with whom he shared but two years of uxorial bliss. Our beloved Elena Filippovna looks distractedly about her, but nowhere does she find her devoted spouse. Her eyes search anxiously, but all she sees . . ." Ivan Ivanovich's voice choked and he rolled his eyes lugubriously. As he stumbled to a halt, as though following his instructions, Elena Filippovna's wandering gaze shifted to the thicket behind him. At first, she gave it only a vague, indifferent glance, but only for a moment. Then, incredulously, she focused her vision on one spot.

A pair of magnetic, arrogant eyes were staring back at her from the bushes between the grave and the masses of lilacs. Fixed on her alone, they radiated an intensity that filled all the surrounding space with a cold white light.

". . . and sees," Ivan Ivanovich continued, "absolute emptiness, an inexplicable void, as it were, which silently encloses her . . ."

It was as though she heard the words in a dream, distant and incomprehensible. Those compelling eyes were attacking her, taking her body. It seemed as though they wished to penetrate her, to devour her, completely ingest her. Unable to bear so all-consuming a visual embrace, Elena Filippovna lowered her eyes, seemingly searching the inner tranquillity her sorrow demanded.

She was appalled anew at what she now saw. What shocked her even more (setting her heart beating wildly at the very thought) was that the others could see too. But despite her horror, she seemed utterly incapable of action; she could not look away. Confronting her, sticking out from behind the funeral drapes, through the green half-shade of the foliage, was a huge, throbbing, distended, indecently human object consisting of scandalously scarlet flesh: a proudly erect male member.

This organ seemed to live an independent life of its own, admitting no connection with any body. Immense, powerful, its dimensions strained the imagination. And yet, considering the circumstances, it was somehow absurd, at the same time. Nonetheless, it contained within itself a kind of eternal reality; its clear, unbelievable summons evoked an echo in previously unsuspected depths of the young woman's soul. Incredibly, Elena Filippovna felt a sudden surge of relief and self-confidence. Her heart slowed, leaving only a throbbing in her temples; she no longer feared the others noticing. She and it—that triumphant, inviting member—were enclosed in an impenetrable wall.

She was being overwhelmed by a passion, a desire to see the whole of the tree that bore so dizzying, entrancing, so stupefying a fruit. Imperceptibly she raised her eyes, awed by this deluge of new emotions. Looking through the greenery where she had encountered that cold, piercing gaze, she could make out an insolent young face that displayed a mixture of ennui and cruelty. Full, curved lips smiled at her mockingly; a mop of fair hair crowned the head with childish curls. Elena Filippovna gasped, and broke into bitter sobs.

". . . But your sorrow, dear Elena Filippovna," Ivan Ivanovich droned on, reciting his speech, "will be completely vanquished by the mighty winds which fill the sails of our socialist state. The wonderful successes of our Soviet industry, in which your late husband, our friend and comrade played such a part, make it wrong for us to lock ourselves within the prison of our own private, personal emotions. Moreover, permit me to say, without offending the tears of our deeply respected Soviet widow, that from her example (*your* example, dear widow) one can be reassured of the superiority of the Soviet ethic, staunchly leaning upon the strength of the collective, of which every one of us is merely a member . . ."

"*Member . . . member . . .*" The word echoed in her ears. Taking a grip on herself, gradually calming down, she stared at the orator in disbelief. *No!* she thought. Ivan Ivanovich was no *member*—other than a paid-up member of the Party and possibly one or two other organizations. Her husband had been that kind of member too.

But here in front of her was a true *member*. Not a member of something or other. It was an emblem, not merely some man who had sprung from the earth or descended from the sky to confront her through the dappled leaves, and it was clearly no part of the world inhabited by Ivan Ivanovich or by any of the others standing behind her.

What she had been made to see, and *he* knew she had seen it, was so sudden a revelation to her, so total and all-encompassing a liberation that she had instantly buried all else; her life had just now begun. Why could she not be alone with him? Ivan Ivanovich would drone on forever. She shifted her devouring, heavy gaze from the man's derisive smile back to his swollen organ, flashing between the light and the shadows. A barely perceptible tremor passed across her lips and somehow, involuntarily, her left toe curled upward. Then a hand emerged from the greenery and attached itself to the organ, remaining motionless for a moment before, suddenly, with a two-finger grip, it began to stroke it up and down.

The movement went on and on. Elena Filippovna had no idea how long it lasted; for her, it seemed an eternity. For it was not only the three-dimensional reality of what she saw that enchanted and enthralled her. Burning waves flowed to her from the huge, coruscating organ and its attendant hand, suffusing her whole being. A piercing tension tautened her breasts painfully, electrifying her nipples, engorged her legs and stomach in languor, penetrated the softness between her legs, her secret recess, and inflicted an unbearable sensation of burning heat on the seat of her femininity.

The organ, she saw, was still growing, swelling to incredible proportions; the gleaming cylinder of flesh, a contrasting lilac in the green foliage, emerged from the shadow of those two fingers, slippery, bloodfilled, ready to glide across the ground or plunge straight into the depths—the obscene and monstrous image of forgotten dreams. The nervous hand moved faster and faster in that single, repeated, voluptuous motion. Elena Filippovna was alone, face-to-face, with this monster; and it was no longer just before her, something removed, but was *in* her. She was no longer its objective but a part of it, totally joined with it in a unified transport of triumphant passion.

An impenetrable silence surrounded her; a dull roar filled her ears. Somehow, Elena Filippovna was still able to distinguish the words which flowed monotonously from the orator's mouth, words that seemed to take flight like a flock of small, gray birds, circling her head and then silently vanishing behind her. She was conscious of her friends and relatives to her rear, but they were all on the far side of the border she had crossed. They were still at the graveside where she had stood with them some thousands of years earlier. For her, all was totally changed.

The layer of corpses had sunk through the ground and in their place life had sprung upwards seeking the sun, emerging as an enchanted garden. Defying the laws of time, it had all happened *instantly*, in a single moment exposing the eternal processes of death, decomposition, organic transformation, and renewal. What was its meaning, this primitive member that had miraculously appeared between tombstone and foliage? By what grace had it been granted to her, surrounded by tragedy, to see the face of the unknown youth, to see his hand, explosively controlling body and blood alike?

Mercy had descended upon her and she was triumphantly reborn; mercy swallowed her whole being to liberate it for baptism, the primal eucharist: the first orgasm. Quick, nervous fingers in a growing frenzy squeezed that huge cylindrical mass of cells, trembling, quivering, until it finally exploded in a celebration of light and life. Simultaneously, something within her tore free of her control, rolled and squeezed her in a prolonged spasm, drawing from her a suppressed cry. A blade of fire plunged between her legs and pierced her throbbing temples with its points—and a wind of joy she had never known cooled her and brought with it peace.

"Elena Filippovna," repeated the eulogist, clearly about to bring his funeral oration to a close, "permit me to recall you from the depths of your sorrow and prostration. Remain with us, who are close to you; with us, who will cherish forever the memory of your vanished happiness and of this never-to-be-forgotten moment when you . . ."

He was unable to finish the sentence. A look of total disbelief passed over his face and, whatever his last words were, they were drowned by noise, laughter, yells, and the piercing shrill of an insolent harmonica. Ivan Ivanovich stood there, frozen, while the others followed the direction of his distracted gaze. Before they could begin to comprehend what was happening, they were surrounded by a pack of youths, boys and girls, dressed in the costumes of the degenerate Western "hippies." They were leaping and dancing hysterically, while two slashed away at guitars.

Esper Ozirisovich tried unsuccessfully to stop them. "Quiet, please! Stop this, citizens! Don't you understand what's going on? This is scandalous! The deceased . . ."

A handsome young man in his late twenties looked at him coldly. "Fuck you, dad. You know you old bastards aren't supposed to be here. You got the word. We've had this planned for a long time. The sanitation people earned the right to have their party here. They worked for it, not like you shit-eating parasites playing at religion. I'll bet this . . ." He gestured at the grave and funeral party, ". . . is illegal anyway. Now, move! Get out of here!" He feinted at Esper Ozirisovich, as though he were going to attack him.

"Please, citizens!" the older man said fearfully, "just give us a moment. Our ceremony is over, really. Let's not . . ." He hastily backed away, trying to hide himself among the other mourners as a knife appeared in the young man's hand. "Just allow me one more word, please!" He was anxious to convince the revelers that he was not a religious hypocrite, nothing of the sort, indeed! "You must understand that the deceased was a director, a leading figure in one of the more important administrative organizations, and I, as a friend and colleague. . . ."

"All right! All right!" the spokesman interrupted. "Now, out! Save your explanations!" The rest of his band were closing in on the mourners, mouthing foul curses and blowing cigarette smoke into the women's faces—all this, you understand, to the accompaniment of strumming guitars and shrilling harmonicas. "Help them get moving!" the leader shouted. "There are enough stiffs around here already!" He looked at Esper Ozirisovich again. "Out!"

Hooting and howling, the youths began to herd the already scurrying mourners down the paths that led to the gate. Elena Filippovna's friends formed a close ring around her to protect her in her sorrow, totally unaware, of course, that her grief had already been dissipated, even before the gang's arrival. Sorrow was no longer what she felt; pushed along, she barely had time to bestow one final fond glance upon the spot where, among the leaves and behind the obelisk, the miracle had occurred. No one was there now of course; there was only a leaf to catch her eye, gleaming in the sun, a leaf bending down beneath the weight of a heavy drop of whitish liquid. She had no time to see more, and allowed herself to be led away.

"Wait a minute!" the gang's leader shouted.

Ivan Ivanovich, prisoner to his conditioned reflex of automatic obedience, halted. As he turned to look back, the others came to a stop too.

"The princess stays. She deserves a little fun." He accompanied his words with a gesture that left no doubt about what "fun" consisted of. He advanced on Elena Filippovna and Ivan Ivanovich reluctantly moved to protect her. The others exchanged frightened glances.

"Sidor!" The cool, sarcastic voice brought the young man to a stop. "What the hell do you think you're doing? Take my advice and quit fucking around. These people are under my protection."

The stranger who had suddenly intervened was a young man of about twenty-five. He wore dark trousers and a light-blue shirt. His corn-colored hair framed a typically Slavic, rather childlike face. His clear, cold, blue eyes gave him a cruel, almost unpleasant expression, emphasizing the disdainful set of his mouth and the premature wrinkles under his eyes and at the corners of his mouth.

Holding himself rigidly erect, he stood by the new grave, clearly confident he would be obeyed. And, in fact, Sidor, who had pushed Tsanatovsky aside and was about to pull the young widow away from her friends, immediately dropped his hands and actually thrust them behind his back, completing the gesture with an exaggerated bow to the newcomer.

"All right, all right, Timur. No harm done. I wasn't planning to steal your princess. It was only a joke." And turning to his companions, he shouted, "Come on, gang, let's hear some music! Get to work on those guitars!"

Elena Filippovna, up to that moment, had not been able to grasp the situation; but from the time the blond youth appeared she had not taken her eyes off him. She stared at him, shocked. The same eyes! The same insolent expression, which never left his face, altering neither for his former ecstasy nor for his present sarcasm. The same man! He flicked her with a quick glance. His cold, clear eyes didn't change but it seemed to her that his lips curled in an ironic smile.

Then he turned away.

Everyone hurried to follow Ivan Ivanovich and Esper Ozirisovich Tsanatovsky along the paths. Behind them, two guitars rent the air, and the youths and their girls bawled out the tune discordantly, parting their ranks for the departing mourners with comically exaggerated respect.

We met at dusk;
She was very bold.
Was it with lips or hands
That she took me?

I melted like candy,
Fell in love—like a fool,
ready to carry her foul body
away in my arms.

And I could hardly wait
till the day, when she came
all broad and flat she was,
just like a flounder.

Timur walked up to the gang's leader. "I'll see you soon. We have business to discuss."

"At your service, Timur," he replied with formal respect, but there was irony in his tone. The mourners, scurrying down the path, were too far away to hear these last words. Timur turned and ran after them.

Catching up with Tsanatovsky, he exclaimed, "That was really disgraceful! No respect for the dead. Turning a Soviet cemetery into some kind of a delinquents' playground. That kind just have no respect for decent people. Steps are going to have to be taken; we'll have to get together on this, Esper Ozirisovich. As a matter of fact, you ought to know something's already in the planning stages."

"We are most grateful to you, Timur Anatolyevich," Tsanatovsky replied. "Not only I personally but all those present, especially the unfortunate widow. Isn't that so, Elena Filippovna?" He turned to her. "May I introduce you?"

But she remained silent, averting her eyes.

"Please forgive her," Tsanatovsky said. "She's really overwhelmed with grief, you know, and after what's happened here . . ."

"I understand," Timur assured her. "May I ask who the deceased was?"

"Afanasy Leontyevich Kondratyev, both a friend and a highly respected man."

"Ah, well, well," Timur said a little too casually. "But remember, something is being planned that will interest you. Meanwhile, good-bye."

He shook hands with Tsanatovsky and tried unsuccessfully to meet the eyes of the widow who had hidden herself among her friends. He bowed slightly to the others and made his own way to the exit.

2. *Meetings in a Restaurant*

Outside the cemetery gates, Timur turned right, and then right again, entering a quiet dead-end alley where his Volga waited. He always left his car at a discreet distance from his destination.

He looked around carefully. No. There was no special reason to worry about it; but it was always better to be extra-careful. Timur typified a type endemic to civil service—here, there, everywhere. Reassured, he strode purposefully to the car, and slipped behind the wheel.

It was three p.m. He rode straight through the city, cutting across noisy, crowded streets which, at that hour, overflowed with people. And he let his thoughts wander . . . So, her name is Elena Filippovna Kondratyeva. It rang no bell. Kondratyev must have been a comparative nobody among directors-of-projects . . . but, then, judging by Tsanatovsky's speech—and he was actually the Director of the Bureau of Funerals—Kondratyev couldn't have been quite *that* unimportant. And yet . . . the funeral party had been so small, only relatives and close friends; and not one official speech—all of which indicated that the dead man couldn't have been very highly regarded. Which meant . . . which meant . . . ah, well. Esper Ozirisovich's motives for appearing must have been personal. But really, what difference did it make? It was the widow who was important, not her ex-husband.

How violently she'd reacted! The bitch had almost sucked

him into her. There she was, so delicate, so fragile in her widow's weeds, so serious, so grief-stricken . . . but, in actuality there was something primal about the creature! Damn it, it was *she* who'd captured *him*! He never bared his prick like that unless there was something special about the person; it had to be someone who could really, truly feel—a sexy broad, or a young guy—or some veritable Queen of Lust. There were no shortages of these in Moscow. But, ordinarily this was nothing more than a casual gift, a form of salutation, a little something to serve as a ray of light in a kingdom of darkness. And it was only for a few moments, and with no manipulation, and *absolutely* no ejaculation. Just a fleeting apparition for those who fancied that sort of thing; or conversely, for those who would never reveal their interest but, later in private, would dwell on it repeatedly, concentrate on it, recall the details and arrive at a totally new understanding of themselves.

Yes, this revealed something that had been hidden deep in the mind, obscure, unconscious. *That* was the explanation for his graveside gesture. An insulting appearance—and an immediate disappearance. A heavy stone tossed into the dull ditch of routine existence, existence based solely on the rules of hypocrisy and inhumanity. Actually, it was a *cry*—probably too generous for such dead souls. "Hey, you, what are you doing? Wake up! I've got something totally new for you!" And it was true; she was just a prisoner, buried alive. Dressed in stone (where had he read that, in some novel or other?), someone to wound, to insult at the moment of deepest grief. And then to vanish. But something in her face had startled *him*.

It was the duality—the voluptuousness—the expression of sensuousness and depth born of woman's mysterious past. It's something frequently seen in women with slight squints; and in it there is always secrecy and complicity. Ah, she spread her net splendidly, by the slight movement of her feet, the trembling of her lips, the quivering of her nostrils . . .

And, finally, it was perfectly obvious that she had been completely hooked, body and soul.

It was that expression which had called forth his condescending gift, the look of the quivering victim. Never before had he reacted in this way—known this feeling of complete and staggering victory coupled with so sweet a defeat. Why had he been unable to stop? The challenge of her ironic smile had melted in the air and a boiling current had flowed between them, linking them in a transport of passion, in a reciprocated heat that compelled him to go on to the end.

She, damn her, had been able to arouse him. And therefore he had to meet her again and crush her, or, simply convince himself of her limitations—prove to himself anew that paradise comes not from women, but from God, who gives life to the woman-mother vehicle.

Timur dismissed the matter from his mind. When it suited him, he would look and find her. It was as simple as that. He had other things to think about. That business in the cemetery, for instance, had only served to convince him things were going as he thought. It confirmed his belief that no decent, honest citizen could obtain a proper burial, let alone untroubled rest or peace, and provided him with solid, new evidence he would be able to use in the future. It was clearly essential to take steps—to act instantly, as he had pointed out to Esper Ozirisovich (that bandit!). Naturally, he wouldn't stick his neck out so long as he was dragging down enough money. But, as no one knew better than Timur, matters were coming to a head and it was this that had taken him to the cemetery—to find out once and for all how things stood. He'd been thinking about his idea for a long time. And, he had his fingers on the very pulse of Moscow while he trotted around the city on business for their co-operative; he had a wide net of acquaintances.

Tomorrow there would be a conference to consider his proposition, which he considered brilliant. Surely such an idea could never have entered the minds of even the Politbureau, much less the academicians. Probably only Pakhan himself could even have understood it. Valery Borisovich, their chief (known as "the advocate" because of his legal background) had thought Timur was joking the first time he'd mentioned it.

"Stop kidding around, Timur. You're always coming up with these mad ideas. But we have to talk *seriously* now." This, mind you, so that they could discuss a new model urn for ashes, to be made of some imitation-wood plastic! Seriously!

"But, Valery Borisovich," he had insisted, "I *am* being serious!" And as he explained, the chief had warmed to it, seen the possibilities. The old fox—shrewd, cautious, always thinking of himself; no wonder he'd done so well as a lawyer! But he had wanted time to consider the legal consequences. Impatiently, Timur had pushed him. "What's illegal about it? You can see the whole thing; you understand it. This business is a gold mine! They'll be pinning medals on us! Has anyone thought of a better way of keeping the memory of our builders of Communism forever fresh? The memory of the vanishing generation of Stalin's sons, who with fire and sword literally *created* our socialist country—and who, now at an increasing rate, are being put into the damp earth, niches piled one on top of the other, where they end up *nothing*! It's obvious there isn't room for them all at the Kremlin wall. But look how many worthy people there are—from politics, science, the arts, industry! You can see that, can't you?"

Still, Valery Borisovich hesitated. Clearly, the whole thing was too much for him. The scale of Timur's plan frightened him. "You're right," he conceded, "but it might cause trouble. We can't foresee where this might lead. You can look around and see for yourself; the current line of products—coffins, graves, all that—isn't going so badly. So why take on extra headaches? Your plan is simply too big. You want to create model cemeteries for the bourgeoisie—I beg your pardon—for the leading figures of our new society. Fine, but knowing how to start doesn't tell us how, ultimately, this might end. Oh, I don't doubt that eventually we'll succeed . . . These people, well, they're super-sensitive when it comes to matters of honor and respect."

The chief clearly wouldn't be hurried; above all, he wanted to consult Horace Evsevonovich, that Colossus of the Future, who had shown such astonishing success at producing their coffins and other funeral appurtenances. Of their group, he had the sharpest eye; he examined everything with peasant shrewdness. He would get to the root of the matter immediately; possibly more important, he would be flattered that they had asked. It was, after all, he who would provide the soil of the collective farms in which the bigwigs of the capital would find their final rest.

Since Valery Borisovich was naturally of a prudent and suspicious nature, his first thoughts were of all the possible intrigues and secret jealousies that would normally endanger such an ambitious scheme. But, offhand, he simply could not see where the danger lay. A famous man is offered a pleasant, restful plot in the finest Soviet soil; a monument is erected to him; he is constantly shown the greatest respect; and, naturally, the entire region benefits from the subterranean presence of all these celebrities. Who could fault that?

And thus the chief was finally convinced. So, tomorrow, at the general meeting of the entire co-operative, the proposal would be considered and Timur saw very clearly that it would be accepted. Once Valery Borisovich and the Party Chairman were converted to it, there were no difficulties—there would be none. Marina and Gleb Vyacheslovov, those two characters, were on his side, of course. Timur's schemes always delighted them.

And there was Avdotya Zakharovna, a woman who combined a fertile imagination with insatiable greed. She would immediately grasp the possibilities; that was what he liked about her. Avdotya Zakharovna, his darling Dunya, still so lovely—yes, incomparably so, even in her mid-forties! She was old enough to be his mother, but she was all woman. Could you find anyone to match *her* among your young Moscow girls? It had been she who had seduced him and taught him what womanhood meant. His mind dwelt on her as he drove, for Timur was on his way to Vnyakovsky Airport to welcome

Dunya back to Moscow from the Caucasus. He wondered what she would be bringing with her.

Once past the Leninsky Prospekt, he made good time and found himself at Vnyakovsky with a half hour to spare. In the airport restaurant, he ordered a shot of Stolichnaya and some zakouskis to nibble on; while he waited he studied the other patrons. Sharing his table were three Georgians, two men and a middle-aged woman. They were involved in an animated discussion, full of gestures and flashing teeth. Timur decided they were simple rustics, come to Moscow on a buying trip. They had more the look of business people than of professionals or workers. It occurred to him that they might be involved in some shady transactions for a small enterprise back in Georgia. Both men wore grand mustaches. Though they went on chattering through them in Georgian, his presence seemed to make them uncomfortable—not that Timur could understand anything they said. When he sat down the woman stared at him and then turned away with a grimace he interpreted as disdain, as though she considered him an interloper. She made it obvious that she intended to ignore him.

Across the room, several tables were filled with foreign tourists, each party accompanied by its Intourist translator. Probably headed for Kiev or Armenia, some southern place. There was a sprinkling of all age groups, though men and women in their fifties seemed to predominate. The men had dulled eyes, florid faces; many wore gold-rimmed glasses and gaudy shirts. The women, wearing glasses too, had blue-tinted hair and dresses in an assortment of garish colors. All carried books, and maps, and cheap cameras. Their coats and jackets were thrown over chairs. Timur assumed they were Americans.

From under one table protruded a pair of long, unnaturally white legs, terminating in red plastic sandals that revealed patches of almost transluscent skin. The feet contrasted strangely with their surroundings, weary bodies sagging more like jello than flesh. The two legs were stretched out at full length, widely parted, and slightly bent at the knees as though their owner were greatly in need of a rest. She was probably sitting on the very edge of her chair; Timur's eyes followed the legs upward until they encountered the hem of a light blue miniskirt, then searched under it to find the inner thighs where they joined at the trunk, merging into the groin in secret shadows. It was as though the two cool, rounded legs grew out of this eternal darkness. The feet were obviously female, and had the smoothness of youth. The bottom one nervously kicked off its red sandal; it fell with a clatter and the bare foot pressed against the floor, reminding Timur of nothing so much as the suckers on the tentacle of an octopus.

The vision disturbed him profoundly. He searched for the rest of the enigma and found, floating above the backs and heads of the other customers, two absolutely rectangular shoulders, a long neck rising from them like a column of steam; and then, framed with a navy-blue silk kerchief, a face that was neither masculine nor feminine, but rather a geometric mask displaying two rows of plastic teeth, shining in a fixed smile that was outlined by cinnabar-painted lips. It and the eyes, encased in the rectangular platinum frames of her glasses, were aimed directly at Timur: in a parody of seductiveness. Everything on that face was polished and functional, streamlined, frozen into a laboratory image of life. Its age could only be conjectured from the very perfection of its immobility, though there were other barely detectable signs for the student that indicated the simulated woman who owned it must be nearer the century than the half-century mark. She'd been born, say, somewhere in Mississippi, or wherever it had been that General Lee's guns fired their last salvo. Daughter of the American Revolution, totally confident of its eternal effectiveness, she looked down at Timur as though she were the Statue of Liberty, or atop some skyscraper like the United Nations; she was a living testimony to the technological progess in the art of human restoration attained by America's laboratories and manufacturing industries. And even the invitation she projected was a part of the rehabilitation plan: one must exercise regularly to keep all that plastic equipment in good shape; one must practice diligently with those artificial instruments for seduction or their dollar value will decline.

Timur gazed at her in admiration, giving her the same look he reserved for the new Cadillacs and Buicks sometimes seen on Gorky Street, or for retired generals scintillating with decorations, or for top party functionaries, formed of the best gray Soviet steel—not very versatile, certainly, but highly utilitarian robots, roughly handcrafted, artisan-style work; appropriate for their tasks and even useful in emergency conditions; remarkably resistant to such acids as doubt or feelings. What is the difference, Timur asked himself, between this American woman and a woman Minister of Culture in the world's most progressive government? The one is embalmed in a bath of chemical sediments and polymers; the other in dogmatic pronouncements and the holy revelations of Marx and Lenin.

The loudspeaker announced the arrival of the plane from Tbilisi, and immediately afterward, the departure of the flight for Kiev. The American miniskirt whirled by Timur at shoulder level; she held a small umbrella pointed down at her miraculously preserved feet. The hand holding it, sharply contrasting with the feet, was covered with dried spots of gray, set off by a large diamond in an old-fashioned setting, which seemed to have sunk in ashes.

When the tourists had left, Timur moved over to the table they had vacated. Ordering more zakouskis and another vodka, he had to convince the harassed waitress that he was waiting for friends and was not monopolizing a table for himself.

Our Soviet restaurants make no concessions to the dizzying pace of a modern airport; obstinately, they remain in the days of Tolstoy and the English Club of Moscow; therefore, by the time the waitress returned, she was naively pleased to see that Timur had not lied and that his table was indeed communal. He had been joined by a party of three. There was a thickset air force major with a shaved head; a young girl of about thirteen—the Eastern type, possibly from Azerbaijan, with large, dark, liquid eyes; and a swarthy woman with very black, curly hair. She was one of those rare, fortunate creatures whose beauty flowers with age, and is enhanced with each new decade. Avdotya Zakharovna, Timur's beloved Dunya, did not, in fact, seem younger than her forty-odd years—she was radiantly settled in the present, as though she had finally reached the point of perfect and definitive maturity. She held herself with a self-confidence that told the beholder she knew her beauty had conquered time.

"So tell me how it's going, Tim," she ordered. "Everything under control?" One eye, unseen by the major, closed in a sultry wink. The question was obviously rhetorical, for she immediately turned toward the officer. "Tim, comrade major, is the son of my poor husband's sister; my niece and I will be staying with him while we're here." She nodded toward the girl, having now filled in Timur on what her act was.

Despite this, Timur was feeling somewhat annoyed and awkward; he had no idea what Dunya might have going with the major, who had inexplicably appeared accompanying the other two.

"Yes, I quite understand," the officer rumbled pompously, staring hungrily down into Dunya's amply filled bodice.

"As I told you, Avdotya Zakharovna," he continued, "I am completely at your service while you're in Moscow, and I assure you I shan't begrudge any time spent with the widow of a hero of the Soviet Union."

So, that's how it is, Timur thought, relaxing, amused at the greedy glance that accompanied the patriotic words. Everything was clear; this was Dunya's latest conquest. She had probably wasted no time in letting the officer know of the great socialist services her husband had rendered. Dunya had married a test pilot chosen for cosmonaut training, who had been killed on an experimental flight. Posthumously, he had been awarded the title of Hero of the Soviet Union, and his widow received a substantial pension. Quite naturally, her consolation for her loss lay in the success of her country's cosmonauts and she took joy in the honor of being with the nation's finest sons whenever possible—people such as the major himself.

Yes, Dunya had mastered Soviet rhetoric, there was no question of that; and she knew exactly how to puff up the egos of these idiots—the bloated, strutting roosters: "I'm grateful for your generous offer," she continued, beaming at her captivated victim, "but I'm really very familiar with the city; I've friends and relatives here, you see, and, anyway, I couldn't take up on your valuable time."

"Nonsense! Nonsense!" the major countered hurriedly. "It would be an honor and a pleasure . . ."

"More pleasure than honor," Dunya interrupted with a bluntness that startled the man. Not giving him time to analyze that, she went right on talking, turning to Timur. "We made friends with the major on the plane. He was very kind—a true Knight of the Blue Star. His help with all the red tape and the luggage was invaluable."

Timur had it all now. Dunya had brought in a load of illegal "goods"—that was why she'd picked up the major. He was a perfect cover. Oh, you wonderful windbag, you priceless melon head, you haven't the slightest idea what you're mixed up with! You probably carried her latest shipment of hashish right through customs. Dunya always brought in a load for Timur and her Moscow friends. She was the biggest dealer this side of the Urals.

"No, no, Avdotya Zakharovna," the major modestly protested. "To the widow of such a hero, all of us—all Soviet flyers—are as a family."

Dunya suddenly tired of the role of hero's widow; now that her knight errant had outlived his usefulness he could go fly on his own. "And *you* certainly wouldn't want to commit incest, my dear major," she prodded him.

Though he was obviously shocked, the major unexpectedly rose to the occasion. "Avdotya Zakharovna, you amaze me! You've learned to joke like a soldier!"

"Naturally, naturally," Dunya answered with approval, for

she far preferred the coarse directness of army men to the wordy vagueness of the party man's approach.

"Seriously, though, dear lady," the major resumed. "As I was telling you, both for the party and the service men who were their comrades, it has become a problem to give our fallen heroes the proper last respects . . ."

The conversation was unnecessarily long and moving in directions he would as soon avoid, Timur decided. "Avdotya Zakharovna," he interrupted, "they are waiting for you; and I have things to do myself . . ."

"Yes, yes, Tim, you're right. My niece is tired, and I too am exhausted by the trip—not to mention the change of climate. Once again, I want to thank you," she told the major, "for all your kindness, and to tell you how pleased I am to have made your acquaintance—no, no, we'll pay the check," she hastened to add, beckoning the waitress.

"Certainly not, Avdotya Zakharovna," the major said, matching her gallantry, and rose. "That would be most improper—and I hope you will give me another opportunity . . ."

"I don't think . . ." Dunya began; but then thought it would be nonsense to refuse his good offices—one never knew when he might become useful again. She went on, more smoothly: "I should be pleased to, comrade major—if you will let me know when and where I might find you."

The officer hastily scrawled an address in his note pad, tore it out and handed it to her, and the two parted as friends. Timur, Dunya and the so-called niece left in a hurry and the major, ordering another vodka, settled down to contemplate the happy thought that Russia still contained many a stalwart wench.

3. At the Country Villa

Avdotya Zakharovna had had a long, hard life. She had been born in the Crimea, in Alupka, the product of a tempestuous if short-lived affair between the former Brigade Commander of Budenny's First Cavalry, and a young Moscow actress. When the child had been no more than two months old, the star had had to go on tour, and left the baby in the care of a Crimean Tartar family. Little Dunya was fated never to see her mother again; she had, in fact, no memory of her at all. Her father was then working in a circus as a horseman and hypnotist, and he could do no better for her than to leave her with the kind Tartar peasant woman. Thus, Dunya's first spoken words were Tartar.

When she was nearly four her father came for her and took her to Batum. He was a very strong man, handsome, bewhiskered, born a Cherkess, a descendant of horsemen and horse traders. He was something of a lady-killer, and in Batum he found himself a new wife: a chemist, no less, from the intelligentsia. But the science of chemistry did not combine well with the science of Cherkess lovemaking: the young graduate of N—— Institute spent her nights testing materials for the first Five-Year Plan, while the former hero of the Civil War, the charmer of Poti and Lobuleti, spent an equivalent amount of time in the Batum taverns. Dunya grew up by the mercy of fate, surrounded by kindhearted neighbors.

Soon her stepmother was swallowed up by sanitoria, crushed under demands of love, creative chemistry, and tuberculosis.

Her father had become involved in Black Sea contraband, and eventually vanished without a trace; Dunya never even learned if he had escaped to Turkey, or if he'd been sent to Siberia along with other anti-social elements in the Party. Tamara, a Georgian prostitute, became her latest mother; this was when she was about eight. And Tamara's professional instinct told her that the combination of Russian and Cherkess bloods in the little girl would one day soon produce an exceptional woman. But Tamara genuinely loved her, as a mother. She took her to Tbilisi and established her as her own daughter. She saw in the girl, in fact, the one opportunity fate had given her, a chance to bring new meaning to her ruined life; and so she helped Dunya to go out among people, displaying her natural endowments, making use of them in the best possible way—avoiding the weakness and sentimentality which had been the cause of Tamara's failure in her profession. Tamara (who had been in the "trade" some twenty years before, in Moscow) didn't sing pioneer songs to Dunya, but the songs prostitutes sang as they were paraded off to camp:

> My white road blanketed
> By cocaine, the silvery powdered snow . . .

The seeds Tamara planted found fertile soil in Dunya, who had inherited from the Cherkess stallion his ingrained sensitivity combined with a masculine strength of disposition; and from her mother perseverance and the ability to study and learn. In addition, as it turned out, luck was added to that genetic pool.

When she became an adult, she fell in with the circle that surrounded the mightiest and the most terrifying man in the Caucasus, and later in the entire country. Like many other girls, she was taken from the streets at a sign from the bespectacled minister who roamed the world in search of young flesh for his master's harem, chasing around the streets and alleys of the city in his car. But what for others meant slavery and tragedy, became for Dunya the beginning of a brilliant career. She developed not only into an indispensable companion in dissipation, but a magnificent swindler as well, and a remarkable organizer. Then—due to a variety of changes in higher echelons—fate brought her once again to the Caucasus.

There, on the Black Sea, she became acquainted with a young test pilot, born in Central Russia, and bearing the legendary name of Pugachev. He had been chosen for astronautical training, and, before taking off for school, was spending his leave there at Gagrax. Their meeting immediately led to a passionate affair, and soon after to marriage. For several years Dunya was a loving and sensuous wife, and in fact her life might have continued quite differently if her Leonid hadn't died a hero's death along the infinite road to the Cosmos. For Dunya it was the end of any hope of a normal life. Chaos reigned all around her: dishonesty, selfishness, absurdity. There was nothing left but to plunge straight into the maelstrom, going headlong into a wild life of adventure—taking vengeance, in short, on everyone and everything, because of everything and nothing. The passive role of a hero's widow was not her sort of thing.

Leonid had also picked a life-style that involved rebellion against reality—challenge to the world. Dunya remembered how they had read Essenin together—not the lyrical writer beloved of sentimental lovers, but the desperate, tragic poet:

> Ah, how gay is today with the dew
> Of the alcoholic river.
> The harmonica-player with the caved-in nose
> Sings of the Volga and Cheka.
> There is something evil in the gaze of idiots,
> Recalcitrant in awkward speeches:
> They are sorry for the silly young men
> Who ruined their lives on the spur of the moment,
> Sorry for those whom stern October
> Fooled with its snowstorm.
> And already, with new daring,
> The secret, the hidden knife in the boot
> Is sharpened . . .

And so Dunya came back to the Caucasus, returning to the world from which she had fled in search of life, returning with hope, but with anger and dry calculation, finding an endless new pleasure in being able to perceive exactly what she wanted. She lived her third youth in the full bloom of her powers, armed with experience, and with friendship reserved for those who had not yet lost their influence. Influence is something she learned to use better than anyone around her—without compromising herself, as the others seemed compelled to do. She soon found herself the center of a network providing every possible illegal service, particularly to those whom the criminal code defines as "maintaining illicit places for the use of narcotics and scenes of debauchery."

Gradually Avdotya developed in herself an ambition commensurate with her business instinct, an insatiable greed which never yielded to her insatiable sensuality. She pushed her pawns with great care, so as not to lose stupidly, and, she always had someone, in reserve, to cover up for her—someone who, naturally, did not know much about the details or the full scope of her activities. Besides, she knew how to be generous with those who were close to her; their welfare was a very small price to pay for the position she had attained in society. And her various deals grew along the same lines.

She became involved with Timur by chance. He'd been passing through Tbilisi on the co-operative's business, and noticed Dunya in one of the cafés. Thanks to that infallible instinct (or is it an inexplicable fatality?) which brings together the sex-maniac and his willing victim, he had not hesitated a second before coming out with his exhibit. The act in itself could not fail to attract Dunya to him. Along with the incredibility of it all, and the almost abnormal size of the exhibit, was Timur's shining face, in which she immediately recognized lack of control, traces of belated adolescence, and premature senility; he became for her the visible symbol of her exclusiveness.

Thus was born the delicate and ambiguous friendship, in which she was both mother and prostitute for Timur. Dunya, for her part, felt raped by him every time, all the more as for a long while she never reached a climax; and now this feeling was accompanied by the astringent savor of incest. This is, in short, how Avdotya Zakharovna was introduced to the funereal business, soon attaining a rather important position thanks to her abilities and specialized talents. Since then she often came to Moscow, usually arriving in town the day before the meetings of flourishing organizations dedicated to providing prompt, adequate, and first-class services for deceased citizens and their families.

Timur's Volga quickly crossed the city from the southwest to the other end of the capital. Avdotya Zakharovna had counted on entertaining the young girl with the astonishing view of a large capital city, but she sat in the back seat, stunned and completely withdrawn. Neither Dunya nor Timur intruded on her privacy. While driving, Timur, in a low voice, brought Dunya up to date on some of his thoughts about the business at hand; and every now and then glanced in the back mirror. The child's immature, delicate body resembled a stalk reaching toward the sun to gather strength and life. The body, poised lightly on the edge of the seat, breathed and quivered independently; the face was immobile and lived within its own dreams. It was not the little girl who looked out of the window—the buildings, the avenues, the streets, the people themselves flung themselves instead through the window into her huge, wide-open eyes. The car ran along Dmitrovsky Chaussee. They had just passed Bytyaka. On the left stood the blocky, prison-like hulks of the new residential area of Novokharinsk.

The dacha of the lawyer Valery Borisovich Tarakanov, where they were headed, lay in a pleasant wooded area a few kilometers out of town. Avdotya Zakharovna turned to the little girl and asked, "Are things all right with you, darling?"

"Dildor is tired," she whined, blinking her eyes and beginning to cry.

"All right, all right, darling, nap a bit. We will be there soon, and you must be as beautiful and sparkling as the stars in Baku."

Timur smiled to himself: *the old procuress, she certainly knows how to flatter her little kitten*!

The dacha was situated on a cliff in a secluded place among white and black birches, whose trunks resembled animals, perhaps long-necked giraffes. They were expected. A large whitish sheep dog jumped out to greet them with a friendly bark. Across the lawn at the doorway stood a very erect, tall, thin, middle-aged woman with a Byzantine face. She was wearing a black and violet flowered dress of heavy silk. Around her neck were amber beads, and both wrists were encircled by silvered Oriental bracelets. This was Olga Borisovna, the sister of the master.

She led them to a spacious dining room bathed in rather dim twilight, the typical spring color of the environs of Moscow. Her greeting was reserved and laconic. Only to Dildor did she turn with a caressing gesture; she kissed her lightly and drew her close. The little girl went to her trustingly, as though this was the person she had expected to meet at the end of her long journey.

The large room gave a pleasant impression of solid comfort. There was no particular style. The furniture was mostly old Russian—a couch from about the time of Tsar Paul, a small bureau of black and red wood, Karelian birch. Conspicuous among all this was the piano (Olga Borisovna had once studied at the Conservatory.) About the round table of Russian Empire style were chairs of the style of the early 1900s. In the same style were the lampshade over the table and the stool next to the couch. On the walls hung paintings by Konchalovsky, sketches by Soudekine and Sapunovsy, landscapes by Ostroumova-Lebedev. In a glassed-in bookcase, two shelves were occupied by rare Yussupov china.

No one paid any attention to these precious rarities. To Dunya and Timur they were familiar, and Dildor simply couldn't evaluate them. Olga Borisovna served them tea and prepared them for the imminent arrival of the master. She turned to the little girl: "And for you, I prepared a *plombière*.

Do you like ice cream? Come with me, little Dark-Eyes," and she led her away.

At that point Tarakanov entered the room, a man of about seventy, with quick movements and smooth black hair. His small face seemed dried-up and in some ways he reminded one of an old Japanese. He was dressed in a gray suit, obviously of foreign material; nor were the tie and soft brown leather shoes native products. He bowed respectfully to Dunya, smiled to Timur, and, settling himself in the armchair, said, "Just a few words about our affairs. You, Avdotya Zakharovna, have undoubtedly heard from Timur about our plan—which is to be the subject of discussion at tomorrow's conference." Dunya nodded vigorously in agreement. "I don't want to hear your opinions now. Give the matter your most careful consideration until tomorrow. Let me add one word. Tomorrow I shall vote for it. Timur knows how difficult it was for me, but I have finally decided to participate. Nevertheless, it must not be forgotten that the plan can yield the expected results only if it is conducted with foresight, intelligence, and *tact*." He stressed the last word.

"Timur has explained it all, and it came as a surprise, but I am absolutely delighted," exclaimed Dunya. "Timur never betrays my expectations; he always comes up with something novel. This is not only lucrative, but strange and even dangerous."

Thc lawycr grinncd. "Pcrsonally, I am pcrhaps in complctc agreement with you, Avodtya Zakharovna, but why so emotional? We must avoid sentimental overtones in such an important and serious undertaking. Tomorrow we must submit the proposition to people whom you know well and who, with the exception of Marina Maximovna and our secretary, will never agree to such a presentation. I have already worked on Savely Sevastanovich, but you can understand that, in order to get the proposition accepted, it is necessary to present it in the best possible light. I take this upon myself, not in any way to push aside Timur Alexandreich, of course, whose whole idea this is. But to get them to accept it, I am introducing it, as Timur and I have agreed; so that the proposition should be looked upon, so to speak, objectively, as though naturally emanating from our present activities, and even, as though from somewhere 'high up', from someone who has a lot of *influence* there, obviously unofficially, but incidentally, as if it somehow reached us in the nature of casual advice. I would say this is encouragement."

"Yes, yes, that's quite right; this is the way to handle it," agreed Timur.

"Marvelous!" Dunya couldn't refrain from laughter. "From above, *from above*—that's how it works in our Russia; our people are accustomed to it. Everything from above: mercies and misfortunes both."

"OK: we're all agreed?" Valery Borisovich interrupted her. "Now, about something else. I saw the little girl—very sweet. Tell me, Avdotya Zakharovna, is she prepared already?"

"Yes, a little," answered Dunya. "In the country we prepared a celebration for her, but after that first time she has not had another man.

"We slept together, of course." Here Dunya winked gaily. "A wild, unconscious little animal, but with certain gifts," she concluded with pride. "All that's needed is skillful hands that won't spoil her. What about you, Valery Borisovich?"

"No, thank you. I know you had me in mind, but I have other plans. At this stage it is essential that we have a protector from higher up, perhaps someone important like Frolov, and the little girl . . . In the beginning she will stay here with me. We'll try to educate her. Meanwhile, she will be amused: Mokh is full of envy."

"Ah, Mokh," laughed Dunya, "he is the one that should be tried for corrupting the young—I have never seen a dog more human in its carnal desires. And he knows how to act tactfully, as you just put it, Valery Borisovich!"

"Don't forget that we trained him—wanting to perpetuate the old traditions of Catherine's time, when the nobility provided their hunting dogs with the services of peasant girls. Russia didn't lag behind the West in her erotic fantasies in those days! Perhaps you recall the painting in the Tretyekovsky Museum, in which a peasant woman is suckling the nobility's puppies with her own infant beside her in the hay? . . . But now, if you please, let us go to the table. Olga is already impatient, since you arrived somewhat late."

"Timur," Dunya asked, "please get my yellow suitcase out of the car. I have some gifts there for our hosts."

In the suitcase were several bottles of Georgian wine, fruit, and other Caucasian delicacies.

"And I have something else," announced Dunya in honeyed tones; "a small portion of hashish for cheerfulness and courage."

"Avdotya Zakharovna, how often have I told you not to get me mixed up in this?" the old lawyer protested, "Perhaps in the Caucasus all this is all right, but here it is an entirely different thing. And, if you will permit me, I consider this both unnecessary and dangerous for you."

"Valery Borisovich, dear, don't get upset. I know, of course, that Timur provides you with it."

"For my own personal needs only," Valery Borisovich defended himself.

"I know, I know, that is exactly why I decided to bring you just the merest bit," insisted Dunya. Naturally she did not reveal that in the car was a large consignment which Timur was to deliver on order.

As usual, the table set by Olga was resplendent with china and crystal, and displayed many dishes of purely Russian cuisine which had already become difficult to get in restaurants.

Dinner was not as exotic as might have been expected in a household of such refined tastes, but country-style, substantial and abundant—home-grown marinated mushrooms, borsch with prunes and black mushrooms, beef (a roast baked in a casserole), and excellent ice cream with raspberry jam.

Afterwards they all sat down to play *preference*. Valery

Borisovich enjoyed Dunya's unfortunately rare visits to Moscow because she played avidly, passionately, with all the force of her masculine temperament. Timur, though he played like a professional player, lost twice. Olga Borisovna was circumspect, and broke about even.

At last, everyone was ready for bed. Although the intimate relationship between Dunya and Timur was well known and Olga Borisovna was a woman of liberal tendencies, she nevertheless arranged separate rooms for them—not from hypocrisy, but out of respect for their freedom.

Naturally, Timur, wasting no time, quickly found himself in Dunya's room. She was waiting for him with anxious hands and, under her blouse, unrestrained, bra-less breasts.

"Ah, you're here so soon," she said triumphantly, "and I thought you were tired of me!"

"Oh, you're a fool," teased Timur. "Tonight I have nothing better to do."

"And our little girl, doesn't *she* appeal to you?"

"No; only women who are no longer young appeal to me," answered Timur in the same vein.

Dunya sat down beside him, studying him through narrowed eyes, with complete calm. "Look, look at the old woman—" and bared one full breast. She held herself in check for a moment, letting Timur satiate himself with the sight of this mature feminine beauty, then lowered her head, grabbing the wide, dark nipple with her own lips and muttered: "Now I'm going to suck it. Could a little girl do that?"

"It's enough that you know how to suck this." Timur pointed to the bulging place in his trousers.

Dunya dropped her breast and said, "No, that's not enough, my boy. Come here." Unable to wait, she went to Timur herself, pushed him toward the bed, and made him sit down.

"Right now! I'll take it out myself, if you can't make up your mind. Dunya isn't one to wait that long. I'm all wet already."

She took his hand and pushed it under her skirt, where it

encountered something soft and hot under the cloth of her panties. Timur's fingers moved, pushing the nylon aside; they lightly touched the coarse hair and immediately sank into the soft greedy depths.

"Do you feel what kind of a beastie this is?" she whispered in a muffled tone, spreading her legs apart. "Strangle it, throttle it, annihilate it!" And, taking Timur's other hand, sticking it in her mouth, she hotly licked his fingers and nibbled on them with her lips. Leaning over him, she unbuttoned his trousers and took out his enormous tool. It was not erect, but swollen and elongated, and in this state appeared even more obscene and disgusting.

Timur took his hand out of Dunya's mouth, took his instrument with his thumb and forefinger, lifted it slightly and slowly began to masturbate while with his other hand he continued to root around between her legs.

Dunya leaned over to get a closer view of the oversized tool which was growing in length and thickness and hardening. Then she suddenly moved away from Timur; his hand, which had disappeared in her depths, slid out, wet up to the middle of the palm.

"And now, everything off me!" Dunya cried out in a choked voice. "You have to give it to me in the rear too, you son of a bitch!" She tore off her clothes and planted herself in the center of the room, allowing herself to be gazed upon, confident that her whole body did not belie the beauty which carnality gave her face. Then she approached the dressing table and put her foot on the little stool next to it.

"Here, now, in front of the mirror," Dunya barely whispered, and, turning her back to him, bent slightly forward. "I want you to stuff it in slowly from behind. I want to see how your big tool goes into me . . . Here, Timushka, that's it. Good! Look how it opens up and swallows him."

In the mirror, she saw her lead-tinted breasts with their dark, wide, brassy nipples. Below in the black spot between the thighs, she tried to see the lilac-colored mucus-like stuff, showing through the hair, and its forced swelling, accommodating to the meat cylinder as it penetrated her, became a part of her, advanced and retreated, forming with her a single burning object.

Timur silently set to work. His boyish face with its blond curls and the cruel expression of its lips, insolent and tragic, the mask of a second-rate Hamlet on a provincial stage, hung immobile in the mirror over the woman's body. The eyes, whitened in a fever of blazing ice, were the only signs of life in this face, where not a single muscle moved. Those eyes bored into the shiny surface of the mirror and insultingly penetrated the bobbing, wild flesh of the breasts and naked belly, but in them was dissolved the febrile matter itself which, spontaneous and exultant, revitalized the mucus beneath the copulation.

"Oh, oh, Timushka, finish, finish," moaned Dunya, all spent from the exhausting, though expected and realized, spasms of deeply felt emotion which, meanwhile, overpowered her even more by its unimaginable intensity.

Timur maintained the same tempo. A smile touched his lips; he knew what Dunya wanted of him at this moment—that he end his penetration of her with a show of incredible strength. Her body became passive and he slowed his movements; then he halted and, with incredible renewed strength, squeezed all the muscles of the body which he continued to control.

But Dunya was already independent; she turned to face Timur, almost touching him with her breasts, throwing out a challenge.

"Ah, you know what I want now! Come, show yourself a hero!"

With a slight movement she disengaged herself from his instrument. She went over to the bed and there awaited him, in full readiness, hiding her face in the pillow, raising and pushing out her rear. In this position the thrust-out, raised buttocks resembled gigantic olives. A narrow, dark cleft divided them. All this gave the impression of brutish and healthy musculature and emphasized even more the soft, damp hairy mass of her female organs.

"Stick it up my rear," she whispered, turning a smiling, mischievous face to Timur.

With his tremendous log, which threateningly hung in the air gleaming with damp female mucus, Timur in two leaps was next to her and covered her with his body.

"Hold on, mother dear! Just watch how I break through."

Embracing her with a firm hand, he pulled her to himself, supporting her rear in such a position that the head of his member at first pressed into her, and then began to beat a path for itself within her. Feeling how the hard rod opened up the breach in search of the living flesh, Dunya relaxed her muscles with voluptuous moans. Everything within her was aflame with desire and she gave herself to the monstrous cylindrical apparatus whose penetration she awaited so passionately and which became an inseparable part of her being, of her flesh.

He thrust inexorably into her to his full length, and his powerful body, dry-skinned and pale, froze at this moment of utter mastery of the dark-skinned, fleshy body of Dunya. The masculine organ then began to move again, back and forth, an endless beat. With one hand he strongly stroked one of Dunya's buttocks, with the other, which had circled beneath her, he massaged one full firm breast.

She accepted his ravishment, trying to control her heavy breathing, and then with all her might gave herself to him, and with all her fiber demanded more—absolute—fulfillment.

Her hand frenziedly teased the strained clitoris. It was prominent and swollen, like a hard acorn. This was Dunya's pride—the center of all her strength and virility, which allowed Dunya to consider herself equal to any man, no matter where—in bed or on the street. This clitoris was not only the focus of sensation, independent of her body, sharp and feverish, but of the violent, all-consuming orgasm. In white heat, Timur took her furiously, shaking her whole body, and rough, insulting obscenities poured from his mouth. Dunya's muffled moans echoed them, periodically interrupted by deep sighs of voluptuous lust. She continued masturbating until suddenly she froze: Dunya tensed, shivering all over, and let out a long, animal wail. Timur suddenly withdrew his penis from the shrinking orifice and erupted seeds of passion on her dark rump. His face was an inscrutable, cruel mask.

4. *Collective Farm, Sheaves of the Future*

The collective called "The Sheaves of the Future" was not one of those which correspondents of big, important, metropolitan newspapers single out to spotlight as examples of the success of Soviet agriculture. In spite of the fact that it was no more than a hundred *versts* from Moscow, for instance, it could still be praised—and quite recently, too—for its success in remaining an untouched corner of that Old Russia we all know from the paintings of Peredvizhnikov. Whoever approached it along the only road connecting it to civilization would see (even before the turn which shows the village itself) the road disappearing between two low-lying hills, on one of which stands an undersized hut, a cart with shafts pointing toward the nearly always gray horizon, and a pile of rotting hay. This picture—made so familiar by Russian writers from Turgenev to Chekhov—had always symbolized the Russian village; and, until very recently, as has been said, was entirely characteristic of the collective, The Sheaves of the Future.

The collectivists, despite their circumstances—forgotten by God as long as He existed, and after that by the inhabitants of the Kremlin—consoled themselves with the following line of reasoning:

"Foolish the bird that fouls its own nest."

Hope, in Old Russia, sprang eternal, and the collectivists, by refraining from any befoulment (such as criticism), managed to hope that eventually better times would come. "Not for nothing," they told themselves, "was this place called the Collective of the Future—one of these days, those legendary Sheaves are going to ripen!"

And so, dreaming and hoping, they soothed themselves with the knowledge that they had not invented the collectives, and could not have created it. Not all by themselves: the entire place was the work of some very powerful Party leaders—of Government Authority. There had to be a reason for the drastic change that had created "The Dry Ford," where very few sheaves grew at all, but only potatoes and cabbages. Authority, after all, as everyone knows, looks sharply and far.

The peasants, then, of the Dry Ford—not to mention the entire country—lived constantly by their faith in The Sheaves of the Future, and all the everlasting misfortune and foul weather they bore with Faith, a faith which never deserted them, any more than the consolation that Authority was farseeing ever left them.

Recently, though, there had been many changes among the collective's chairmen. The people changed, too, but two things united them: first, they wholly shared the collectivists' faith in those Sheaves of the Future, and considered it their stern duty to pursue that faith when different higher authorities, taxes, and agricultural changes allowed it; and, second, they had begun to doubt the honesty of the world as, perceiving the violent contradictions between hope and reality, every chairman sought his consolation in the temporary illusions of vodka—in which each, finally, drowned.

But the hopes of those who know how to hope are realized in the end. And recently the situation of the collective The Sheaves of the Future had become enviable—had even begun to have something in common with its prophetic name. The collectivists were unable to understand to what secret movement of fate they were indebted for this new prosperity; but since the past was full of hard-to-explain secret movements of fate that had only resulted in new misfortunes, they felt it ridiculous to inquire after the secrets now, when things were prospering.

It all began when Horace Evsevonovich Baranov became chairman of the collective—or, to be perfectly accurate, shortly after that, when he started fulfilling his duties. He had been born in Dry Ford, and, as a young man, had gone off to defend his Soviet Motherland. He returned with a fairly impressive bag of trophies and medals, but the main thing the war gave him was the precious baggage of information and experience.

Unlike many of his Army comrades, he'd managed to collect a great deal of valuable knowledge from his sojourns in various countries being liberated by the fine soldiers of the Soviet Army. In spite of the fact that his name had the connotation of *stupid—superficial*, this particular Baranov was keenwitted and inquisitive, meticulously fulfilling his soldierly obligations but, at the same time, quite able to assess his surroundings; and what he saw was forever imprinted on his mind. He soon noticed, for instance, that the farther our conquering armies penetrated, the more opulent were the Western fields and villages they passed through. In the days of victory (and directly following his entrance into Austria with the Army of Occupation), Horace Evsevonovich kept his head, and made, quite consciously and thoroughly, the best use of all the prerogatives of the conqueror.

No: he was not one of those benighted *muzhiks* who, having conquered, loots the first cellar and the first delicatessen, and rapes the first strange *baba* he sees on the street. Not that he was above such things, you understand: he looted and raped; but he was also observant, taking note of everything that might, in future, be of value. But besides all this, he was lucky; he came to the attention (not, it must be said, strictly by chance) of one of the commanding officers; he became that man's orderly. This gave him an opportunity to become even more closely acquainted with Austrian life. The country had been defeated; it had been occupied by its conquerors, but when Horace Evsevonovich compared what he saw with what he had experienced in childhood and adolescence (as an inhabitant of a collective no more than a hundred *versts* from the capital of the victorious Soviet government), it didn't seem as if occupation forces could do much to The Sheaves of the Future: everything, it appeared, had already been done. And right then, in his village (to judge from his mother's letters), his gloomiest memories were being acted out all over again.

As a soldier he had suffered cold, and thirst, and hunger, and every form of danger, and animal fear, and passion—but never again could he fall prey to the terrible, hopeless, endless poverty of his childhood and youth on the collective. Never again; but the collective remained the same—if possible, a little worse. Because, they said, the country had been through a war—or for some other reason. It had been difficult to find an explanation. But at the same time he was seeing, there in the West, how people got to their feet, recuperated before his very eyes, tackled their work, created their own little islands of happiness; and he thought, "Such fools—such shallow, inarticulate fools! Could they conceivably imagine what impenetrable darkness has collected in my native land, locked in a cell, put on a chain—like the brown bear at the market who escapes when someone is careless and leaps on the crowd, wild and hungry. That darkness, that final blackness, will spread throughout the world, destroying as it goes, sucking the world into its own impenetrable nothingness, its Russian nothingness . . . its sham surface colors, its gray army steel . . ."

Such things lived in his mind as they did in the mind of any Russians: the darkness, far beyond the reach of any philosophy; the result of vague, ancient history, crying for punishment; the result of the horrible and fatal October uprising that had forced whoever lived through it to start all over again on the ravaged, flooded land, dragging out a miserable existence there where people struggled for—something, but not knowing if their work would renew life or if some evil force would destroy that life—or what they had to call life. But to people like Horace, who despite such thoughts saw life renewing itself, sensed the reality in the tangible circumstances surrounding him, that newly perceived force was able to drag him from darkness, make him try with all his might to pull everything useful from his very convenient position among the occupying forces. He never forgot that "one doesn't go to a strange monastery with one's own entourage"; there were a good many circumstances in which he turned things to his own advantage—in fact, had he not been a Soviet soldier faced with the return to his socialist native land, one might have predicted with absolute certainty a brilliant future for him in business; most probably, he'd have become a wealthy shopkeeper in Styria, or an Austrian landowner.

One fine day, however, he was demobilized, and discovered the entirely different lot for which fate had prepared him—in Dry Ford. He had had a brief earlier try at being chairman of a collective; but it had taken him very little time to realize that there were more lucrative positions for him personally, and positions of more use to the people as well. While a soldier, he had learned a good deal about "arranging things," and this priceless know-how came in extremely handy in his native land, in those postwar times when it was difficult to pinpoint exactly what was lacking—everything being lacking, after all, from bread to boots, and everything having to be recreated and rebuilt.

He knew, as an "arranger," how to procure the needed items at the right moment—nails, glass, wood, bricks, anything and everything. He began as a dealer in "sundries," and soon found himself an irreplaceable part of all organizations for regional building. And so he became an operator—one of those people who do not, officially, exist, on whom society frowns, and whom the law hounds, but without whom the Soviet economic machine would grind to a rather rapid halt. People of this sort are always labelled one way or another: speculators, hucksters, "remnants of capitalism and individualism"—but in the end, thanks to them, government planning, whose life is on paper, is translated into a life of reality, from the distribution of slippers to the arrival of vacuum cleaners, or railway carriages. In this army of anonymous and unacknowledged Heroes and Builders of Socialism, Horace was still a long way from Generalship (or whatever term can be used for such people as "the king of lipsticks"); he was mostly a local entrepreneur. But he knew how to exploit his front-line buddies from the old days, and made good connections with the new local organizers for the Party; an enterprising and open-handed pal, he seemed certain to get ahead. Of course, you've got to have a foundation under your feet at all times, and his innate caution never let him forget the old rule: "Measure seven times, cut only once." Besides, he attempted constantly to give everything in his life at least the appearance of legal solidity, since "God protects the protected."

So, carefully swimming in his shallow waters, mixing easily with the authorities in his local region—flattering one while silently noting, for future use, the sins and shortcomings of another—he won for himself the position of a man much needed by many—and feared by some.

His appointment as chairman of the collective farm, Sheaves of the Future, seemed little short of a trap. To the blissfully ignorant it appeared a just recognition of the virtues of a resourceful man who enjoyed widespread and fully deserved respect throughout the district; in short, it was an excellent choice, and he was fully expected to provide that unique, efficacious and resolute stimulus that was destined to budge the collective's petrified and ponderous economy. But people in the know were fully aware that this ostentatious promotion was fraught with dangers for Comrade Baranov, threatening to compromise or even cut short that aspect of his activities in which he had hitherto excelled and which had made him so indispensable to those around him. But neither the first group nor the second suspected the full extent of Baranov's ambition. A big ship has to keep its sights on the horizon. Not only was he fully aware of what he was doing when he agreed to allow his name to go forward, but he had in fact been trying for some time past to bring about this desirable result—with the aid and co-operation of the local Party Secretary, Mikhail Nikolayevich Mephodiev, "for a hundred rubles is no great fortune, but a bit at a time from friends will also add up to something."

It had all begun when Baranov came to see Valery Borisovich Tarakanov about a certain matter. From that time forth, the wily lawyer had continued to remain in business contact with this cunning, resourceful peasant, who, although clumsy and crude, was nonetheless a past master of hypocrisy and dissimulation. The lawyer had long since retired on a pension, but this only smoothed the way for his private business; we have in mind not so much his legal consultations in high places, but rather—and he was greatly helped in this beneficent service by his important connections—his participation in those multifarious "combinations" that are never referred to in public, but are nonetheless decisive for the welfare of our country, that oil the rusty wheels of our planned economy and ensure that all essential cogs in the machine get replaced the moment they break down. In practice, the lawyer fulfilled at the highest level the same functions that Baranov fulfilled at his much more humble local level. But it was essential to harmonize them into a single whole, for dialectical materialism teaches us that quantity is transformed into quality; the lawyer was a carnivorous hawk, a boa-constrictor, while Baranov remained but a small snake and a country barn-owl.

Apart from this, Tarakanov, together with Timur and a number of others, had launched an extraordinarily delicate and extraordinarily profitable enterprise that we may call the "C Business." For in our country all national forces are justifiably concentrated on the development of socialism and on the speedy transition from socialism to communism, where everyone without distinction will have his slice of bread and butter, and the progress of Soviet science will eliminate death. It is generally held that the phenomenon of dying rates no particular attention or energy; although it is accepted that death is a black mark on our society that is destined to be erased in the not too distant future.

Thus, when a Soviet citizen dies, especially if this takes place in Moscow or one of our larger cities, his relatives and friends suffer not so much, or at least not only because of the sorrow it brings, but equally because of the dreary purgatory that awaits them when the remains depart from the house or hospital in search of their last resting place in a cemetery or crematorium. In itself this is a matter not one whit easier than finding a self-contained apartment with only one or two rooms.

Hard on the heels of the moment of death appears a peculiar character who has usually already had a skinful and who, for a liberal reward, will agree to remove the corpse. But then follow hours of standing in endless lines outside the funeral bureau, filling in forms at the registry office, paying shamelessly hiked fees without a murmur, and writhing helplessly in an agony of uncertainty and suspense while the talk turns to open funeral trucks or special buses, which rush the coffin with its unfortunate remains at top speed over the final processional route to the grave. And if you think that there at last the loved one is destined to rest in peace, you are simply unacquainted with the state of the "death problem" in our country. For all this is only the beginning. From the moment you get inside the cemetery walls, you have to struggle unremittingly simply to get the grave dug. And how many weeks, months and sometimes even years do you have to wait before you can erect a monument to the dear departed, or even a marker, or at the very least a headstone?

But, as is well known, in those areas where the long arm of a planned economy cannot reach, the situation is always saved by the resourcefulness and flexibility of the Russian character, or of one of the minorities, who are not averse to picking up a ruble on the side. And so it was always possible to find obliging types who would come to the aid of families in their moment of grief, not forgetting to ask, of course, for a special price for rescuing them from thankless cares and endless lines. All this activity, however, was inconsequential and disorganized, with no co-ordination and underlying logic, until Timur Yamshikov and Valery Borisovich Tarakanov took the matter in hand. With his cold precision and his qualities as a young leader, ubiquitous and not in the least squeamish, and aided by a small band of faithful followers, Timur conquered the funeral brokers, and persuaded stubborn individuals by force. And, after that, everything remained under his direct control, which in itself was a guarantee of smooth operation, provided no interference came from outside. This was unlikely, however, since all channels led to the lawyer and himself. The lawyer, meanwhile, took care of the finer aspects of the business and kept up the necessary contacts; and from the moment when their enterprise expanded and Baranov entered the field with his collective farm, he had taken on the role of director of a fairly sizable and complex undertaking.

The Sheaves of the Future, one might say, had at last attained its promised future, "hanging onto his gills and tail," to paraphrase Mayakovsky. And all this thanks to the new chairman, Baranov, and the lawyer. What did it matter that the edifice of this future rested on coffins, graves, gravestones, obelisks, busts and suchlike funeral appurtenances? Was this really of any significance, given that the collective farmers of Dry Ford were at last having a taste of prosperity? For it was they who produced this collection of funeral objects that were such rarities in the multi-millioned metropolis, which was so miserably and unsatisfactorily supplied by the organizations officially existing for that purpose. But all this became possible only after Comrade Baranov had occupied the post of chairman of the collective. Until then the "C Business" (Cemetery Business), if so we may describe it, was unable to develop normally, like an ordinary enterprise for the manufacture of funeral accessories, and resort had had to be made to the services of jobbers.

Having made the acquaintance of Baranov and evaluated his outstanding capabilities, Tarakanov outlined to him the various possibilities of a deal. He described to him the activities of numerous small and large collectives in the immediate vicinity of Moscow, and also in other districts, which succeeded in making a fat profit not out of hard and thankless labor in the fields, but by producing articles out of polyethylene and polystryrol, colored items, door-handles, electric plugs, etc., etc. "So why don't we follow their example and specialize in some similar commodity in short supply?"

"But what exactly do you have in mind, Comrade Tarakanov?" asked Baranov.

"Death accessories, Comrade Baranov!" replied the lawyer, hastening to explain to the stunned but still interested peasant the full variety and extent of those commodities and the kind of profit they produced. Baranov quickly caught on and gave his assent. Naturally, when he became chairman of the collective, the business could but gain from it, and continued to develop along broad and well-organized lines.

Baranov showed himself to be indispensable, speedily taking full control and fully justifying the confidence placed in him by the lawyer Tarakanov. Not only did he take direct charge of the production side and himself acquire a major part of the raw materials, but he also displayed an original talent for diplomacy, whenever it became necessary to draw in the local peasants and present the business to the local authorities. For each of them he found an appropriate rationalization, giving them to understand that such activity was not in the least to the detriment of the collective's aims or their customers' requirements, but on the contrary corresponded to the legitimate desires of their sister collectives and was even a valuable contribution to Soviet life and culture.

To those who did not know him well, Baranov came over, particularly in his official capacity, as the very type of a collective chairman, exactly as they are described by so many of our slick writers that go in for painting rose-colored pictures of the bucolic, pastoral life. His speeches were overloaded with pithy proverbs and folk sayings on the one hand, and on the other with that gray stodgy terminology that comes straight out of the newspapers, or one of those interminable speeches at conferences. Thus they contained all the features deemed typical for local agricultural managers.

Not only Mephodiev, whom he adroitly succeeded in twisting around his little finger, but all those in the district who were representatives of Soviet law and order, considered him one of their own. He was a firm believer in the old adage: "the law's like a willing horse, point it correctly and it will always follow the course." And even if it did get around that one or two of his machinations were on the very borders of legality, or even crossed them, nobody would ever dream of pointing the finger at him—Horace Evsevonovich Baranov. For all his actions were for the good of the common cause, and took place under the banner of mutual personal profit, with the participation of all, so that none could have the least interest in letting such details reach the ears of the public.

He was far more cynical than anyone could possibly have imagined and he kept to two golden rules: "I'll scratch your back and you scratch mine," and "gold is heavy, but lifts you instead of making you sink." Money and comfort were the palpable measures of his efficiency and success. All those recondite little tricks he was able to fall back on to achieve this end, and all his hypocrisy, not only came to him without the slightest effort, but were manifestations of his real character and even afforded him pleasure. The thing that caused him most torment was the necessity, enforced on him by our loudly proclaimed, but spurious Soviet morality, and the existence in his village of public opinion, to conceal at all costs the marks of his success and superiority, and all the manifestations of his own true nature. In this he was aided by the atavistic customs of hypocrisy, false modesty and skillfully concealed cunning that over the centuries have become second nature to the Russian peasant, at first under the influence of the gentry and then under constant pressure from the new regime. So that the Russian breadth of Horace Baranov could not help but seem pitiful, pathetic and broken-backed.

Therefore, whenever his will flagged and he was dragged into the green swamp of melancholy, he would lock himself in at home and drink himself under the table. The only person in whose presence he was able to be himself was Glafira Trifonova —Glasha. Glasha was lame and cross-eyed. Some years ago, when she had been pasturing a pig in the meadow, Baranov had come across her just when he was under the influence of one of his periodic fits—as rare as they were irresistible—of animal lust. And he raped her. At first he had been frightened by what had happened and promised Glasha the earth in return for silence, taking her into his house as a cleaning maid. But then he saw that it would never even occur to her to broadcast her shame.

Baranov had never married. He always said that he hadn't time for affairs of the heart. His old mother, with whom he had lived, had died soon after the war. In all likelihood, he had failed to marry because of his physical inadequacy. While still a boy he had suspected that he was somehow different from others. But it was only in Germany that this was finally and painfully brought home to him, carrying with it a burning sense of shame and humiliation that he was never to forget. Until then, Horace had never known a woman. In Germany he was twice put to shame, first with one prostitute and then another, who laughed disdainfully at the pitiful proportions of his masculine organ. Even in erection it looked like the penis of a boy, and this seemed all the more peculiar and incongruously grotesque in a man with such a strong and masculine physique. It made an indelible impression on him and since then he had avoided the company of women, fearing comparisons and new humiliations. He found compensation in eating and drinking and devoted himself body and soul to his "work."

But the incident with Glasha proved in this respect to be his salvation. He felt confident with Glasha, because she had never known other men. No one had ever experienced the slightest desire for this silent and timid little girl, who had been so deprived by nature. Just like an old woman, she used to dress in black and keep apart from the others. At Baranov's she managed the entire household and gave herself to him with meek obedience on those rare occasions when Baranov surrendered to the urges of concupiscence.

Glasha came into his life like an obedient animal, and Baranov was able to talk to her as to a faithful dog. And, like a dog, all she discerned in his words was his mood, for the meaning eluded her, or else was a matter of indifference. This was a peculiar kind of guarantee that she would never pass things on and never betray her master.

"Listen, Glasha," said Baranov to her on that same evening that the lawyer, in quite a different district near Moscow, was greeting Timur and Dunya, "tomorrow we have a customer coming. It goes without saying, of course, that one's OK, but two are better. Anyway, we've also got to get Mikhail Nikolayevich along. He's always buzzing about like a fly near a jam pot, insists on reading the instructions and hasn't got the vaguest idea what he's talking about. Because, Glasha, you'll never believe what a whopping great project is coming along soon. Bigger than anything you've ever seen. Say what you like, but Tarakanov's a real ace, and an ace of trumps at that. And once you know him, Glasha, it's useless to try to guess ahead. Anyway, it's all right, you can't have too much of a good thing. Does it make any sense to you, simpleton? The dead tell no tales. Come on, drink up, my girl!"

Already well on the way to being drunk himself, Baranov poured out a full glass of Armenian brandy and pushed it over to Glasha, who was sitting across the table from him. They were in the new house that Baranov had built after his mother's death and had equipped with all modern conveniences: television set, refrigerator and imported Finnish furniture.

Glasha jerked her head back and grimaced.

"Drink, I tell you. You may not be pretty but at least you're happy," said Baranov, raising his voice, "so say thank you—and for the brandy I'm offering you too. It's a special brand, three-star. Go on, drink up, don't sit there sniveling!" and he himself emptied his glass at a single gulp.

"Oh, I can't," responded Glasha tearfully, hunching herself up in a ball. "I'm not used to it, it makes me feel sick."

"If you don't begin you'll never get used to it, you village gnat," blustered Baranov. "And what about me, have you become used to me yet? All right then, get used to my brandy too, my young lassie."

"Oh, don't make me, Horace Evsevonovich; I can't help it, it makes me sick," said Glasha stubbornly and fixed her eyes on the table.

"And does this make you sick too?" bellowed Baranov, leaping up from behind the table, red with rage, and then slapping her with all his might across the face.

She lowered her head in silence, making no effort to evade the blow. The unhealthily pallid skin became covered with red spots along the whole left side of her face. But she made no attempt to move away, a fugitive light kindled in her eyes, and they rolled like a beaten animal's.

Baranov sat down again and continued to stare wrathfully at her. He poured himself another full glass, watching her all the while as a cat does a mouse when playing with it.

"Playing stubborn, eh?" he gritted through clenched teeth. "I'll show you, you dumb bitch!"

Big and ponderous, with his check shirt unbuttoned at the neck, he got up from his chair and went around to Glasha. She remained sitting in the same position, but seemed to grow smaller in proximity to the bulky Baranov. He snatched up Glasha's glass and pressed it to her lips, pressing down on her head with his other hand. But the girl's lips remained tight shut. Removing his hand from her head, he continued to press the glass against her lips. Her head tilted back. Encountering resistance from the tightly closed lips and teeth, the liquid ran down her chin in a golden stream and then over the bluish skin of her unnaturally stretched neck.

"My God, that's valuable stuff you're wasting," bellowed Baranov, beside himself with rage, then up-ended the glass of brandy over her closed mouth before hurling it to the floor.

Instantly he began to rain one, two, three, innumerable blows down on the young girl's face.

She groaned feebly and made a motion with her hands as if to protect her face. But Baranov seized her tightly by the shoulders forcibly lifted her off the chair, continuing all the while to hit her about the face, then carried her bodily across the room and threw her onto the divan. She rolled over face downwards and Baranov continued to rain punches on his victim's hips and waist. Glasha's puny body went limp under the impact of the blows. She stretched her arms out in front of her and buried her head in a cushion—her body seemed to emanate a strange sense of peace—and whimpered softly, like a wounded animal. Or was this her special kind of mating call?

Baranov turned her over and fell on top of her. His tiny, erected organ slipped into her and sank into her sheath—aided, without his realizing it, by the woman's eager legs.

Glasha continued to whimper chokingly, hiding her face in her hands. Baranov grunted and labored on top of her, crushing her fragile body with his weight. But her thin legs, bared to the thighs and raised in the air, were now trembling and her face, still buried in her hands, expressed submission and assent. Glasha undulated her waist and strained upwards to increase the pleasure, and to draw in still further that inadequate appendage of Baranov's great body that he employed for copulation.

Glasha whimpered and blubbered, while Baranov's movements grew faster and stronger until he let out a hollow groan and subsided.

She waited for several minutes, crushed by the weight of his sweaty alcoholic body that seemed to grow heavier and heavier. Then, with a series of agile, animal-like little jerks, she extricated herself from underneath. Baranov's body sprawled across the divan; a moment later, turning on his side, he began to snore.

5. *"Public Convenience"*

Horace Evsevonovich Baranov sat at the midpoint of the big conference table belonging to the collective farm, Sheaves of the Future. His body was squeezed tight between the back of his chair and the table, and his belly oozed over the table between his propped elbows like well-kneaded dough out of a tub. Set deep in his broad, fleshy face, which sloped in waves to his chest and shoulders, and drowning in the engulfing mass, were his tiny little eyes, beneath the bristles of his straw-like brows.

He was flanked by Valery Borisovich Tarakanov, Timur Yamshikov, Avdotya Zakharovna Pugachova, the local Party secretary, and a young woman of extraordinary beauty, with ash-blonde hair plaited and twisted neatly into a bun. She seemed to have stepped down from a painting by Vasnetsov and one might have wondered how she could have landed up here at this meeting and among such people. Next to her sat a strange-looking old man and a dark-eyed youth.

Also present were Tsanatovsky, director of a funeral bureau, who had long been connected with them; Smirnov, manager of the funeral transportation department; Mikhalkov, who worked in the store that sold "funeral accessories"; and Sofronov, the collective's chief bookkeeper. They were all complete mediocrities whom the lawyer was able to manipulate at will, men capable of any deception, any enterprise, so long as it guaranteed them the possibility of continuing to grow fat in jobs already provided or promised.

The table was covered with a red calico cloth that was clean, rather than the usual dirty one; the standard model of ostentatious chandelier hung from the ceiling; and on the walls hung a multitude of framed photographs illustrating the collective farm's idiosyncratic output: miscellaneous coffins, graves, stelae, headstones, small memorial stones and photographs set in marble. Over all reigned a plaster bust of Lenin, inscribed: "Lenin—our beacon and leader". And on either side of the bust, a bit lower, hung portraits of the General Secretary of the Central Committee of the Communist Party of the Soviet Union and the Chairman of the Presidium of the Supreme Soviet.

The eyes of those present slipped from one to another of this collection of photographs—their juxtaposition endowing them with an absurd, an irreverent meaning.

Baranov turned to Tarakanov.

"Valery Borisovich, how shall I put it, our people often say to me, 'Work's work, Comrade Baranov, and we understand that, and we know we're doing our bit for socialism, but one thing isn't clear to us. The more goods we produce for the dead and the more we fulfill and overfulfill our norm, the more people there are who must be dying in our country. And that, so to speak, is the sort of thing that can only serve imperialists and zionists. And so it turns out that for business reasons, the more people that die the better, whereas for political reasons, the fewer goods we turn out the better. And that's what's worrying us, Comrade Baranov,' said one of our workers to me the other day. As for me, Valery Borisovich, I must admit that at first I didn't know what to say. 'Don't stick your neck out,' I said. 'If that's the work they've given us to do, that means they know what they're doing. It must be right and helpful to our cause and it's not for the likes of us to worry about the contradictions of world politics.' "

"It's only an apparent contradiction!" interjected Mephodiev, the Party secretary, abruptly.

Everyone looked at him with astonishment, for he had never

been noted for impulsiveness. Normally dull and listless, in spite of his comparative youth (he was not yet thirty-five), slightly balding and with a penchant for wearing gray, he was always extremely cautious in his statements and preferred to weigh matters up before expressing an opinion. This time, however, a sensitive nerve must have been touched.

"An apparent contradiction!" he repeated after a pause and regarded the collective chairman almost with irritation. "And I am surprised, comrades, that such ideological illiteracy is still so deep-rooted in our people. You were right, of course, Comrade Baranov, to reply by affirming the wise policy of the Party, but that's not enough, comrades, that's still insufficient! We are for Leninist democracy, we are for Leninist humanity in everything and everywhere. But the point is how, what does it mean, in what sense are we to understand it? In the sense, comrades, that the time is long past when people would be satisfied with directives from the center and would trustfully wait for the achievements of socialism to follow automatically. Today the people sees our triumphant successes in the cosmos, in the international arena—for instance our decisive rebuff to imperialism in Czechoslovakia—and understands that if the state is preoccupied with such extraordinary initiatives, it cannot possibly have time for the home populations and its minor desires. Yes, comrades, that's the way it is and . . . and . . ." He was obviously growing confused and had lost the thread of his thoughts, a frequent occurrence in the presence of the lawyer, for when Mephodiev tried to shine he always got tangled up in a maze of theoretical speculation. He looked about him distractedly but his gaze met only the laughing eyes of Timur and he grew even more confused.

"Christ, what a windbag!" thought Timur.

Then, putting a serious expression on his face and staring meaningfully square at Mephodiev, Timur mockingly said something of which only the second half was fully audible:

"And . . . hot air-OLOGY . . ."

"Yes, that's it!" beamed the party secretary. "Ideology today must be fully primed for battle and the Soviet people clearly understands that it is essential to be prepared and that it has to do its homework, but at the same time it must be fully aware of our Soviet motivation. And it follows from this that we have to help the people and clarify the essence of various phenomena. The contradiction that Comrade Baranov outlined to you, as I have already said, is only an apparent contradiction and that must be clear to every schoolboy, if only because of the simple fact that death is a phenomenon that doesn't always depend on the Party and such-like organizations . . ."

At the point where he said "doesn't always," Tarakanov raised his eyes to the secretary and grinned openly, but the latter was obviously carried away and not realizing what inspired it, grew even more confused. He pulled himself together at once, however, and went on:

"Yes, comrades, men leave their jobs and, if you'll pardon me, die. And even if fewer people die here than under the rapacious conditions of capitalism, nevertheless they die—from old age, from hardship, from various accidents. And so it emerges, comrades, that our task—given that it is out of the question for the time being to prevent such a social defect—is to help people in death, just as we help them in their lives. Everything comes to us from the Party. The Communist Party gives us birth, raises us, instructs us and sets us on our feet. And the same Party sends us to the grave and erects memorials to us. And this is a great encouragement, comrades, because when it sees what pains are being taken over its death, the laboring Soviet people does not spare its efforts while still alive to see that the greatness and might of its Soviet homeland and its devoted Party continue to grow and prosper.

"No, no, it is not my intention to become demagogic," he hastened to add, remarking a fleeting shadow of impatience in the faces of his listeners and seeing a direct hint in Baranov's eyes. "I'm talking to the point. What I have just said was by no means empty phrases, but a humble attempt by a humble party worker—if you will concede me that status to clear up certain obscurities so that you, comrades, and especially Comrade Baranov, can explain them to the collective's workers. Make them realize that the work the collective has undertaken, thereby raising their living standards from the pathetic to an enviable level of prosperity, is at the same time an honorable contribution to the welfare of our homeland. By the manufacture of coffins, urns, memorial plaques and obelisks they are doing their bit to hasten the triumphant march toward the final victory of socialism. And let them know that they too, as a mark of eternal gratitude for their honorable labors, will have a first-class memorial plaque erected to them in the name of the entire, progressive Soviet people!"

Having concluded his speech, hoarse with emotion and drenched in sweat, the Party Secretary looked triumphantly over to where the lawyer was sitting. The latter smiled back encouragingly and a faint shadow of condescension passed over his lips.

"Our weeping willow's hit the target today," he thought. Then, turning to the chairman he said aloud, "Comrade Baranov, I think we should express our gratitude to Comrade Mephodiev for his pithy speech and for clarifying once and for all the patriotic character of our enterprise."

"Yes, yes, of course," said Baranov hastily. "Allow me, comrade, to express to you the gratitude of all present at our meeting. But now it is time to explain why this conference has been called. It is our task to consider routine problems of our auxiliary business and also, more important, to give our attention to one particularly significant and promising new initiative. For this purpose I would like to call on Comrade Tarakanov."

Everyone turned to look at the lawyer, who at this moment was ordering certain papers in front of him.

"Well," he said, after a pause, "I am pleased that Comrade Mephodiev has, as it were, anticipated and so to speak given his blessing to the initiative that it is my duty to outline and recommend to you. It concerns the same line of business that has so far aided the development of the auxiliary economy of the collective, Sheaves of the Future, whose basis is none other than that honorable labor on the subject of which Comrade Mephodiev has just expressed himself so appositely."

At this he raised his eyes to the secretary, who was so enraptured by this mark of esteem that he stopped mopping the sweat from his bald forehead with his checkered handkerchief.

"Yes," continued Tarakanov, "that honorable, socially useful and above all profitable labor that ideally combines the interests of the state with those of individual citizens. Let me briefly explain the core of the matter. I think it will prove to be as extensive and as promising as our present enterprise. But first of all I must tell you that the idea for this new undertaking has, so to speak, authoritative backing."

Here Tarakanov turned accidentally, as it were, toward Mephodiev and looked at him meaningfully. "Yes, hints have been dropped in circles where they never waste any words," and he again looked meaningfully in the secretary's direction, but this time the latter did not understand what was behind this persistent attention. "Well, the point is that, knowing what it is that we here are engaged upon, certain highly placed personages have let it be known to me in friendly conversation that they strongly deprecate the pathetic and disgraceful condition of our cemeteries. Furthermore, they put directly to me the following question: what can be done to improve this state of affairs? 'The statesmen of Old Russia,' said one of them to me, 'and also the leading representatives of the exploiting classes continue to be honored and esteemed even beyond the grave. They have always found a durable and honorable refuge in aesthetic and memorial cemeteries. So why should the leading representatives of the first socialist state in the world have to be hid in anonymous, featureless graves, situated (even worse) in ancient, dilapidated cemeteries where they are exposed to desecration by rowdies? There's not room for everybody beneath the walls of the Kremlin and it's high time the more prominent of our dead citizens were honored in some way over the others!' "

"Quite right! I remember my uncle saying exactly the same thing during a conversation with some generals who were friends of his," interrupted the woman with the ash-blonde hair. Her light silk dress of a fashionable shade of light brown was deeply cut in front to reveal the tempting beginnings of her high, generous breasts, which were adorned with an antique medallion hanging from a thin gold chain.

"Thank you for the validation, Marina Maximovna, but I would be grateful if you would postpone your invaluable observations until later," said the lawyer with a sour smile—he hated being interrupted.

The young woman grimaced with displeasure. "Pedant!" she thought. "I said it purposely to give him some support. Everybody knows who my uncle is."

This was only partly true. Even if everybody present knew that Marina Maximovna was living in a KGB general's house, only a few were aware that, far from being her uncle, he was her patron and lover.

Tigran Oganesyan, a young Armenian sculptor who worked with the collective, seized the chance to stick up for her.

"Marina Maximovna," he said, looking across at her with such unbridled affection that she automatically recoiled, "made an extremely relevant remark that seems to me to support precisely what you were saying."

"Perhaps," said Tarakanov, "but protocol demands that the speaker should not be interrupted, even for support. I am sure that you will all have an opportunity to voice your—I hope positive—opinions. And so," he continued, raising his voice somewhat, "it is absolutely clear that ideas of this nature, once uttered at such a high level, amount to definite instructions. This became clear to me when it transpired that the speaker was not thinking of measures to halt the disorders or calling for greater vigilance on the part of the police. No, the root of the matter went deeper than that. But in order to get a clearer indication I said, 'What we need is a brand new cemetery—not even in town perhaps, but somewhere outside. Maybe the government would set aside . . .' 'No,' he replied, 'it wouldn't be discreet, we're not talking of some luxury store for government officials, you know. You're the man with experience, try to think of something.' "

The lawyer stared hard at Mephodiev, watching to see what his reaction would be. The secretary hadn't missed a single word Tarakanov had been saying and his attitutde had changed gradually from one of simple attentiveness to outright worship. His gaze and posture were the embodiment of willing assent and eagerness, which spoke volumes more than words could have.

Tarakanov grinned complacently and continued.

"And so, comrades"—he used this word only when it was unavoidable, as at today's meeting, or in similar circumstances —"your chairman and Yamshchikov and I (he avoided mentioning that Dunya was in on the secret so as not to offend Baranov and Mephodiev) have given a great deal of thought to this matter and, with your permission, I will explain to you the plan that we regard as most feasible. The collective farm is in a position to make a piece of land available for this purpose. It's a pleasant area, peaceful and relatively close to Moscow, bearing in mind that our clientele will consist of people for whom sixty miles is no problem.

"Here, in the midst of our calm but majestic Russian countryside, they will find a deserved last resting place far from intrusions, disrespect and tumultuous disorders. Our production resources, which we shall have to expand considerably, will remain here, with the further advantage that we shall no longer have to cope with shipping difficulties. And that, I feel, is everything. There is nothing more for me to add. I am no lover of idle words, but it would not be untoward to emphasize that this new initiative [he again glanced swiftly in Secretary Mephodiev's direction], which carries the hopes of the personages I mentioned earlier, will provide the opportunity for yet greater service to our country and will give a noteworthy stimulus to the further expansion not only of the collective's economy, but also that of the whole region. We will all share in the glory.

"Here we shall create a model cemetery, a genuine monument of art that will become the pride of every Soviet citizen and the birthright of the nation. Here our most eminent citizens will be laid to rest. They will come here at the end of their glorious careers. We will raise monuments to them that will enshrine their memory, simultaneously educating our youth and providing a warning to the enemies of progress and socialism. That is our task. We shall rely upon the creative talents of our architects and of sculptors such as our young friend Oganesyan," the lawyer Tarakanov smiled at the gathered company and accompanied it with a brief, gracious gesture in Tigran's direction, "and on the skilled work of our craftsmen. And naturally the significance and artistic quality of the finished ensemble will depend upon the financial resources of our chosen clientele. This, however, will present no problems. I have finished what I have to say. Let us proceed to a discussion of the matter. Each of you is invited to offer his opinion. Do not forget, however, that everything that takes place in our country takes place for the sake of man, life and happiness."

His speech was followed by a pause and Tarakanov pulled the jug toward him and filled his glass with water. Most of what he had had to say had been intended for the secretary's ears. All the others already knew, though some of them, including Baranov, the chief bookkeeper, the director of the funeral bureau, Mikhalkov, and Sofronov needed to have an official and formal presentation of the matter before they would take part in it. Only Timur and Dunya fully understood the grotesqueness and deceit embodied in Tarakanov's words about highly placed personages.

Mephodiev was wrapped in thought and two deep, vertical furrows in his forehead bore witness to the desperate working of his brain. He was aware to the very depths of his being of the political significance of this enterprise and of the importance of the decision that those present, under his leadership, were to take at this meeting.

Timur's vanity, by contrast, was suffering heavily because his idea—and it was the sort of idea that could have come only to such a devil-may-care young fixer like Timur—was here being depersonalized and, worse still, was attributed to those apes at the ministry. He was aware that this had to be done for the sake of appearances, but nonetheless it tormented him.

"We have given lengthy consideration to what Comrade Tarakanov has just outlined to us," Timur began, and saw that he had anticipated the party secretary Mephodiev by a mere second—the latter was already straining forward, mouth open, to offer his measured opinion. "I thought from the very outset and I still think that we are bound to realize such a brilliant project, a project that only a farsighted and creative mind could have brought to our attention." And Timur thought to himself contentedly: "Stick that up your ass and let the lawyer and Dunya remember just whose creative brain it was!" Then he continued aloud, "Those farsighted minds that are leading us along the path to communism know that memorials and cemeteries will serve to embellish and glorify it still more."

At these words Tarakanov frowned. Secretary Mephodiev, who considered it both his duty and his right to speak first, once the proposition had been made, in order to orient the others, was somewhat taken aback. "This young hoodlum," he thought, "is a pretty suspicious character, and his social origins haven't been cleared up either. Look how he jumped in before me. He's not even a member of the Young Communists. Still, he went straight to the political root of the matter. Oh well, at least we're bringing up our youth in the right spirit."

"Comrades," Mephodiev said, turning to the others, "I concede that the previous speaker," and he waved his hand vaguely in the direction of Timur, content for the time being to deprive him of his name, "has anticipated me and put the matter in a nutshell. After what he has just said and after

Comrade Tarakanov's report, I have nothing to add. I agree completely, and reserve the right to speak again later at the conclusion of our meeting."

This seemed to him the most dignified course to take after having been deprived of the chance to expatiate at length and in detail in support of this new undertaking. But the others maintained an embarrassed silence, because if there were no possible objections from the secretary's point of view, then the meeting had lost practically all its purpose.

Dunya was the first to break the silence, and of course warmly supported the enterprise in the name of the Georgian Marble Combine, whose interests she was representing. Marina Maximovna could not resist the opportunity to get in another dig at the lawyer. She again underlined the fact that her "uncle" had also expressed a desire to see such a cemetery come into being, and she let it be understood that this circumstance was in itself a highly encouraging factor, once you took into account the special circles that her uncle frequented. She added that in her opinion it would be a mistake to let the future clients have too big a say in the esthetic design of the memorials, since this might lead to bad taste and destroy the artistic value of the ensemble.

Tigran Oganesyan lost no time in supporting Marina. He announced that Marina Maximovna had given expression to that "delicate, spiritual sensitivity that is the hallmark of the Russian woman" and proposed that all funereal projects be made subject to inspection and approval by an artistic commission before they could be built. It went without saying, of course, that he himself would be a member of the commission.

An elderly writer, Gleb Matsa, said that the new cemetery would have to locate its roots in the old Russian tradition of burial mounds, and added that while the esthetic merits of the memorials were under consideration, there should be control of the epitaphs as well. As they all knew, he himself had collected dozens and dozens of epitaphs during his journeys through Russia and abroad. He proposed that they be published in a glossy booklet which would serve as a guide to the cemetery's clients.

The chief bookkeeper raised the highly relevant question of how they were going to obtain their clients and how they were going to let it be known in the right circles that such an enterprise was being undertaken.

He was answered at once by the secretary, who rightly remarked that if it was true, as Comrade Tarakanov had explained, that certain highly placed personages had voiced this idea, then they themselves would nominate deserving corpses, and it would be indelicate, to say the least, to open the gates of the cemetery to all and sundry without distinction.

The final word was spoken by Tarakanov, who clarified certain technical details of the undertaking and announced that, so far as suitable clients were concerned, he would not fail to seek clarification from his highly placed contacts. On the other hand, he considered it quite a good idea for the others to spread the word in circles as might conceivably be interested in this new undertaking.

With this in mind it was decided that some of them—Tarakanov himself, Timur Yamshikov, Dunya, Gleb Matsa, Marina Maximovna and Tsanatovsky—would exploit their wide circle of acquaintances in order to make the necessary contacts.

The conference continued for almost four hours. The collective farm's boardroom was filled with tobacco smoke, and Baranov, tired and sweating but at the same time extremely self-satisfied and proud of himself, couldn't wait for the drinks and snacks to be served as a reward for all this mental strain.

Two pretty young collective farm girls were already setting out the table with the best that Sheaves of the Future had to offer. This was not, alas, the fruits of the collective's labor in the fields. It had been bought in the capital on the proceeds of their income from coffins, gravestones and similar appurtenances of death.

But what difference did it make? The generous nature of this primordial Russian peasant, Horace Evsevonovich Baranov, elevated by Soviet power to the role of manager with a horizon that was far from narrow, genuinely rejoiced at this chance to do his guests proud.

And when the collective's lands were graced with that memorial cemetery that had been the subject of today's meeting, what abundance would then flow over the land, thanks to that silent marble, those sober memorials and those glorious graves!

6. *And the Cashier Counted Click, Click, Click*

By the time Timur and Oganesyan appeared at the party the mood of the assembled guests had already passed that point at which people are still arguing, when pairing off with girls is still within the bounds of decency and the guitar—an indispensable part of such affairs—has ceased to be a mere accessory and has taken on a major role of its own. When all suddenly fall silent, as though at a command, their eyes staring into space; when you seem to be teetering on the edge of an abyss, beyond which the mystery of life begins, and every glass brings you closer and closer to infinity; when each object around you—the turntable of the record player, Tolik's drawing on the wall, the supple curve of a girl's neck—seems somehow displaced and unnaturally enlarged by a telescopic lens, concentrated in its materiality, in its only apparent banality (for in truth this only masks its essence, which is full of significance)—then the guitar, this oracle of the absolute, and the song it accompanies, conquer the whole of that space won from disorderly cries, and reverberates in the soul as an echo of that unique sound by which the surrounding world expresses itself.

A youth in black trousers and polished ankle boots was playing the guitar and singing. His long fringe of dark hair had been brushed to the left side of his face, where it half covered a burn mark running from his temple down to his cheekbone.

From his chair in the center he was controlling the mood of those present, who kept to the sides of the room.

Three youths and two girls were sitting tightly squeezed together on a low sofa. All the rest were scattered about: sitting on sofa cushions on the floor and leaning back against the walls. One extraordinarily young guest, still a schoolboy practically, had squeezed himself under the table, which was littered with dirty plates, leftover good and empty bottles and glasses and had been pushed back against a wall.

When Timur and Oganesyan arrived, the youth with the burn mark was softly intoning—and slightly lisping—a song by Galich, with his head bent to one side and his eyes half closed. His face expressed not the slightest sign of surprise at their appearance but remained impassive and immobile. He merely flicked his eyelids up and fixed them with a glance for not more than a second; then, continuing to play and croon softly, he quickly dropped them again.

Timur took a swift look around. His glance fell on a loose-limbed, pale-skinned man with thinning blond hair, and instantly he tensed and raised his eyebrows. This character, who was obviously locked in mortal combat with his true age and straining with all his might to resist the galloping onrush of his fifth decade, glanced back at him with sky-blue, innocent eyes. Timur averted his gaze.

The thirty-five-year-old blond was an artist and decorator. He loved to play the role of a nonconformist and was followed about by a troop of pupils and disciples. But he was never short of official commissions either. His new gray-blue Volga matched his pink and white face very well. And everyone was fully aware that he was a master of compromise. Several years ago, when it seemed that a lot more latitude was going to be allowed, and when it looked as though many barriers and many constraints were going to be abolished, he had been one of the first of those young artists who had stood out in their words and deeds as freethinking iconoclasts. But at a time when the others were running into all sorts of difficulties and obstacles, although they had been far less outspoken, he, on the contrary, seemed to provoke no displeasure in the Artists' Union and was able to exhibit in all the big exhibitions, at the Kuznetsky Bridge and in the Manezh, and take on fat commissions from industry, not even disdaining mass commissions from the state. And he even managed to get a grant to stay at an artists' residence abroad.

And now, when the wind was blowing in a different direction, it didn't seem to affect him at all. He simply ceased proclaiming himself in public as the founder and champion of iconoclasm. When among friends, he was the first to criticize the situation of art and other aspects of the country's cultural life, disregarding the possibility that his words might reach those who would most like to know about them. But whereas his friends stayed out in the cold, on the fringes of cultural life—and it was common knowledge that they were constantly being subjected to all manner of pressures and suppression—he himself continued to flourish.

Timur had known him for a long time now, unlike the others, who had learned of his existence only during his brief, but fairly dramatic rise to fame. Timur had numerous contacts in the prominent, wealthy families among whom the artist enjoyed great social success, carrying out the commissions of stately family heads to paint portraits of their wives and daughters, or even of the pastersfamilias themselves, who were high ministry personnel, various kinds of managers or responsible officials. And Timur, who moved in the same circle and who received commissions from these same wives and daughters—for rather a different kind of objet d'art—often used to run into him.

From their very first meeting the painter had treated Timur with great friendliness, and despite the latter's attempt to stay at a cool distance, had insistently sought his acceptance. But this constant flattery only aroused Timur's suspicion and put him on his guard. He carried out his own sort of reconnaissance and what he learned about the painter turned out to be much worse than he had supposed. He was informed that the painter occupied himself with "work" that had very little to do with art, but that, in all probability, "inspired" his creative brush and enriched his palette. He was not just a common or garden informer, but a thoroughgoing professional secret agent.

Nobody paid any particular attention to the arrival of Timur and Oganesyan. One or two glanced absently in their direction, but at once averted their eyes and plunged back into their thoughts, or perhaps sensations. The fact that they were followed in by Galya, a tall, slim girl, with green eyes who was a friend of the host, was sufficient to reassure anyone who didn't know them; this guaranteed that Timur and his companion were friends of the family.

"Wait a bit," said Galya. "Vadik will finish soon and a lot of them will be going home."

Suddenly the guitarist threw his head back, speeded up the rhythm and his fingers began to race over the strings. In a strong, somewhat sharp voice he ended the last verse, rapping out the words as if clicking up numbers on an abacus:

And the cashier counted click, click, click
And the cashier counted click, click, click

Ah, what a pleasant subject. . . .

The guitar fell silent and he reached to the table for his glass and emptied it with a single gulp. Somebody half-heartedly applauded.

"I dunno about Little Red Riding Hood," exclaimed the youth sitting under the table, "but the whole country's cash-boxes are doing nothing but going click, click, click!"

"Hey, you under the table, keep your mouth shut! Secret Chinaman!" grumbled somebody else. "That's not the point."

"Timur!" exclaimed the artist, coming toward him. "Let an old man welcome your coming and honorably retire from the field of battle. I leave you in excellent company and wish you an abundance of sensual pleasures and the blessings of passion."

"Begging your pardon, but what *is* the point then?" insisted the youth under the table who had been called a secret Chinaman.

"The point, junior, is genes," replied an athletic young fellow who was sitting on the sofa with his arms around a pretty brunette. "It's not ideology that will create the men of the future, but biology—and that in a dozen years or so. It all comes down to what genes the future government prefers."

"A typical professional distortion of biology students," retorted Oganesyan with a touch of irritation.

"That's the way it's going to be. Genetics laboratories will prepare master blueprints according to the aesthetic canons laid down by the government. It will mean an end to your caprices, maestro."

"All right, boys, who are we dumping tonight?" called the painter from the doorway, where he was taking leave of the host. The three who had accompanied him there were already standing beside him. Then two others rose and joined them on their way out.

Ed, the host, who was tall and skinny, just like his girl friend, had a permanent smile on his face that revealed huge, horsey teeth. Only now did he emerge from the next room to see his guests out. When the painter and his retinue had disappeared, Timur went up to Ed in the hall.

"Do you know who he is?" he asked, his voice lowered and jerking his head after the departed artist. "He's a well-known informer."

"He came with Vitaly, I couldn't very well keep him out!"

"Watch your step! What I'm telling you is straight from the horse's mouth."

"OK, I've got it. Now listen, I've got a couple of things to tell you. First, Zyama Silach has put the finger on that auxiliary cop, you know, the one who was giving them all the business in the fifth district. He made life miserable, he did, everybody hated him, even the quiet ones. Zyama had a girl friend and this character started bugging her. That's no way for a decent

Soviet girl to dress, he'd say, the son of a bitch, and he also started getting at Zyama, saying he was a loafer, a parasite, a social enemy, and so on, in the same insulting and threatening tone. And then he tried to get the girl to inform on Zyama. Well, Zyama had already warned him to steer clear and not to keep bothering him for nothing, because he was just a stinking shitkicker and thug, and he'd better get the hell off if he knew what was good for him. This time he lost his cool; it had been going on for too long and it was time to teach this obnoxious windbag the score. Wham—Zyama let him have it with his knife. That cop, he says, went dead white even before he croaked—just stood there, propped up against the wall, like a living corpse. Well, Zyama had to finish him off, of course. The trouble is he's got no alibi. Can you think something up and take care of him?"

"M-mm, I guess so," said Timur slowly, emphasizing the complexity of the situation, and then added firmly, "Yes, I'll do it. What was the other thing?"

"You see that stocky guy over there? He's one of us," Ed continued.

"I know. So what?"

"Well, his uncle's a well-known scientist, his name's Dermoshchenko; he was really famous in his own time. But nowadays he's being suppressed. He used to belong to Lysenko's group and now they've been discredited and aren't allowed to work. That young man is a biologist too," he nodded in the direction of the athlete sitting on the sofa, "and he says his uncle's nothing but a fossil now, a dinosaur, totally decayed and senile, especially now they've discredited the Lysenko outfit. The thing is, he complains he's not being given a chance to carry on his research on a collective farm (better late than never after the rubbish they put out!). His speciality is shit, well, you know, manure—he's supposed to be perfecting fertilizers. But he says that chemical fertilizers are worthless, that you have to stick to nature and make use of our country's natural wealth. And his nephew seems to have told him that he might be able to find him a collective farm, where he could go and live quietly and wallow in as much shit, that is to say manure, and play around with as much fertilizer as he liked, so long as he didn't interfere with farm production, and if he would agree to stick up for his collective farm colleagues. 'They'd meet you halfway,' said the nephew, 'and you in turn, if needed, would express your gratitude to them by your actions.' Naturally the old man was overjoyed and fell over himself to thank him. 'I see the younger generation is not forgetting its old scholars,' he said, 'and I thank you for your trust.'

"The point is," continued Ed, "you can give him a place and let him make the most of his manure. Then rumors will go around that there's some experimental work being carried out at your collective farm and that a well-known scientist has chosen your particular farm, Sheaves of the Future, as a place to conduct his experiments. And that will bring you prestige and respect. And the regional party will react favorably too. Furthermore, he belongs to the group of party members that fought against cosmopolitanism under Stalin, and you know that it's raising its nasty head once more. It's not a bad idea. What do you think? It's mutual aid, and from our point of view an auxiliary anti-tank defense that we can't afford to ignore."

"OK, it's a deal," answered Timur just as coolly as before. He turned to look at the biologist, as if inviting him to come over. The latter rose from the couch and approached.

"That's a bright idea of yours," said Timur, "thanks. I'll talk to the boys about it and let you know what they say. As far as I'm concerned it's on. But," his tone suddenly changed and his bright cold eyes chilled the young biologist, "what do *you* get out of it all?"

"I hate his guts," retorted the other sadistically. "Let him drown in his lousy shit."

"OK," said Timur, "that gives me the picture."

All this time Vadik, the guitarist, had been immobile, his eyes half closed, head lowered, sprawled back in his chair—it wasn't clear whether he was perhaps dead, asleep, or had simply retreated into himself, and was roaming the realms of his own solitude.

The athletic biologist returned to the sofa and whispered something in his girl friend's ear. She started to laugh noisily. His arm encircled her neck and his hand disappeared inside the neck of her blouse. While he sat there, cradling her breast in his hand, two other girls, blind drunk, laughingly started climbing over Tigran Oganesyan, pulling at him and fighting each other for possession. Tigran was sprawled out on the floor, reclining on the cushions that had been tossed there, and the two girls thrust their fingers into his thick black hair, pretending fright, and pulling out the hairs one by one: "Ouch, ouch, it's biting! He's got millions of them in his hair!" Then one of the girls suggested they examine the hairs on his chest as well. In a flash they had unbuttoned his shirt, exposing the dark, hairy, tanned chest of the young Armenian.

Vadik, meanwhile, had started strumming his guitar again.

> Figs are now grown by Eskimos
> And the Sahara's knee-deep in snow.
> Those bastard scientists, just for a bet,
> Have turned the whole world on its head . . .

The secret Chinaman suddenly felt sick (from too much drink, evidently) and left the room. Galya had put the bottles Timur brought on the table. The two of them were now sitting on the sofa, crowding the other pair. But the athletic-looking young biologist and his girl friend were now locked in an endless kiss and nothing in the world could penetrate their nirvana.

> The tropics are where the poles were
> And Tokyo's swapped with New York,
> Whether it's rabbits they deal with, or man—
> The scientists couldn't give a damn!

Ed was in the next room with his girl friend, while in the main room the two girls continued to struggle with Tigran's body, having almost completely stripped him by now. They were sweating and panting and uttering shrill whimpers from time to time; their state evoked contemptuous pity. One of them was bending low over Tigran, so that the people sitting on the couch had a full view of the backs of her plump, naked thighs. Galya was also fairly high by now. Her green eyes gleamed and she kept trying to tell Timur something. He did not reply, however, but sat there motionless, staring ahead, and it was impossible to tell whether he heard her or not. Galya was considered a highly desirable prize. She had a type of beauty that only recently, during the past ten years or so, had begun to appear—and that very rarely—on the streets of Moscow: slender and fine-bred, full of pride and a barely perceptible promise that concealed both sensuality and strength, and a fearless, haughty face. She had been discovered by Slava Zaitsev.

> It's five weeks now since I slept with a girl,
> For five weeks now I've been going around ill.
> My buddy is no better off,
> They say he's been poisoned to death.

The unstoppable Vadik went on with his song and the soft sounds of his voice and guitar gently permeated the room. Nobody paid any special attention to him, but everything that happened was possible only because of his magical presence and his sorcerer's instrument. The combination of music, liquor, arguments, shouts, silence, warm young bodies under the pressure of fancies and desires—all this created a new dimension, a previously non-existent space in which everyday time came to a halt and free truth triumphed. Such things happen rarely, because in this agglomeration of a thousand factors, it is sufficient for merely one factor—for instance one of the people present—not to merge with the general mood and the magic disappears, everything succumbs to gravity and remains in the unbreakable grip of workaday reality. But when the chains are broken and the prison walls trampled down, the world becomes ineffable and all that is banal and ugly seems lofty and inspired.

"I was waiting for you to come," said Galya.

"I know," replied Timur, continuing to stare straight ahead.

The pair beside them remained in their unbreakable embrace, their hands wandering in search of secret places exuding warmth.

"Why can't you understand, or why don't you want to," persisted Galya, "sometimes it seems to me that you just don't want to think about what I could do for you."

"That's not true," replied Timur, coming to life at last and turning to face her. "I can see you and I understand you. You are wonderful, incomparable. It's that I'm a blockhead."

Vodka's what I recommend,
So as not to go round the bend,
The stoker says vodka in plenty
Is the best cure for strontium-90 . . .

It was difficult to make out what was happening between Tigran and the two girls. A writhing mass seemed to be thrashing about in the corner, a multi-limbed animal snorting in low tones—discernible as bursts of muffled human laughter.

"But why, why?" insisted Galya. Her slender fingers ran in quick little steps over Timur's muscular hand, then paused in anticipation and suddenly dug into the skin with terrific force, leaving behind two deep indentations like the marks of stiletto heels on the sun-softened asphalt of a midsummer pavement. A few moments later two little pools of blood formed there.

Timur didn't move a muscle, but merely looked indifferently at his hand. Then he turned his impassive gaze on Galya and asked ironically, "And what now?" A pause followed before he continued: "How boring this life is! I'm finished. I exist only because I long ago ceased to exist. All my happiness is inside me and only inside me."

Vadik, who was still playing the guitar, reached once more for his glass on the edge of the table and emptied it into his dry throat. Then, watching Timur intently, he continued his song.

I believe it, yet can't believe
That an end will come to my grief,
And the globe goes spinning on,
And still the direction is wrong.

Galya raised her head, her green eyes gleaming and her chin proudly tilted back.

"Here's my hand," she placed her palm in Timur's, "burn it, mark it with the emblem of your cowardice!"

A harsh grin was the only reply to her words. Timur had so turned in upon himself that his cheeks were pallid and gave heightened color to the scarlet tip of his cigarette. Calmly he took Galya's hand, turned it palm up, stared for a moment at the tender, helpless wrist, and then coolly pressed his lighted cigarette against it. Galya did not draw her hand away. Timur, to prevent the cigarette from going out, raised it over the bluish skin; the glowing spot continued to burn, fed by a fraction of a millimeter of oxygen.

And the globe goes spinning on,
And still the direction is wrong . . .

Vadik repeated the last couplet and aimed a friendly wink at the two of them. His face had difficulty in expressing anything like friendliness, impeded by the long slits of his eyes, the gray skin and the terrible, violet scar that disfigured it. Even when the eyes did try to form a smile, the rest of his face showed nothing but a monstrous grimace.

He finished his pizzicato. And only then did his eyes, turned upon Timur and Galya, fill with a new expression, as they realized at last, it seemed, the full import of what they saw. A gambler's gleam came into the eyes. Then they ran swiftly around the room, as though inviting the others to share the sight with him. But all they found there were bodies absorbed in their own pursuits.

The three of them were alone. And of the three, Vadik was the odd man out. But as soon as Timur sensed that he was the object of attention, that Vadik was participating in this little scene, he felt revolted by the whole affair. The game with Galya was serious and cruel, concerning the two of them alone, and had nothing in common with false show or a cynical bet between men.

He removed the cigarette. He was sorry for what he had done, he could not tolerate a third person's having seen it, thus endowing it with a totally different meaning.

Only then did Galya remove her hand, grimacing with pain. She groaned angrily, contemplating her violated wrist. Her eyes clouded over, then she turned to Timur and in a clear, calm voice said:

"Thanks. That souvenir will never go away."

"Get me a drink, dopey," said Timur, "what the hell game do you think you're playing anyway?"

Galya stood up, went to the table, filled a clean glass with vodka and returned to Timur. "Can I have some?" she asked, standing opposite him and raising the glass to her lips. Bending forward slightly, she offered it to Timur. Her eyes were filled with the desperation of love.

With a single swift blow, Timur knocked the glass from Galya's hand—it shattered to pieces on the floor. "What are you up to now? I asked you for a glass of vodka, not a cupful of slobber!"

Vadik placed his guitar on the floor, got up from his chair and went over to the corner where Tigran was entangled with the two girls. He dug the toe of his shoe into one of the girls. She raised her face to look at him.

"What do you want?" she exclaimed. "To have me?"

"Let's go into the corridor," he said in a not very friendly tone. "I don't like it in here."

The other girl moved to get astride Tigran and with all four hands they guided the instrument of lust into an anxious receptacle. It fitted perfectly.

Galya retreated to the table. Timur followed her, carefully picked out a glass, calmly filled it without haste and drank it off, not paying the slightest attention to Galya, but looked first into the corner, where two human bodies were jerking rhythmically, and then at the couch, where the other couple had also yielded to lust.

"Galya," he said with restraint, "there's another way of doing it, isn't there?"

"Yes," replied Galya hastily and agitatedly, in a voice that was barely audible.

What had happened to her pride? Her mystery? Her charm? Only devotion, adoration, the thing that was called love, identification and dedicated passivity could lubricate their secret passages and this led, in the final analysis, to impulses of quite a different character. He recalled the episode at the cemetery and the widow who had participated in his satyriasis with such transports of union and ecstasy. And again this image pierced him, taking his breath away and kindling in him the fire of revenge, of retribution for what he couldn't find here now, but that had been given him, so it seemed, by that woman at the cemetery. He was aware that this was an illusion, a reflection of his own imagination, an image that he himself had created at his own command. He had no doubt that Pythia, in reality, had been a vulgar strumpet. He knew that the widow was like all the others and could offer him nothing that was new, only the same old moist, slippery flesh, passively exhaling warmth and an acrid tang.

He moved close to Galya, with a swift movement pressed his firmly erect penis to her yielding body, crushed her in a forcible embrace and ran his tense, avid tongue over her lips. Galya went limp in his arms. Supporting her with his right arm, he used his left to push up her skirt, baring her high hips. With his knee he separated her legs—yielding, quivering with desire and ready for anything—those long legs that had looked so inaccessible earlier.

He was aware of her desire, but did not accept it. Galya was panting for air with parched lips, and tears welled in the pools of her eyes. Still standing, her body had been forced back over the table by Timur's body, resting on the empty bottles and dirty glasses. With one hand, whose bony relentlessness she could feel on her soft skin, he tore away the thin cloth of her pants and aimed his rapacious rhinoceros horn at the spot where woman's flesh is most vulnerable and destined to be pierced and split. Her eyes remained motionless in gratitude and ecstasy. Angrily, Timur felt himself plunge into something that was endlessly receptive, yielding and welcoming. His anger made him drive deeper, farther, in search of an end, but there was no end, and to sense himself and her better, he withdrew and attacked again. And then he did it again and again, desperate for resistance from this body that gave itself to him without pride.

Galya closed her eyes and compressed her lips so as not to cry out from the sharp, piercing pain that rose from the pit of her stomach to her throat and cut off her breath. Timur could find no bottom, Galya was a richly plowed field, but Timur's plowshare was sharp and cut a deep furrow in the flinty earth. Through the sharp, shooting pains Galya felt the onset of a powerful lust that overcame everything else. He possessed her, she belonged to him totally, but to a certain extent it was also a victory for her, although she knew she owed it to the contemptuous magnanimity of a warrior who abandoned the vanquished on the field of battle. She almost lost consciousness in a rushing wave of excitement and satisfaction, which followed inexorably as a result of his unceasing, almost mechanical thrusts. Not with her body, but somewhere deeper, with her soul, her consciousness, she registered the birth of his spurting emission. Timur jerked his penis out and for a few seconds watched the copious sperm of his ejaculation as it splashed from his male flesh. Trying not to touch it with his fingers, fastidiously he tucked his penis into his trousers and closed his fly. Then he left the room and went out onto the balcony. Day was just dawning. Neatly strung diagonally across the street, the street-washers, those hard-working denizens of nocturnal Moscow, crawled over the gleaming asphalt like slowly moving beetles.

7. *Dog is Man's Best Friend*

Valery Borisovich Tarakanov had just finished shaving in the brightly lit bathroom of his country villa. Once more he examined himself in the mirror, checking to see whether his youthful cheeks were smooth enough, and rejoiced at his achievement. Shaving for him was always a long drawn out and meticulous exercise, because for dozens of years now, Valery Borisovich had always used a cut-throat razor. Even when the safety razor had made its appearance he rejected its use, and was even more contemptuous of that barbaric recent successor, the electric razor. He followed a similar line in everything, wherever possible, and particularly in the small things of life, which are all that can offer us a bare minimum of freedom in this fearsome age of ours. For him it was a duty to remain faithful to a given style of life, to the style he had grown used to in his stepfather's house in pre-revolutionary St. Petersburg.

His stepfather had been a rich and famous stockbroker, one of those representatives of our then nascent financial bourgeoisie—subsequently to be swept away by historical events—that combined admiration for the political order, morals and culture of the West with a sincere attachment to the best traditions of the Russian nobility and a genuine nostalgia for it. It was in his house, among the circle of his friends—which included the most prominent names and greatest fortunes in St. Petersburg—that the young Tarakanov had been formed. His mother, whom his stepfather, twenty years older, had married after she had been left a young widow with two small children on her hands, had died of consumption before he was five. One could say, in fact, that Valery had hardly known her, because toward the end she had lived abroad practically permanently in the sanatoriums of Switzerland and the Italian Riviera. The stepfather had supervised the education of the two young orphans, though he had been able to manage it only partly with Valery's sister, Olga, who was much younger. Valery's stepfather had wanted him to have a career in the law and had sent him abroad to visit France and Germany. But the Revolution put an end to all that. Stricken with paralysis soon after the events of October 1917, the stepfather died in the terrible winter that followed. The young Tarakanov, meanwhile, was living in Moscow, where he decided to stay, trying to make certain that nobody would recognize him. And he also tried to forget the house and circle in which he had grown up, emphasizing his own surname, his father's name, the name of his mother's first husband—it was a name like any other, with no reason to be remembered for anything, particularly since its original owner had long since passed away.

And so Valery Borisovich Tarakanov succeeded in completing his legal studies without complications, thus fulfilling his stepfather's desire, and then worked at his specialty and adapted to the new and constantly changing conditions of life in Moscow, for that was the only thing to do under the new social order. But his intelligence, his cunning, his tact and his caution were such that he not only remained alive, but even won for himself the modicum of prosperity possible to acquire in the new conditions of life. And he managed it in such a way that he never drew attention to himself nor got in anyone's way, but remained always in the shadows, far from the official posts that many sought out of vanity. At the same time he spun around himself a dense web of important contacts and highly placed friends. Not only did they give him a feeling of security and guarantee him against trouble, but they also provided the platform from which Tarakanov, during this latest period, had been able to launch and develop his various commercial enterprises, including the "C Business."

It was precisely this commercial activity of his that turned the ageing Tarakanov's thoughts back more and more to the world of his youth, to that time of commercial and financial excitement in which his stepfather had been active and which, for half a century now, had disappeared as if forever. The long decades of his activity as a lawyer now seemed to him like an extended intermission and occasionally, perhaps as a result of the feebleness of age, he caught himself thinking. "Who knows, perhaps Russia, after decades of bitter, internecine struggle, will live to see the dawn of new, freer relations, when enterprising people will at last occupy their proper position in the life of the nation and the concept of economic life will become more flexible." The very growth of the country's productive capacities, together with the complexity of contemporary production technology, had reached such a stage that they were threatened with degeneration and death by suffocation unless these forces found new channels for free outlet and nourishment. Everyone knew this. Many of the people Tarakanov mixed with voiced the same thoughts in one form or another, especially those who were more aware of the pressures generated by comparisons with the West and of the nature of contemporary public opinion.

Such initiatives as the car production plant at Togliattigrad and numerous, similar but smaller-scale, agreements with the West seemed to him a good sign in the context of his own hopes for the future. In this he found both moral justification for his own activities and a fresh stimulus, particularly now when they promised to become really important, thanks to the project for a memorial cemetery.

"Huh," thought Tarakanov, "they've had to turn to capitalist industry and bring in Italian specialists to produce Signor Automobile. In order to produce the Bologna—symbol of technological bad taste and boring uniformity—they had to bring in a whole factory from abroad and then have foreigners swarming over it for six whole months in order to teach our workers how to run it. And the result: an expensive, clumsy product of low quality. We, meanwhile, are forced to produce our artefacts at a loss in order to satisfy the demands of the population, operating at the borders of legality, twisting and turning this way and that, and covering our tracks like common pickpockets. Why, without us this whole ponderous machine would seize up and grind to a halt! Always in Russia our best people have perished before their time, the national genius has been suppressed and foreigners have had to be called in to carry out tasks that we were more than equal to ourselves. How many pairs of capable hands there are in Russia, how many inventive brains—just give them their head! And a stimulus! They'll weave you such a magic carpet as will cover the whole of Russia, and from there the wise, ingenious, inventive thoughts of the Russians will take off and fly up into the cosmos. Down with our chains, down with autocracy, be it tsarist or Soviet, for all they do are hold us back and crush the life-giving shoots, for above all they are frightened of their own people and demand only one thing from them—loyal subjection. They have drafted their own kith and kin, children of the same mother earth, into a military colony, where the soldier is forbidden to think aloud, forbidden to use the language of man to say what he is thinking to his brother man. But man is born to think! And it was just such a brother-man-soldier who laid the foundations of cybernetics, when marshals and generals hadn't even dreamed of such a thing in their comfortable party beds. The very first mention of cybernetics brought down the full wrath of the autocracy: it was proclaimed to be against the law, non-existent—Antichrist in the temple of Marxism—and then suddenly Simple Simon woke up, raised his hands with surprise and intoned: the lack of cybernetics has resulted in the lack of computers, the lack of rockets, the lack of space satellites, and the retarding of progress into the cosmos. For them, of course, the main thing was that the cosmos—whose infinity could not be comprehended inside those narrow foreheads (and they rejected divine assistance)—should be dotted with red flags. So cybernetics was rehabilitated. But then the boneheads dug their heels in over plastics, semi-conductors and aeronautics. Chemistry reared its head like a black nightmare. But then even here, as usual, the plain soldier, sometimes even the nameless inmate of a prison institute, had to come to the aid of castrated science. Go on, let us search, invent and think our human thoughts! Can we go on like this? Who among us thinks? Marshals and generals, great strategists, the fathers of mankind. 'Hey, you over there, shut your face!' they yell if anyone steps up with a tentative suggestion. 'Don't get in our way! The voice of the individual is less than a squeak. Everything must go through the strict hierarchy of the bureaucracy—that's where to begin!' The Party! The brains of the working class, the managers of the class, the strength of the class, the glory of the class! And what does the Party brain work at? Security measures are the immortal creation of the Party. But what lies behind the red banner carrying the slogan? We have become the laughing stock of the world, we have to imitate foreign automobiles, cameras, overcoats and a thousand other things demanded by the greedy philistine for lack of any thoughts in his head. We are behind in everything: in light industry, in agriculture, in chemistry, in electronics. It was this last defect, blast it, that cost us the moon. The delicatessens are empty, caviar has disappeared and even the modest pickled cucumber has become as hard to find as pineapple . . ."

Tarakanov cursed his seditious thoughts about the fate of Russia and buried them at the back of his mind. He had no wish to poison the satisfaction that his excellent shave had given him and his delight in the enchanting June morning of the countryside just outside Moscow. He glanced through the window and a smile formed on his lips. His firm nostrils, hairy and sensual, quivered imperceptibly, as though sensing game or catching the aroma of cakes baking.

In a glade between the birch trees Dildor was romping with

Mokh. Her straight black hair streamed in the air and bounced against her back. The angular profile of the young Azerbaijanian girl was poignantly noticeable. The gracious movements of her long, tense legs energetically propelled her light slender body, already at the point of flowering into the full-blown woman she soon would become.

She ran barefooted. The panting dog ran after her. Dildor ran up to a fir tree, turned in a flash and sank down at the foot of it, leaning her back against the trunk. The dog came running —and stopped in bewilderment. The laughing Dildor raised her bent arms in the air and repeated the movement several times without stopping. Joining her hands to form a wedge, she tenderly beckoned to him.

Mokh stood up on his hind legs, growing suddenly tall and large, and held the stance a few seconds. He looked comically human and clumsy, with his tongue hanging out to the side from a mouth that seemed to be smiling; and his smile revealed two rows of white, threatening fangs. Then, carefully and tenderly, he placed his front paws on the girl's shoulders, pushed his muzzle into her face and thrust his tongue against her cheek, then licked her all over, using it like a quick-moving palette knife.

Laughingly, Dildor bent her head away, trying to escape Mokh's bold assault. Her fragile hands pushed against the animal's ribs and with the tips of her fingers she felt the strange vulnerability of his ribcage with its prominent ribs, protected only by the taut skin, which in turn was covered with soft down. Through her fingers she felt a sensation of tenderness and embarrassment flow into her.

"Sit, Mokh!" she exclaimed.

The dog obediently did as he was told and curled up at her feet. But the moment Dildor leaned forward and came close to him, he rolled over on his back, presenting a picture of submissive surrender and utter devotion. He gazed at her with almost human eyes that were filled with sensuousness. And, indeed, in this position his ribcage, stomach and penis (exactly like a grown man's in its hairy sheath) suggested the participation of equals in the game that Dildor had just thought up, and in which all the natural elements of two living, aroused bodies were to be employed. Sex was an essential factor in this game, but both Mokh and Dildor were unconscious of its external manifestations, and this testified to the innocent spontaneity of childlike creatures, in whom sex is an essential, crucial, but deeply buried instinct.

This always happens when close relations are established and a friendship is struck up between a domestic animal—a horse, say, or a dog—and a young girl at the moment of her transition from childhood to adolescence. If the animal is a bitch or a mare, these relations are of quite a different character and do not evoke the same feelings of attraction and delight in the girl. And the same is true of friendship between a boy and a bitch. From this one may conclude that it is precisely the unconscious knowledge of the real possibility of sexual relations that secretly excites the girl. Generally it expresses itself in reciprocal erotic tension: for the girl, the dog or the horse is transformed into the image of man in his primeval, natural state, powerful and masterful; for the animal, of course, the opposite is true—the young human female becomes his mistress, his goddess. How many stories have been written on this theme, especially in English and Scandinavian literature. Upbringing, environment, fear—all these leave definite sexual traces in the young developing woman. But far more often than we imagine, excitement of a purely erotic nature, masked by friendship and devotion, is complicated by and expressed in ambiguous caresses, immodest physical contact and tender indulgences. Children never tell adults of this—neither their parents, nor, in later life, their husbands. Occasionally, but not very often, a friend of the same age may be informed about it, but then she is lost track of as the two grow older.

In this happy situation Dildor possessed three specific advantages: Mokh was not only a good-natured and intelligent dog, but he had also been trained differently from most other animals. He had no idea how to be aggressive and was hopeless as a house dog, but on the other hand he knew perfectly how to perform various erotic exercises with human partners. Secondly, this hospitable house, the villa in which Dildor now found herself, seemed to her, after her impoverished village in the depths of Azerbaijan, like a fairytale castle. And lastly there were these kind people who had taken her in and who were caring for her and cherishing her, enabling her to bask in peace, happiness and freedom.

Tarakanov and his sister, Olga, when speaking in the girl's presence, made it a rule, with cunning indirection and suitable hints, to imply that they found it perfectly natural that a girl of her age was almost certainly a woman already, almost certainly had already had men friends and could think of nothing but love, could desire nothing more for herself than love, joy and satisfaction.

When alone with her, Olga Borisovna taught Dildor how to care for her body and her hair, how to hold herself, how to make up her eyes and numerous other tiny stratagems and intimate secrets that were a real revelation to Dildor. She shared with Dildor various memories of her childhood, when she too had had a faithful dog for a friend, had been inseparable from him, had shared his games and his food and had much preferred him to the nasty, stupid boys who had only hurt her (at this a shadow passed over Dildor's face), whereas her Jack . . . And then she told her how Jack had been shot, how she had been inconsolable for months, in faithfulness to her loyal friend, and then had decided to resort to the use of her own hand. And since, at this point, Dildor had been puzzled, Olga Borisovna had exclaimed in astonishment: "What, child, don't you do it! But you're a southerner, where's your eastern blood? Don't tell me you don't know how to do it! There's no pleasure in the world like that we can get from gently rubbing that little button in our pussies . . ." It should be added that Dildor didn't always understand everything that she heard in Russian, and spoke it even less.

Russian was a foreign language to her, learned in school; at home in the village she had spoken in her native Azerbaijanian, or rather in one of its numerous dialects. In this respect the Tarakanovs were extremely useful to her, for they spoke the purest literary Russian of old St. Petersburg, which sounded strange and out of date on the streets and in the offices of the present capital, but here, in the countryside outside Moscow, in this villa set in natural surroundings, furnished with antique furniture and filled with books bound in gold leaf, this language sounded both beautiful and natural. And as often happens at that age, Dildor was growing by leaps and bounds. Suddenly she was showing astonishing progress.

Dildor lived in a world of enchantment and remembered nothing of her former life; and she had decided not to dwell on the question of how long this enchantment was likely to last. This morning was somehow special, everything in nature around her suddenly seemed brand new. The air smelled of fresh grass and foliage; it was rich with the coolness of water and the azure of distant sky. It was languorous and at the same time vibrant. Dildor felt her life merge with this mysterious world that beckoned to her so insistently.

While Mokh, still in the same position, was regarding her with eyes full of that resigned cunning that only dogs possess and pulling at her shoulders with his broad front paws, trying to recall her to the game she had suddenly dropped, Dildor discovered that he had suddenly grown strange to her and that she had lost all interest in their game. Mokh too had suddenly ceased to express that mysterious hairy force (though he remained just as close to her and just as different as she was from all adults) that had dictated her actions and drawn her into the joyous interplay of two equals. He was once more an animal, her dear, darling dog. And she was his mistress. He was obedient to her. And now she had decided what they should do.

Thoughtfully she ran her eyes over his body and her gaze lingered on his black balls and furry penis. It was the first time in all these days that she had examined it so frankly. It wasn't at all repulsive, nor even frightening. Not so frightening, at least, as his black lips and sharp fangs. She guessed that it was soft and strong, like his tail, that it could have no resemblance to the one she had not even been able to glimpse, but that had crushed her like a thick, blunt log, that had burst its way into her without ceremony, inflicting a piercing pain upon her, ruthless and revolting, like Mohammed himself from their native village, a brutish, abhorrent rapist.

What did he want with her? Why had he done it? Dildor knew what the boys and girls used to do in such circumstances, how the bull used to cover the cow, but what had that to do with the way he had thrown himself upon her, like a jackal, when she was on her way home all unsuspecting, and had then sent some strange men to her house to announce that she was now his. Her father had agreed with old Mexeti that the best thing would be for her to go away. But this episode had nothing to do with the way her pussy (as Olga Borisovna called it) felt tucked away down there between her legs. Where nobody could see it, except she herself, when she was in private and examined it with curiosity and excitement, although she had not the least idea how it could possibly turn into what everyone assumed it would; sure, this was entirely normal, it really had to turn out that way, because that was where children came from when they were born, and that was why people married and cohabited, and this was what women used when they did things with men, just like the animals. But really—how?

When Olga Borisovna gave her her bath, she told Dildor that she was extremely pretty, that her pussy was pretty as well, that she was an utterly charming little woman and that it was stupid to worry about what Mohammed had done to her—after all it wasn't such a tragedy, he hadn't spoiled her in any way and she was no different from other girls. It was best to forget that she bore this scar, for it was all nonsense.

Dildor quickly glanced around her to see if anyone was about. No, all was quiet. The windows of the villa about fifty yards away were blank and silent. There was not a soul in sight. Then the girl sank down at the foot of the fir tree.

"Mokh, come here!" she commanded him.

The dog rose to his legs and obediently came up to her, wagging his tail. He immediately tried to lick her, but Dildor stroked his head and pushed his muzzle away from her. With her other arm she encircled his neck, holding him beside her. Mokh wagged his tail happily, reassured and grateful.

Dildor removed her hand from his muzzle while continuing to hold him beside her with her other, and gently began to stroke his stomach, gradually sliding her hand lower in search of that which had long since aroused her curiosity. When her hand, as if by accident, reached the spot, she quickly jerked it away again, watching to see what the dog's reaction would be. Mokh remained calm and indifferent to what she was doing. Then, with the tips of her fingers, Dildor began to stroke the fur encasing the dog's penis, not so much afraid as closely attentive to the results of her actions. Mokh remained calm. She pressed a bit harder and her fingers could feel the soft throbbing flesh of the penis. It seemed to her as if the dog moved and she looked into his face. Mokh turned his head and seemed to look at her questioningly. But Dildor knew him well enough to understand the agreement expressed in that look and in the dog's whole behavior. This encouraged her and she grasped the penis with her whole palm. Her heart was beating strongly. Again, she looked about her carefully.

Birds were chirping loudly in the trees surrounding the villa, but she did not hear them. Her ears were filled with a persistent, continuous buzzing noise into which she sank deeper and deeper so that it formed a background against which the sound of her beating heart and Mokh's breathing seemed very close. Now it was no longer curiosity, as before, that impelled her, but excitement and anticipation, as though she were expecting something to happen. It was strange, but it was precisely the calm warmth of Mokh's body, which she still encircled with one arm, and the misty gaze, full of gratitude, that he turned on her, that reassured her and gave her the boldness to continue her action.

But what did she want from him? To touch him *there*, to discover how he was made, to do something new on this morning that was so new for her, something new for herself, because this morning she felt everything differently from before; she seemed to herself both bold and brazen. And then, somewhere at the bottom of her stomach, yes, that was it, just there, she felt the pulse of independent life, and also some sort of strange, unfamiliar sensation that made her want to laugh. It wasn't that it itched or burned, although there was a hint of that at times, but that her body bore something reminiscent of an open wound, which brought her not pain, but on the contrary was the glowing source of pleasure, something that endowed her legs with the strength and desire to run, something that sought an outlet in search of something else, wishing to crush this "something" or else to be crushed. And now, caressing the dog, she noticed that not only was it gay and amusing, but that the impatience rising within her was becoming a voluptuous fever and her entire being was in commotion.

The captive of her own actions now, Dildor stroked the dog's penis along its entire length, feeling its shape in order to ascertain where it began, where it ended, how it was made and what mystery, what secret it contained within itself. And perhaps without her realizing it, her hand grew more insistent, trying to hold even tighter this newly discovered shape. In continuing these researches she involuntarily squeezed his balls and the animal let out a resentful yelp. But Dildor quickly adjusted the action of her hand, fondled Mokh's ears soothingly and tenderly spoke to him in her own language. The dog fell silent. It even seemed to Dildor as if he was enjoying himself; she could see it from his face and open muzzle and sense it in his breathing. And it seemed to her as if the thing she was stroking had grown bigger and longer. She bent down to see whether this was her imagination or had really happened, and what she saw exceeded even her dreams: the penis she held in her hand looked back at her like a fiery red weapon, so red that it seemed bloodstained or inflamed. The sight of it evoked in her a novel sensation of both disgust and pleasure and she continued to gaze at it at the same time as she continued to stroke it, carried away by what she was doing and wondering how it would all end. But evidently her clumsy and unpractised caresses, even if they had afforded him a certain pleasure to begin with, now only irritated and disturbed him. Suddenly he turned his head, thrust it down towards his stomach, sniffed it, together with his reddened penis, and suddenly started to lick the latter with swift strokes of his tongue.

A moment later he shuddered all over and Dildor jerked the hand away that had encircled his neck in sudden surprise. Having lost all contact with the dog, Dildor remained sitting on the grass. Then the dog suddenly placed its forepaws on her shoulders, pressed its stomach up against her hand and commenced to rub it rhythmically back and forth against her hand, which at once felt the pressure of the strong burning flesh of his penis. She realized that her shoulders were a support for Mokh, but were too low for him. She straightened up so as to make him more comfortable. The animal's tenseness, the violence with which he carried out these actions, which, apparently, afforded him great pleasure, finally conquered Dildor. She yielded herself up to his jerky, exciting movements and this opened up to her a world of new, totally unsuspected sensations, endowed her with a fury she had not known before and a ruthless, feverish desire to experience that which her partner was experiencing.

She passed her hand over her crotch and inserted a finger beneath the elastic of her pants, lifting, as she did so, her light summer skirt and exposing her still childish legs and hips. When her fingers lighted upon the bigger lips of her sexual parts, which had been violated and wounded at such a tender age and perhaps for that reason now parted so distinctly, she experienced a feeling compounded of relief and rage. Ah, so here it was! Here was where she had to touch it, that strange little creature, and at that moment she started to become a woman. Carried away by this new sensation she leaned her body forward and Mokh was thrown backwards. But not for long. In an instant he leapt between her legs, hungrily thrust out his moist nose and began to push it towards the spot that she was rubbing. Dildor did not take fright. Her deep instinct told her that this was a kiss and that she should yield to it. With her right hand she continued to fondle her own flesh where Mokh had insistently thrust his nose and with her left she pulled off her pants, fully disclosing the flower of her lust. This crowned her pleasure: to feel it free of the cloth, naked and exposed and bathed in streams of fresh air.

Mokh, it seemed, had been expecting precisely this. Thrusting out his tongue, he commenced violently licking the pink petals of flesh. Occasionally the dog's hot, rough tongue touched Dildor's fingers and she withdrew her hand in order to experience the tongue better; its burning, tormenting contact pierced her from head to foot. Her head was aching from its odd angle, but she felt so inexpressibly happy that she desired nothing more.

Dildor was unaware that the whole of this scene was being observed from the villa.

"The girl's life has begun," said Olga Borisovna and there was both sorrow and excitement in her voice.

"Yes," responded Tarakanov, lowering his binoculars, "she will remember this and be eternally grateful to us. It is thanks to us that she has been able to recover so quickly from the shock to her system and gain control of herself. Be gentle with her, Olga. I, unfortunately, have to leave. I've got an important meeting in town. With Frolov."

Olga Borisovna's face looked serious and troubled.

"Be careful, Valery," she turned to her brother. And then she added cheerfully, "Oh, Marina called; I forgot to tell you; Dildor distracted me. She asked me to remind you not to forget June 24."

"Ah!" exclaimed Tarakanov joyfully. "Excellent! That will be a day to remember!"

8. *The Man from Underground*

The night was quiet and warm. The gilded cupolas of the Kremlin churches, the marble, the cement—everything had a soft sheen in the impassive moonlight; and the drowsing center of Moscow was suffused with sweet airs. On Red Square, in Gorky Street, in Kalinin Street, the ceaseless human flood had subsided and quiet had taken over from the endless crowds of Russians and non-Russians, of visitors of all nationalities from the innumerable regions of the boundless Soviet Union and of foreigners from all corners of the world, who by day exceed the number of Russians in this part of the city. Now it was totally deserted. Night enveloped everything and only the sharp beams of passing headlights snatched strips of asphalt, stone and cement out of the blackness and slid over the endless windows of the administrative and public center of the Soviet capital. The doors of the Bolshoi Theatre had long since closed behind the last of the departing spectators. The dolls and toys in the department store, "Children's World", maintained their inert existence outside of time. Most of the buildings were plunged in that dumb inertia that is characteristic of a city's business and administrative districts at night. With the exception of the Hotel Metropole—of whose night life the average Muscovite is totally unaware—undoubtedly the most alert building in that part of town and at that time of night, the most active, the most pulsatingly alive and the one where the most concentrated work was being done was the building on Dzerzhinsky Square that enjoys an unenviable notoriety under the name of "The Lubyanka", in which the Committee for State Security (otherwise known as the KGB) has centered its activities. Thousands of invisible threads extend outward from this building over the entire country, threads for observing, decoying, confusing, entrapping and paralyzing the citizenry, while thousands of others branch out and multiply and succeed (even without the sophisticated apparatus of modern communication and an army of agents) in conveying the sufferings and hopes, the groans and messages of the prisoners, linking their hearts with thousands of other human hearts throughout the land.

It was precisely here, right next door to the most awesome building in the whole city and land, in this triumphal sacred district at whose heart lies the Kremlin, where the state's magnificence and might are celebrated, where foreign tourists and delegations come to salaam before these manifestations of the state's power, where the whole architectural ensemble, especially at night, takes on an air of severity and grandeur and the walls, those jealous guardians of their secrets, bear down on frivolous nightbirds foolish enough to disregard them, threatening to crush them—it was precisely here that there lived an inoffensive-looking little old man whom, for all his inoffensiveness, the KGB would almost certainly have seized had it known of his existence, if only because his existence was strange and inexplicable and also because it was quite exceptional and quite unlike the existence of anyone else. This man was Gleb Vyacheslavovich Matsa, the elderly writer who had spoken of burial mounds and epitaphs at the conference of organizers of the "C Business."

It would be incorrect to say he "resided" in this district of Moscow, since Matsa was not named in any household register or on any list of the district's registered inhabitants; therefore, he not only didn't reside here, he didn't even exist. The basement of the building at the very heart of showplace center Moscow, in which he had fashioned his lair, was officially designated as a store belonging to the collective farm, Sheaves of the Future. People working in offices situated in the same building, it is true, and also some of their visitors, were occasionally amazed to see quantities of coffins and plaster and marble busts being unloaded from trucks beneath the poplars in the yard and then disappearing rapidly down the steps leading to the low entrance to the basement, through the energetic efforts of stalwart and efficient unloaders. But each one of them thought that if anything like that was taking place it was bound to be in order and therefore bound to be legal, and so each saved his amazement for the far stranger things that are happening in our native land. It was also true that the janitor and various other visitors to the house quite often met this curious little old man during the day, with his quick movements, careless clothing and a sharp, not to say fierce expression in his eyes behind the lens of his glasses, as to make even the loaders cringe. But there was nothing at all unusual about this: they took the old man for a storekeeper or simply a watchman.

Nobody realized—except for the participants in the "C Business", and not all of them—that the spacious premises of the basement were not entirely taken up by the store. What the loaders saw in the depths of the basement when they carried the things in was a solid wall pierced by a single, small iron door. It went without saying, or seemed to if you followed the logic of the situation through, that this door led into a mysterious underground refuge bearing some official function, where surely the fire extinguishers were kept and access could be had to water pipes, electric cables and all the paraphernalia connected with the normal running of a large city building. The loaders and other casual visitors to the store had never known this door to be opened.

But sometimes many hours, and even days, passed during which not a living soul, even for a second, came near this basement at the base of that enormous pyramid. And who could suspect that the sole possessor of a key to that door was none other than old Gleb Matsa? Behind the brick wall he had two rooms and a bathroom. The rooms were quite tiny, but they had central heating and a telephone ("their" man in the telephone service had found no difficulty in taking a wire in to make an extension to the legal telephone belonging to the store). Furthermore, there was a tiny iron staircase leading from Matsa's bathroom up into a trapdoor in the ceiling, whence access could be had to the closet beneath the stairs inside one of the main entrances to the building. Matsa had a key to this door too—it had not been difficult to arrange this through some of Timur's friends for whom copying keys was part of their trade.

And so Gleb Vyacheslavovich Matsa was in every sense of the word a man from underground. But even if he lived underground, he nevertheless had a comfortable self-contained apartment with two rooms, telephone, bathroom and front and back entrances —and he didn't have to cope with people living over him in a communal apartment, nor with neighbors sharing the same landing, nor with a house manager, nor with the housing department, nor even with the cop in charge of their block. He belonged neither to the category of "underground men" who inhabit basements from necessity, nor to those who are proclaimed to be outside the law and are accused of conspiracy. All this was remote from him. He simply lived there, and this was just the best way out for a man who cherishes his personal freedom and who values his personal right to solitude. And there can be no doubt at all that not a few inhabitants of Moscow would have envied him his underground residence, if only they had known about it.

Naturally, to reach Matsa's den you had to thread your way through an extensive series of basements piled high with coffins, headstones, statues and suchlike funeral attributes, but few would have minded in the least all this funeral frippery had they been the owners of a similar two-room apartment. Incidentally, there had already been an impressive precedent: the Master in Bulgakov's wonderful novel, *The Master and Margarita.* It was the Master who put the idea into Matsa's head.

When you stepped over the threshold of this residence you

found yourself at once in a wholly different world, a world that had nothing at all in common either with this grim cold store of reminders of the grave, or with the external world, of which it was both the continuation and the conclusion. The visitor's feet passed in a single step from bare concrete to a soft and vividly colored Caucasian carpet, and he was at once enveloped in an atmosphere of warmth and coziness. Two things completely dominated this room: paper and cloth. Paper was represented by an enormous number of books that filled the shelves lining the walls and were scattered about everywhere, lying in heaps about the floor and in corners. Apart from books, the room was also filled with drawings, lithographs, engravings, photographs and illustrations from newspapers and magazines that chaotically plastered entire walls, in some places even overlapping, so that not a single spot was left free. Here could be seen drawings by Vrubel, lithographs by Feofilaktov, sketches by Roerich, reproductions of several of their paintings and a copy, done in oils, of Somov's watercolor, "Death and Harlequin", that was larger than the original. Behind glass hung the covers of the first numbers of pre-revolutionary art magazines, such as *World of Art*, *The Golden Fleece* and *Apollo*, and also a cover from the post-revolutionary *Lef*, together with reproductions of pictures by Malevich, Larionov and Lissitsky. But all this was lost in a welter of old maps, newspaper clippings and pencil sketches by unknown artists on odd scraps of paper.

At first, these thousands of objects aroused one's curiosity and the desire to linger over each one of them in turn. Then, instinctively, the glance would travel upward to encounter the sole gap in this mass of paper—a single tiny window that served as the sole inlet for light and air. The glass was frosted, and when the light was on in the apartment, the window was covered with an opaque black cloth of the sort that old-fashioned photographers used to use. It was decorated with the figure of a naked woman of an unbelievable shade of pink, whose mound of Venus was covered by a luxuriant tuft of golden fleece.

Beneath the window was a tall desk with a slanted top like a lectern. Such desks were used during the last century for writing while standing up. Over it hung an office-style lamp with a green glass shade, while beside it was a high round stool. Everything else in the room was low and soft, recalling rather the furnishings of a nomad's tent in Asia than a contemporary European apartment. The opulence of cloth, leather and wool was represented by a low wide divan on which rested a mountain of cushions and pillows. Cushions slipped from it on all sides and tumbled to the carpet. Pieces of beautifully woven native tapestry that could have been from the Carpathians, the Caucasus or even Central Asia—it was difficult to be certain in this anarchic profusion of color—covered the shelves, the round table in the center of the room (whose height did not exceed that of the low divan) and even a saddle that was situated next to the divan.

Astride the saddle, with his short trunk erect and his palms resting on his sharp little knees, looking full of dignity, sat the owner of this hospitable cave, Gleb Matsa. He was facing the divan, on which, reclining on the cushions and holding a porcelain cup in her hand, sat a blonde young woman, the very one that at the Sheaves of the Future meeting had referred to her important uncle and who was now arranging for the memorable meeting to take place on June 24. Matsa was saying something, and as he spoke his big prominent ears moved on either side of his small, naked skull and seemed even bigger than they were; and the countless wrinkles on his forehead moved with them, now contracting, now spreading, like tiny waves rushing up the smooth motionless expanse of his skull, as up a beach, there to flatten out and expire. His little green eyes, whose fierce expression inspired fear in those who did not know him, now glinted playfully and were completely friendly, although still as penetrating. It seemed that deep down inside them there flickered a tawny flame of unquenchable feline vitality.

"As you can well imagine, Marina, that character almost ran into us. But Timur braked, backed up and stopped him. After that it turned into a cursing match. I don't know how it would have ended if it hadn't turned out that he was from Mnas and Timur, it seems, even knew how to speak the language."

"Well, after a fashion, I suppose, but Timur's father really was from those parts. He worked in a factory there and after that went panning for gold," explained Marina.

"What? What's that you say, Marina? A gold prospector? A workman and at the same time a gold prospector? Did I hear you right? How—independently and not in a co-operative? Do you mean to tell me that that was possible at the very height of the Soviet era? But you know that all mining for gold, just like all other sorts of mining in our country, is the sole prerogative of the state and is under the state's direct control!"

"Yes, but not everywhere, it seems," responded Marina thoughtfully. "Timur told me that in the Chelyabinsk Region in the mid-thirties there were many workers who, like his father, abandoned the factory to go looking for gold. There was no way of stopping them and the authorities were forced to accept a compromise. What's more, at the gold-buying points, where it sold for forty rubles a gram, payment was made by vouchers, and in the shops these precious vouchers were exchangeable for no less precious goods. I don't know how it is now or whether things have changed very much."

"Now isn't that marvelous!" exclaimed Gleb with childish delight. "This old Russia of ours never ceases to amaze you with its fantastic revelations—even when you are as ancient as I am. I don't mean about the gold, but the people. The people who contrive to wriggle out of all possible kinds of imposed schemes and throw off even the strongest shackles. But where did they look, those gold prospectors? In the river?"

"River? What on earth are you talking about?" laughed Marina. "No, the amazing thing was that they found the gold in the fields. There was wheat sprouting all around, while the gold just lay there in the ground. They just used to wash the earth as they plowed."

"So Timur's the son of a worker and gold prospector!"

exclaimed the old man gaily. "What a combination. And possible only here in Russia—or perhaps in America too," he added after a moment's thought. "That explains a lot."

"But, Gleb Vyacheslavovich, you don't know Timur's mother. She was an extraordinarily erudite and intelligent woman," Marina went on enthusiastically. "And her mother, Timur's grandma, was a celebrated teller of folk tales and is still alive and living in her village." Marina placed her cup on the large round table and settled herself more comfortably on the cushions, her generous swelling form clad in silks that parted to reveal a white plump, but beautifully sculpted knee. "It's no accident he's done so well," she added seriously.

"I had no idea you were so well acquainted with the details of Timur's biography," commented Matsa, somewhat surprised. "I've also known him for a long time, but I didn't suspect anything like that."

"He's reserved," sighed Marina. "He only told me one or two things because I insisted. Ordinarily he's quiet, reticent—and he doesn't much care for me," she concluded unexpectedly, her eyes flashing angrily, deep and blue as a bottomless pool.

"Now, now, none of your coquetry," Matsa smiled indulgently, "what woman's wiles are these? Who doesn't love you? He not only deeply admires you, but truly respects you as well."

"Oh yes, of course," retorted Marina spitefully, "he loves me, respects me and admires me, but he doesn't desire me."

"But this antediluvian old fellow here desires you, even though as a boy he used to sit on the knee of Alexander Blok," said Gleb Matsa jokingly, taking in at a glance the monumental splendor of Marina's young female flesh stretched out on the divan. " 'The Muse in spring's raiment appeared to the poet,' " he added ironically, saying this more to himself than to her before continuing: "He doesn't desire you because you are too much alike. Love between similar natures is the most difficult of all, though once it triumphs it is also the fiercest: as intense as incest, as savage as onanism and as vital as sodomy."

"Do you really think we are similar, Gleb Vyacheslavovich? I'm just a simple woman . . ."

"Yes, a woman," Matsa interrupted her, "and maybe even simple, but at any rate with a Russian soul as desperate as a bottomless abyss."

He got up, went over to the table and poured another cup of tea for Marina and himself. Marina sat upright and watched him pour it. Just as at the meeting, the two perfectly white hemispheres of her breasts bulged from her décolleté. In the warm deep provocative valley between them nestled a crucifix instead of the medallion she had worn that day. The tiny ears peeping out from under her heavy blonde hair seemed fragile under the weight of her sapphire earrings. When he had poured the tea, the little old man returned to his saddle.

"Gleb Vyacheslavovich," said Marina, "you often speak about Russia and the Russians as if they were somehow special. Why is that? Don't you think this specialness is nothing but a cover for their grayness and stupidity, their monstrous and deformed natures? It can be used to justify tsarism, the revolution, Stalinism, Khrushchev, the idiocy of the present government and our celebrated passivity. Maybe there's a grain of truth in it somewhere, but all the same it smells. If we have to live without hope of achieving the kingdom of God here on earth, then I agree with our youth: let's live normally in a modern humane way and throw out all these nostrums and this useless hypocrisy. Russia won't suffer from it and won't disappear. She can only gain, because she is being ruined and paralyzed by all the brocade and velvet that her governing peasants have used, from Ivan the Terrible to the Soviets, to hide her sores and her glorious nakedness."

"And is it you saying all this to me?" smiled Matsa, "you who are one of the few Old Believers left alive?"

"What's it got to do with my faith?" retorted Marina severely. "I'm not talking about myself. For me, for us, all earthly power is sinful. But whoever believes in earthly institutions, if he's logical, is bound to reject the theory about Russia being special. This has always been a cover for the most hideous bestialities, starting with the tsars and continuing right up to Stalin and even to the present day. It's a convenient credo for those who are in power, for those who have been unlucky in life—cowards—and for those who are inclined to justify all forms of power. 'It can't be helped,' they say, 'communism's a utopia, but western standards don't fit us. Russia's different, she has her own ways.' And with this the circle is closed."

"The circle is closed; everything is justified; everything is as it should be," added the old man, completing Marina's thought. "But I'm against all that! And you know I'm against it. Russian singularity contains both resignation and rebelliousness, but above all unpredictability! That is what we have to rely on and there's no need to deny our originality."

"How shall I put it," Marina struggled to express her idea better. "All I'm saying is that I'm no writer and no philosopher, but it seems to me that all this is inside us, it's ours and no one can take it away from us; we apply it without thinking about it. But whoever tries consciously to exploit it, on the other hand, no longer serves the truth. And it has always been that way, from the Slavophiles of the past to the Slavophilism of today. Lenin and the Bolsheviks made a revolution precisely by negating the specialness of Russia, in the name of modern progress and western ideas: the French Revolution, industrialization, the commune, Marxism, and so on. But then elemental Russia devoured everything and came out on top again."

"Yes, the revolution lived only for a single morning, while Russia is still copulating," grinned Matsa. "Russia's a whore-mother: the orphan revolution was raped and thrown out onto the streets and then some secret policeman murdered her without knowing who or what he had murdered."

"The secret police don't need to murder anyone any more," said Marina thoughtfully, "they are the masters now."

"And that's why I talk about Russia and believe in her," Matsa almost shouted in a piercing voice, now growing heated for the first time. "Because I can't conceive of the fascist being here, of the Russian retreating before him, of Russia being already dead and buried—It cannot be, it cannot be!" he repeated twice, as though speaking to himself in tones of anger and disbelief. "It will all crumble to dust and Russia will be resurrected."

"But Dostoyevsky prophesied," said Marina quietly, a smile on her lips, "that there would come a new breed of men, gray nullities who would destroy everything and set up a nonlife, an anti-life. An Antichrist would come—only after that everything would come to an end . . ."

Matsa argued with passion, almost trembling. He did not gesticulate with his hands, but kept them on his knees, where they opened and closed convulsively. Marina gazed at him with enchantment; her tiny lips, parted and gleaming, revealed a row of white, even and perhaps slightly too large teeth.

Once again Matsa thought, as he had done in the past, of how similar she was to Gorky's Marina in *Klim Samgin*: that same heavy beauty and the same name, the same teeth and the same love of serious conversation. Only Marina Kerzhentseva here before him was no street trader, but the mistress of a KGB general. Still, what difference did it make? Marina Zotova could quite easily have been the same. The thought of this similarity titillated and at the same time annoyed him, for he was no lover of the later Gorky—it was too obvious and lifeless, the boring monologue of a philosophizing old man. But, as he detected the shade of Zotova in Kerzhentseva, he couldn't help acknowledging a semblance of reality in this fictional phantom and hence a certain vital strength in her creator and his novel.

"Goddam it!" he exclaimed, and Marina thought this had to do with the argument they were engaged in.

Matsa got up again and left the room. When he returned, carrying a bottle of vodka, Marina was sitting on the divan as before, but her naked legs now stretched its entire length as far as the table. Her tiny pink puffy feet rested on the dark varnished wood beside her empty cup, between a glass holding a spray of lilac and a pile of books. The book on top was a numbered copy of Butkovskaya's 1912 St. Petersburg edition of Beardsley, with an introduction by Evreinov. Marina was naked as far as the waist, her full silk dress cascading down to the left in myriad folds and pleats. Sitting there calmly in a perfectly respectable pose, she was slightly arching her naked, softly rounded belly, the fleshy button of her navel and her muff covered with light amber hair. Her large plump thighs were slightly parted to reveal the still lips of her sex. In this position she looked as if she were preparing for a gynecological examination. But the distant look in her eyes and the tense expression of her mouth suggested a condition more like the sudden onset of a fit.

The old man continued to behave as if nothing at all had happened.

"Here, Marina, cool and fresh, just as it should be. It's Wyborowa—Polish. I'm not such a maniac for everything Russian, you see. Anyway, it's vodka and that means it should be disposed of in a minimum of time. One can also drink brandy, of course, but then it has to be French or at least well-aged American, and not some of your three-star Georgian poison for upstart party bosses. Oh, how beautiful you are!" he exclaimed suddenly, scrutinizing her from head to foot. "You are as naked as death or rock, as a cold fish on a golden tray. You can feel the Spanish fly, eh?"

"Fly?" asked Marina in reply. "What fly?"

"Spanish fly, my beautiful lady!" laughed Matsa. "I put some in the tea, because disgusting old Matsa doesn't always have faith in himself. But then, why 'Spanish'? It's got just as much right to be called Russian. They fly in June, these green rectangular beetles—here as well as in Spain, and also in Sicily, I believe, but that's it, as far as I know. From time immemorial they've been caught, dried out in paper bags, crushed and used for poultices and dressings. Man has always tried to arm himself with anything that enables him to extend his powers. In Brazil and Mexico they have coca, damiana and hundreds of herbs and mushrooms . . . Dangerous, did you say? Well, it's not impossible. You just have to know whether the game's worth the candle. Naked desire dictated by hormone demands leads only to simple acts of sex. Eroticism is born here," he struck his forehead, "and nature has given us everything we need to strengthen and sharpen it. So why abstain? We don't abstain from crab and celery, do we?"

Spreading her legs wider apart, Marina placed her hand between them, covering her light hair, but leaving her fingers slightly parted so that her swelling lips remained visible between them. Whether this was a clever game or unconscious, it was difficult to say. Probably the former. The hand remained motionless. Everything in this large ripe body was motionless, as though resting. Only her breasts rose and fell, her eyes burned, and waves of feverish heat emanated from her.

"And how did you manage to find it, this fly I mean?" said Marina with an effort, as if from far away.

"How?" responded Matsa cheerfully. "I went hunting for it. It wasn't possible, I thought, for such an ancient tradition to disappear completely without trace. And in the end I was lucky. I came across a man at Tishinsk market. We chatted about this and that. He raises bees and has preserved the secrets of the old mead distillers. He's absolutely soaked in genuine old Russian traditions. We became friends. He told me about this green wonder in our forests. He knows them well, of course, for they are usually found in the vicinity of beehives, these mysterious dangerous insects . . ."

"Dangerous insects," echoed Marina distantly, as if relishing these words.

"Yes, dangerous, because you only need to make a mistake with the dose or overdo it and you're a goner. Death by poisoning. Your kidneys are totally destroyed. And death is accompanied by an unstoppable sexual frenzy. That is why I was fascinated by this stinking insect, the bearer of lust and at the same time of certain death, an omen, already present in nature's chemistry, of the bond between eroticism and eternity."

"What?" asked Marina eagerly.

"Between two absolute dimensions." Matsa settled himself

once more on the saddle and gazed enchanted at Marina's sex. "The poison has already penetrated your mask, the poison is flowing through your fingers, your eyes are poisonous, like a serpent's. So let congress take place. Perform your sorcery!"

"Yes, yes, let them be joined together! Let them burn as I burn!"

"Burn, burn to ashes, witch!"

Marina's fingers worked frenziedly between her legs and the liquid azure of her eyes traveled downwards along two almost palpable metallic trajectories.

9. Frolov's Dream

"What queer people are running around Moscow nowadays," thought Avanchel Frolov as he settled down in his armchair in his fifth-floor apartment on Television Street. As he had got out of the car that brought him home that evening he had noticed a man and woman on the sidewalk in front of his apartment block.

The young man had a shock of blond hair and a cheeky provocative face, with the eyes of a tough. As for the young woman with him, one could say with certainty that she was very pretty in spite of a slight squint. She was strikingly elegant, and Frolov instantly attributed this to the foreign clothes she was wearing. The young man, although no child, exhibited signs of retarded infantility in his face; he was also fashionably dressed, a fact which displeased Frolov.

But the strangest thing of all was that such a frivolous and suspicious-looking young man then got into a new, coffee-colored Volga. Before doing so he held the door wide open for a bit with his right hand, while holding on to the young woman with his left. He was smiling unpleasantly and it seemed to Frolov as if he were holding the woman by force and perhaps even trying to drag her toward him. But her face, as Frolov looked at it, kept changing its expression, ranging from fright to condescension, and he concluded that they were simply playing some peculiar and badly thought-out game known only to themselves and no one else.

Once home, Frolov calmed down again and with relish consumed the excellent fish soup that old Lukeria had skillfully prepared for him under the strict supervision of his no less skillful wife and cherished life's companion, Larisa. Then he downed a generous shot of vodka, pouring it from part of the service that had been presented to him in Hungary at a reception given by Rakosi, when he was there with a Party delegation. Frolov was a connoisseur of the creative arts of the fraternal peoples from the socialist countries. Apart from this Hungarian dinner service, he had furniture from Yugoslavia (goddam it, fancy letting a country like that get away! With that beautiful Dalmatia! A foothold in the Mediterranean!), lots of Bulgarian carpets, electrical equipment from East Germany (Ulbricht's our man, well tried and faithful), Czech crystal (there we bloodied their noses when we had to) and even sheepskins from Albania (to hell with those fleabitten shepherds, they're half Turks anyway and have nothing to do with the working class!). All this was the result of innumerable trips he had made after the war as a respectable and responsible citizen, and as an old member of the Central Committee of the Communist Party of the Soviet Union since the time of the Eighteenth Party Congress.

Settling his ponderous body comfortably in a leather armchair, Avanchel Frolov lit up a largish Cuban cigar (among his friends he liked to say that the only good thing Khrushchev ever did was support Castro—thanks to his love of cigars. He didn't care for their rum, nor for their music and dances, which to him smacked of indecency; and as far as their sugar was concerned he had no interest in the matter, since he had long been a diabetic. Let the long-suffering Soviet people have sugar as a compensation for all the bitter pills it had had to swallow from all those imperialist aggressors. But cigars were another matter, these you could accept with a clear conscience from those brigands over the ocean).

And at this point the thought of those lascivious Cuban dancers (he had never been there himself; by then the time had passed when his services and his experience as a leading party official of the thirties still counted) reminded him of the couple he had seen on the sidewalk. There was also something strange about the two of them. And yet he would bet they were both Russian. The young man was certainly Russian, and the girl too, probably, despite her foreign finery. The thought preoccupied him. How could such types suddenly appear in Moscow? For the thing that really bothered him was that they were by no means lone examples, not simply birds of passage who had accidentally alighted on the city; he had previously seen others like them. While Stalin was alive such a thing was unthinkable. And even for several years after he had died everything had stayed the same, except for the occasional eccentric throwbacks to the past that turned up here and there. But they were definitely relics of the past, whereas these were still young, the children of victory. And we had been brought to this by the rotten line adopted by Khrushchev at the Twenty-Second Congress, this is what came of blackening everything, of destroying everything, of giving in to demagogy—or even worse, to the most disgusting Dostoyevskianism, kowtowing to the unconscious instincts of the masses.

Oh yes, here they were traveling about in their Volgas! While we, old fools that we are, are preparing to speed up the production of automobiles for them! But at what a price! All they do is hold up the traffic and paralyze the city transportation that is so vital to the state and to a planned economy! And what for? To take their girls for a ride! My god, the nerve of it! Back, back, back! What has got into their stupid heads? That the Soviet system is English democracy? Or French wine? Or a Togliatti vinaigrette? Our aim is the greatness of Russia, the greatness of Communism, for Communism cannot prevail without Russia's greatness and greatness demands sacrifices, discipline, order and an iron grip! That's what He understood perfectly. He led the people with a firm hand, and the breath of greatness was in everything, and this breath, thanks to Him, inspired the twentieth century. He knew how small man is, how petty and bad, and how he has not yet grown sufficiently to fulfil his high tasks. He corrected Leninist idealism, He understood that man cannot be changed, that man always goes against his own interests, that socialism has to be constructed against his wishes but in the interests of his own welfare and happiness, that to give the people their freedom is too dangerous: the people will dance like a bear at a bazaar. The people need a wise father, the whip, fences in order to achieve greatness and create history. But they cast Him down into the mire, they threw His remains to the dogs—and why? In the name of the dubious and ambiguous humanism of the philistines and petty bourgeois, in the name of the people's welfare, as if the people know where their true welfare lies and what they really want.

The people deified Him, while He whipped them, crushed them, punished them and rewarded them. And they didn't give a damn for that clown who offered them a corncob as though it was the golden fleece, and they also know what to think of the gray efficiency of this new lot . . . At any rate they have realized at last that He was a great man and so now they're dashing around trying to put things right again. They've realized that He was a symbol, a symbol of our greatness and strength. To renounce Him meant to lose everything, to break everything and to destroy everything. Yes, I too used to shake and tremble before Him and didn't know what would become of me on the morrow. But the fact that I joined the Central Committee at the Eighteenth Congress Committee even after His death proves that He knew how to pick genuine, faithful and dedicated servants of the Party. And even afterwards they weren't able to get rid of me. And what didn't I endure and what wasn't I accused of: "being too divorced from life, dogmatism, superficiality, excessive love of talking . . ."

But I held out. I have had to live into my seventies, when I shall not be active for much longer, to see the first new rays of hope. But how they mocked at His remains when they removed them from the mausoleum, and how suddenly the former greatness of our triumphal sessions and congresses disappeared from those marble walls! All that was left was trivia, day-to-day cares about houses and bread and meat for the people. And the state? And its faithful servants? And we who gave up our lives to the people's cause without getting a thing in return?

He belched as a sign of good digestion and gratitude for the fish soup and glanced distractedly at the suite of rooms of his spacious apartment, which he occupied with his wife and Lukeria.

"Yes, it's true that not many in our country live like this, but perhaps it's better that way, and healthier. I am obliged to reward my body with this fish soup, this armchair and this lovely apartment for all the fears, sacrifices and sufferings, the absolute daily dedication that my unconditional service to the Party has cost me and costs me still. Can there be any moral satisfaction in that? An ideologically sound Party leader needs some moral satisfaction, at least at the end of his life. But no, He had had to endure humiliations and insults even after His death. Yes, yes, His remains . . ." A postprandial languor was stealing over him, but again the thought popped into his head: "The remains of our revolution, of our greatness, must be brought back to life and given back to the world . . . And who will work the miracle? Avanchel Panteleimonovich Frolov, that's quite clear . . . clear . . . clear . . . Yes, that's what I must do. Never retreat, always be in the forefront." That was what his name meant, it bound him: Avanchel—*Avangard Chelovechestvo*, "the Avantgarde of Mankind". He had chosen it himself as a boy in place of the completely unrevolutionary Yefrem . . . His eyes closed, drowsiness overcame his thoughts, his mind sank into oblivion and the last thought that came to him was: "Today that lawyer is coming to see me to get my support. That's not at all a bad idea of his: a cemetery for us, a cemetery for the glorious sons of the Soviet Union. There I will get my well-earned rest, that in itself will be a moral compensation . . . but before that . . . before that there is something I must do . . . Oh yes . . . bring the remains back to life, the remains of the revolution . . ."

. . . He was in the Kremlin, in the conference hall of the

Central Committee, but the Presidium's table was missing and the windows were covered by black shutters. The gilt chandeliers had been extinguished, but a soft violet light was reflected off the marble walls and suffused the whole interior. The enormous hall was empty. He was alone. But he knew why. A catafalque stood in place of the Presidium table, as tall as a tower and with a black coffin on top of it decorated in silver and red.

Frolov was standing at the foot of the catafalque, but could see what was in the coffin: the remains of a young girl of extraordinary beauty, who lay there with closed eyes. One might have thought she was sleeping, but Frolov knew she was dead. An invisible orchestra was playing somewhere in the distance, and together with the music came the solid but ill-defined sound of thousands of feet walking, not heavy and measured, but muffled as if by canvas and cotton.

Frolov knew why this was. He also knew that the Party and people had chosen him to carry out this important mission. He was their last hope. Everything was ready: the hall had been decorated, the girl laid in her coffin and placed on top of the catafalque, the orchestra struck up, everybody retreated, leaving him alone with the dead girl, and the people waited silently in the background, somewhat as in *Boris Godunov*.

But Frolov saw that the coffin was too deep and narrow for his massive body and that he would not be able to squeeze into it and share it with the girl. It was completely hopeless. And now he didn't know what to do. He realized he couldn't take the body out of the coffin, for that might have seemed indecent. And anyway, how could he get the girl's body down from such a height? And where would he put it? On the floor? That might seem like an insult to the revolution.

Besides, he had only just noticed that the floor was teeming with fleas, lice and other revolting insects, so that it gave the impression of being alive.

Frolov was in despair; he had proved incapable of carrying out the important task entrusted to him by the Party, the people and by Himself. Meanwhile the girl in the coffin was rapidly turning black. Starting with her feet, the black stain crept implacably upward, penetrating into every part of the dead girl's white transparent body. But Frolov realized that it wasn't only a question of color: this blackness represented some sort of matter that was devouring the girl's flesh—porous, rubbery, moist and apparently sticky. And he, Frolov, was impotent in the face of everything that was happening and slowly gave way to despair.

"It's over!" proclaimed a thunderous voice from the back of the hall.

Frolov turned and saw a smartly dressed young NKVD lieutenant standing there holding an enormous hourglass.

"Comrade Frolov," said the lieutenant, "the time allowed you has run out. You have failed in the task set you by the Party. Because of you the revolution can no longer be saved. On the orders of Comrade Stalin, I have to hand you over for trial by a military tribunal, which will sentence you to be shot."

With his head bowed low, Frolov walked toward the lieutenant. He was convinced of his guilt. His grief and pain were so great that shooting seemed to him a relief and a release.

But suddenly the doors of the hall opened wide (only now did Frolov notice that the lieutenant must have entered by some secret passage), the chandeliers lit up, and who should enter and cross the strip of red carpet, accompanied by a large retinue, but Stalin himself, wearing his field jacket and with a pipe clenched in his teeth.

He came up to Frolov, short and completely confident of himself, removed the pipe from his mouth and said in the purest Russian, without an accent:

"Comrade Frolov has served his country and Party well, he's a personal friend of mine. I invite him to our banquet."

Behind him came a smiling Molotov and others. Making signs with his eyes Poskryobyshev motioned to Frolov to turn around, but the latter hesitated to turn his back on Stalin. But since Poskryobyshev insisted, he stretched his neck up a bit, peeped over his shoulder and saw long tables gaily decorated for a banquet, with couches along the walls. At the far end stood the catafalque still in position, with the coffin on top. The tables were being served by young girls in Russian national costumes. In one corner an orchestra was playing softly on national instruments.

Everyone took his place at the tables, with Stalin sitting at the head, beneath the catafalque. Beside him sat Beria. But Stalin chased him away and sat Frolov at his right hand instead. What is more, from time to time he would fork some delicacy or other from one of the myriad trays offered him and feed Frolov with it. The girls were pouring drinks for the guests. When one of them approached Frolov to fill his glass, he saw that her sarafan had a stunning slit right down the front, extending from the floor to the navel of her naked belly.

He turned to Stalin, fearing that the latter would have noticed the way he looked at her. But then he noticed with horror that Stalin was wearing only his tunic and that his legs were naked and short and pink, like a piglet's, only they were covered with spots and with red and gray hairs. He averted his eyes and looked around him. Now, nobody was eating. Many of them had the sarafan-clad girls on their laps with their hands thrust into the slits, embracing and kissing them with total abandon. Others were doing the same with the women and girls who had been invited to the banquet. And a number of guests were making love in the most indecent and outrageous way on the couches.

"Comrade Frolov," said Stalin, turning to him, "you can see what good fuckers our people are, yet you didn't want to use your heroic prick for the salvation of the revolution. Why did you disappoint us, comrade? But I believe in you: you'll still be able to do it. But now, to justify my faith in you shove it up my ass as hard as you can."

Frolov turned to stone, his horrified eyes wandered around the room and he could not believe his ears, hoping that this was one of Stalin's vulgar jokes.

"What does it mean to be a member of the Central Committee, Comrade Frolov?" exclaimed Stalin indignantly. "To be a CC member means to be at the disposal of the Party and at the personal disposal of its general secretary. And so I order you: up my ass! Understand?"

Saying this, he leaned over the table and propped himself on his elbows so as to offer his ass to Frolov. On one cheek was tattooed a picture of the Spassky Tower in the Kremlin.

Beria, Malenkov and Mikoyan stared at the unhappy Frolov, shaking their heads. Khrushchev laughed nervously, pointing at him and whispering something to Suslov.

"But I can't . . . I can't!" groaned Frolov, his teeth chattering. And with horror he regarded Stalin's pink buttocks, flabby, stinking like carrion, with their tattoo, and the vertical cleft, which He himself was holding apart with His hands. "It's too much for me," he groaned.

Then Stalin jumped up enraged, and poked poor Frolov with his index finger:

"Shoot this swine! Shoot them a-a-all!"

. . . Frolov started up from his chair. He was covered with sweat. His heart was pounding furiously. What nonsense was this he had dreamed? Yes, yes, it was that mixed salad . . . Ever since he had had that stroke the doctor had put him on a diet. But somehow he could never resign himself to it; it was too much for him. What, what? He tried to gather his thoughts, because ever since the stroke his brain had been slightly fuzzy, his mind tended to wander and sometimes he got into the most awkward situations. He had also said that in his dream: it's too much for me . . . That meant there must be something in it, it wasn't such a senseless dream after all. He strove to recall the details. It had been the result, of course, of his indigestion, which had befuddled his mind. Where on earth had such a disgusting obscene image of Him come from? And yet everything had been so real, so clear and so logical. Gradually the initial fear and shock he had experienced at the end of the dream began to fade away. All that remained was that inexplicable but powerful impression that prophetic dreams usually do leave with a man, inspiring him to search in life for omens that correspond to the meaning of his dream.

By the time Tarakanov had come, Frolov, who could never be accused of capriciousness but who, with the onset of age and arteriosclerosis had grown quite weak (and besides suffered sharp transitions from numb indifference to a state of great excitement), had made up his mind. He was resolved that Tarakanov was the very man through whom he, Frolov, would bring his life to a worthy climax by linking his name with the creation of a memorial cemetery, which many, like himself, deserved, and by beginning to prepare in it a place for himself such as he had earned, and a funeral appropriate to his rank and position, and finally . . . He dared not admit it to himself, but he felt that some decisive impulse was directing his steps and that finally, when he had accomplished that which he had failed to in his dream . . .

On this account Tarakanov found him in an excellent mood when he arrived, permitting him to hope for the support and protection he had come to beg of Frolov . Frolov met him with far more enthusiasm and hospitality than he had dared dream. And before proceeding to the subject that had brought them together, he even told him some of the latest Moscow jokes about Mao Tse-tung.

The lawyer Tarakanov felt himself at ease and responded:

"Tell me, Avanchel Panteleimonovich, who won the war, Germany or Russia?"

"What do you mean?" snorted Frolov. "Russia, of course."

"All right, and what is the difference between Russia and Germany on the twenty-fifth anniversary of our victory? Don't you know? Listen, the difference is that almost every family in Germany has a car, while almost every family in Russia has someone in prison."

"Aw, these wicked tongues," commented Frolov, but without any particular emphasis, revealing his weariness. "They're hoodwinking us with this business about automobiles! What are we going to do with all these automobiles? Let me tell you, Valery Borisovich, that in our country even the prisoners are a productive force. They are working—and always have worked—for communism, for its future greatness, and they can be proud of it, for the nations who go chasing after automobiles will always be small fry who leave no mark after them."

"Hm," grunted Tarakanov under his breath. "You're talking about freedom of choice, but I'm not sure you're right. The question is much more complicated than that. The point is that automobiles set everything else in motion, and for the people they are the strongest stimulus possible at present. And because of that they act simultaneously as a lever for further economic development . . ."

"Yes, well, all right," interrupted Frolov, who was growing bored with this conversation. "Let's get down to business. Tell me about your projects and what you need."

Tarakanov needed all his diplomacy and discretion to present the C Business to a man like Frolov as an irreproachable and logical enterprise. But he knew that this was not a hopeless task, that for the great leaders of the world's first socialist state, its grandeur and might took precedence over everything else, and they were willing to go to any lengths for the good of the cause and had so far stuck firmly to this principle. In that sense there was no difference between the old and the new generation of Soviet leaders. He was well aware that he had to strike exactly the right note in his description of the business, and knew he must not depart in the slightest, one way or the other, from the version he had given to the secretary of the district committee. Of course, the present conversation would be quite different from the earlier one, but not in its essence, only in form. Both for a humble secretary of a district committee and for a long-standing member of the glorious Central Committee moving in the higher echelons of the Soviet leadership, the essence of the project had to rest upon a firm socialist foundation and to show what advantages the Soviet state and its lawful representatives might derive from it. It all had to tie in skillfully with the immortal legacy of Marxism-Leninism, and in a creative form at that (we're no Talmudists!).

Throughout his life, Tarakanov, like thousands of our other citizens, had been obliged to perform mental gymnastics of this kind, thereby making an enormous contribution to the astonishing renaissance of the art of sophistry, which has earned the right to a twentieth-century existence solely thanks to Lenin's revolution. And he was a master of his trade.

As for Frolov, on this occasion, as always, he showed himself a born politician, broad-minded and politically erudite, like all architects of the socialist system and founders of the Soviet state, faithful to Lenin's incorruptible principles, but always ready to apply them in a new way to the unexpected contingencies of practical life. When Tarakanov described the ceremonial graves and memorial cemeteries filled with monuments that would immortalize the fathers of the Soviet state, his eyes grew warm and delicious waves of satisfaction engulfed his heart at the thought that he would be among the first guests of this posthumous sanctuary, and that none other than himself had been requested to give his consent, offer his assistance and lay the foundation stone.

His name would be recorded in the annals of revolutionary history, he would become known to posterity as the founder and the creator of a colossal new structure! He was deeply moved when Tarakanov described the rows of collective farm workers with their hammers, chisels, trowels, and floats ready to begin turning out marble tombstones, busts, and gilded epitaphs. And when he mentally pictured the endless rows of tombs and graves spread out in the distant future of the project's triumphant realization, when beyond radiant peaks glittering in gold and marble splendor, there rose the cemetery, invisible until then in all its vastness and beauty, he felt involuntarily obliged to set Tarakanov's mind at rest by promising him his active assistance. Moreover, he tried to convince him that people like himself, Frolov, had not lost their power and influence in high places and in the Soviet government apparatus, and that their voices still carried decisive weight in important undertakings. These explanations were entirely superfluous for Tarakanov, for on this occasion Frolov could hardly be accused of exaggeration.

Frolov was in excellent spirits as a result of their talk, and he even dropped his usual dry tone of address and ventured a reply to the joke that the lawyer had presented him with at the beginning of their meeting, which had left a nasty taste in his mouth.

"You know, of course," he said to the lawyer, squinting slightly, "that speculation like this carries the supreme penalty—death . . ."

He uttered this unsmilingly, and did not finish the phrase; his face meanwhile assumed an almost grim expression, since he wanted to add something very funny but couldn't find the right words.

Despite all his experience, Tarakanov was taken aback by these words, which he thought entirely inappropriate, considering the benevolent attitude that Frolov had so far shown him.

"But what has speculation to do with it, Avanchel Panteleimonovich!" he mumbled pitifully, "why, you yourself . . ."

"Aha, you're scared!" Frolov let out a laugh, gratified for many reasons—his joke had been a success; he had experienced in actuality his power as a member of the Central Committee in the eyes of his visitor; and, lastly, this visitor was such a petty and insignificant creature that he was afraid of an accusation like that, in spite of the immensity of the undertaking that he was defending, whereas if that undertaking had been the brainchild of a member of the Central Committee, someone like himself, Frolov . . . "Aha! You're scared!" he repeated, laughing. "It won't do you any good, Comrade Tarakanov," he said, shaking his head, "it means you yourself don't see the full significance and importance of this business, you don't have sufficient faith in the principles of socialism. But I'm telling you, Comrade Tarakanov, this business of ours is a serious, honorable, fundamental affair of state! And this alters everything, for it determines its essence . . ."

By the time they had finished, both were fully satisfied with one another. Frolov promised that he would take every opportunity of supporting the interests of the projected cemetery at a higher level, and in addition he would even lend his worthy presence—after all, he was still a Central Committee member—to the meeting at which a start on the project at Sheaves of the Future would be announced, and at which the foundation stone would be laid. Frolov, for his part, extracted from Tarakanov a promise that a prominent position would be reserved for him in the cemetery, and an appropriate vault constructed, and furthermore, that his attendance at the opening ceremony could coincide with the moment when he would at last accomplish what he was supposed to accomplish . . .

10. *On the Sidewalk*

The strange pair that had so offended the thoughts of Avanchel Panteleimonovich Frolov and aroused his indignation consisted of none other than Timur Yamshikov and the widow, Elena Filippovna Kondratyeva.

How did they come to be on the street where Frolov lived on that day at that time, she on the sidewalk and he standing by his Volga holding the door wide open? First, it should be pointed out that Kondratyeva lived on the same street several houses further on than Frolov. Then, of course, one would have to relate how Timur found out as much as he could about the widow, learned her address and at once went about arranging a meeting with her.

He purposely did not phone her in advance. He was aware that his voice alone would not manage to return them to that state of blissful contact between equals, total and overwhelming, unforgettable and full of vibrant promise. No, only his physical presence would be able to resurrect all that. Therefore he had driven to her street, parked his automobile a short distance from where she lived, then climbed the stairs to her apartment and rung the bell.

He was not kept waiting long. An old woman opened the door and fearfully peered at him over the chain that stopped the door from opening more than a crack. When asked whether Elena Filippovna was at home she growled that she wasn't.

"What do you want, young man? I don't know you, do I?" Her voice expressed distrust and was challenging, but Timur paid no attention.

"Can't you tell me when she'll be back?"

"How should I know?" replied the old woman and shut the door.

He descended the stairs without waiting for the elevator. Near the bottom he collided with an extraordinarily tall and skinny young man whose Adam's apple was remarkably prominent. He was helping a mongoloid girl to climb the stairs. The girl, whose age was hard to tell, goggled at him and attempted a crooked smile.

"It's good for her to go up and down stairs," remarked the young man, as though apologizing. And since Timur continued to stare at him in amazement, added, lowering his voice: "It's radiation, you know. I expect you heard about it down in——. Everybody knows, but don't say I told you. She's just an unfortunate sick girl, if you see what I mean."

He turned his back on Timur and went on helping the girl, who in turn craned her short neck to look at Timur with her glazed watery eyes. Timur practically ran out the front door and hurried back to his car.

It was four o'clock in the afternoon. He moved his car a bit further back and parked it closer to the metro station. If she came home by taxi he would be sure to see her from here, and if she came by metro then he would be able to intercept her on her way to her apartment. Of course, there was always the chance that his patience would run out before she came home at all.

He decided to wait for no more than an hour. Switching on his portable tape recorder, he started listening to a Duke Ellington concert that some physicist friends had recently given him, and then picked up the latest number of *Foreign Literature* with *A Hundred Years Alone* in it. But in spite of the fact that, unusually for him, he liked the novel, his eyes frequently wandered and took more interest in what was going on around him than in the exciting adventures of the Buendia family. There were few passers-by in this part of the town, everyone was in a hurry and nobody paid any particular attention to him. He took out his Ronson lighter and lit a cigarette. But two girls who were animatedly discussing something as they went by suddenly fell silent at the sight of him. Then he saw in his rear-view mirror how they turned to look back several times and exchanged remarks about him.

After waiting for twenty-one minutes he saw her. Again, in his rear-view mirror. But she was still too far away. It was only because, since the day when he had first seen her, the image of this woman had constantly lived in his retina, where it had been engraved by his memory and subsequently multiplied by his imagination, that he was able to recognize her from so far away.

In the gleaming mirror her short figure stood out from the crowd (because of its special quality), and followed its own trajectory, leaving in its wake a track of curiosity and indignation.

The Moscow crowd invariably makes a spectacle out of the few visually prominent figures that come its way, so that the city streets are turned into a special kind of theater in which the vulgar, inquisitive and sensation-hungry crowd both thirsts for scandal and at the same time condemns everything that doesn't fit into the narrow framework of its own preconceptions. Such bitterness, which finds expression in indignation and noisy aggressive outbursts in speech and in print, cannot be explained away by our people's innate feeling for the theater. This is the embitteredness of people who most condemn that which they themselves would like to be, but haven't the nerve to become.

Elena Kondratyeva was like a piece of litmus paper defining people's reactions. Extraordinarily beautiful, extraordinarily elegant and, moreover, dressed entirely in foreign clothes, she did raise not the slightest doubt in those who were observant, for there was a Russian purity about her. But her essence remained concealed, her beauty inaccessible, and it seemed she somehow had different co-ordinates from the rest. Yet at the same time her whole personality radiated delicate, but sharp and penetrating sensual signals, somewhat similar to certain persistent and ethereal passages in electronic music.

To make contact with this woman's beauty and inner self was possible only through the medium of a special kind of code, something like an ultrasonic language. It was by such code that Timur and Elena had understood one another when they met. It went to the heart of the matter. But it is well known that our human envelope is an aggregate of conditional reflexes, which exists independently of our true nature and can even contradict it.

Timur watched her figure growing larger in the mirror. When she was quite near, he got out of his car and calmly walked toward her. But when he was halfway he halted, so that she could see him properly before she drew level.

And that was how it went. She suddenly caught sight of him. Her head spun. She was immediately sure that he hadn't turned up in her path by accident, but had been waiting for her. But she continued walking, not looking in his direction and pretending not to have noticed him. Only for a fraction of a second, at the moment when they were abreast, did her eyelids tremble as she threw a swift glance in his direction.

Everything was as she had expected: his cold piercing eyes enveloped her with their insane, insolent self-confidence; they seemed to want to absorb her, to devour her down to the last little brain cell. His face was as she remembered it from that memorable day at the cemetery—youthful, with signs of fatigue, with the ironic grin of a satyr, with soft childish curls—and then it lost its form for her and disintegrated into a shapeless blob.

"Elena Filippovna!" he said softly, but insistently.

She continued walking, as though not hearing him, trying not to glance in his direction.

It seemed to her that if she raised her eyes to look at him, he would at once read in them her shame, as though she had already given herself to him in her lonely widow's bed, aroused by the associations recalled by the sight of his figure, his eyes that were devouring her, and his penis, which had revealed to her for the first time the meaning of the male organ. It was this latter that had played an evil trick on her: ever since the day of her husband's funeral, when it had appeared before her in its triumphal erection, she had been ceaselessly aware of the existence of her sex, until then modest and neglected, and unable to give tongue, but now aflame with ardor. The memory of the ecstasy and the voluptuous delight she had expereienced on that morning of death, transforming her grief into total, criminal exultation, had tormented her thereafter so fiercely that one evening she had accomplished something of which earlier she had simply had not the faintest concept. In her bed, unable to fall asleep, she began to stroke her soft, furry mound, her hot, moist vulva; she imagined him standing before her with his gigantic phallus like a shining apparition in the darkness. Then she was seized with passion and opened her legs wide, burning with shame at her licentious position, and this bashfulness flowed through her with a delicious tremor, despite the utter darkness and solitude that existed in her bedroom. Pulling up her nightgown, she touched the lips, tense with arousal, discovering for herself a pleasure she had not known until then; then she ran her finger over the spot where the rush of blood was particularly hot and the sensations particularly acute and intense. With her other hand she touched her swollen breasts, and then began squeezing the nipples. Her whole being was flooded with a frenzy that drowned both the desire and craving that had made her oblivious to everything around her, and the joy of which she had simply never had the faintest notion. The image of him there in the darkness in front of her, with his mocking smile and his penis throbbing and endlessly disgorging seed, had driven her to delirium, madness, complete loss of self-control, and she had sunk to such depths of degeneracy that she could still feel herself burning with shame.

If she were to look at him now—and she knew this for certain—he would surely realize everything, and would think that she wished for nothing but to give herself to him, belong to him, satisfy all his loathsome desires. But she had not the least intention of glancing at him; between them, her, Elena

Filippovna, and this impudent, insolent fellow, this tough, perhaps even criminal, there was, and could be, nothing in common.

"Elena Filippovna!" repeated Timur harshly and his eyes glittered.

She walked past him and continued on her way. With a quick movement Timur caught up with her and walked along beside her. She paid no attention to him.

"Elena Filippovna," said Timur in a low voice, drawing out the syllables sarcastically, "are your feelings only to be awakened at cemeteries?"

But she did not respond even to this, remaining distant and aloof and continuing to walk forward. They drew level with the Volga.

Suddenly Timur seized her wrist with his right hand, tightly so that it hurt. She did not resist him or react in any way. She was simply forced to stop while he opened the door with his left.

It was at this moment that a ponderous man emerged from a black government Zis, about a dozen paces away from them, and crossed the sidewalk to enter the imposing foyer of an apartment building. He allowed his glance to rest on them for a moment, but neither Timur nor Kondratyeva noticed him. And in any case, they could never have imagined that their very appearance would provoke such a flood of thoughts in him that would take him so far, or that these thoughts would, in a certain sense, eventually link him with Timur, even if only in a distant, roundabout way.

They were busy with their absorbing game. He with trying to understand her true nature, she with trying to fend off this young man who had so suddenly burst into her life again unasked, even though till now she had wished with all her heart to meet once more that young fair-haired faun from the cemetery. A composite of accepted rules of behaviour, conditioned reflexes, generally accepted norms—all this stood between them like a solid wall. The glorious miracle of mutual understanding that had united them at the cemetery could not be repeated in this street of conventional and habitual gestures.

Timur kept hold of her arm, feverishly devouring her with his eyes. She stood there indifferently, waiting for him to tire of this game. Bystanders might have concluded that they were a quarreling couple.

At last she gritted through clenched teeth, turning pale:

"Let me go . . ."

Timur suddenly released her arm, pushing her away slightly as he did so, slammed the door loudly behind him, and the Volga shot away from the curb.

"Whore!" he muttered angrily to himself. "Pretending now she's untouchable. Well, we'll see who wins. You'll be mine soon enough, my beauty!"

In an hour he had a date with Tamara Denisova, a well-known Moscow nymphomaniac. She was the wife of the director of one of Moscow's innumerable scientific research institutes who simply didn't have the time to pay any attention to her because of the sheer load of work he carried in his ultra-responsible post. Gossipmongers used to say that, actually, he knew perfectly well about his wife's adventures and, what is more, had married her for that reason, that he himself encouraged her in this and that he used to make her tell him all the details afterwards when she got home. And that that was the only way he could get any sexual satisfaction. But Tamara refused point blank to confirm these rumors even to her closest friends, even to Timur.

Timur decided first to drop in at the Exhibition of Soviet Economic Achievements in order to calm his nerves. One day he had jokingly said to a writer he admired that this exhibition struck him as a faultless copy, carried over into life, of some of those old religious colored prints depicting paradise. This impression was particularly reinforced in June, when the sky over Moscow seemed particularly high and wisps of white cloud stood out clearly as they clung to the azure. But still it couldn't be denied that one experienced at all points in the exhibition a sensation of complete detachment from reality. And in this relaxed atmosphere the unbelievable bad taste of it all dissolved and was forgiven. The buildings of the twenties, on the other hand, and the hybrids of the recent past—with pretensions to being modern—introduced a note of dissonance and discomfort. But if this was so, then perhaps Stalin had even here displayed his inspired intuition? Maybe he had more understanding than the foremost and best-trained contemporary specialists in architecture and town planning? No, it couldn't be, it went too much against the theory of probability.

He walked down an avenue framed by the most incredible fairytale pavilions of this surrealistic world. He knew where he could get a glass of Bacardi and meet one or another of his pals. And at the bar he indeed caught sight of Alik and Vitya. Both were about eighteen. And both belonged to that class of young men who, after a first outburst of rowdyism, had swiftly concluded that it was both safer and pleasanter to drown their boredom and bitterness in the arms of ladies from the cream of society. From time to time one or the other of them would make a slip and get sent up—"take a trip to Mazhaisk" as they said—but then invariably turned up in Moscow again when his term was over, and the cleverer ones even got hold of clean papers. Timur himself was up to his neck in all this.

Alik and Vitya were already well primed with rum. Timur had a few more glasses with them. The bar was manned by a fat flabby blonde with brightly painted lips. She made no secret of her greed and hungrily prompted tips: a typical outskirts tart.

"Listen, Alik," said Timur, "are you free this evening?"

Alik had dark hair and soft features, which made him look effeminate, but despite his appearance he was worth several tough lads in action. And Timur knew that Alik was a first-rate stud.

"Yes, friend, I am, things are completely stagnant here," lisped Alik somewhat absently. "Why, have you got some goodies?"

"Call me in an hour at this number, here," Timur handed him

a piece of paper with a number on it. "Well, so long, friends, see you later."

Timur paid the bill for his own two glasses and for what the others had drunk before his arrival. While Timur was getting the money out, the fat barmaid's hand fiddled with the front of her blouse and undid the top button. Timur regarded her pityingly.

Tamara, extremely amiable, attentive and ingratiating as usual, was waiting for him at her home.

"Ah, how marvelous that you came in time! You know, it was only because of you I stayed so long," Tamara smiled coquettishly. And only Timur knew what leaden weights, what ballast weighed down her desperate body and what voracious insatiability lay behind her exaggerated show of welcome.

"I was supposed to have gone down to our villa already to get it ready for Fedya, he's flying in the day after tomorrow," she added with the same coquettish but somehow crooked smile.

By Fedya she meant Fyodor Apollonovich Denisov, her esteemed and no longer youthful husband.

"What do you have to do at your country place?" Timur regarded her with suspicion, for this didn't at all coincide with his plans.

He was making his usual check on her, for he knew that Tamara was capable of dreaming up the most unheard-of and fantastic situations, which could quite likely turn out to be genuine. And all just to show how much she was loved and desired and at the same time how ordinary her life was, never going beyond accepted standards. And for others it did indeed seem like that, and perhaps objectively it was like that, but she secretly considered it to be the reverse.

"Nothing," said Tamara. "I merely said that I would get everything ready before Fedya came back."

"But I was hoping . . ." rapped out Timur.

Tamara stretched herself and looked at him closely and in surprise.

"There's always room for you down there, if you want . . ."

"No, I can't," Timur cut her short sharply. "Do you want company down there? I know a guy who's absolutely phenomenal . . ."

"Why do you talk to me like that?" said Tamara in an insulted tone, which may even have been sincere. "Who do you take me for? Some old street whore? But anyway, who is he?" she added, unable to resist it, an expression of submissive curiosity on her face.

"A friend of mine," replied Timur. "He's seen you and you've completely turned him on. Anyway, it's not important. Let's forget it."

"What do you mean, forget it?" protested Tamara, falling for Timur's trick, sorry now that she had spoken, and aroused.

"It's not important, let's forget it," snapped Timur. "I warned you when I called you that I was coming on business."

Tamara tried her hardest to look interested, but suddenly she seemed to have grown gray, listless and unattractive.

"Yes, yes, that's quite true! What was it?" she exclaimed with exaggerated interest.

"It's very important," replied Timur, "and our friendship depends upon it."

Tamara was genuinely interested now and asked in a worried tone of voice:

"What do you mean by that?" It wasn't so much a question as a pitiful and pathetic snivel. "What are you trying to say?"

"I mean that for me it's extremely important," said Timur with emphasis, "and if you refuse to help me—this is the first time I've ever asked you for something—I will remember it and neither I nor my friends will want to see you any more."

"But what is it, what do you want to ask me?" gasped Tamara in a low voice, thoroughly alarmed by now.

She looked at him feverishly, in complete contrast to the words she was uttering. Her long slender hand slid from her hip to her belly, pressing hard, and came to a halt beneath her breast. At the same time she sighed deeply and her eyes became huge as she stared at Timur.

Then Timur told her briefly, without frills and perhaps even a trifle roughly, what it was he wanted from her. This was to persuade her husband to order himself a plot and a substantial memorial in their projected cemetery. The important thing was to get a major advance from him. Then he would be offered as many different models to choose from and as much technical assistance as he desired.

Tamara listened closely, without interrupting and expressing no surprise. But when Timur had finished she said:

"It's impossible. It's madness! You won't find any clients, because none of our people believe in death and nobody gives a damn about a cemetery. And then, as soon as the alarm is raised the whole thing will blow up."

"Listen, cut the babbling or you'll put a jinx on us!" said Timur sourly. "I didn't ask for your opinion, but your help. We're counting on your husband being one of our clients."

"But he'll only laugh at me and ask if I want an Indian mausoleum for myself where I can have my romantic orgies while waiting to die."

"Well, so what?" grinned Timur, "that doesn't change anything. I take it that you understand what I want and that I can count on you. Otherwise it's good-bye. Got it? And now I have to go," he added, glancing at his watch and standing up.

Tamara jumped up as lithely as a cat and entwined her arms about his neck.

"I'll do everything you say," she said, slobbering a lingering kiss on his cheek with her moist lips, "but stay just for a minute."

"No," said Timur unmovably, pushing her away. "That guy I told you about will be calling in a minute. His name's Alik."

Tamara stood a few steps from him. With a smile hovering on her lips she unbuttoned her robe, which parted to reveal her small, adolescent-looking breasts.

Timur went out without a word.

11. Pavlik

The telephone rang in the hall. A fair-haired lad with a pallid face and oversized hands, who had been sitting awkwardly on a chair facing the couch on which his mother sat with a friend newly arrived from the Caucasus, chattering about the most trivial and absurd subjects, leapt up and rushed to answer it. He had just been waiting for a chance to escape from the flood of trivialities and for more than half an hour had been intending to do so, but somehow he just couldn't bring himself to ask his mother's permission to go out into the yard and play with the other boys who lived, like himself, in Old Petrovsko-Razumovsky Lane. He almost always had to meet them without his mother's knowledge. "Daddy doesn't like it, daddy doesn't like it," she used to nag at him over and over again. "These boys come from a totally different background and you mustn't mix with them. They're uneducated and rough. When we finally get an apartment in the right block in the right street, appropriate to your father's position, then you can play with the neighbor children, but not with these, heaven forbid. You've got nothing to learn from them and in any case they're older than you, which isn't good." Well, okay, he was only fifteen while Igor and Yurka were sixteen and seventeen, but so what? It was quite untrue that he had nothing to learn from them! Just the opposite, in fact, he had learnt lots of things from them already, not the least important of which had been his first astonished realization of the fact that he was no longer a child, no longer a mere appendage of his parents and a schoolboy by profession. He had realized that he had his own character and his own independent position in the world.

"Stop!" commanded his mother imperiously. "I'll answer it. You know you're supposed to answer the telephone only when I ask you to."

She got up from the couch, a thirty-five-year-old, somewhat plump but pleasant woman, a typical wife who had fallen behind her husband as he continued to make progress in his career and instinctively compensated for her subconscious feelings of inferiority by an excess of sentiment, and it was this excess of sentiment that drove her to ever greater feats of marital infidelity. Before rising she had time to whisper in Dunya's ear:

"It's my . . ."

Going out into the hall she closed the door tightly behind her and Dunya remained alone with the boy.

He watched his mother disappear through the door with an expression of barely concealed outrage and suppressed protest, having firmly made up his mind to ask for permission to go down to the yard the minute she returned. He was cunning enough to realize that his mother probably wanted to be alone with this old friend whom she hadn't seen in so long. Perhaps she would even be pleased to see him go.

But now he was quite satisfied to be left alone for a while with his mother's friend, who had nothing in common either with his mother, or with her other friends. He even felt slightly confused. This woman was in all probability the same age as his mother, but he was hardly aware of it. She wasn't affected by the problem of age. The way she behaved and talked, the way she looked—everything indicated that she was not "one of them," that she had nothing at all in common with "their" world, that she lived her own strange and enchanting life, which, although it attracted censure mixed with feelings of doom and terror, nonetheless irresistibly fascinated him with its charmed air of mystery and adventure. There's no help for it, adventure is adventure and it's useless to try explaining it, and the mystery was woman: that is to say, the essence of what he sensed in Dunya, although without being aware of it.

"Well, what's up, Pavlik, why are you looking at me so sulkily, and angrily? In love, are you?" said Dunya immediately without a pause, winking and smiling. "She's waiting downstairs for you, is she? And mamma won't let you go and meet her. But I'll tell her I have something to tell her in secret and ask her to send you for cigarettes, shall I?"

"Who asked you to butt in?" thought Pavlik irritatedly, but at the same time was grateful that she didn't launch into a description of how she had seen him as "a teeny-weeny boy," and that she attributed to him a girl friend that he didn't have but was already longing for day and night.

He glanced at her, not knowing what to say. Dunya responded with a look that was sly yet friendly, and smiling like an old friend with whom he had shared lots of tricks and pranks in days gone by. But Pavlik sensed something else in that smile, something that disturbed him. And he realized the cause of this disturbance when he looked at her body, at her so feminine breasts, at her legs shamelessly crossed so that her bare knees were prominent and he could even see, somewhere at the back, a strip of bare thigh.

He had noticed it at once, but didn't dare look while his mother was there. And even now he felt ashamed of his eyes, which pounced on this woman's body, disobeying his orders and independently of his volition. It was dangerous and Pavlik was completely absorbed in his anxious efforts to hold his gaze back, as though holding on to the leash of a dog that hurls itself upon a visitor, disregarding its master's command. This struggle took up so much energy that he was unable to speak and his thoughts got all mixed up in his head.

He was glad when his mother returned. But so disconcerted was he by his confusion that he missed his chance of asking her to let him go.

"Dunya, darling, forgive me I beg you, you simply can't imagine how sorry I am, but I absolutely *must* dash this very moment," she said swiftly, making a conspiratorial face at Dunya. "You do understand, don't you? It's terribly urgent and I won't be long. But you stay here with Pavlik. He'll keep you company. And soon my husband will be back, my jealous master. He'll ask you where I am and you can say that Katya called: there was a chance to get hold of some luxurious foreign underwear and I had to make up my mind at once, with not a moment to lose. He'll understand. And in the meantime you can tell him about the cemetery business," she laughed nervously. "I think he'll be pleased. He's still grieving over his father—he was an important factory director, one of the men who built our industry up into what it is today, yet now everyone's forgotten him. And that distresses my husband. And you know, I think he himself is beginning to get ideas, he's no longer so young as he was, you know," she added coquettishly, changing to a bantering tone, but glancing cautiously in Pavlik's direction ("I hope he doesn't understand!"), although it was too late to worry over what effect her words might have now.

But Pavlik had long since got used to his mother's giddy flights, and attributed no meaning to their underlying content. He was angry at himself, and at her, and at this woman, whose arrival he had so looked forward to in the hope of getting a chance to escape, at least for a time, from his mother's oppressive surveillance. It was precisely this hope that had caused him to linger on in the lounge after his mother had called him proudly to present him to her old friend. And now he was a prisoner, face to face with this woman with whom he would never have chosen voluntarily to remain alone. She was agreeable and in some strange way attracted him, but at the same time her presence inspired him with inexplicable dread and yearning. It was as though he had been bound hand and foot and thrown into a pit from which he had no chance of escaping into the sunlight.

His mother took her leave of Dunya, promising to return as quickly as possible, and kissed Pavlik on the temple, saying:

"Entertain Avdotya Zakharovna until your father comes."

Pavlik cast a look of desperation at her but said not a word.

He realized that there was nothing he could do, that he would have to remain where he was with this woman he hardly knew, who, apart from everything else, possessed the strange gift of arousing everything inside him and setting in motion something that had nothing to do with her, yet for him was extraordinarily important, perhaps everything: his strength and secret riches, something that enabled him to feel he was somebody, rather than the nonentity he felt himself to be in the company of his parents, or at school, where he was considered an average well-behaved pupil. With Igor and Yurka this strength was transformed into freedom. At home it was destroyed: he couldn't breathe, he couldn't exist! But this woman, this stranger whom his mother had taken into her home as a friend and who was now completely at her ease in it, aroused in him some sort of new sensations. She represented everything that was condemned and suppressed in their home. And therefore she was the cause of a dilemma, a contradiction that, because he was unable to resolve it, reduced him to the condition of slavery. By staying here in the room with her, he was slavishly carrying out his mother's instructions. But apart from that he was the slave of circumstances that had completely upset him, and in this condition he was fully aware that he himself was to blame, because he, Pavlik, was such a depraved youth, because this practically middle-aged woman excited him so powerfully, because he felt himself to be under her spell and completely enslaved by this friend of his mother's. Not even Yurka, who had long since started to run after girls, could have sunk so low.

He was jolted out of these reflections by the voice of Dunya, which seemed sharp and loud to him, like a cry.

"Do you smoke, Pavlik?"

She had already lit a cigarette for herself, although she smoked rarely. She calculated, however, that it might help to melt the coldness and tension that had come between them.

Pavlik nervously shrugged his shoulders, as though struck by the impact of two mutually contradictory answers that were both on the tip of his tongue. No-o! He didn't smoke in this world where he was sitting with this guest, just as he didn't argue and didn't swear, but on the contrary, was overflowing with respect for the work of his father and others like him, for their morals and ideology and for his homeland. On the other hand, yes! Of course he smoked, although rarely and without enjoying it, but that was in that other world, genuine and human and simple, in which Igor and Yurka lived, where things were called by their real names—not as in the newspapers and at school and at home—where he felt himself a person and not a thing.

And now, here in this room, a new conjunction was taking place, a realignment of planes: this woman was asking if he smoked. Was this ridiculous straightforwardness on her part, or was she making fun of him? Or was it a refined form of hypocrisy? What if he lit up, or simply said: "Yes, I do, thank you," and she immediately went and spilled the beans to his parents? He writhed and emitted an inaudible monosyllable. But then he instinctively guessed that he had to answer properly and that his answer might prove to be far more important than the actual act of smoking.

"Yes, yes, sometimes," he managed to get out at last, but then added hastily: "Mamma doesn't know about it."

This last phrase was somehow both a warning and a plea to her not to give him away to his mother. But at the same time it meant that he was jumping into the well with his hands tied, and he was fully aware of it. He had not only owned up to smoking, but had put himself in this woman's power by asking for her sympathy and asking her to keep his secret, hooked by her witchery, and not as an equal with another equal, but as a sort of lower being, like that time with Yurka when he had begged his friend to let him go with him on his hunt for Mercedes badges. Then, as now, he had felt frightened but fascinated, as though he were plunging into an abyss, aware that he had voluntarily thrown himself in head first because it had both horrified and attracted him with its promised joy of liberation.

"I can well imagine that your mother doesn't know," said

Dunya, warm, smiling and friendly, "my husband also doesn't know that I smoke," she lied shamelessly.

Pavlik looked at her in surprise, with a grateful expression on his face. Dunya leaned forward to offer him her pack. As she did so, Pavlik, who was sitting on a chair somewhat higher than the couch, caught sight of her breasts in the cleavage of her blouse. He completely squashed two of the cigarettes before managing to extract a third and when, at last, the difficult operation was accomplished, Dunya leaned forward once more to let him light his cigarette from hers.

Then she straightened up and said:

"It's best if they don't know. I like forbidden things myself, don't you?"

Pavlik blushed and looked away from Dunya, who was staring directly at him. He was also caught out in something else, something stronger and more mysterious, something that pursued him ceaselessly and was an indissoluble part of him. With a motion of his hand, which he tried to make as natural as possible, he endeavored to cover the spot where his trouser-legs met. He was afraid that the obvious bulge there would give his secret away. But he couldn't conceal the other signs: Dunya had already noticed the dark rings round his eyes, the feverishly drawn face that seemed somehow more handsome and delicate because of it, while his childish features derived from it a vitality that was otherwise missing. Dunya had not put this down to tiredness from excessive studying or spring anaemia, as obtuse parents and school doctors are wont to do. There was something quite different behind it and the correctness of Dunya's guess was confirmed by the motion of Pavlik's hand and the deep blushes that suddenly transfused his face.

"Hm, do you do it often? And you've still not had your first woman, eh?" said Dunya.

She leaned forward again in order to flick the ash from her cigarette and Pavlik again caught sight of her plump, ripe breasts. Leaving her cigarette in the ashtray, she again straightened up. He did not reply. His face was aflame, his eyes were earnest and burning, and the fire emanating from him and from the object he hid in his hand transferred itself to her and he offered himself to her. Then, deliberately fixing her unwinking eyes upon him, she slowly parted her legs. Beneath her skirt she was wearing nothing at all: there was just her naked sex.

"Shall we play a little forbidden game ourselves?" she asked softly, opening her legs wide with a voluptuous shudder of excitement. Pavlik's eyes were riveted there, carried along on an irresistible tide that surged through his feverish virgin soul. "At what time does your father come home? Does he ring the bell before entering?"

"It's early yet, not for another hour," replied Pavlik, recovering the gift of speech in the face of minor concrete problems such as he was used to dealing with in his other pranks. "He doesn't usually take a key with him. He's almost sure to ring. But mamma said she'd be back soon."

"Oh no," said Dunya soothingly, "your mamma will be even later. But do you know how to keep a secret and hold your tongue? You won't tell anyone about what we did?"

"No," said Pavlik in a low voice, shaking his head vigorously.

"Not even your friends?"

"No, I won't tell them, honest I won't."

"Listen, if you breathe a word to anyone I'll be sure to find out and then you'll be in for it. Joking with me is dangerous. I have faithful friends and you'll have to spend an unpleasant quarter of an hour with them if anything goes wrong, got it?"

"Aha," nodded Pavlik, who was by now completely bewitched by her mysterious hints, which revealed her in quite a different light. Dunya! This was an adventure for you. But who was she? A crook? A spy? What did it all mean?

"Come over here," said Dunya, her voice suddenly soft and caressing again.

When he sat down next to her on the couch, she put her plump motherly arms about him, drew him to her, put her face up close to his and said in a tender and understanding tone of voice:

"You very very much want to have a woman. That's all you

think about and that's why you've so withdrawn into yourself, like a little porcupine. And when you are alone the fever completely devours you, isn't that so? How many times a day do you do it to yourself?"

"Twice or three times," he answered trustfully and growing bolder, but still turning red once more. "But how do you know?"

"I know, I know, my dear boy," said Dunya with great tenderness, nervously unbuttoning his shirt and stroking the skin of his thin boyish chest.

Dunya's heart was now beating more, perhaps, than Pavlik's. In all this she was experiencing not only the pleasure, which she had not had for a long time, of enjoying such a youthful and immature body, but also the profound and piercing joy of contact with the virginal world that contained the boy's body. How satisfying to take him by the hand and lead him over the threshold to where genuine earthly life began.

She stretched her hand down to where earlier, when sitting on the chair, Pavlik had held his own and where now could be detected a prominent bulge.

"Oho, you're not such a boy at all, but a real man!" exclaimed Dunya in surprise, pulling out the already sizable prick of the youthful masturbator.

These words enabled Pavlik to throw off the last traces of shyness. With a sudden sharp movement he plunged his hand into the opening of Dunya's blouse and took tight hold of her breast. Then, with his other, he forcefully gripped her knee.

"Patience, patience, little one!" laughed Dunya. "There's no need to hurry, we're not rabbits. We're people and you have to use your head a bit. I'm sure you've never seen a naked woman before. Do you want to now?"

She got up from the couch and in an instant stripped off her skirt and blouse, beneath which she was wearing nothing at all.

"Can you see how a woman is made? How much flesh and blood and life there is in her? Man's nature is concentrated in his prick, but a woman's whole body is the incarnation of her nature."

Saying this she stroked one breast, running her finger round the dark circle of her nipple. Her other hand meanwhile slid down over her belly toward her soft female orifice. She was aroused by the stare of the stunned Pavlik. Standing there shirtless, with his prick sticking out of the opening in his trousers, he was looking at her in a state of complete stupefaction. And she was excited by this sudden but spontaneous turn of circumstances, which seemed to her like a gift of the goddess Fortune. She had come to this house to talk of cemeteries and the dead, but instead had encountered this rare confrontation with life.

"Well, what are you staring at like a blockhead? Now you get undressed as well. Do you like the look of me?"

She went over to Pavlik and while he sat on the couch, pulling off his trousers, pressed her belly to his face until she felt his hot desire somewhere at the bottom of her belly. At that instant she toppled over on top of him, drawing his young fragile body down with her so that their two bodies became entwined and it seemed that her plump arms and legs would crush him in their passionate impatient embrace. She rolled over on her back with him on top of her, his hands wandering over her body. Taking the sign of his manhood in her hands—his most precious possession—she introduced it into her, setting him an example with the motions of her body. Copying these motions, he learned to be a man.

Almost at once she was overwhelmed by her orgasm, hastened not so much by Pavlik's movements as by her own excitement. He also came inside her, overcome by the urgency of youth and his excitement.

Dunya helped him to get dressed quickly and went off to put herself in order. She quickly pulled on her skirt and blouse, just as quickly rinsed herself in the bathroom and then set about tidying the room so that nothing could arouse suspicion. Picking up the butt of Pavlik's cigarette, she pressed her lips around it so that traces of lipstick were left behind. Then she threw it back in the ashtray. Finally she settled down again on the couch. Pavlik, combed and tidy now, was all set to hurl himself upon her again, but Dunya held him off, saying:

"No, no, not now. They might come back at any minute. Do you want to come again?"

"Please," blurted out Pavlik in a tone of pleading.

Dunya bent down, unzipped his pants, pulled out his once more swollen prick and fastened her mouth on it. Pavlik ceased breathing. Dunya's fellatio was both skillful and affectionate. She worked at it without haste, calling up waves of voluptuousness in him that were incomparably stronger than those he had experienced during his first and premature possession of a woman. Dunya would not allow him to touch her, fearing that she would lose her head once more, for there was very little time left. But she was not strong enough to ward off Pavlik's hand, which plunged once more into her burning furnace. And the very thought of it was enough for her to experience another powerful orgasm. In order to stop herself from crying out she sucked on Pavlik's prick so hard that she hurt him and at the same moment swallowed his sperm, which he ejaculated into Dunya's hot mouth with a groan of voluptuous pleasure.

They had not had time to exchange a single word before there came a ring at the door. It was Pavlik's father. When the boy opened the door to him he asked:

"Is Avdotya Zakharovna here? Is she in the next room with mamma?"

"Yes," said Pavlik, "but mamma's not here, she went out."

"Where on earth to? Was it a long time ago?" asked his father.

"No, not long," lied Pavlik. "I think she went to see Orlenina to buy something from her, I'm not sure."

Irritated by this news, Rubkin went into the lounge where Dunya was waiting for him. Having greeted her, he turned to Pavlik and said condescendingly:

"Now say goodbye to Avdotya Zakharovna and go and get some fresh air. We have to talk business. But mind you keep away from those tough kids in the yard."

12. The Representative of the "C Business"

Tarakanov hadn't the faintest idea how he could fulfill his promise to Frolov. The latter had made himself quite clear. "I shall attend the solemn opening of your memorial cemetery for the glorious sons of our native land only if you guarantee that I shall there be able to carry out my important mission. What's more," he had added, "it is essential that the two events be linked, because for me they are indissolubly bound up with one another. If I take part in the establishment of this cemetery I shall be lending my name to an event of the first magnitude, but at the same time it is essential for me to be able to fulfill my mission: to bring back to life the remains of the Revolution. Therefore, I beg you to inform me when everything is ready."

The lawyer wasn't sure whether Frolov's words were the result of a terrific upheaval that had occurred over the past few weeks in Frolov's unhealthy and obtuse mind, threatening to end in total mental disability, or merely the result of mephistophelian hypocrisy. In either case, the important thing was to have his protection and he had already promised that he would attend personally. That in itself was no small success. When he had lied at the meeting about having support from above, he had not expected to be so lucky or to have his words so quickly justified. The whole business, of course, was founded on hypocrisy. But if you ignored the material basis of the matter and concentrated instead on the prevailing mood, then the whole thing appeared in quite a different light. How many times had he noticed that some groups regretted the absence of the very thing that Timur had formulated with such genius—yes, yes, genius, thought Tarakanov, convincing himself more and more as his thoughts took on a more concrete form. All those top dogs, the cream of political, economic, art and literary circles, were sensible of approaching death and regretted that after death there would be nothing to distinguish them from the ordinary multiplying masses, nothing to record their memory with tangible grandeur for their successors.

But not one of them would have dared to take the matter into his own hands. They were all imprisoned in their own rules of behavior, their own prejudices and their own fears. They also needed a decision to be handed down from on high, that is for someone like Tarakanov to take a personal risk, open the way and find a method of realizing the possibility without breaking the rules of Soviet legality and Soviet morality.

"I beg you to inform me when everything is ready," Frolov had said. As if it were the easiest thing in the world to find a dead girl for him." What a fool I am," thought Tarakanov. "I thought Dildor would be the perfect bribe for Frolov, but now it turns out he had his own little plan the whole time, though there seems to be something mystical about it: a virgin, he said, but she absolutely has to be dead." The fact that it had to be a virgin didn't seem so important to the lawyer, though goodness knew Frolov was quite capable of checking up. But who knew what changes that part of the body underwent after death? Do they contract and get smaller, or do they, on the other hand, grow slack and open out? He would have to ask Yakov Moiseyevich, his doctor, about it . . . But there remained the problem of acquiring a dead body: where on earth could he get one? If the worst came to the worst, Timur would help him procure the body of some young woman soon after she had been buried in one of the Moscow cemeteries. "After what the Black

Hundreds did in the Jewish cemetery at Kiev (real organized desecration) and after what happens annually on the night of Judgment Day in our cemeteries, which are raided with impunity by our surviving remnants of fascism, no one can accuse us if we remove the body tactfully and without leaving a trace, for an excellent cause."

These were the thoughts of Tarakanov as he crossed Moscow in his ancient Moskvich. Tarakanov, apart from anything else, was an excellent driver of the kind you don't often find in our great land. He had learned to drive before the revolution, and not in some broken-down old wreck but in his stepfather's Benz. But he had never bothered about expensive or foreign automobiles, favored by those who were destined to become clients of the C Business. He knew the automobile's value—it was simply a means of transportation. And besides, he preferred to remain in the shadows, so that his old Moskvich was the perfect answer to his requirements.

He came to a halt outside the Central Journalists' House near Suvorovsky Boulevard. Tarakanov remembered it as it was when it had been a mansion belonging to the millionaire merchant, Postnov. But now, since Adzhubei had had it completely redecorated, the interior was completely modern.

He had an appointment here with Sergei Petrovich Shchedrin and their meeting was to be exclusively about business, although it was bound to be warmed by a long acquaintanceship that in a certain sense might almost have been called actual friendship. They had known one another for years. Shchedrin had had a brilliant career in journalism and had held a wide variety of posts. For many years he had been a foreign correspondent and now held an important post in the domestic press. Not only did he regularly read Tass's "white bulletin", but sometimes the "red" as well. His contacts were broad and unexpected, extending from several ministries to the censorship office, from research institutes to the Writers' Union, and in all levels of society. He had even managed to visit that fabled science city that figures nowhere on our maps and is buried deep in Siberia

—in certain Moscow circles it is known as Kitezh. Shchedrin was inordinately ambitious and openly cynical, at least with Tarakanov and other of his friends. In all probability he was a genuine cynic, but not all the way through, because he had too many weaknesses. Tarakanov could never feel completely at his ease in talking to him, because he was never sure exactly where Shchedrin drew the line between seriousness and joking. He could tell the most outrageous stories, but in doing so he fixed the listener with such an intent stare of his gray eyes that the latter felt ashamed to laugh. That is why Tarakanov was usually on his guard when discussing with Shchedrin things that had nothing to do with the C Business. This, however, was what he had come to talk about today and Shchedrin was not the sort of man to turn Puritan or go sneaking to the police. On the contrary, knowing his weaknesses the lawyer was sure he'd take the bait.

They hadn't met for some time, but Shchedrin hadn't changed in any way: tall, bulky, sweating in the summer heat, well but sloppily dressed, he was the spitting image of Gogol's Manilov. With his invariable amiability he conducted Tarakanov to the journalists' restaurant and they sat down. It was difficult to talk to Shchedrin about anything away from a table, food, drink and the chance to drag out the formalities of eating to the utmost. And all this was readily available here in the restaurant of the Central Journalists' House, which couldn't be said of many rendezvous places in Moscow.

They were surrounded by those special breeds who are eligible to eat in our "closed restaurants". Perhaps even more than India, our world is divided up into castes; we have cafés, restaurants, theaters, concert halls, cinemas and shops that are closed to the general public and intended only for particular castes: leading party workers, economists, writers, academicians, journalists, artists, painters, and so on.

Although, as usual, there were many outsiders in the dining room who did not belong to any of the special castes, it was possible to note a common denominator in all those present.

The consciousness of belonging to a privileged minority, and pride in this fact. Even the most innocent are infected with this virus the moment they find themselves in these enviable surroundings, and this binds them to the existing order of things. These social centers that are closed to the masses differ from one another only in the most insignificant nuances: thus the inexperienced visitor is unlikely to notice the difference in atmosphere between the Journalists' House, the House of Writers and the House of Composers—these new clubs of an aristocracy that has been resurrected under a new sign and in a new form.

Tarakanov's idea that "there was nothing new under the sun," which he was now defending so earnestly, began to irritate Shchedrin and even seemed to him in bad taste. So he changed the subject and drew Tarakanov's attention to the excellent broth that they were now delicately supping from silver soup bowls. Tarakanov grasped the reproach and said smilingly:

"If I'm not mistaken, Sergei Petrovich, isn't that Shakovsky over there at the third table to my left, the editor-in-chief of *The Unfine Arts*," he nodded discreetly in the direction of a refined-looking man in gleaming eyeglasses, with a tiny pursed mouth like a chicken's posterior.

And that is precisely who it was. He was sounding off about the decadence of the West, although every time he went there he practically killed himself trying to get as much of it as he could. He was the most convincing sort of representative of our prospering new order of Jesuits.

"Still, you have to admit that he was *le physique du rôle*," said Tarakanov, who loved to show off his ancient store of French expressions in the presence of erudite companions, "at least he's a decent-looking sort of fellow and not one of these lop-eared peasants."

"Do you know French well, Valery Borisovich?" asked Shchedrin. "My generation is better acquainted with English. But no other language has such a subtle erotic vocabulary," he added, wrinkling up his crafty gray eyes with pleasure at the thought.

"In that sense we ourselves are complete savages," responded Tarakanov warmly, "we're still a race of peasants, and on top of that we've got an overdeveloped sense of sin which was nurtured in us for centuries by the Orthodox church and is now supported by the mysticism of the present regime. Sex for us is an animal activity which we have to be ashamed of—necessary for, but unworthy of man."

"Everybody does it, but nobody talks about it," interjected Shchedrin.

"Yes, and this silence is preserved even when they are actually doing it," continued Tarakanov, who was very fond of this subject. "That proves that for us it's a taboo. And it is characteristic of a taboo that nobody tries to define it in words, for words have the capacity of bringing objects to life, duplicating them in reality, like a mirror, dragging them out of the unconscious into the light of day, but already altered and after having been subjected to censorship. And only here does man's power over nature begin, that is to say, civilization. And eroticism begins here too, for everything that precedes it is nothing but simple sexuality. Erotic language comes into being at precisely this point, created by recondite possibility and necessity," Tarakanov heavily emphasized this last word, "the necessity of using it, for language is an instrument of cognition, of thought. And when the definition of an object has been formulated, the latter needs a language for its development."

"You've got into very deep waters now, you know. Why, we don't have any sort of refined erotic language at all, we don't even have a proper terminology for naming the most elementary sexual actions, except for those few we avoid using and that serve only as a vehicle for us to express anger and irritation, but never outbursts of passion."

"Well, of course, this shows our false consciousness of the object," said Tarakanov, "these are the fruits of our sexual repression. But at the same time it also represents the pangs of liberation, the freeing of the word, and its use outside the constraints of the past. We see this process taking place among many nations, particularly among the lower orders of the population, and with us this is a historical phenomenon. Obscenity, as a symbol of sexual repression and the weapon of primitives, has become the weapon of our peasant millions, who although they are situated at the lowest level of cultural development have become the principal force in Russian history. This has given a special coloring to our life here, to Soviet society since the thirties, and it has had its limiting effects. This is the source of our official moralism, the outdated moral precepts with which our life is saturated, beginning with school, and of our inability to create a new code of ethical standards or at least to try to in the spirit of Marxism. This is the source of our inferiority complex toward other countries, our imitation and at the same time denunciation of the bourgeoisie, the colossal hypocrisy that has infected every single aspect of our life."

"I absolutely agree with you: everything comes from our peasant and his primitivism. The workers have nothing to do with it. This is a big subject, Valery Borisovich, and we've already gone pretty deeply into it. The essence of what you're saying, if I've understood you correctly, is that 'you can't make a silk purse out of a sow's ear,' is that right? Maybe that's true, but just let's wait for the next two or three generations to come along. Today our workers all stink of manure, or at least ninety per cent of them do, but through their grandsons they'll grow into a true working class, and this new class, the ruling class, will steer the country in a new direction, will tackle new contemporary problems."

"Yes, Sergei Petrovich, but maybe it's already too late: today's primitive has been in control for fifty years already, and he's done everything in his power to cripple and stop this process, and maybe he's already succeeded. Russia today is one of the most reactionary powers in the world. You say wait a hundred years, but that will be too late for us. But still, I wanted to show you something," and the lawyer picked up his leather briefcase from an empty chair, removing some papers from it and spreading them out on the table.

As always, the animated discussion had made him appear more youthful, the tasty food and wine had imparted a healthy glow to features that seemed untouched by age, and a sly gleam appeared in his eyes. But he was exaggeratedly controlled in his demeanor and one could only admire the style with which he bore himself as he handed a file to Shchedrin and said:

"Do take a look at this. This is a detailed exposition of the plan I had the pleasure of telling you about in general terms, and with which you can acquaint yourself more closely. I hope this plan of our projected activities will meet with your approval and will arouse your personal interest. It would be a great honor for our . . ." He almost said "firm" but at the last minute corrected himself and went on: ". . . . for our enterprise to be able to count on a client as esteemed as yourself."

Neatly typed out on a sheet of paper was an exhaustive description of the entire C Business. An appendix contained a list of various samples of graves, together with their prices. For instance, a simple grave with a headstone, a grave with a headstone and memorial bust, a grave with a proper monument, a family grave, and so on. Then followed a complete photographic documentation of the cemetery under construction. Then a list, which was more like a fantastic anthology, of suggested funeral inscriptions for customers to choose from. This last was naturally the work of Gleb Matsa. As for the photographs, they began with pictures of the site which the collective farm, Sheaves of the Future, had set aside for the cemetery and on these Oganesyan had done charcoal sketches of projects for a monument entrance to the cemetery and its entire façade. Then followed a whole series of drawings, sketches and photographs of various other accessories.

"Read it through at your leisure, think about it, and then I'm at your disposal. If you have any doubts, your humble servant will be at your service at any time of the day or night," went on the lawyer somewhat verbosely, but with a sense of his own dignity, and lit up a Cuban cigar.

Shchedrin was engrossed in reading through this astounding documentation. Raising his thick eyebrows slightly, he replied:

"The Russian revolutionary spirit allied with American practicality, I see. What an extraordinarily elegant confidence trick!"

The lawyer didn't bat an eyelid and Shchedrin went back to his study of the documents.

"A remarkable piece of trickery, Valery Borisovich," he repeated his conclusion, neatly arranging the sheets of paper again with his soft fleshy hands. "Congratulations! That alone makes it worthwhile helping you. Put in my order, please, for model number 7G. I can certainly be of use to you," he added, with an ironic gleam in his eye. "I can get extra orders for you. What commission may I count on?"

"Up to twenty-five per cent," said Tarakanov coolly.

"Excellent. Let's have a drink at the bar. To our collaboration!" exclaimed Shchedrin, getting up from the table and slapping Tarakanov on the back from where he stood. But the lawyer left him at this point, because he had one more little chore to do.

That morning he had given a lift as far as the center of Moscow to the chairman of Sheaves of the Future, Baranov, who was due to meet Dermoshchenko to come to a concrete agreement concerning the formalities connected with the scientific assistance promised to the collective. But Dermoshchenko had suddenly been called that day to the Academy on the Leninsky Prospekt by his teacher and patron, L., and it was impossible for him to refuse this summons.

Their meeting was postponed till seven o'clock in the evening and since the lawyer was lunching at the Journalists' House with Shchedrin, Horace Evsevonovich Baranov had gone alone to the restaurant, Uzbekistan. The lawyer had promised to join him there just as soon as his lunch was over. But a strange thing happened to Baranov in the Uzbekistan. When he entered there were no places free. Then he noticed a man with black hair and a mustache who was just finishing his lunch, and so he stared at him meaningfully. The latter paid no attention at first, but then began to smile at him. His smile seemed strangely inviting. Baranov decided that he must have been drinking and was giving him to understand, in his own peculiar way, that he was about to finish up his lunch and continue on his way, thus leaving his seat free for Baranov. And indeed, after this long performance, the man finally got up. As he left the room he passed right next to Baranov, practically pressing up against him with his body, and whispered in his ear: "Sorcerer!" Baranov concluded that he must have been really plastered and sat down at the table. After waiting a while for the waitress and ordering his meal, he decided to go to the toilet. But there, the moment he entered, he caught sight of the man who had given him his seat and at once the latter rushed up to him and kissed him full on the lips, hissing in his ear once more: "Sorcerer! You've put a spell on me!" Baranov held him off with both hands, but in silence, because he wished to avoid a scandal, and returned to the dining room.

He finished his meal and drank up, but since Tarakanov was a long time coming he was forced to go on ordering things to eat and drink. As he waited for him, the chairman caught himself thinking, not indignantly but ironically and good-naturedly (perhaps because he had reached the same degree of intoxication and was sitting in the same chair), about his adventure with the man with the mustache. Following his train of thought, he glanced about him, and the amazing appetite of the crowd filling the restaurant assuaged his imagination, which had hitherto been dwelling on various dirty thoughts. They were eating and drinking, the women were not bad looking and the men were jovial and masculine. This calmed him down and he surveyed with pleasure the general spectacle of these members of the Soviet public, for whom strange happenings, unnatural and foolish fantasies did not exist, but whose pleasures were, on the contrary, the well-earned, concrete, ethical pleasures that reality around them had to offer.

He was at first surprised, then pleased suddenly and unexpectedly to notice Avdotya Zakharovna seated at one of the tables. It had been a real mistake not to trust her completely in the past. Just look at her now sitting there so self-satisfied and comely, and completely natural! A real Russian woman. And who was she with? What? An airforce major! Baranov looked long and hard. He sensed at once that the couple not only knew one another, but were even on very intimate terms.

To come to this conclusion he had, of course, to watch them for some time. This entailed no difficulty, since Dunya was seated with her back to him while the major facing him did not know him. And anyway, Baranov was no fool; thanks to his country cunning, no one noticed his interest in the couple sitting opposite him. What he saw was truly interesting and fascinating, although it conflicted with all the accepted standards of behaviour in public places. Baranov, however, was not unduly troubled by this fact when he considered that Dunya's consort was not only a member of the armed forces, but a high-ranking one at that.

Only a man who had merited his country's trust could take the liberty of doing what the major was doing. He had removed one of his boots, utterly oblivious to the fact that he was in a restaurant filled with the most respectable clientele in the very center of the capital. True, none of his fellow-diners had noticed anything, but the major had gone even further. His bootless leg was resting not on the floor with his other foot, but was stretched out in a horizontal position so that it disappeared somewhere between Dunya's legs and was moving slightly up and down. As for Dunya, her legs must have been spread-eagled, because her right knee was positioned far out at an angle to the chair and Dunya's back, while her left leg extended parallel with the leg of her consort and was resting against the base of his abdomen. Baranov had a perfect view of everything, seated as he was directly opposite the major. "Lucky nobody else is being put at their table," he thought with faint uneasiness, "the waiter must have had his palm well greased by the major."

Dunya's foot, also shoeless, was gently rubbing against that erect bayonet that was an accessory not of the major's uniform, but of the major himself. Performing this feat with brazen calmness, the pair smiled insolently at each other and swilled their Tokay like a couple of clowns.

Actually, the major had cast a fleeting glance at Baranov, who, he thought, was the only person in the room who might be able to see their furtive contact. But Baranov's fleshy, sunken eyes seemed so vacant and expressionless that he stopped worrying. As for Baranov, he was not the least bit shocked, but was at that precise moment placidly wondering at this sexual silliness. Not only did he regard it as trivial and unimportant: he simply could not understand what pleasure they could possibly derive from such activity. His diminutive prick spent most of the year in hibernation, like a tortoise; it preferred to doze in comfort in its shell, and considerable effort was required to make its tiny tip peep out from under the shell and show the slightest sign of life.

He could see them, but their words were inaudible in the general noise. And he was already getting bored when he suddenly observed that something had happened between them and the position had changed.

The major jerked his foot away, the foot that had been between Avdotya Zakharovna's legs, and nervously pressed it against the foot that had remained on the floor, as though trying to hide behind it. He sat back stiffly in his chair and his face became serious and thoughtful.

Avdotya Zakharovna also rearranged herself and gazed at him, expectantly, attentive and serious.

The major was saying something to her. Baranov strained his ears, but in the noise of the crowd it was difficult to make out any words. He stopped looking at them and became lost in his own thoughts. But he guessed that the pair were no longer employing the language of their feet to amuse themselves, but had got down to concrete business talk.

"Do you remember, Dunya, the opinions we exchanged at

the airport?" the major asked her. "You said yourself that the military in our country carry a considerable weight and that they'd gone up in the world."

"Of course, and I can say it again, my dear," Dunya answered unhesitatingly and passionately, adding, as though prompted by an instinctive caution: "And my husband used to talk to me about the purity of those who devote their lives to the welfare of their country."

"Precisely, my dear Avdotya Zakharovna!" the major's honeyed voice cut her short. "That is precisely what I wanted to talk to you about, especially now that we have got to know each other so well and have known real intimacy." He patted Dunya's knee lightly, as if trying to emphasize their complicity and the mutual trust that had been established after their having slept together, as if, in meeting her in a restaurant and arousing her to sensual play, he had been acting quite naturally. "That was precisely why I asked you to meet me today; I wanted to have a talk with you . . . or rather, to tell you a little secret, something very important for us." He leaned forward, his neck stretched to bring his face nearer to Dunya's, and said in a lowered voice: "Our country, Soviet power, they need us. Because, and you are well aware of this, certain people are trying to start a fire, but the spark must be extinguished before the fire starts! Certain people are already weaving the nets of a cosmopolitan conspiracy; and we must call things by their proper names—Zionism is rearing its ugly head! Their aim is clear: to undermine the unity, the traditions, the very soul of the Russian people . . ."

"Zionist plot?" whispered Dunya, arching her black, neatly pencilled eyebrows, with an expression of surprise and attentiveness. Not sure what the major was driving at, she nonetheless realized that the conversation was taking an entirely unforeseen turn and tried to defend herself: "But who are you talking about? And why now, why at this precise moment?"

"Oh, come now!" replied the major, puffing himself up. "We're Russians, true Russians. Our Soviet Union is a fraternal union, but how many Cains there are still in our society, just think for a moment! And even in our midst, in the army and in first-rate jobs, there they are, these Cains . . . yes, yes, all Jews are basically the same, people in whom the voice of their blood, their race will speak out sooner or later, and who will follow the voice of their blood and enlist with the Zionists. And there's no doubt about it, they're a cunning people, subtle, capable of years of feigned loyalty, but they all have the same aim—sabotage and conspiracy. That's who we're talking about, my dear. And you, Avdotya Zakharovna, are just the one who can help us, who could even, I might say, accomplish a feat that would do honor to the memory of your glorious hero-husband. You can help us tear the mask off these vile creatures whom Mother Russia's warm bosom has nourished, and who are just about to bite . . ."

Dunya began to understand. She was aflame with anger and scorn, and flickers of memory recalled the terrible, shattering humiliations she had suffered on Caucasian soil. Russians—us? Did anybody in the Caucasus ever regard us as the Russians' equals? Yes, of course, there had been a lot of talk about equality and fraternity, but in practice, in reality? Moscow dictated the laws and the Russians were masters as always. Yes, of course, they were "big brothers"! Not a bad expression, so nice and patriarchal, a rose-colored image of their domination, and especially of their conceit and their invincible sense of superiority. Yes, Russian blood flowed in her too, but she remembered how repugnant to Lenin Great Russian nationalism had been, and she knew the position of the "sister"-republics too well not to realize what a wretched life they had as the Cinderellas of the "fraternal family of peoples". What had Zionists to do with it? Maybe they were even worse than these people, but they served as a cover-up, simply something to hide behind! That was it! As if she didn't understand! She wanted to answer the major straight with a few strong words. After all, she'd slept with him because she believed that somewhere in the depths of his soul he wasn't a bad sort, a good old square, but it turned out he was a bastard! Taking into account the positions that each of them held in this life, she made an effort to suppress her emotions, as Tarakanov had taught her, and said, with exaggerated modesty:

"Help you? Me? What are you thinking of! You really don't know me."

"No, forgive me, I am sure you could do it. You are intelligent, attractive . . . What would it cost you to win any man, let's say a general, an interesting man, a connoisseur of women. A bit of a hangover, a grain or two of dope . . ."

Dunya gasped. Drugs? What did it mean? Did the major know anything? . . . A tremor ran through her body. In order to suppress it and not give herself away by an incautious gesture or word, she grasped her glass and downed the Tokay, watching the expression on the major's face. But it did not alter; he smiled at her again, and once more stroked her thigh with his fingers, which were as unctuous as his words.

"What do you mean, drugs?" she asked, alarmed, giving him an uncomprehending stare. "What do you think you're saying? How dare you speak to me, a widow of the Cosmos, like that?"

"Don't be afraid, what is there to be frightened of? When it serves a just cause? We'll arrange for you to be supplied. Briefly, this is what you have to do. We are asking you to capture this general called Imyarek. He serves in the Caucasus and he's got lots of high-level connections, but he's not one of us. First and foremost, he's a Jew by nationality and so defenseless in the face of international Zionism, and apart from that he's the sort who might open the doors wide to revisionism—or worse. With your help we can render him harmless; it'll be an easy matter for you. All you have to do, dear Dunya, is become his mistress. And you'll drive him out of his mind!" the major whispered, gazing at Dunya, his eyes filled with meaning, bending over the table towards her and lightly brushing his lips against her cheeks. "You'll make him your slave, a slave of love, you'll get him on cocaine and he'll feel he's a magnificent stud in spite of his age. Well, in short, he simply won't be able to go on living without you. And you'll tell us all about him: his friends, acquaintances, contacts, and so on. But it won't be for very long, don't worry, my dear," he hastened to add, observing traces of anxiety on Dunya's face, which she was unable to conceal. "Not for long, since all we have to do is come to the crunch, and as quickly as possible. So, at a particular time and in a particular way—which we'll agree on later—we'll arrange for him to be caught red-handed, in a scandalous situation, drugged with cocaine—everything that is absolutely incompatible with his honor as a military man, and his morals as a communist and a Soviet citizen. He'll be finished. And we'll leave the rest to the legal organs: they'll see to the application of the law. As for you, I hardly need say that you'll come through it all safe and sound, and more—you'll be given moral and material compensation . . ."

"Oh, you swine!" Dunya screamed silently as she heard him out. "You mercenary, you filthy spy! And who's it for, yourself, you bastard? Or your Black Hundreds?" But she had to stifle the cry in her throat, and this hurt her and caused a searing pain. The fear which had earlier flashed through her when the major mentioned drugs had proved groundless. And now everything coalesced in a nervous, hysterical laugh that the major interpreted as an amused and eloquent corroboration of his words. But the answer Dunya threw at him, looking straight into his eyes with a steady gaze that suddenly became icy, was quite different:

"When I sleep with a man," she said, enunciating every syllable distinctly, "it's because I like him. I thought you were a man, an honorable soldier like my Leonid. I prefer other games to the power game."

"And I thought we were friends," answered the major, disappointingly. "But I can see you're no friend of mine. I only hope everything we have said here will remain between ourselves. I can demand that much at least from a woman, who cannot maintain the standard set by the hero who gave her her position and the respect she still enjoys . . ."

"That's enough!" she cried abruptly, getting up. It was not so much the offensive meaning of his last words—uttered purposely by the major—as his ignorance of Dunya's past and present, that was important to her at that moment. He had no cause to blackmail her, he couldn't hurt her, and he could not possibly conceive the whole truth about her. So to hell with him! Poor old melon, full of water. He wasn't even worth knifing.

When Tarakanov finally appeared, Baranov said nothing to him about his encounters. Behind the wheel of his Moskvich, Tarakanov once more rehearsed Baranov on how to behave and what to discuss with Dermoshchenko. Despite the fact that Baranov had never suffered from modesty, he was overwhelmed by the thought of meeting such a celebrated scientist, about whom he had heard so much and whose picture he had seen more than once in the newspapers, but the lawyer explained to him once again that it was the duty of Horace Evsevonovich Baranov, Chairman of the collective farm, Sheaves of the Future, personally to invite the scientist to carry out experiments on his farm. Tarakanov left him at the front entrance of the house where Dermoshchenko lived. The Chairman tightened his belt, emboldened by Tarakanov's words, and prepared to carry out the military operation that had been entrusted to him, although he was far from being sure of himself and felt very much out of his depth.

13. Marina's Confession

The church was plunged in deep gloom and gave every appearance of being empty. Anyone peeping in from the narthex would have had difficulty in making out the altar through the open royal doors, beyond the iconostasia, the partition that separated the nave from the choir, with its ark and seven-branched candlestick. And the icons of the Savior, the Mother of God and the saints were even harder to see.

But the church was not empty. As often happens in the absence of the usual throng of worshippers, which by the force of its very vitality occupies the center of the stage, thereby modifying the character of the place, its spiritual quality and its true essence, this church was always ready, at moments of peace and quiet, to shelter those rare visitors who liked to come and linger in its dark alcoves and secret corners. And only the experienced eye of a frequent visitor would have been able to detect two figures by a bench against the north wall, not far from the analogion, the pulpit.

They were black and motionless and their outlines merged with the surrounding darkness. One was standing, while the other sat. The latter was dressed in the invariable attire of Russian priests: a cassock and long stole over the left shoulder. The tall standing figure with covered head was also dressed in a black or dark dress that did not reach the floor, and was apparently female.

She was speaking in a very low voice, standing there without moving her arms, looking into the face of the priest who sat before her. The priest's heavily wrinkled face, framed in a gray beard, with dark melancholy eyes, looked as if carved from stone.

". . . and that's why I haven't been to see you for so long. Often, during my long absences, I think that it is useless for me to come, because you say I am an incorrigible sinner incapable of entering the temple of the Lord. But I feel bound to the Church. Everything you consider a mortal sin is for me the holy of holies, the shortest and purest path to communion with the Holy Ghost."

"That's heresy, I've told you before, Marina," interrupted the priest severely, "and I've already given you your penance for it. Do you do it?"

"Y-yes," said Marina, hesitating slightly, "but not for all the things you call sin. My position as a worshipper here is ambiguous and it's not my fault, Father Mitrofan. You . . ."

"What do you mean, it's not your fault!" exclaimed the priest, interrupting her. "You desire to remain in a state of heresy, and according to the rules of our Orthodox faith I cannot accept you into the bosom of the Church."

"But how can you say that, Father Mitrofan?" said Marina softly and plaintively. "Why, the *Khlysti* are one of the original sects of the Old Believers, they have never renounced the faith of their ancestors."

Without waiting to be invited, she sat down on the bench.

"Yes, but they gave themselves up to pagan and sacrilegious behavior, to 'satanic singing and dancing', to 'blasphemous acts' that are unacceptable to our Church and are looked on as sin and heresy. Thou shalt not commit such acts! . . . They are repugnant to God and cursed by the prophets! Today this sect has been almost extinguished, yet you are endeavouring to resurrect it. Not only are you in a state of heresy yourself, but you are trying to spread it. And that is unforgiveable."

"What pagan and sacrilegious behaviour have you in mind?"

asked Marina indignantly. "What's the most important thing for a believer? Communion with God and with his divine essence—the Holy Ghost. In the course of this communion, man is cleansed of all his sins and himself becomes divine. That is what God desires of us, that is what the Church should strive for, and all its rules and rituals should be subordinated to this end. If this isn't done, there can be no communion with God and therefore we are deprived of God's mercy."

"The Lord said: Thou shalt not commit adultery."

"Yes, and the Lord also said: Thou shalt not kill. Yet how much killing has there been in the Church's name; to ensure Her victory, and how much killing has She herself condoned? But you won't give me absolution and you refuse to confess me, even though I . . . we don't even commit adultery, for what we do is something quite different. Just as every Christian, swallowing the sacrament, enters into communion with God through his flesh, and just as the more devout Christians mortify themselves with penances and don hair shirts, thus using their bodies to elevate the spirit and attain communion with God, so do we do something similar. When we dance naked, lashing our bodies and singing songs at the same time, at first slowly and then faster and faster to fever pitch, so that our frenzied flesh is transformed into spirit, and when, finally, our bodies combine, are joined and copulate, they no longer exist as sinful matter, cut off from God, but participate in spiritual congress, and this is the spirit of infinite joy exulting in them, derived from their communion with God and the pure happiness of residing in Him and His creation. And thus is achieved the perfect union that He desires between His divinity and His creation. In this union we who are in flesh and spirit a part of His creation are enabled to commune with the Divine Spirit with our entire being—our flesh and spirit and the flesh become spirit—and identify with It. How far this is from adultery, which I too consider a sin, for the two things are completely different. Can you not understand this?"

"It is a distortion of the Church's teaching to turn sin, error and disobedience into the path of salvation! You are sorely mistaken, my child! It is only because I have known you for many years . . ."

"Father!" exclaimed Marina imploringly, but in a tone that conveyed controlled strength and a conviction of her own righteousness. "Don't talk like that, listen to me! You say it's disobedience, pride—maybe it is. But then Christ Himself disobeyed His Father in order to show men a new road to salvation. And as for adultery, that's just an empty prayer act, without feeling, which will never ascend to God, whereas our ritual copulation means praying with all our being, a perfect union of the flesh with divinity. And you, the servant of God, can you condemn us? Condemn us and forgive people of little faith, hypocrites and pharisees?"

Father Mitrofan looked at her as she sat there, pulsating, vibrating with the flame of certainty and righteousness and with genuine passion as she made this confession of faith. He gazed at the young woman intently and his face suddenly softened and took on an expression of indulgence mixed with uncertainty.

"Marina," he said smilingly, "it's not for nothing you bear the name of Kerzhentseva. The town of Kerzhenets has been the stronghold of our faith since the Great Schism; it has been the cradle of the Old Believers, and you have that same staunchness in your blood, the same obstinacy, and also that implacable pride and the yearning for direct access to God, the pugnaciousness and the self-reliance—you want to find the best way to God on your own. Who are the Old Believers? They are the ones who have remained faithful to the Orthodox Church as it was up till the time of the Patriarch Nikon and Peter the Great. We are distinguished not by the spirit of innovation, but by loyalty to the faith of our ancestors. And just think: it was our schism that led to the formation of the various sects, you know the ones I mean—the *Molokanye* (Milkites) who drink milk during the fasts; Evtimy's *Byeguni* (Runners), who spent their lives wandering from place to place, renouncing material goods and fleeing from civilization; the *Nikudyshniki* (Useless Ones), who renounced civilization in their turn; then the *Doukhobors* (Soul Wrestlers), who formed free communes with no church and no marriage and made their way to America; and finally your *Khlysti* (Flagellants). But they are all mystics—a tiny pool in comparison with the human sea for whom the church ordinances exist, which were created for the common folk as a well-beaten path for coming closer to God. The human race walks on level ground, while these few have ascended to the mountain tops and desire to fly. The people sail in the ship of the Church, while they have hurled themselves into the sea in order to come quicker to God. They left the Church and broke with it, yet you have come to me for the absolution of your sins . . . Are you listening to me, my child?" The priest imperiously demanded her attention, for she was beginning to grow confused. "I have known you since you were a child, when your mother became my spiritual daughter. I baptized you, it was through me you entered the faith. I am recalling this now because I am convinced it is a good thing and you ought to remember it. Everything began for you on a certain day—you know the day I mean." Father Mitrofan suddenly fell silent. He was a good judge of people and knew Marina extremely well. He had purposely invoked a bitter episode in her memory, and for a good reason.

"Father!" exclaimed Marina sorrowfully. "Why think of that? Why cause me pain? That day is buried in my soul, in my innermost being, like a tumor that pretends to be dormant, but that suddenly tightens with pincers of unbearable pain. There will always be an empty compartment in my brain and poison in my blood. I strive not to remember, I try to live as if not only that day, but all the other days and even years before it had never existed, as if I came into the world already seven years old, in 1949, as if I began life there in that orphanage. And I did not come here, Father, for you to invoke bitter memories in my soul. You have no mercy, it is not Christ speaking in you, but Lucifer . . . But please don't be offended, I don't mean to insult you. You are right, it all began on that day. I only realized it recently. Earlier I used to remember it and burst into tears and suffer terribly, but that was simply the memory of it, and I used to hope that gradually it would grow blunted and fade away. I had my life before me; I was eagerly looking forward to the future, to the new, beautiful, joyful life that was to come. I was a child, a little girl, so that was perfectly normal—right? That day was part of the past for me, a mere sign of what was to come later. But nonetheless I remembered—remembered perfectly—how they had come during the night. I didn't hear the bell, but I woke up afterwards because of all the rumpus."

Marina was speaking now as in a dream or in a delirium, staring motionlessly into the dark.

"They charged about all over the place. There were four of them. The floor was strewn with papers. Mamma and Papa were dressed and looked serious, they didn't notice that I had got up and was standing there barefoot, in my nightdress, in the doorway to Papa's study, staring with fright at everything that was going on. Nanny also got up and led me away to the kitchen. She talked to me and stroked my hair, but I was terrified. Then they called me and Nanny took me into the hall. Mamma and Papa kissed me and said they would soon be back—in a month or two, they weren't sure exactly when—and that I should be a good girl. Then one of the men there said 'Get going!' in a voice I can still remember better than Mamma's and Papa's voices, and I can still remember the submissiveness with which they obediently did as they were told. I had never dreamed that they could be so submissive toward anyone, much less toward someone who in comparison with them was absolutely nothing. Then they hung seals on everything in the apartment and said it wasn't ours any more and that we'd have to leave. Nanny went off to some people she knew, but nobody wanted me; even Mamma's sister who lived in Ufa refused to take me in. Then I was put in an orphanage. Still, what's the point of going over it all again; you know it already."

She glanced at Father Mitrofan and seeing that he was listening to her with profound concentration, the expression of his whole face encouraging her to confess, she continued automatically:

"It was an orphange like any other, and had everything you'd expect to find in an orphanage, both good and bad. I was an excellent pupil, always top of the class; and twice I was transferred to other orphanages. Then one day I was called to see the director and told that my uncle had come. But what uncle? I didn't remember any uncle; neither Mamma nor Papa had ever mentioned one. My Ufa aunt, Mamma's sister, had never married. But he had already completed all the formalities and took me away with him. He told me that I would go to school in Moscow and I was just glad of the change, the chance to go to school in Moscow and the fact that I wasn't alone in the world, but actually had an uncle. The other girls envied me. And he was reasonably good to me. He paid a lot of attention to me, he was unmarried and we lived in the apartment alone, except for a woman who came in to do the cleaning. He was an officer in the KGB. And he personally told me, and brought the documents to prove it, that my parents had been posthumously rehabilitated, and I was very grateful to him. One day he told me that in fact he was not my real uncle, and that in actuality, we were not linked by any bonds of kinship: he had some distant relationship with Mamma that was impossible to define. I graduated from the philosophical faculty of the university just at the time when he was promoted to general in the KGB. Immediately after this he bought himself a villa thirty miles down the Zagorsk road—you know what a marvelous house it is. We were already lovers by this time. I'm not complaining, maybe I could have expected nothing better from life. And anyway, life must go on. I am free, I have everything I need; he's not very jealous, and I fulfill his demands on me as a woman without regrets and even with some degree of satisfaction. But there's something else . . ."

"What?" said Father Mitrofan.

"I don't know, everything seems to have changed just lately, or maybe it's just that we look at things differently now. When I was a girl at university we had such high hopes."

"But that has nothing to do with you personally."

"Why not?" objected Marina. "We have retreated into ourselves, we seek in ourselves that which we can't find around us. Oh, I know why I turned to religion! But I don't want to find in religion the same system of commandments, dogmas and rules that surrounds me everywhere else. In that case I prefer our mutilated and distorted version of Marxism, for at least there's a hope that it will change for the better. We have grown up now. A primitive ideology can no longer satisfy us; we long, we thirst for theories and universal values. How ridiculous, though," she smiled bitterly, "in a world where science is daily exploding universal theories and values."

Father Mitrofan grew gloomy. She was slipping away from him; she was stronger than he had thought. He guessed that her interest in sectarianism had grown out of her deep dissatisfaction with the life she was leading and that was why he had made her think back, so that she would look at her life as a whole once more. Secretly he hoped to find in all this the free end of the thread that made up the tangled skein of her faith; but now she was too far away.

"When you first came back to me, were you already a follower of the *Khlysti*? Or was that still only a thought, an idea?"

"Yes and no," replied Marina with a distant smile. "It wasn't an intellectual temptation for me, if that's what you're thinking. No, practically speaking I was already prepared for it when I discovered the historical existence of everything and its philosophical explanation. What's more, I discovered it by my intuition of life and of our relations with the secret life and with divinity. Then I came to you, but there had already been an important meeting in my life before I came."

"What meeting?" blurted out the priest.

"Shall I tell you about it?" smiled Marina, who felt that she had got the upper hand over the priest. "They exist, you know, and are walking about among us. Who? Flagellants! And not like my uncle, who acts merely under the influence of his instincts and out of a desire to run away from reality, but as a religious sect."

"But how, where?" interjected the excited father.

"The meeting took place in Moscow," replied Marina coolly. "But they are everywhere, all over Russia, and their number is undoubtedly growing, because our country now offers excellent soil for the growth of all kinds of sectarianism. But why am I telling you all this? You have already refused to confess me."

"But how can I possibly confess you when you warn me in advance that you don't repent and when you continue to defend heresy?"

"And if I do repent?"

Father Mitrofan felt a pounding in his temples from the terrible anger that rose within him: she was making fun of him! But he restrained himself; he did not want to break the last thread that bound him to this believer, who differed so strongly from the usual women who came to confess. No, he did not wish to drive this strange young woman away, this woman who lived with a man invested with great power and who knew of things that he hadn't even suspected. In a calm and friendly voice he said:

"Do as you wish. But confess to me as a spiritual father and not as a clergyman."

"All right," replied Marina. "I'm sure Christ has forgiven me already and that he does not regard me as being in a state of sin," she smiled to herself, "for being what you call a heretic. But I do need a spiritual father; I have to speak to a man of the Church about my spiritual life."

"Go on, my child, I'm listening," said the servant of the Church in a low voice. "Begin with the meeting. Was it a man? What did you do with him? What did he say to you?"

Since it was not a confession according to the rules, but simply a talk with her spiritual father, he did not deem it necessary for her to stand before the icon of the Savior. It also seemed superfluous to him to say such prayers as "Thrice Holy," the Lord's Prayer or "Lord Have Mercy On Us," and so on. He contented himself with a brief "Blessed Be Our Lord" and settled down to listen to Marina, who was just beginning her story.

"Yes, it was a man, and we got to know one another at an art exhibition. We talked about a great deal and he turned the subject onto sectarianism. I was extremely interested. He opened my eyes to all sorts of things in that sphere and seeing my interest, began to tell me about the *Khlysti.* I had never dared hope for so much! We talked for a long time and he saw clear through me. I didn't tell him anything about my uncle and the nature of our relationship, I just let him think that the experience was nothing new to me. We went to the baths together. He had some switches and there in the family baths we whipped one another. We couldn't sing or cry out because others would have heard us, but he was a real man of God, he never saw me as a woman, but simply as a sister in faith, and he knew how to ascend into the skies with a switch in his hand. And only when we were both up there did he unite with me, and together, like children of the Word and the Holy Ghost, we achieved divine ecstasy, divine communion . . ."

"In such a place!" blurted out Father Mitrofan.

"What importance does the place have for true believers? God is everywhere!" retorted Marina.

Once more Father Mitrofan felt the hot blood rush to his temples, but again he held his anger in check. Not for nothing had he been through a hard school.

"Tell me, Marina," he said, pretending not to have noticed the young woman's self-assurance, "what did he tell you about the sect? Are there many of them? And where do they meet?"

"He told me that if I would go with him to a small town beyond the Volga, he would show me the spot where they gather in great numbers to pray to God and perform their secret ceremonies. He told me that I shouldn't recognize any church, not even that of the Old Believers, that we should pray alone to God and strive to understand His mysteries ourselves. He told me that the next time he came to Moscow (he doesn't live in Moscow), he would be able to arrange a gathering of brothers and sisters, for by then there would be a place for us to meet."

"Hm-m," grunted Father Mitrofan, "can't you be a bit more exact about it, you're being very vague, you know."

"Exact about what?" asked Marina suspiciously. "I hope you're not in the same service as my uncle."

"A spiritual father has to know all the details of the temptation and sin in order to be able to judge and to guide the erring soul," replied Father Mitrofan solemnly. "Didn't your uncle notice the traces of the whipping?"

"Yes, but he put it down to our own exploits, which I would like to tell you about, for they constitute a genuine sin! Because he and I and our two maids, Marfa and Iksana, do it only for sensual pleasure. He's very fond of these exercises, because it's the only way he can make love, but it's impossible to pray with him. I try to do it to myself, but it's quite different; you need the participation of others in order to ascend. He likes me to whip him with a switch and for Marfa and Iksana to do the same, but he doesn't pray at the same time; he gets excited without praying and he even puts his general's tunic on—the tunic's absolutely essential—and only then does he desire me, takes me, possesses me, while the girls have to go on whipping: they have to whip him, me and each other, it's always the same. But for me it's a sin. What do you think, Father? Can't you see the difference, can't you see it's a degradation? I try to pray, but only my flesh gets any pleasure out of it; my soul doesn't detach itself and fails to rise into the sky."

"It is difficult for me to say, my child—there is nothing about it in the church books," replied Father Mitrofan, for the first time showing an interest in the classifications of lust. "I would like to be clear about everything, to be sure. I can say nothing, I am a simple servant of God, but if in the sacred . . ."

"Father Mitrofan!" exclaimed Marina, interrupting him. "Russian priests have always been fond of food and the flesh. Don't contradict me, you know it can't be denied . . . So why don't you want to rise above everything and soar in the sky, for you are a deeply religious man?"

"And to think I have to sit and be lectured to by her of all people," thought Father Mitrofan to himself, but aloud said: "It doesn't seem to me that my life is in contradiction with the precepts of the Church. On the other hand I cannot take it upon myself to give my own version of Christ's teaching. The Church guides us from the cradle to the grave, my child! The Church accepts us into its bosom when we arrive in God's world, raises us, teaches us, nourishes us and comforts us with its presence when we die! The Church gives us burial and keeps vigil over our earthly remains after our soul has accepted its last communion in preparation for eternal life."

Marina suddenly had a vision of something quite different, of Mikhail Nikolayevich at the collective farm meeting, and this vision merged with the figure of Father Mitrofan, while the latter's words seemed to be transposed into the corresponding words of the Party secretary.

"Good-bye, Father Mitrofan," said Marina, standing up. "I see that you are unable to help me, but our conversation has once more confirmed me in the belief that each of us must seek the truth inside himself, rejecting established and organized truth; truth is impossible to know, but we must strive for it eternally, and in that striving lies the secret of life, creation and the divine spark in man."

"Wait," said the priest, trying to detain her. "Let's go on talking for a bit, come back to me soon. You will come back, won't you?"

"I don't know." She turned toward the exit.

"Marina!" the priest called in a deep expressive voice. "Stop, wait!"

Marina halted, but without turning back.

"Look around, Marina, look at your spiritual father."

Without moving her body, she turned her head and looked back over her shoulder at Father Mitrofan.

He was sitting in the same place as before, beside the analogion, but his cassock was open in front, revealing his stomach. In the gloom of the empty church it was just possible to make out a small gap a fraction lighter than the surrounding clothing. Rising out of it from the pillow of black hair covering the priest's stomach was a long, thin, quivering phallus that terminated in a sharp, scarlet, but violet-tinted little head. His sleek white hand was resting horizontally at its side and seemed to be pointing to where she should fix her gaze. And this was in sharp contrast with the animal look of the flesh, the blackness of the surrounding hair and his gleaming black cassock. There was an expression of cunning in the gleaming eyes that he fixed on Marina.

Marina uttered not a word as she remained motionless, with her head turned back over her shoulder. With her two hands she lifted her skirt waist high to display the two perfect hemispheres of her high buttocks, rounded and tenderly pink. For a moment she held that pose without moving, grinning sarcastically at the clergyman. Then she lowered her skirt and said:

"Are you satisfied now, Father?"

Then she turned to face forward again, and with swift decisive steps made her way out of the church.

14. Ah, the Smell of Shit!

Foma Kharalampiyevich Dermoshchenko was in seventh heaven. He would never have supposed that at the end of his long scientific career, when its best pages had already been turned, when the general situation was no longer favorable to the scientific school to which he belonged, when voices were being raised everywhere demanding that he and his colleagues be put on trial, the clamor having reached even as far as the head of the school—that he would at the end of his life meet such a brave and intelligent collective farm chairman who would offer him a permanent base for carrying out his scientific experiments.

And how he had introduced himself! He had been overflowing with respect bordering on reverence, practically holding his cap in hand, like a Tolstoyan peasant in the presence of his master. One had to admit that our country folk, while remaining natural, had still not lost their admiration for our scientific achievements and still believed in them. This Horace Evsevonovich (just think, what a primordial Russian name, it had the fresh smell of plowed earth about it, it came from the very depths of Slavdom) definitely had dignity, it was at once apparent that he was both experienced and quick-witted. Dermoshchenko was an excellent judge of peasants and knew the countryside well. His slogan in his scientific work was: keep in touch with everyday practice and give "genuine help to agriculture."

Naturally he had nothing whatever to do with these Morganists—Mendelians—Weissmannites who merely built castles in the air with their drosophilas, completely divorced from reality. But how many concrete proposals they, the genuine biologists, the Michurinists, had made before the war, and then after that redletter "discussion" in '48 and right up until '63! Yes, it was easy to say now that not one of them—literally not one— had made any contribution at all to the development of agriculture.

But the road of science is long and hard. Granted it was true that there was nothing to show for it and that, even worse, their proposals had, as they said, brought only tragic losses to agriculture—granted! But what did that matter on the historical level? Stalin, who clearly saw the struggle of two competing systems on that level, understood perfectly that their group was the only one that stood for dialectical materialism in biological science.

Stalin (and he was helped in this by our promptings) didn't hesitate for a moment, when it was necessary, to sweep away two or three thousand false biologists and their colleagues, including Vavilov and Dikussar. And Khrushchev too, although he could be harshly criticized for many things, was not without his own form of genius—take, for example, his project with the corn. He also realized that Michurinist biology was working for the future. And it was far from being accidental that the collective farm's name included the word "future."

Yes, it was no accident that fate had brought him here. Now was the very moment when, after over thirty years of effort, hard work and, most important, terrible bloody battles to exterminate the Morganists—Mendelians—Weissmannites, his group was at last on the verge of success: soon they would reveal to the world their astonishing achievements, which would give their fatherland the possibility of getting oats from wheat, robin redbreasts from chicken's eggs, and build up a flourishing communist agriculture. And then, at that very moment, they had been banned, and biology had been handed over to scientific traditionalists! Thank God the Party apparatus still had people in influential positions who understood and remembered, otherwise they would all end up like poor old Yakushkin. No, no! It couldn't go on! And now here was proof of our correctness: the people itself had held out its wise and munificent hand and had sent for this purpose a genuine representative, Horace Evsevonovich Baranov, who had been here a week already and things weren't too bad at all. On the contrary. He had been assigned two rooms in a small house that also contained a workshop, or something like it. He lived in a small cabin that was kept neat as a new pin by his landlady, a quiet and obliging widow. What more could he wish for? His spirits were uplifted, he was reborn in the bosom of Russian nature, of the Russian village. It was mid-June, when everything in nature sang its triumphant song, when animals, plants and trees (what a pity that nobody had planted them in clumps!) sprang to life again and everything was filled with the exultation of summer, confident that it would last forever.

He found it a little strange that almost no one went into the fields to work, while the village girls looked more like factory workers. Probably there was some sort of craft being practiced on the farm, he realized that at once. But what of it? It could do no harm to a healthy agriculture! And in any case, he had no time to poke his nose into other people's business—he had no time even to occupy himself directly with the types of grain being grown! He had to check out the results of his manure experiments against practice. But above all he had to continue his researches into methods of analyzing manure and to do that analysis where the manure was produced. Ah, what odors there were when he went into the cowshed, what exhalations, and what sweet aroma rose from that rich and blessed substance! It was a long, long time since he had been able to plunge into it like that, as into an oxygen bath, soothing and revivifying. And then the incomparable pleasure (his scientific conscientiousness had, over the years, grown into a passion and a genuine taste for it) of gathering samples, rooting around in the different layers and digging down ever deeper in order to familiarize himself with the various stages of maturation, and even to learn to distinguish the particular characteristics from each individual breed of animal. Who could understand such things better than he? Even his colleagues belonging to the same school of thought, even the very leader of the school—all seemed somewhat at a loss in the face of such enthusiasm, such insensitivity to the research material, such creative dedication (yes, it was the correct expression for it: creative!). He knew that many considered him a maniac, a madman, a scientific degenerate, but what did they know about it, such cold, dry individuals? Could they not understand that to create something in science you have to bury yourself up to the neck in your research material, submerge yourself in it, breathing in and testing its scent, its aroma (alien and objectionable as it is to lovers of flies and genes), soaking yourself in it until your personality completely dissolves in it? Here on the collective farm, Sheaves of the Future, he had found a magic land of plenty, an abundance of the substance he loved. Yes, that was right, loved, why not say it at the top of his voice? He had done it once in his life, in Moldavia, but the manure there wasn't really Russian, there was something Rumanian about it, or even Turkish. Here in Dry Ford he felt that the manure was primordially Russian, there was something about it that found an echo in his soul and inwardly moved him.

It was so nice here that he decided this year to refuse his usual free ticket to the Crimea, where he had been planning to go on holiday with his wife and thirty-year-old unmarried daughter, and to spend the whole summer here on the farm. Two months of absolute peace, during which he could sink bodily into his experiments, abandon himself to the object of his researches and freely merge with it in its natural element. What wouldn't he have given for such a possibility? And now it was being handed to him on a plate and was rescuing him, what is more, from the irksome presence of Katerina Antipovna, who even at her age was still the demanding wife she had always been, and still insisted on being satisfied by him, and this after thirty years of married life; for she had never realized that he was unable to separate the joys of love from the object of his scientific passion. Oh, how much he had suffered during the past twenty years, ever since his whole being had begun to feel genuinely alive only when inhaling the aroma that had become a revelation for him!

When he came to think of it, he realized that he had had this proclivity even as a child, and that even then there was no doubt that this would be his vocation, his scientific destiny. One day when he was about thirteen his mother had told him laughingly how, when he was two, she had once caught him guzzling one of his elder sister's turds. And from that day on, Foma seemed to hear a call and experienced an insistent desire to follow it. He immediately dashed to the bathroom, leaned over the lavatory pan and with a beating heart started to sniff up the elusive smell that seemed to be slipping away from him. Afterwards he began to watch for his mother's and sisters' trips to the bathroom. He would pretend to be in agony from waiting to go, whenever one or the other was on the lavatory, and would force them, with his complaints and pitiful howling, to come out again as quickly as possible, so that he was able to go in afterwards and enjoy the stink of their ordure.

At that time it was merely the stink that attracted him, but it was a special stink that irresistibly drew him, calling forth an echo from the innermost depths of his being. And there, one day, he made a real discovery: the blood drained from his face and rushed downward, and down there something hard came into existence that answered the signal of his quivering nostrils and erupted in a spasm that merged with the exciting aroma that pervaded his skull and made his heart race, a spasm of unfamiliar intensity and pressure, with a distinct and piercing culmination that at once receded and marked the end. It was his first ejaculation.

From that day on, he found it difficult to keep away from lavatories: at school, at youth camp—everywhere they brought temptation. How many times had he risked being discovered bent low, sniffing eagerly at some choice morsel while masturbating at the same time. How many times had he been forced to pretend he felt ill, complaining of shooting pains in his stomach, in order to explain at home or in company his constant and inexplicable visits to the lavatory, which everyone noticed sooner or later. How many complicated excuses, how many cunning tricks he had been forced to resort to, not to be deprived of those fortifying scents that were as vital to him as air or his daily bread! Thus he was always ruining the flushing mechanism of the lavatory bowl, or something of that sort.

This went on for about two years until—horrors!—he was caught *in flagrante delicto* in the school lavatory. Subsequently, Dermoshchenko erased that day completely from his memory. He also erased everything that had led up to it and from that day forth he was transformed. He drove this demon, this shameful mania of his, so deep into his unconscious, that he was able to enter these places with head held high and without a trace of excitement. Not the slightest emotion was aroused in him, no matter how high the stench inside. He felt nothing, neither pleasure, nor revulsion. He lived like other young men of his age: he finished his education and took up a career in science. Then he married, and though it was impossible to call the marriage happy, he enjoyed fully normal conjugal relations with his wife for the first ten years. But then, suddenly, everything changed.

It happened immediately after the triumph of the Michurinites in 1948, when hundreds and hundreds of nonconformists were thrown out of the university and the various research institutes, and dismissed from all research and teaching posts and rounded up and arrested. It was precisely then, when Michurinites were taking over all the university posts and laboratories, when boundless horizons were opening up for their research projects, in this favorable creative atmosphere for new and bold ideas, that Dermoshchenko, in search of an original subject for his scientific research, hit upon an idea that came from the depths of his unconscious mind: manure! How much work there was to do and how much to reveal about this substance that was produced in such abundance by all living creatures: from horses to sparrows, from cows to men, and that so unwisely, for the most part, went unexploited. But apart from his practical aim, which consisted in aiding his country's agriculture, and its economic situation in general, by means of a rational exploitation of these biological byproducts, he set himself also to achieve a lofty scientific and even philosophical task. By establishing once and for all the absolute identicality of these byproducts within the species, he thereby, by a different route, confirmed the inspired theory of his teacher concerning the non-existence of the intra-specific struggle, and thus, in his own way, produced confirmation of that crucial parallel theory of scientific socialism, namely, that the idea that "man is a predatory creature" is a lie; he is only made into one by capitalist society, which tries to keep him that way in order to rule him more easily. By analyzing both the common and the distinguishing characteristics of all the possible varieties of excrement of all species, he arrived by that same original path—through the back passage—at a definition of those species that were amenable to cross-fertilization and could provide useful hybrids, for this was at the very root of Michurin's theory: crossing, hybrids, planting in clumps.

Thus, well-armed morally and ideologically, that part of his unconscious—his poor ego—that had so unjustly been given short shrift by his illiterate parents and idealistic teachers, surfaced once more, and this time with barely controllable force, although, unfortunately, not with complete freedom. This lack of freedom was to be explained by the persistence of ancient prejudices that ought to have been rooted out of our society and destroyed. For our society was still held captive by bourgeois taste in many—in all too many, alas—of its aspects, ranging from food to concepts about smells and odors, about what is clean and what dirty. All those paints and powders and things that his wife and all those other women plastered on their hair, lips and face were dirty, but it was impossible to consider a normal natural product dirty. Where had he read that Eskimo women used to rub their bodies with their own urine? Now there was the popular wisdom of people untainted with capitalism, who had retained their primitive communes and natural economy! And then it was sufficient to take children, those tiny representatives of the species who were still uninfected by ideological hangovers from the past—did they not often swallow their own funny little curly turds, just as he had done in childhood, and did they not associate their intestinal evacuations with sexual satisfaction?

At the collective farm there was indeed no shortage of raw material: shit, manure, both animal and human. He had been here only a few days as yet, but had already fully satisfied himself on this point. Such abundance made his head dizzy and even caused him to lose his bearings, like the starving man who, after going hungry for so long, is suddenly faced with a banquet. But he did not hurl himself upon the food, did not take advantage of the liberality of the spread (although one or two morsels came his way), but measured all this spiritual, olfactory, edible and sexual food, which was being constantly renewed, against the two months he had ahead of him in which to gorge himself on these riches.

But despite the fabulous abundance and quality of these victuals, despite the colossal ease with which it could be obtained and despite the fact that it would never run short, Dermoshchenko yearned poignantly for, and was pursued by an insupportable longing for something that only the Moscow lavatories could give him. Who knows, maybe it wasn't only their special aroma, the complex product of the stagnation and fermentation of the deposits of feces and urine of thousands of men in these closed institutions, that had served in this capacity since time immemorial, that called him irresistibly back; no, it wasn't only that, but also the danger he was exposed to there, the danger of being recognized—for he was a member of the academy, wasn't he, a well-known and respected figure. What would happen if he was caught unawares and made a public laughing stock? A psychoanalyst would probably have said that he was in a state of regression, that he was experiencing a return to the period of his sexual maturation, when secretly, in the shadows of the lavatory, under threat of being recognized, he had attained the peak of satisfaction. But Dermoshchenko detested psychoanalysis, a harmful, anti-Marxist pseudo-science—no less so, probably, than genetics—and therefore would not under any circumstances have accepted this explanation of his psychosexual pathology.

Usually he used to change into old clothes before visiting public conveniences and tried not to be very noticeable. In his personal automobile he always kept some shabby cheap clothing in reserve, that enabled him to disguise the severe expensive suit of a scientific luminary and take on the appearance of someone who could have been a laborer or truck driver, or perhaps some provincial hick up from the country.

Thus disguised today, as on many occasions in the past, he set off for Komsomol Square, which boasted three whole railroad stations with their corresponding public lavatories and metro stations. He left the collective farm, Sheaves of the Future, drawn by a terrible nostalgia for the Moscow toilets, counting on returning home that same evening. But now there was nothing that could hold him back.

It was the end of June and the day was unusually hot, as often happens in Moscow when summer arrives with a bang. It was 11 a.m. and the asphalt was already soft, with the marks of women's high heels all over it. The air was motionless, being stirred only occasionally by the waves of heat emitted by the surface of the street. Foma Kharalampiyevich, despite the heat, walked jauntily in the direction of Kazan Station. Arriving at the entrance, he climbed some steps and set off diagonally left across the station concourse. As he did so he glanced briefly to the right in the direction of the platform, where whole families were bivouacking while waiting for their trains: for the most part they were simple people and mainly Asiatic-looking. He reached the entrance of the station lavatory and descended the first few steps.

While still on the steps the compact stench of the lavatory was wafted up to him from below. Dermoshchenko's nostrils flared to inhale as much as they could of the blessed aroma, while he descended further, plunging into this gaseous material that was something more than air, consisting of floating chemical particles of the substance that was being uninterruptedly discharged down there by myriad human bodies. He not only breathed deeply from the pleasure of it, like a termite in the heavy, damp, conditioned air of its nest, but was also drunk on this gas, which not only nourished his lungs and stomach, but also, with its smell, his epithalamus, nerves and sexual apparatus.

He entered the large public lavatory, which was spacious and oblong in form. Along the walls a number of men squatted over holes about a foot in diameter set directly in the floor. The expressions on their faces were concentrated, tense, occasionally tragic and at times shamelessly relieved. The two rows of holes were situated opposite each other. Each defecator could observe the simultaneous evacuations of several other persons, and if he had neighbors to right and left of him, could feel their animal presence, hear their grunting and groaning and smell the fruit of their exertions. In this heady atmosphere, the whole scene presented a picture of a genuine bacchanalian Valhalla of defecation. All that was lacking was music by Wagner.

Dermoshchenko at once spied an empty place, occupied it, lowered his rough trousers, exposing, with a shudder of excitement, his naked buttocks, squatted on his haunches and attempted to ensure that his shirt in front suitably concealed his prick. He had worked out a special technique that enabled him to hold it without anyone being able to notice where his hand was.

But his prick needed no helping hand. It was already aroused. Immediately in front of him, no more than twenty paces away, a hard cylindrical turd was slowly being squeezed out of an arch formed by the squatting limbs of the citizen opposite. To the right of the latter, a similar arch was expelling great gobbets of dark runny shit. And all around equivalent processes were taking place. At this, Dermoshchenko's prick, as though endowed with a sixth sense, with its own vision and hearing and, above all, sense of smell, swelled and expanded in response to a familiar summons. The orgasm came of itself, as though called up from the entrails of the earth, from the stinking magma that seethed beneath the perforated floor and seemed to be flooding the entire vault below, the entire substructure, streaming out under the houses, under the city, under villages and the countryside and the entire earth's crust.

It was precisely at that magic moment that Dermoshchenko noticed, with horror but also with concealed delight, that the third citizen to the left had rivetted his gaze on the space between Dermoshchenko's suspended buttocks and the floor. The effect of this gaze directed at the seat of his sensations was to make the last spasms of Dermoshchenko's orgasm sharper almost to the point of pain. But he noticed simultaneously that the other was in the same state as himself and experiencing the same kind of sensation. They exchanged glances. But when all was over and the last drops of semen had dropped into the hold, Dermoshchenko again acquired the capacity to think, and realized with horror that the face of the other man was familiar. Where had he seen it? And when? He asked himself these questions with a sinking feeling in the pit of his stomach as he wiped himself and pulled up his trousers, trying to glance at the other covertly without being noticed.

And then suddenly he recognized him: this short sixtyish man with the look of a Crimean vintner about him, with red face and tousled hair, was a noted writer who had taken to the bottle; for thirty years now he had been unable to finish his last book. Dermoshchenko ran out, not daring to look at him; climbed the stairs and went out into the square.

Had the other recognized him? No, it was out of the question, he consoled himself. The writer wouldn't bother about him, he was too high up in society, he lived in a completely different world, and anyway he didn't live in Moscow. It was pure chance. But then, what chance! Whoever would have guessed? So he too understood . . . Two prominent personalities whose paths had crossed thanks to the mysterious workings of fate, not recognizing one another in their highest act of self-expression.

Dermoshchenko set off on his usual tour around Moscow's public lavatories. He knew where to go. He had collected valuable material from all of them. In his pocket he had a stock of small clean pieces of material of various colors, specially chosen by him. And he also carried glue used for mending broken china cups and porcelain figurines, but which he used for sticking cloth and cardboard. In Kazan Station itself he would have stuck one of these pieces of cloth inside one of the holes, just below the rim, but the unexpected encounter with the writer had thrown him off balance. Still, it didn't matter, he would go back there later.

He visited two urinals and a lavatory with cubicles. In the two urinals he quickly picked up the two pieces of cloth he had left a week ago, which now were no different in color from the material they had been stuck to and over which, for a whole week, rivers of yellow fluid had been running. He already had two new pieces ready and covered with glue, while the used pieces, peeled from the urinals, were carefully put away in tin boxes. In the cubicle he was able to do finer and neater work: carefully he rubbed a piece of ribbon on the darkest part of the bowl, where the brown crust was particularly old and impressive. Then these scraps of ribbon were also put away in special boxes.

In the second urinal another incident occurred. When he had finished his painstaking work and had already turned to leave, he caught sight of a gray unprepossessing man who had been standing behind him. Dermoshchenko at once realized that he had seen everything. As in the Kazan Station lavatory, he hastened toward the exit, but at the last moment he glanced back out of the corner of his eye. The strange man was curiously examining the spot where he had glued his fragment of material, which decided him to make his departure with even greater speed.

He visited two more lavatories, where he repeated the same operation. Sometimes, between stops, he allowed himself to rest on benches along the boulevards or dropped in here and there for a glass of lemonade. At one point he even ate some ice cream. Finally he grew tired. The heat was intolerable and he thought with pleasure of his cool cabin at the collective farm. No one knew he was in Moscow, least of all the other members of his family. He rode out to Sokolniki Park, had lunch in the restaurant there and relaxed in the shade of the trees. Then he made a last tour of inspection of the park urinals. And in the evening he returned to Dry Ford, well satisfied with the time spent in the city and with the harvest he had been able to bring back with him.

15. The First Stone

A deep depression had hung over Dry Ford ever since early morning. There was no breeze, not even a stirring of the air, only the motionless dust gleaming white on the farm tracks and paths. And only occasionally was there a flurry of movement on its smooth surface, caused by sparrows bathing in it or searching for invisible grubs. The sun had heated the fields and woods, the barn and the roofs of the houses to an unbearable pitch and now was peering gloatingly through the pall of haze that had turned the sky gray. The pines and aspens, elms and birches were choking in the heat and had given up all hope of evening freshness.

On days like these, neither evening nor night bring freshness with them. The air appeared to have become utterly still, shrunk within itself and almost palpable, as if consisting of molten metal and enclosed within a restricted space, beyond which, it seemed, there was only a void. Such days can only be compared with the bitterly cold days of winter when the frost is at its worst, the only difference being that in winter the air is molten stainless steel, whereas in summer it is molten lead. But in both cases time comes to a halt and the place into which it is poured is transformed into neutral space.

At one o'clock in the afternoon a cock suddenly crowed. This cockcrow, which was sharp and despairing and unusually long drawn out, made an unpleasant impression on the residents of

Dry Ford. At three o'clock came the ominous and repeated hoots of an owl. No one at the collective farm, Sheaves of the Future, had ever heard an owl hoot during the day.

At half-past three Glasha died. The village boys playing by the pond all suddenly stopped at the very same moment. A strange gust of hot air wafted its lonely way through the village. And then everything became motionless as before, and the boys returned to their game.

Glasha was alone when she died. She had been forcing herself to do the housework, in spite of not feeling up to it, when suddenly she felt obliged to sit down in the living room in a state of exhaustion. That was how Matryona found her when she came with the milk. And she immediately rushed to the office to tell Baranov the sad news.

By the time he reached home a large crowd had gathered in the yard and everyone was offering comments on the event. Inside the house Glasha was being attended by Nadya, the nurse. She told him a doctor should be sent for to establish the cause of death, for a doctor's report was required by law. Baranov phoned Dmitri Petrovich, but asked him to come on his own and not send an ambulance. The doctor arrived at ten and diagnosed heart failure.

Before he had even gone to Dry Ford, Baranov had managed to call Tarakanov, and the lawyer had called Frolov and arranged to meet him at his home the following morning. Then he warned Timur, Marina and Matsa. None of them had known Glasha and none had expected such a stroke of luck. Who would have thought that fate would take such a turn and a girl would die on the farm?

Glasha had never had a father, and her mother had died in a railroad accident. She lived with her aged grandparents, although she worked all day at Baranov's and often stayed the night there. The old folk at once asked that the girl's body be taken to their house; the grandmother was very religious and Baranov even suspected her of being an Old Believer, although he had never been able to get anything sensible out of Glasha on this subject.

Nor could he refuse them this request, since Glasha's grandfather, in his day, had been one of the first chairmen of the collective farm. He came to an agreement with them: it was decided that that night and for the whole of the following day, Glasha's body would remain at their house, but that in the evening it would be moved to the club. Baranov insisted on this, explaining that the collective farm would thus be showing special honor to the granddaughter of a former chairman and assistant to the present one (officially Glasha had been Baranov's housekeeper). In truth it was an extraordinary occurrence, but so many extraordinary things were happening so regularly in Dry Ford that nobody attached any special significance to it. But it was important to Baranov, because he intended to make the dead girl's body available to Frolov the following night.

And only now did Baranov feel a pang as he became fully aware for the first time that Glasha was dead. His heart contracted. He thought about how gentle and humble Glasha was, how she had understood him and had eased his loneliness.

But this thought did not bother him for long. Tomorrow Yefrem Panteleimonovich Frolov, full member of the Central Committee of the Communist Party of the Soviet Union, would be honoring the collective farm, Sheaves of the Future, with his visit. In his presence, a short solemn ceremony would be held to announce the opening of the cemetery. After that, Frolov would spend the whole day in Dry Ford and visit the "C Business" workshops. This would endow the whole enterprise with a facade of legality and serve as excellent camouflage. Mikhail Nikolayevich, their Party Organizer, the Regional Party Secretary, the local authorities and the residents of Dry Ford and the surrounding districts would no longer doubt that they were engaged in something grandiose and fully official. Everything was going swimmingly.

At ten p.m. another strange occurrence took place: Timur arrived, accompanied by his grandma. He told Baranov that the old lady, who had been a teller of folk tales for thirty years in the Urals and was now staying temporarily with her daughter,

Timur's mother, in Moscow, had expressed a desire to participate in the all-night vigil beside Glasha's coffin.

Glasha was lying on the table. The tabletop had been spread with straw and then covered with a clean sheet. The old women of the village had already washed her and dressed her in the best clothes they could find and had wrapped her up to the chest in a handsome dark shawl, on which rested her two wrists enclosed in sumptuous cuffs. Around her neck hung a scrap of material that probably had a prayer sewn inside it. This apparently took the place of the small wreath on the forehead (with a representation of Christ, Mary and John the Baptist) demanded by the full Orthodox ritual. There was no ikon in her crossed hands, but there were two in a corner of the room and both had candles burning before them. Small beeswax candles also surrounded her body.

When they entered the chamber, Yefrosinya Danilovna, Glasha's grandmother, was reading from the book of psalms. The only light in the chamber came from the dancing candle flames, which threw trembling shadows on the dead girl's face and on the features of the black-clad women crowding around her.

With the arrival of the newcomers the women all turned to stare, somewhat discomposed. But Baranov motioned them with his hand, and the expression on his face indicated that these were friends. He looked at the dead, motionless Glasha lying on the table with her eyes closed. She suddenly seemed unexpectedly beautiful to him, as he had never seen her during her lifetime, and this embarrassed him.

Timur remained respectfully by the door, but his grandmother crossed to join the old women sitting along the wall. She whispered something to them, and was at once taken into their circle and given a seat among them.

Yefrosinya Danilovna continued reading from the book of psalms. Her husband was standing to the side with a serious, preoccupied expression on his face. In the uncertain candlelight and monotonous drone of the psalms it seemed at times as if the dead girl's face had come back to life. All went on for an extremely long time, but the chamber remained just as crowded as at the beginning: there were also younger women, and even some men. Timur did not move, astonished by this extraordinary scene, and waiting for the wailing to begin.

When she had finished reading the psalms, Yefrosinya fell silent for a moment and then turned to the women crowded along the wall. The one sitting next to Timur's grandmother (why had she approached this particular old woman when she had not known any of them?) stood up and in a quiet voice began:

O, you tall hills, you Vorobyov hills,
Vorobyov hills outside Moscow!
There is nothing you have borne, O hills,
You have borne nothing but bitter stones . . .

The woman who had started this wailing was not really old, although she had sat formerly in a black headscarf among the group of old women. She could barely have been fifty, taller than average, noticeable when she rose from the bench, and with a strong, almost masculine face. Her plaintive song would continue on low notes for a while and then suddenly soar up onto a long-drawn-out high note that tugged at the heart as the mourner went on with her wailing lament:

. . . A young gray eagle has perched on a bush,
In his claws he holds a black raven,
He does not rend him, but only asks:
"Where did you fly to, where were you flying?
Whom did you see, raven, whom did you see?"
"I saw a marvelous marvel, a body all white,
A snowy white body that hadn't been shot . . .

It was only at that that the people in the chamber and those crowding outside seemed to be silent, absorbed in listening to this ancient lament. In reality they were singing together with the wailing woman, responding with all their hearts to the words of this Russian plaint, which raked the ash from the soul and gave everyone on such rare, though funereal, occasions the chance of deep spiritual communion with one another, united by this ancient Russian form of mourning.

Timur yielded to the general mood. Listening to the songs and gazing at the dead girl, he recalled the quite different songs that had already eaten into his soul, sung to him by his grandmother when he had been sent as a boy to the Urals to spend his holidays with her.

The room brought back a flood of memories, and he felt the white-hot emotional tension of the people in it, but instead of plunging into the swampy mourning that sucked painfully and exquisitely at his soul, he was aroused by it all and the fire of exhilaration flared up inside him. A cry welled up in his brain and swelled till it was irresistible; and simultaneously he had an urge to do something that would destroy the unctuous state that prevailed around him: violence upon violence, because all these people that surrounded him had forced him into this vicious funereal circle. Funereal? Just as his brain was formulating the word and apprehending its meaning, a memory circuit in his head was set in motion, evoking a more recent recollection; at this point his gaze, which had been ranging uneasily over the crowd for some time, came to rest absent-mindedly on a figure that was directly linked with this recollection. Could there really be two persons so alike? Despite the feeble candlelight, Timur could see that it was not she, although her resemblance to the other woman, to the widow at the cemetery, Elena Filippovna, was astonishing. There before his eyes, in the crush of people standing in the doorway, was an exact copy of the other woman, not merely a sister, but a twin. And although Timur was at that moment less than ever inclined to allow himself to fall prey to mystical hallucinations, his heart missed a beat. He stared at her in a frenzy, measuring her, undressing her with eyes that were malicious and resentful of the delusion that was trying to ensnare him.

This "facsimile" was in turn staring back at him; perhaps it had been her look of combined rapture and submission that had caught his attention? To her, this dashing city-dweller was immensely attractive: the hero of the dreams and repressed hopes that now irradiated from her, like a message signifying his instant and utter conquest of her.

The soft, shimmering light seemed to exist exclusively to engender illusions and to insist on a pitiful attempt to give the form and features of this young collective-farm girl the thrilling intensity of that other woman, the genuine one, by imitating the authentic, sombre glitter of Elena Filippovna's eyes, her quivering bosom, her trembling lips and hands. The light endeavored to emphasize the amazing likeness of form, concealing the body's true contours, and was abetted in this task by the funeral laments, the accompanying hum of the mourners, and the whole extraordinary, strained, ritual atmosphere.

Unobserved, Timor tiptoed stealthily to the door, abandoning all this eerie witchcraft and its cunning trap: "You're not the one I'm after! Well, so much the worse for you, bringing me a vision of her! All the same I'll eat you up, although you're certainly not my Little Red Riding Hood, and it's your fault, you're so like her!"

Finding himself next to the girl, he brushed lightly against her, pressing his tumescent penis to her thigh, envenomed by the savage sensuality of this combination of death and tree-resin, old shawls and the stagnant aroma of the summer's night, the village and the ancient laments, the candles and the burial of hopes that cloaked a mocking taunt.

The girl could not, or simply did not want to move, and Timur's hand streaked like a fish through the tangle of human bodies, slid between her legs and began travelling upwards to her breasts; then it suddenly halted in its restless flight and settled calmly upon the girl's elbow, its light contact hiding its latent power; a moment later her arm was helpless in Timur's iron grip. His hot lips hissed into her ear "Let's go!", but no one around them heard a sound or noticed any unusual movement. Timur slipped outside and the girl followed him, as though tied to him by an invisible thread.

At this point the wailing woman introduced a new theme:

. . . And I look, I see, poor unhappy soul,
I look, I see, and bitter is my sorrow,
Standing at the porch, beyond the door,
Our carpenters and all our lusty lads:
For whom are they building that unmossed cabin?
For whom are they chiseling that log of white oak? . . .

There was no choir of wailing women, because that custom had long since disappeared from these parts, and still less was it possible to imagine in this place the whole theatrical production as it had once been played out by the women mourners, with every single part accompanied by a chorus from the moment of death to the moment of burial. Nevertheless, such was the character of the people present that each one of them subconsciously repeated the whole ceremony under his breath. Sensing this atmosphere of participation, and out of love for her art, Timur's grandmother rose and with an expression of commiseration and grief on her face, began in a plaintive wail:

You are prepared and ready waiting now
For eternal life without end.
You have been bathed here like a bee in honey,
Like a flawless jewel on a golden dish you lie outstretched!

Katya too was outstretched like a jewel upon a dish, and those jewels were set tinkling and threaded on Timur's golden thread. Her instinct subconsciously obedient to the ancient custom, Katya crept stealthily through the crowd of people clustered outside the door and her slight, agile figure disappeared behind the hut. She knew he was there, close by, ready to sink his claws into her, carry her off with him and devour her with his all-consuming fire.

The moon shone obliquely on the path, and there was pitch blackness to both sides of its shaft of phosphorescent light. The dark summer's night, warm, palpable and filled with scents and fragrances, enveloped Katya. She flattened herself against the wooden wall of the hut and stood motionless on the sharp boundary between black shadow and white light.

There was not a soul near her: the muttering laments of the wailing women were muffled and unintelligible by the time they reached her and merely increased her sense of the remoteness of the world and of other people, sharpened her feeling of utter solitude in this night that was so hospitable and full of passionate promises. Katya strained her ears and instinctively leaned forward.

Her head and neck emerged from the shadow and were caught in the gleaming white shaft of moonlight. Timur, waiting on the other side of the road, once again had the impression that he was seeing a ghost. He gave a soft whistle in the night, and as Katya recoiled, frightened, back into the darkness, trembling with expectation, Timur shot across the path of light and swooped hawk-like upon her.

Silently his strong, sinuous body wound itself about Katya in the darkness, gripping her like a steel spring, while his lips scorched the girl's tender white neck with a searing seal, piercing her with their imperious desire.

Timur knew that from that moment on, his victim would be passive and completely yielding, totally devoid of any will of her own and subject only to his will, obedient to her master's every wish. But the thrill of his first swoop, of the first blood drawn by his hawk's fangs, would not be repeated, and he would find all that followed boring and redundant.

The girl stayed passive only during the fleeting moment when Timur seized her and left the imprint of his voracious mouth upon her neck. Without removing his lips, Timur released his hold and his hands tore a way through her light clothing in search of bare skin. But Katya tensed and her neck, earlier obedient to his lips, now shrank away; then she managed to free her right hand and her nails scratched hard at Timur's face, down past his ear right to the shoulder and then over his chest.

Timur almost swore in his surprise: how could he have guessed that she would react like this; besides, the scratches stung his skin. Grasping Katya by the neck, and aware of the sensual fragility of her bust, his left hand gave her a vigorous but controlled slap in the face. Her face flinched at the blow, but not a sound escaped her lips. Her eyes widened and became filled with the same feverish, sombre gleam that he had already seen in the eyes of Elena Filippovna at the cemetery, and at their recent encounter when she had rebuffed him. And this, even more than the resemblance in their features and figures, made his heart leap again. The girlish eyes, wide open and glittering feverishly, were looking straight at him, while her lips, soft with desire, quivered as they parted to meet his.

"How beautiful you are," thought Timur, "you young thing, you burning candle!" He bent over the blooming lips and brushed them lightly with his hot mouth: but only for an instant, and then studied her motionless, dilated eyes. That was enough to convince him that the frenzy lurking in them was unmistakably a manifestation of life and desire. He seized her arm and without uttering a word, dragged her after him along the wall, taking care to remain in the shadow as he did so.

It seemed to Katya that he dragged her down a long, unending, narrow passage that led at first between houses, huts and buildings, and then turned into a tunnel that descended not into the ground, but apparently into a dense forest, a sea of green plants and leaves on either side and above her head. Her feet moved noiselessly, and all around her there was a whispering and a rustling, and fingers, not of flesh, stretched towards her, touched her and caught hold of her dress, avid and insistent. But she knew that she must continue her flight, must go forward, and that no one was dragging her along; it was only her own reflection she was pursuing, that part of herself which held sway and alone had the right to allow her to be herself. And the more enticing and dominating that part became, the stranger and more enigmatic it remained for her herself as it abused its powers.

Trembling and exhausted after her long flight, she became aware that she had stopped, without knowing why; then she realized that something irreversible was happening: something enormous that belonged to her, something unknown, was assaulting her, trying to reach her and become a part of her. As a nightmare, looming larger than all our fantasies, breaks away and turns against us, violating the innermost recesses of our soul, so Katya belonged to him. She herself had created the idol that fed on reflections of the image of the young blond-haired man who came to the collective farm periodically in his car, probably from Moscow, and then disappeared again for a long time, who strode through the village with a proprietary air, handsome, sure of himself and independent, and paid no attention to the girls of Dry Ford, every now and then giving them glances of indifferent curiosity—not a victim but a true master of life. And this idol was doing precisely what she had longed for it to do: it was devouring, transforming her, depriving her of one life to give her another. Like the shadow of a gigantic shroud it suffocated her, oppressive and enveloping, alluring, superb and murderous.

"My little wild candle, I'll snuff you out and set your little flame alight again," thought Timur, coming to a halt in the dense undergrowth beyond Dry Ford. Releasing Katya's hand, he at once gripped her in his embrace and for a moment was suffused with the pleasurable feeling aroused by the beauty of Katya's slim figure and her beautiful face, dappled by the moonlight's sensual sheen. He thrust his hard, avid tongue between her curling, eagerly straining lips, forcing them apart to accept him; he explored the inside of her mouth at length. Katya responded greedily to his kiss. Her hands, which had earlier scratched him, now firmly clutched his back. With the palm of his left hand he supported the girl from behind, while his right hand pulled up the hem of her dress in search of the desired spot. His penis, erect, militant, stretching the cloth of his trousers, was already pressing against her girlish thighs. She felt the enormous, fleshy bayonet, but her inexperience and her dazed state prevented her from appreciating its merits: she aspired merely to a fusion of their beings, and was ignorant of the means of achieving it.

He bent over her, the strength of his kiss forcing her head back, and if his hand had not been steadying her back, she would have toppled over. Then, gradually relaxing his hand, and bending further and further over her, he lowered her gently onto the cool night grass. Their lips separated and Katya turned her head, sensing that he was lifting her skirt and exposing her thighs. She had nothing on under her skirt, and her finely moulded legs and small round belly shone with a fragile luster in the limpid moonlight. And above the fragile, silvery, lunar flesh, like a wild stallion galloping exultant and free, Timur's huge, earthly rod reared its blunt, violet head. He took shrewd aim into the small dark triangle of hair, the soft valley between the two warm dunes of tapering, perfectly chiselled form. The stallion poked its muzzle at the tiny, carnivorous flower, voracious as a python that risks being choked to death by the victim it has swallowed, torn asunder by a particularly large choice titbit. Timur held this position awhile, revelling in the shameless contact of their swollen organs. He increased his pressure ever so slightly, and suddenly realized that the girl was a virgin. "So, my girl," he thought, "you took a fancy to Timur, but you don't know that for him it's triviality." He glanced at Katya's face as she lay back on the grass, her eyes closed, and in spite of its resemblance to Elena Filippovna's, he no longer saw it as a replica. On the contrary, it was new, unfamiliar and inviting in its untouched freshness. With a swift movement he uncovered her small, unripe breasts and, by a hand on the small of her back, raised her slightly into a more comfortable position: and then his enormous, stiff penis began its inexorable advance. Katya jerked her head around and glanced at him, her eyes vacant and dilated, deep and yawning chasms. Her lips did not utter a sound: only her white, tightly clenched teeth gleamed in the moonlight. Timur's penis penetrated her, stained with the blood of her maidenhead, and set about its ageless labor.

It was late in the night by the time Baranov and Timur left Glasha's hut. Many had already departed, but the nocturnal vigil was still continuing and the crowd around the dead girl was as thick as before. All these living bodies breathing feverishly around the corpse, the dying candles suffocating in their own smoke, the wailing voices of the women that filled the entire surroundings—all this formed a real ship sailing darkly over the bottomless heaving sea.

But morning came, and with it, freshness. For many inhabitants of Dry Ford that ship had never set out, nor had there been any death; and normal daily life went on as before. The morning was taken up with chores, but behind everything was a sense of expectation, for the visit of a Central Committee member that day had already been announced, together with an important public meeting at twelve noon.

Busiest of all were Baranov, the Chief Bookkeeper, Timur and the Regional Party Secretary, who had come to instruct and prepare people beforehand. There were many automobiles: Marina and Matsa came; Dunya came in a taxi; and then there were Esper Ozirisovich and the lawyer, together with Frolov.

In a convenient spot on the site set aside for the future cemetery, somewhere near its center, where a level meadow stretched between two low hills, laborers and carpenters had been busy since dawn. Now a platform had been erected on the flattened ground and equipped with a strip of red carpet. A table on the platform was covered with a red calico tablecloth, and held a jug of water and an empty glass. Around the table were a number of chairs.

By the time Frolov, the collective farm chairman, the Regional Party Secretary and other local dignitaries (who had been invited by the Secretary on his own initiative) had arrived, together with our friends from the "C Business", about two hundred had gathered under the blazing sun in patient expectation.

Baranov sat at the head of the table, but Frolov was introduced by the Regional Secretary, who read several sentences from a scrap of paper, breaking off from time to time with excitement, his voice occasionally rising to a scream and at others sinking to a barely audible croak. The honored guest also delivered a speech, streaming sweat in the noon heat, reading from a sheet prepared for him by the lawyer, and adding merely a few greetings from a few of his comrades. He then added on his own account, in a tone suitable for a government representative when speaking to the people, that the death he had just been informed about, of an honest daughter of the laboring collectivized peasant masses, although depressing, at the same time marked this day of the cemetery's foundation as a special one, and therefore he personally, and comrade X agreed with him, and comrade Y supported them, and at the instance of comrade Z, he was proposing that she should be the first to be buried in the new cemetery. The chairman of the collective farm introduced the other dignitaries, who illustrated, appealed, and assured . . . The Regional Secretary welcomed . . . And then the others spoke, including Esper Ozirisovich. Tarakanov, Timur, Marina and the others were absolutely dying of boredom, but it was even worse for the ordinary people: they suffered in silence and mentally sent the whole lot to the devil.

The dead girl, meanwhile, was lying on the table. The heat increased and grew even more unbearable as the afternoon wore on. And it set about its destructive work. Glasha was no longer as cold as she had been in death, through the night. The temperature of her body continued to rise and inside her the unstoppable process of disintegration set in, although her face remained clear and attractive, touched only by a slight shadow of sickly languor.

As had been agreed, the old people gave up the body at dusk and it was transferred to the club. Baranov made arrangements for the entire farm collective to pay its last respects to the dead girl. Past the girl's corpse on the catafalque in the club's main hall filed the representatives of local society, faithful to their duty, but totally indifferent to what was going on. The young pioneers came too, wearing their red scarves, with their rebellious curls tightly brushed down for the occasion. By eight it was all over and no others came. Glasha remained completely alone.

She remained alone till midnight. At that hour Dry Ford was fast asleep. Only from somewhere in the distance came the drunken singing of some youths. A light breeze ruffled the leaves and swayed the branches of the trees. The houses looked into the street with blind windows: complete silence reigned in them. It was impossible to see from the street that they were still awake in Glasha's house. Yefrosinya Danilovna was still chanting prayers. At exactly midnight a cock crowed. Perhaps he was asking that Glasha's couch, as in the old days, be carried into the yard for the cocks to crow over three nights running. But Yefrosinya didn't remember that custom.

Baranov locked himself in and drank himself under the table. He didn't want to know.

At the dead of night, two men noisily approached the club. One was stout, bald and wheezed heavily; the other was tall, elegant and had light, economical movements. He led the fat man to the entrance, like Charon in modern dress; then he deferentially opened the door for him and politely disappeared into the night.

All remained silent for a while. Then Timur and two youths, who had been placed on guard in the darkness to make sure nothing went wrong, heard a cock crow. Silence followed. But suddenly it was broken by a low, plaintive grunting that gradually increased in volume until it was loudly hoarse and jerky, with a hysterical note of despair.

Only much later did a man emerge from the club, lurching, his clothing in disarray. It was not very difficult to recognize Avanchel Panteleimonovich Frolov. He took about ten steps and then collapsed heavily on the ground. They lifted him and led him off, supported on both sides, to enjoy his well-earned sleep. Then Timur broke the lock of the club door.

Old Yefrosinya raised the alarm at dawn: it was obvious that some drunken delinquents had broken in the door during the night and had desecrated the dead girl's corpse. Groaning and saying their prayers, the woman fussed over the body and tidied it up as best they could.

The next day, news of the desecration spread through the village. And then the last rites were sumptuous, such as Glasha could never have expected.

Horace Evsevonovich Baranov did not appear for the last rites, but sent word that people could take their leave of Glasha in the way they thought most fit, and could bury her as they wished.

Glasha lay in her coffin that smelled of fresh pine needles, wrapped in the same Russian shawl, but with the prayer amulet no longer around her neck. Her head was surrounded by a nimbus of wild flowers brought by no-one-knew-whom.

All day Yefrosinya remained by the coffin, grim and stony, silently reading the burial service. Her lips moved without emitting any sound, but whoever knew the words of the service could have followed it from her lips. Glasha's grandfather also spent long hours by the coffin, as did Timur's grandmother, although she did not recognize any church ritual but remained faithful to folk songs and legends that were far more ancient and convincing than Christian beliefs and ceremonies.

At six o'clock the truck came. At the head of the coffin they set benches for the old couple and their close friends. The chief wailer and Timur's grandmother also climbed into the open back of the truck. The truck started up and slowly crawled away, drawing after it a train of anonymous old folk and curious children. Then it drove out of the village in the direction of the cemetery, which was situated about a mile and a half away on the borders of the village of Bludnoye. The truck was preceded by Glasha's cousin, accompanied by the village simpleton, who hobbled along carrying the coffin lid. The lid had a cross on it.

As soon as the truck was at a good distance from the club, the chief wailer, wearing a red scarf over her head and holding a green branch in her hand, commenced to wail:

Your oaken home has been brought,
That mossless funeral cabin . . .

She was echoed by Yefrosinya, Timur's grandmother and two other old women who had been loaded into the back of the truck, who all repeated each couplet of the lament:

. . . When they nail down your coffin lid,
We unfortunates will never see you again,
Nor hear your words again . . .

At the cemetery, Glasha's cousin and the simpleton nailed down the coffin lid. Ivanushka, the village idiot, banged his fingers with the hammer, and to avoid swearing began to laugh, but then burst into tears instead.

The coffin was lowered into the ground and covered with earth. Yefrosinya, with dry eyes and without a single tear, struck up and chanted "eternal peace" in a firm voice. Timur's grandmother stood beside her, supporting her, but not singing. The other old women sang.

The wake was held outside Yefrosinya's hut. The food and drink were provided by Baranov. First the old woman scrubbed out Baranov's living room, where Glasha had died, then she scrubbed the whole of her hut. And afterwards she completely changed into something fresh. So did Glasha's grandfather. Yefrosinya's sister prepared the victuals.

When about thirty people had sat down to table (a rumor had gone around that it was to be a rich and substantial feast), one of the mourners handed the bowl with the funeral pudding in it first to the grandfather and Yefrosinya and then to the rest of those present, including Baranov.

Before taking the first drink, Yefrosinya wished Glasha to be remembered with a last funeral toast and poured everyone a drink consisting of a mixture of beer, honey and, instead of home-brewed ale, Soviet champagne. Then everybody ate a great deal, drank liberally and talked of the departed Glasha.

Timur came to collect his grandmother. He reported that in

Moscow he had seen vehicles equipped with firehoses, but he didn't know against whom. Dermoshchenko was also there. He loved the old folk customs and revelled in mixing with the real peasantry. But when Timur mentioned the firehoses he remarked spitefully: "And about time, too. We've got too fond of kid gloves; they used to shoot them in the old days." Everyone present fell silent in pained embarrassment, but the chief wailer saved the situation by striking up, as usual at wakes, a lament of remembrance. Yefrosinya later paid her well for her services.

16. Wonder Boys

"Wonder boys! Clever boys!" Who hasn't heard such exclamations over young boys who are just beginning to show the first signs of intelligence, kindness, honesty? In the circle of their family and friends, at school among the neighbors, in their Komsomol group—everywhere they are praised for these qualities: wonder boys!

In Russia, as in all other countries, there are two classes of such wonder boys. Their progress is watched over with love and sympathy, with understanding and indulgence toward their shortcomings—which they, like all others, possess—and much is expected of them. Needless to say, many of them, as they grow older, disappear from the ranks of wonder boys: certain qualities and vices lead to their being struck off the list of "favorites," who are under the constant protection of their parents and teachers. But nevertheless a large number survive. And at the age of sixteen or seventeen this green harvest of wonder boys, guarded at all times and in all places by the loving vigil of their families and society, begins to show signs of differentiation.

With light and elegant gait they follow in the footsteps of their parents and of the best moral examples held up to them, distinguishing themselves in their studies and taking up the cream of the professions—those which are not only particularly esteemed by society, but also bring more than satisfactory material rewards, thus providing a guarantee for the future and enabling them to provide for their families and their old age. Naturally, these professions can vary considerably, depending upon personal qualities, milieu, chance and opportunities. But almost always they are to be found in that wide selection offered by service to the Party and the state, ranging from the army to the various ministries, from the Komsomol to the Party itself, and so on.

That is for some. But for others a quite different fate is in store. Although still wonder boys, from adolescence on they become prematurely questioning and difficult, showing signs of impatience with the family and surrounding society. Instead of continuing successfully with their studies, they are distracted by useless and dangerous fantasies, read harmful books, avoid the collective, and choose their own friends. Gradually they become critical and sarcastic toward their parents and the representatives of any sort of authority, and have a tendency to band together in the sort of groups that hold out no promise for the future. But the main thing about them is their complete inability to perceive what is required of them in life, what path they should choose, what post they should occupy and the nature of their duty to themselves and others. They cast doubt on everything and are satisfied with nothing. And they are unaware of the pain they cause parents and teachers who continue to reiterate lovingly: "Wonder boys!" but are already shaking their heads with worry and incomprehension. And even if the odd one or two do reform, the majority continue downhill, throwing themselves recklessly into life and becoming fancy dressers, hoods, hooligans, and sometimes real crooks and thugs. In recent times a new species of this breed has made its presence widely felt, in some strange way managing to include all these qualities in its complex psychology, together with great intelligence, an adequate and sometimes superlative cultural training and success in science or one of the arts, although on no account in the realm of social or Party activities or in spheres connected with managerial or state responsibilities. Often they are taken for idlers and loafers, parasites on society, and are rounded up by the police and put away for two or three years for "parasitism," for not being engaged in "disciplined," "organized" production.

These are the two categories, the two breeds of wonder boys—good guys who are known as such to everyone they meet in life—and all because they are born with these qualities. But their circumstances vary and their lives follow various paths: some go to the bottom of society, while others float on the surface like pirate ships that can never come into harbor, like a modern Count of Monte Cristo, or the first revolutionaries that fled from Siberian exile.

And all of them are excellent, wonder boys (even if divided into two categories), likable and nice, fond of mamma, brother and sis, weeping on papa's grave (who died as a result of long years of gray service), the life and soul of parties held among family and friends. And nevertheless the distinction between the two categories is sharp and ineradicable. Two breeds living in the same city, in the same houses, using the same transportation and all riding out to Luzhniki, yet remaining eternal enemies, as alien to one another as the Jew and Arab, although they both belong to the same branch of the Semitic tree. If ever they meet, it is from antagonistic, opposed positions where the contest can never be a draw.

Timur was obviously a lost soul who belonged to the second category of young people. Therefore, his friends, or rather acquaintances, were all the same, for he possessed no real friends and the wide circle of youths with whom he mixed were nothing to him but merely the manpower he needed for the "C Business," for his machinations with certain unsatisfied ladies (and frankly speaking, for his trade in young men), and also occasionally for his own use.

Oh yes, Timur was sufficiently far advanced along the tortuous and recondite path of sex no longer to believe in an absolute difference between beauty and ugliness, youth and age, masculinity and femininity. He had long since discovered that the secret lay not in these factors, but in the spark ignited in him by another being. That creature might inflame you with its beauty, youth, or the primal, provocative signal of the opposite sex, but also (for these elementary reflexes are soon exhausted) with less obvious, more secret signals having nothing to do with the waving banners of beauty, youth and femininity (for him, a man), but which are transmitted thanks to barely perceptible, special qualities that are so unusual that they can only find a response in the parallel qualities of a similar—and at the same time dissimilar—being. These for a long time had now acted as the strongest possible erotic stimulus for Timur—which, however, did not exclude the concepts of beauty, youth, femininity. It was simply that these latter were auxiliary qualities that were not in the least degree alien to his erotic impulses. But they could never have any effect if the person in possession of these elements did not in the first place emit a much more profound and powerful stimulus, a special and more specific signal. And this signal was always the decisive factor for him, much more so than any generally accepted, conventional and sanctioned signal; because for Timur no difference had ever existed, perhaps from his very birth, between what was sanctioned and what was not.

Thus, there had been one long episode several years ago, a burning passion (a purely erotic passion: Timur did not recognize and was practically repelled by any sentimentality in matters of sex, as though they were an inappropriate continuation of mother love) for a poetess who was some thirty years older and, moreover, both lame and unattractive. Similarly, and this was also in the past, he had suddenly discovered one day that not only female flesh was capable of exciting him, and of exciting him so that every nerve was tautened at the mere sight of someone and everything around partook conspiratorially of the central tension. Nevertheless, Timur was a favorite with all the most beautiful girls, such as Galya, for example, who particularly sought out his company. Perhaps it was precisely this feeling of being pursued by girls that made him neglect them. Certainly the thought had occurred to Timur, but he said to himself: "No, it's not true, it cannot be."

It was simply that, objectively speaking, he was forced to recognize their erotic inadequacy (and he had not the least desire to waste time on their erotic education, a form of pygmalionism that offered no sort of guarantee), so that even if he sometimes did manage to extract something from his relations with them, he had only himself to thank for it, and specifically his miraculous power of resurrecting, even if only for a moment, those who were totally dead. From this point of view, a male body on the threshold of maturity evoked in him a far stronger response, rooted in its more open and honest childishness. Such bodies attracted him far more strongly, although (he had found in actuality, and the same was true of girls) only the prolonged initiation of one subject out of a hundred ever produced the desired results. But what results? O, how complex it all was. There they were, all these queers and their "wives," kissing, pushing their tongues into one another's mouths and groping for one another's crotches. Today it was only boys. All from the same crowd. They included Alik, whom Timur had sent to Tamara, Vitya, Borya, Dima and a sixteen-year-old queen called Kolka, who carried a breath of country freshness with him and the aroma of cherry blossom. There were Gora, Volodya and Felix, all of them high on the hashish Dunya had brought and which he, Timur, was handing out to the boys in prudent moderation as a mark of his favor.

Volodya had already finished two joints and was sitting on the couch with a blissful, satisfied expression on his face, his eyes fastened on Vadik the guitarist, the indispensable troubadour of their parties. And in his usual undertone Vadik was declaiming a song by one of his favorite poets, accompanying himself on the guitar:

When the city festivities are ended,
When sinners and the virtuous are all asleep,
The state reservists

Quietly abandon the statues.
Hundreds of thousands, all much alike,
Stream down the road in the bright moonlight . . .

"Volodya," said Timur, "you've already spoken, I take it, with your distinguished daddy? A man in his position absolutely has to make sure of a place in our cemetery."

"Well, to tell you the truth, I haven't quite managed it yet. It's not so simple, you know, and I haven't found the right moment," lisped Volodya in an apologetic tone of voice.

"Look, I'm giving you three days. Don't try to make a monkey out of me, and no more of your fool excuses," rapped Timur shortly and sharply. "You like our hashish, don't you? Well, just make sure you earn it!"

"What, him? How do you expect him ever to earn anything," exclaimed Alik. "When was he ever known to have two thoughts in his head? Papa takes care of everything: automobile, tape recorder, money to burn: he never lacks anything. And nor should he. 'That's what we made a revolution for,' says his distinguished papa, 'and that's why we have socialism, so that our children can live in comfort.' Such is the philosophy of the Soviet bourgeoisie. Only they forget that millions and millions of people are living on a hundred rubles a month (and glad to have it) and are housed in barrack huts . . ."

"In Moscow alone they've proved with absolute accuracy that there are almost two thousand millionaires."

. . . The clock's pendulum comes to a halt,
The hands start whizzing backward,
A single statue goes striding along,
With a thousand copies behind it . . .

"Hey, Vadik, quit it! Sing something a bit more cheerful," protested Volodya.

"Let him be, let him finish it," said Timur with irritation.

. . . I open the window and thrust my head out,
And tremble feverishly as though blazing hot,

For I see the bronze generalissimo
Leading a clownish procession.
He stops in a corner of Red Square,
The genius of all times and nations!
And as in the good old days
Reviews a parade of cripples.
And they are beating their drums . . .

Felix went up to Vadik, a glass in hand. With glazed eyes he stared at him in silence. Fatigue and vodka made his face look older, but in fact he couldn't have been more than twenty-five. It was obvious that he was on the point of exploding. Vadik, meanwhile, went on with his song:

. . . Pink morning of our native land!
The squeaking call-signs are flying,
The bronze general goes back to his retreat,
But the plaster ones lie there in hiding.
Maybe they're crippled for a time,
But even in the ground they preserve their features,
Human flesh they need, the plaster ones,
They will achieve greatness once more
And beat their drums! . . .

As soon as he had finished, Felix downed his glass with a gulp, pointed his finger at Timur and shouted:

"Timur! Find an electric skeleton that will let me have it up the rear end! Get me a skeleton from one of your goddam cemeteries and get an electronics engineer to fit it with a motor. Yes, my friend, I'm in funds. That Georgian cunt of a millionaire paid me pretty handsomely. Millionaires! They're not limited to Moscow. The Caucasus is an excellent breeding ground for the species. But it's all the fucking same to me! I hate the Union, all these Party barracks and this military crap. We're in the grip of a mania. A mania to serve. To serve the people, the Party, the fatherland. But I don't serve anybody. I serve myself and my ass. It completely replaces the lust for serving the Soviet people! Here, suck this!" and Felix thrust out his fingers in an indecent gesture. "What is the Union? An infernal machine for prostituting people, just like America, just like all states. How many good lads get turned into robots, into animals! And that's what they need. The Americans for Vietnam and us for Czechoslovakia. Dictatorship of the proletariat be fucked! Whoever saw it? My father never ordered anyone to do anything; all he found was poverty and hardship, hardship and poverty, war, hardships, hardships . . . and the 'honor roll' at the factory. And now what? He doesn't believe in anything any more. He doesn't believe in communism, and, even worse, he doesn't believe in himself. Everything inside him has been burned out, he has been plundered, he works at his factory like madmen in a lunatic asylum, not knowing what they are doing or why. Forty years ago he believed, perhaps, and had hopes for the coming of socialism, but now he doesn't even have the strength to curse. Unhappy, shy and timid, he reveres his bosses and dares not even look them in the face. He is your faithful working class, as faithful as a well-beaten dog. But I don't want it, fuck it! I curse the lot of them, I don't believe in anything except my ass, and that's my advantage. Queer? Yes, gentlemen, and proud of it! Better a perforated asshole than a fuddled brain. What do they teach our schoolboys? 'I serve the Soviet Union.' Slaves! Mother Russia? But what if I've always hated my mother? She loved various bigwigs more than she did my father, than she did her own children. And Father? They squeezed all his juices out of him and humiliated him. All our fathers were castrated. One wise father was enough, a patriarch. He fucked all Russia—women, men, children . . . The great slob! And now see what's happening! His stooges are continuing where he fucking well left off. Okay, Vadik, play on, goddam it!"

Everyone was silent during Felix's unexpected tirade, a little frightened and a little sympathetic, but also warmed by his words, which inspired them with a feeling of solidarity. Vadik needed little persuading and at once began another song.

While he was playing and singing, Timur went over to Felix

and slapped him amiably on the shoulder. Felix filled a couple of glasses and handed one to Timur.

"Here, have a drink with me, Timur! Today I want to go the whole hog."

The two of them emptied their glasses with a gulp. Then Timur turned and spoke to the whole room:

"Listen, lads!" he shouted. "Now Yamshchikov will show you a trick that nobody's ever seen before—it's sensational!"

He went over to the couch and ordered off the people sitting on it. Then he stretched out full length and pulled off his trousers.

The eyes of all present were fixed on him. He raised his legs in the air, tightly pressed together, and then slowly lowered them over his head, spreading them slightly as he did so. At the same time he lifted his shoulders and head and thrust them forward.

His abnormal penis throbbed perpendicularly in front of his mouth. Timur thrust out his tongue and licked the head of it. With the tip of his tongue he worked neatly and painstakingly, making swift circular movements. From beneath his lowered lids he cast long, self-satisfied glances at the onlookers. These glances were both mocking and pleased.

Under his tongue's influence his penis swelled even more, so that he no longer had to reach for it with his tongue. It pushed straight into Timur's mouth needing room for its implacable advance.

Vadik went on singing indefatigably as he watched Timur's performance. He also showed signs of surprise, but it was well concealed and did not, as in the case of the other lads, express itself in bulging and stupefied eyes.

. . . Don't share your bread with swine,
Don't fall a prey to flatterers,
Don't believe in a clear sky
Or the smiles of shining faces . . .

Timur's young flesh, thick and cylindrical, now plunged into his mouth and with simultaneous movements of his head and waist muscles he sucked and sucked—an awe-inspiring illustration of self-fellatio.

"Wait, Tim!" exclaimed Felix, "let me offer you this golden vessel of mine, which would be glad to accept your radiant seed!"

But Timur continued to rock back and forth, tense with strain, absorbed in the pleasure of this obscene exhibitionism, and terrible in his gymnastic, unbelievable acrobatics.

> . . . So what if we are cradled in glory again,
> So what if our foes are calling themselves friends,
> We remember that a move to the right
> Must always begin from the left foot! . . .

Vadik sang on while all were spellbound by Timur, enraptured and bewildered by this unexpected feat of his. But perhaps Vadik was thinking there was some connection between the song he was singing and what was taking place on the couch.

* * * * *

While Timur was killing time this way, those wonder boys of the other species had already started on work that was to put them on the trail of our friends. On guard over their socialist fatherland, unceasingly watchful in the face of all possible dangers, these wonder boys had already completed a fair amount of highly creditable work. One of them had returned to the building on Dzerzhinsky Square several days ago, all excited and impatient. He strode in to see the lieutenant-colonel who was his immediate superior and triumphantly reported something unusually reprehensible detected by his own keen powers of observation.

He did not say that quite by accident he had been in such and such a public lavatory with the aim of satisfying his natural urges and that a stroke of luck had brought him together with an individual whom he had been instructed to keep under normal observation—a boring procedure forming part of the general duties that gained no credit for a KGB agent. How many people did he have to keep watch on and trail over long days, months, years of service before he could expect promotion! No, he said that he recognized the man when he left his house (all lies!—the man never left his house that day for the simple reason that he had come into Moscow from the country; that lie was to cost wonder boy, Volodya, official agent of the KGB, very dearly in the near future), followed him, without letting him out of his sight, and observed that the individual in question behaved extremely strangely in the public lavatory on such and such a street. For instead of pissing, as one might have expected, he had removed something from the back of the urinal (the agent had not been able to establish exactly what it was, for he was standing behind him). But, he suggested eloquently, the "thing" removed could not have differed in essentials from something that the suspect then stuck there in its place.

"And did you confiscate whatever it was?" interrupted his boss with a timely question.

"Yes, comrade colonel," replied the agent, pulling a small package from his pocket and placing it on the table.

The package turned out to be nothing more than a page from *Pravda* folded over several times and with patches of moisture showing through it.

The lieutenant-colonel gingerly unwrapped it. The paper tore in several places. The more he unwrapped it, the wetter became the paper and soon there came the foul smell of urine and lavatories. With a grimace of disgust, the lieutenant-colonel finished his delicate task, and his eyes lighted upon some torn scraps of soaking wet, yellowish-gray cloth.

"What's this?" the lieutenant-colonel bellowed threateningly.

"I don't know, it's what I confiscated."

"I can tell that," snapped the lieutenant-colonel testily, and pressing the tip of his pencil to his left nostril, held the noxious evidence of crime as far away from him as possible. "Talk sense now, and tell me why you brought this disgusting stuff back here."

"I've already told you: he sticks these things on urinals and in lavatory holes and takes away others like them. He did it in a whole lot of lavatories." And the agent added that he had followed the suspect, that is to say Dermoshchenko, into various lavatories in many different parts of Moscow. In each, the same operation took place, while he, the agent, gathered a harvest of suspicious pieces of cloth left behind by the biologist.

In the third lavatory one citizen, noticing this peculiar behavior, had thrown himself accusingly upon Dermoshchenko and threatened to call the police. To quiet him, the agent had been forced to identify himself to the citizen. But this had caused him to waste valuable time and in consequence he had lost track of Dermoshchenko.

"It doesn't matter," replied the lieutenant-colonel, "he can't get away from us. But what do you think they are? Coded messages?"

"How can I judge?" the agent shrugged his shoulders. "I've done my duty."

The boss let him go and in turn reported to *his* boss. The latter issued orders to a whole slew of wonder boys, who moved into action at once. Some of them submitted the fragments, soaked in the stinking liquid, to all the appropriate analyses to reveal the coded messages in invisible ink. The liquid and the cloth were submitted to a rigorous chemical analysis, for there was no limit to the perfidy of imperialist plots, and therefore what might appear at first glance to be mere urine could quite conceivably be a threat to socialism. Other wonder boys visited all the lavatories in town and searched them systematically, gathering in the process additional valuable material. A permanent apparatus of surveillance was set up in the lavatories: hidden cameras, microphones and similar equipment. Several typewriters over several days filled a multitude of pages, as a result of which the case expanded. It seemed strange that Dermoshchenko had abandoned his home in

Moscow and his place of work. And since nobody could say where he was (his wife was on holiday at this time in Sochi), a search was instituted, for he was to be placed under restricted observation so that they could establish the purpose of such behavior and discover his connections.

17. *Moscow Is Full of Rumors*

Matsa and Tarakanov shared a common passion: horse racing. They often used to meet at the Moscow racetrack, and occasionally went there together, after which Tarakanov would drive Matsa back to his villa where Olga Borisovna gave them supper. On such occasions they usually ended up playing cards, and then Matsa would stay overnight with them and return to town the next day by train if Tarakanov himself wasn't going in. It was at the racetrack, in fact, that they had first got to know one another, during one of those arguments that often spring up at the tote window. After this they continued to see one another and gradually became friends. All this, of course, was a long time before the "C Business" came along. And long before that, Matsa had also introduced Tarakanov to Marina, the daughter of his old friend, Kerzhentsev, who with his wife had long since been swallowed up in the hostile ocean of the camps.

Today they had met at the racetrack by chance, shortly after six p.m., at the tote window. They watched the races together, commenting on the qualities of the horses, their best times over certain distances, and occasionally risking a bet on something they fancied. The races were coming to an end and were not very satisfying for regular racegoers.

"Valery Borisovich," said Matsa, lowering his binoculars, "you know, of course, that they are already talking about our affair in Moscow."

"What affair?" Tarakanov raised his eyebrows, although he realized at once what Matsa was talking about.

"The cemetery, of course; is it that difficult to guess?" a gleam appeared in the old man's gray, catlike eyes.

"Well, what are they saying and who's saying it?" asked the lawyer with barely concealed irritation.

"I don't mean on the streets, but in certain circles. And particularly those that, in the last analysis, interest us most. And as far as I can tell, they are very impressed."

"How did you find out?" asked Tarakanov, softening.

"From B.S. You know, the writer who's about our age—he's better known abroad than here. He's a typical intellectual and ashamed to show too much interest in an enterprise of this nature. He told me he'd heard about it from F, adding that since F has been little more than a corpse for fifty years or more, and has gone more or less completely to pieces, he's got nothing more to hope for than a monument after his death."

"You're being sarcastic as usual again," laughed the lawyer. "But joking aside, let me tell you that the business is making great progress. Timur's already got five orders, Dunya three, and Esper Ozirisovich a full half dozen. I've picked up four. But what about you? Had any nibbles?"

"Valery," responded Matsa plaintively, "you know I live the life of a hermit. You know I have as few acquaintances among the upper crust as I have many among simple people and among those who, through no fault of their own and not because of any lack of good qualities, live at the bottom of society. Do you know what one fifty-year-old friend of mine once said to me—a poet totally dissatisfied with his surroundings? He said that he had sacrificed all that was best in himself to the war, trusting that a complete renewal of life would come afterwards. But now he's completely disillusioned and convinced that we are being ruled by a gang of bandits. All right, he said, make your cemetery, then we shall have a real museum of dishonor and paranoid slaves."

"But you know lots of people in the literary world, don't you?"

"What on earth do you mean, Valery? I wouldn't dare cross the threshold of the Writers' Union, and then, don't forget, I'm not a member. Thirty years ago they stopped printing what I wrote, and what I've written since and what I'm writing now is best not shown to them at all. The best thing about it is that they've completely forgotten my existence, and they mustn't under any circumstances be reminded of it. The writers and poets I meet can't possibly be classed as well off—just the opposite. I do know one or two, like K, who are well off and honest. But what would they think if I approached them with a proposition like this? They're above that sort of thing; I respect and admire them; there's nothing opportunistic about them at all. Therefore . . ."

"Who knows," the lawyer interrupted him, "perhaps it could help us, indirectly, to widen our clientele, or at least to spread the idea among possible customers. I don't want to nag you, Gleb, you've already done a lot for us . . ."

In this way they reached the racetrack exit and started walking down Leningrad Avenue, their conversation ending.

The lawyer was thinking of Dildor, who called him uncle and was growing more affectionate toward him every day. He had noticed that when Olga, his sister, was not at home, the girl did everything she could to attract his attention, combing her hair in front of him, fawning upon him like a kitten, continually passing to and fro in front of the open door of his study and casting long looks in at him, coming in to empty the overflowing ashtray on his desk and asking if he wanted any coffee. Sometimes she settled down on the lawn before his window and read the books Olga had given her to improve her Russian, reclining in poses that she conceived, in her naivety, to be seductive. Yesterday after dinner he had found her asleep half naked in her room with the door wide open. But from the way her body quivered almost imperceptibly as he walked past and paused, on catching sight of her, he realized that she was not really asleep at all. This evening Olga would be out. She had gone to visit an old friend on the other side of Moscow and wouldn't be back till tomorrow evening. Tarakanov, therefore, was in a hurry to get home. And he was afraid that Matsa would want to spend the evening with him.

Not far from the Dynamo metro station, Tarakanov broke the silence:

"Gleb, I've got some urgent business to attend to and I'm not sure how long it will take. Forgive me if I leave you. It's not for nothing," and at this point he smiled, "that I'm called the lawyer. See you soon. We'll meet again on midsummer night, or the night of Ivan-Kupala, as you prefer to call it. And if we follow your persuasive instructions, I'm sure we'll have a pretty good orgy. I'll meet you at the *Prague* as we arranged and pick you up . . ."

He watched Matsa until he disappeared into the metro.Then with swift steps he made his way to his automobile.

The crowds were hurrying past at breakneck speed, as they always did during the rush hour. People ran to overtake one another and dash down the escalators. Many of them, both men and women, but above all the young people, were not satisfied with the speed of the escalators and rushed down the moving stairs, racing them, as if they would soar through the air like birds. They burst headlong into the tunnels and whirled like a flood of pebbles past the quiet, weary and sometimes simply lazy Muscovites, who reverently stood aside for them.

Matsa belonged to the latter group. He stood still on the stairway as it carried him down and followed his usual habit of watching the hurrying, impatient mass of people as they flooded past. Then, tired of this frenzied motion up and down, he fixed his eyes on the passengers standing behind and above him, who also were content to abandon themselves to the automatic movement of the stairs.

His attention was attracted by a young woman of extraordinary beauty, with delicate and at the same time sensual features. Matsa allowed his gaze to rest on this serious, but languorous face, which was turned in upon itself and indifferent to its surroundings. He was incapable of tearing his eyes away, because in that face, in its delicate and elegant features, which were imbued with a consciousness of inner vitality and a hint of provocative sensuality, he was rediscovering the true nobility of the human visage, a quality that is encountered less and less in the world's cities today: the visage of a woman in whom femininity was absorbed by spirituality, by virtue of which it acquired a special force bordering on sorcery. She was one of those beings who, like the transitory passengers of distant planets, where perfection is the norm, pass through the world like accidental, temporary visitors, although they nonetheless belong to this world and are its best representatives.

The woman's deep, dark and alert eyes responded to his gaze. The escalator continued its mechanical descent and Matsa did not know what to do, spellbound by this face, which shone with a quiet, calm light, bringing him life, joy and peace. But she herself spoke first:

"Citizen, why are you looking at me like that?"

"Because you do not belong to this world," replied Matsa, "because you are much more than just a beautiful woman."

Matsa by this time was already at the bottom of the escalator, where she caught up with him, fluttering from the endless conveyor belt. Then she simply took him by the arm and said:

"Today I feel gay; would you like to be my escort? Let's go somewhere, shall we? Do you mind?"

"What? I'd be only too pleased," gasped Matsa, whose heart was pounding like a little boy's.

"Are you a writer? Or perhaps a painter?" she asked, inclining her amiably smiling face toward him.

"I am the speech of forgotten lips, a tower of dormant dialects," declaimed Matsa.

"No, tell me the truth."

"It is the truth, I swear," replied Matsa. "Do you know who wrote those lines? Pasternak. And they fully apply to me. But where are we going? Let's go outside, into the light and fresh air, I want to free you from this crowd. Let's take a taxi and go to Neskuchny Sad or better still, Sokolniki. Agreed?"

"Yes, but only if you tell me who you are. A writer?"

"Without doubt, but for some reason I'm not recognized as such. I write for myself, for the desk drawer, but not, alas, for publication. Anyway, the things I write are a bit special."

"Oh, are they secret? And why don't you publish? And why aren't you recognized as a writer?"

"Oho, so many questions all at once! Later, later . . . Let's get ourselves organized first: a taxi and then a walk."

They were lucky, and found an empty cab waiting at the rank. And what was quite strange was that the driver, with absolutely extraordinary politeness, got out and opened the door for them, and, which was even stranger, addressed Matsa as "sir," an incredibly old-fashioned, forgotten and discarded expression.

Matsa was highly intrigued. He had noticed that the driver was reading a book when they approached, and now he asked him what the book was. The driver said it was *Anna Karenina* and explained that he had read it and re-read it many times. And that he had read many other old novels as well, for he liked escaping into times gone by. Excitedly he told them that as a boy he had been kissed on the forehead by the tsar, and that the tsarina had smiled when the tsar did it. His whole account was full of "sirs" and "madams." And Matsa, astonished and diverted by all this, thought that this monarchist remnant must be an apparition too, a phantom from the past that had materialized just for him in the streets of Moscow. In the same way he had once—he was sure of it—glimpsed through a trolleybus window the absolutely genuine and living figure of his father, who had died before the revolution. But the figure had disappeared in the crowd by the time he had been able to alight from the trolleybus.

In Sokolniki Park, as they were walking down one of the avenues and a few seconds before they told one another their names, Matsa, catching sight of a bush swaying in the wind, suddenly divined that the ravishing stranger walking through the trees with him was none other than Elena Filippovna, the young woman who had produced such an ineradicable impression on Timur at the cemetery, about which Timur had repeatedly told him.

Until then Matsa had managed to evade answering the young woman's many questions, paying her instead a series of recondite and eccentric compliments, and amusing her with light conversation. But she had impatiently taken the bait: she sensed the unusual nature of their meeting and was eager to discover exactly who this interesting and intellectual old man was, for he was undoubtedly connected with literature.

This was confirmed for her when, on one of the avenues, they bumped into a tall skinny man with boyishly fair hair and with the spoiled expression of a little boy on his face, that was scored with deep wrinkles or scars. The man appeared to be talking to himself as he walked, laughing at something, like a child, but his face never lost its tragic expression. "M," said her companion, "is a poet of the intellect, rather than sentiment, clear and rational. He's seventy now, yet he's the most youthful poet of the past decade. He didn't publish anything before that because he was in prison; he's covered the whole of Russia on foot. I'm very fond of him."

Sitting in the cozy restaurant that was situated in a detached wooden house looking somewhat like a former villa, here in Sokolniki, Elena Filippovna returned to the attack.

"Gleb Vyacheslavovich, I've already told you about myself: how I went to teacher's college, but then threw it up to get married and afterwards did no work, and how I recently lost my husband. Now I need to find some sort of job, and I was thinking of teaching literature. But what do I know? I'm perfectly well aware that literature is something different; that it is broad and has nothing in common with the narrow schematicism that they thrust down our throats in school: socialist realism, Gorky, Serafimovich, Fadeyev . . ."

"Well, yes, Gorky's OK," said Matsa, drily agreeing with her, "but Serafimovich and Fadeyev simply don't exist as writers; they're even worse than Ostrovsky, you know, the steel that was tempered. As for socialist realism, please, my girl. Surely there can't be anyone left who believes in it any more? It exists only in the programs of the Ministry of Education and in the Party theses. But let's not talk about such sad subjects."

Elena Filippovna felt toward him like a schoolgirl. But it was not because of his words. She was drawn to him from the depths of her being, not as a disciple to the master, but as a young woman sensible of his physical and spiritual attraction. But the words she spoke were quite removed from this.

"What does literature mean to you?" she asked.

"Do you want a definition?" Matsa raised his eyebrows playfully. "But how on earth can one define it, my girl? It's like life—can you define life? No, it's impossible. Pasternak had some good things to say about this as well. Every definition of life is partial and incomplete. And the same is true of art. Tendencies? In life, my girl, as in art, there are innumerable tendencies, and all contradicting one another. And so they should."

"But surely we need to aid those endeavors in art that make it useful to society and the people?"

"But how can it be managed? There's the rub! Positively and straightforwardly as the Party does it, or our corrupt pseudo-criticism? No-o, spare us! You know, I sometimes wonder in despair whether some spiteful enemy of the Soviet system didn't think up such a useful enslavement of art. Why, what better would serve than the literature and art they encourage—false, evasive and lifeless—to encourage the spread of indifference and disbelief? After all, it's not a question of literal meaning; but of the fact that these soulless scribblings offer an image of moral bankruptcy, collapse and helplessness, and are incapable of concealing the bloodstained sores of our actual reality, although they endeavour to hush them up. Do you think that such hypocrisy is helpful to society and the people?"

"The things you say are all so remote from everything I live by. It is difficult for me to understand it all," said Elena Filippovna meekly.

"The worst thing of all is that we are ruled by stupidity, my dear Elena! Doubtless you passed your exams in dialectical materialism; studying superficially and mechanically for them, unable to figure out what was what, as though the whole thing amounted to nothing more than grade-school arithmetic, and the art of addition and subtraction. But still I hope you have some idea of it, and know about the concept of negation?"

Elena nodded and Matsa continued:

"Well, in the dialectics of social development art can only and exclusively be one of the aspects of the concept of negation, in this it manifests its usefulness and this is its sole function. But here, in the country of socialism triumphant, everything expressing negation is ignored, repressed, strangled—because our rulers are not in the least interested in socialism and they simply couldn't care less about how it develops; all they are interested in is power and the ability of the country they rule to preserve them in power. As their beloved Lord and Master once said, they are like blind kittens whom a tidal wave will eventually sweep away, notwithstanding all their dams and barricades. In any country and in any society, art is one of the basic manifestations of the concept of negation, and as such should enjoy complete freedom. Only thus can it make discoveries, uncover problems and create something new."

"But if it attacks and blackens the very foundations of society and the things the people believe in?"

"So much the better, my beauty," said Matsa, growing excited, as he had during the dispute with Marina. This was a common occurrence with him: he lost all consciousness of his companion's personality and level of development and completely unconsciously bludgeoned them with his arguments. "So much the better! The writer, artist, intellectual has a duty to be seditious and blasphemous, and must know how to spit into the dish he eats from. 'To spit in your own dish'—this favourite phrase of slaves accustomed to live off charity has somehow become negative and is applied even to our greatest sinners: from Zoshchenko to Pasternak, to Sinyavsky, to Solzhenitsyn, whenever they are being held up to ridicule. But objectively speaking, this is the highest praise that can be given to an artist or intellectual anywhere and at any time, but particularly now in countries where communism reigns. For this precisely, to spit in the dish you eat from, is the essence of the writer's vocation! And it's not so easy as people think to produce a good gob of spit!" he concluded laughingly.

"And is that the way you write? When you write not for publication?" Elena Filippovna returned to the question that was bothering her.

"No, I write things of an erotic nature," replied Matsa, "and for the time being they are unpublishable. Even Babel was severely censored. But I'm convinced that Russia needs this sort of thing more than any other country in the world, for we have never had this sort of thing up till now. But I have a feeling that the times are changing. And it doesn't bother me that I have to wait."

"But then nobody will learn of your existence. You won't get your rightful satisfaction in any respect," Elena Filippovna wanted to add "neither moral, nor material," but hesitated, fearing to seem too trivial.

" 'The poet's aim is dedication, not brave success and bold sensation,' " declaimed Matsa once more, quoting Pasternak. "The poet was speaking not only about himself, but was warning all us small fry as well."

"You keep on quoting Pasternak, but what about Mayakovsky?"

"Mayakovsky was a genius who throttled his own gift, as he put it himself. But I don't rate Pasternak higher than Tsvetayeva or Akhmatova. Taking them all together, with the addition of Mandelstam and the whole galaxy of lesser poets, you have perhaps the richest collection of poetry of the twentieth century —Russian poetry."

"Gleb Vyacheslavovich," said Elena Filippovna shyly, "could

I read some of your works? You're such an exceptional man and so . . ." she shied away from the word "old" and amended it to: "mature, that it makes me ashamed to confess that I have a great interest in questions of eroticism. I don't know a thing about it and until quite recently the thought of it had never entered my head. But then something occurred that stirred me to the depths of my being, something that opened my eyes as to my own true nature and forced me to think deeply about a number of things. And I would be grateful if you could educate me even just a little in matters of eroticism and the subtleties of love."

"But eroticism is not a refined sexuality; it is a concept far broader than that and even, I would say, something quite different. Eroticism embraces the human personality in its entirety: it is the essential energy of life and also its object; it is the destruction of alienation in incomplete individuals and their transformation into whole, perfect and higher beings embodied in cosmic or divine—as you prefer—substance, enabling them to become conscious of their egos as parts of the universe. But we will go into that in more detail later."

As she listened to him, Elena Filippovna gazed at him with eyes tinged with mystery and sensuality, which endowed them with a slight squint. Her face retained its slightly haughty expression, but her breast was heaving.

"Yes, of course, Gleb Vyacheslavovich!" she exclaimed. "You were sent to me by fate. To think of meeting a man like you!"

"It was not only fate," explained Matsa, "you yourself picked a man out of the crowd, you intuitively divined a mentor in him. I believe in prophetic signs. You chose me to be your escort and so be it: I will guide you along the difficult and tortuous road leading to an understanding of eroticism. But tell me frankly in exchange for my own frankness, can I rely on you if I give you my works to read; can I trust you? After all, I hardly know you."

Matsa was lying, because from Timur's account of Kondratyev's widow he knew more than enough to draw his own conclusions, and they were entirely favorable: she would never have betrayed him. If Timur had at any time had occasion to distrust her, he would not have kept quiet about it and would have been the first to ferret out the truth.

But Matsa wanted to test her; moreover it had occurred to him that she might be able to participate in their orgy on midsummer night, so that she and Timur could meet again at last and resurrect the inspiration that had visited them at the cemetery. Her answer to such a proposal would be conclusive: if she was playing with him, she would never risk going off with strangers who made a rendezvous with her on the street, and then drove her away to an unknown destination. On the other hand, there was no risk in it for them, because they would drive her back to Moscow afterwards and she would never recognize the place where she had spent the night or remember the way there. And if she tried to make fools of them, Timur would never forgive her, even if it meant resorting to extreme measures.

To Matsa's question she replied:

"Yes, you're quite right, I never thought of it when I asked if I could see them. How suspicious we all are! But what can we do?"

"Give me your hand," said Matsa, "I'll read your palm and then I can tell what fortune has in store for you."

"Oh!" laughed Elena Filippovna gaily. "Here you are. It's the left one, isn't it?" and she held out her hand to Matsa. It couldn't be called beautiful, it was too narrow and twitched, and the fingers were slightly crooked.

Matsa donned his glasses and closely examined her palm.

"Hm, you have a sensual nature, my girl," he said after two or three minutes. "Inconstancy, a love of adventure, kindness, loyalty—as that is possible for a woman . . . But I don't see any tendency to deception or lying."

He paused and made as if to release her hand, raising his eyes to look at her.

"And what else?" she asked impatiently. "Do you see anything else there?"

"Yes," said Matsa decisively, but then stopped, as though reluctant to go on.

"What is it, what is it?" said the woman insistently.

"I see a recent encounter . . . a very important one . . . a man, and then I see crosses, death . . . no, no, don't worry! Don't be afraid!" he added reassuringly, seeing that she had turned pale. "It's happened already; it's all in the past . . . At the same time I see love, voluptuousness . . . strange, it's as though death were transformed into voluptuousness and the latter is still continuing . . . look, here, you see?" he said, pointing to a line on Elena Filippovna's hand. "This line here is a path leading to a man . . . It's all rubbish, isn't it?" and he raised his eyes to the woman again.

Elena Filippovna was clearly agitated.

"Oh, please don't stop, I beg you, go on!" she exclaimed, with a break in her voice.

"I don't know whether I can tell you this," replied Matsa, once more examining her palm closely. "You yourself were looking for an erotic experience. I see that something very powerful took place with this man, and very erotic . . . in the presence of death . . . I see it has left its mark on you . . ."

"Strange . . . amazing!" muttered Elena Filippovna to herself.

". . . And I see that you will soon meet again . . . in a few days . . ."

"Oh no! You can't know that!" responded the woman agitatedly. "That's in the future."

"If what I told you about the past was true, why not accept this as true as well?" parried Matsa.

"But who are you?" asked Elena Filippovna, almost in alarm. "How can you know all this?"

"It's quite simple, my girl. I'm Azazel!" smiled Matsa. "Didn't you guess?"

But Elena Filippovna couldn't guess, because she hadn't read Bulgakov's *Master and Margarita.*

"Who? Who?" she asked impatiently.

"The demon Azazel, who will take you to the man you so

passionately desire to meet. Azazel, who will take you to a witches' sabbath, where you will be initiated into eroticism by that very man."

"No, that's quite impossible!" Elena Filippovna almost groaned. "Why are you making fun of me?"

"I'm not making fun of you at all," replied Matsa. "If I promise you that you will meet him there, that's how it will be. But you must be prepared to follow my instructions."

"I'm prepared," replied Elena Filippovna resolutely, and then added thoughtfully: "It's the main thing in my life now . . . I'm ready for anything."

18. Ivan Kupala's Night

In his office at the KGB headquarters Colonel Dvoretsky gathered up all the material on the Dermoshchenko case and went off to report to the general.

In spite of the fact that for many days now he and his closest colleague, Lieutenant-Colonel Dementyev, had examined, studied, immersed themselves in the unimaginable mountain of reports, declarations, estimates, laboratory analyses and the conclusions of the experimental division, they had had no success at all in finally unraveling the matter and were unable to say with any confidence that Dermoshchenko had been unmasked. On the contrary, the case remained shrouded in obscurity and there were weighty reasons for suspecting that it was of an extraordinary importance, exceeding their first estimates, and that not only had Dermoshchenko been recruited by foreign intelligence, but that the threads led to a sizable organization that had put down solid roots and was in possession of considerable means that were completely unknown to Soviet counter-intelligence.

Not one laboratory analysis had been able to decode the messages on the strange pieces of material that Dermoshchenko had been depositing in lavatories and subsequently collecting. Two of them had revealed signs of something that remotely resembled some sort of letters, but they were so indistinct and misshapen that it was impossible to make them out, and it seemed just as likely that they weren't even letters at all. But on the other hand, each fragment was distinctly numbered in fountain pen ink and bore fingerprints, in spite of the fact that it was completely soaked in organic matter.

"Goddam it!" the colonel swore to himself. "Just look at the sort of place they chose for passing messages, and the disgusting stuff they chose to disguise it with! Talk about killing two birds with one stone. A really cunning trick!"

His only comfort was that imperialist espionage felt obliged to resort to shit in order to operate in Soviet society. "Our society is so healthy that in order to do their filthy work they are no longer satisfied with the dregs and sewage of society in the metaphorical sense, but have to throw themselves head first into the sewers, in the direct and most disgusting sense of the word, and crawl through ordure and stink!" The only thing clear was that none of the means employed had been capable of decoding the secret messages, which meant that those bastards had thought up some new form of invisible ink or, even worse, had thought up god only knew what new chemical or electronic process, to which the cloth was subjected in order to imprint on it, and subsequently read, the coded messages. But there was yet one other strange circumstance: the cloth was of the most ordinary sort of native manufacture.

But the doubts tormenting Colonel Dvoretsky did not end here. How was he to explain the fact that the film cameras set up in the public lavatories clearly showed the figure of Dermoshchenko as he carried out the operation described by agent B week after week, and that the film showed a host of other people coming and going and satisfying their natural needs, but not once did any sort of accomplice appear to collect the fragments of cloth or leave other ones for Dermoshchenko and his fellow spies to collect. Perhaps the group had been warned off by something, by the agent's incautious behaviour perhaps, or else had means of detecting the positions of the cameras and microphones?

Dermoshchenko's trail had also taken them to the collective

farm, Sheaves of the Future. It was obvious that the scientist had abandoned his apartment and work in Moscow and was now living in Dry Ford. But what was not clear was the exact nature of his relations with the farm. The agents who were put on active duty in the farm itself reported a host of strange and contradictory things: the production of coffins and funeral appurtenances (what could that mean?), the coming and going of numerous trucks (that would have to be looked into), earthworks over a considerable area of ground (what was the aim?). The peasants, when they were asked, said something vague about a cemetery, but others knew nothing about it and some even maintained that some sort of underground establishment was being constructed, and that was why some important bigwig had come out from Moscow and why some sort of "engineers" used to turn up regularly. On top of all that, the reports also spoke of a visit to the farm by a member of the Central Committee, Comrade Frolov: what was the explanation?

As far as the scientist was concerned, the peasants said he was interested only in manure, while some supposed that he was trying to make, and indeed might already have succeeded, in making gold from manure. Gold, of course, was out of the question, but perhaps he had found some rare and hitherto undiscovered element in it, which was of great military significance? Dvoretsky was a regular reader of *Science and Life* and was sufficiently well educated to realize what unexpected discoveries science was able to make. And at this point it occurred to him that there might be some sort of connection between the lavatories and the collective farm manure.

Yes, it was a big and difficult case: espionage, science, perhaps even politics, bearing in mind that a Central Committee member was mixed up in it. What were they up to? And what could an underground establishment mean? Perhaps this fifth column was preparing a base on Soviet territory? (And only a stone's throw from Moscow, he thought with a shudder. Was it an international plot to strike at the very heart of Soviet power?)

Dvoretsky decided to act with caution and cunning. He decided not to interrogate either the chairman of the collective farm, or anyone else who might in any way be mixed up in the affair, so as not to frighten them off. But everything was placed under strict observation, agents were scattered about the farm to keep watch on everyone and to question the peasants on any pretext. But the general had no patience, he was putting pressure on him, he wanted immediate results and now had summoned him to give a final report and analysis of the entire affair. Having gathered up all the material he needed to show to General Nedobora, the lieutenant-colonel left the room.

When he reached the general's office, Colonel Dementyev and Lieutenant B. were already there.

"Well," said the general, "what results do you have to offer me? I hope that by now you have moved from hypotheses to facts."

Dvoretsky informed him of the latest developments in the case, trying to synthesize the facts into a single, coherent whole. Then he expounded his theories and hypotheses.

"It's all decidedly vague," responded the general coolly when the other had finished. "What's your plan of action?" This question was addressed to both Dvoretsky and Dementyev.

"To maintain our vigilance and by comparing any new facts we learn with those already in our possession, to establish the exact nature of the case. And then we will take the appropriate measures."

"My opinion is somewhat different: it would be expedient to begin by arresting Dermoshchenko, the collective farm chairman, and even the party organizer down there," said Dementyev. "In this way we would be able to put a stop to their actions, which, whichever way you look at them, appear to be dangerous, and afterwards find out what it was all about."

"We shall do neither!" rapped out General Nedobora, with a hint of malice in his voice. "The KGB's aim is the liquidation of all actual and potential enemies. We must act decisively and without delay, energetically and on a broad front. Let me inform you of a new fact that throws considerable light on the case and that has only just been communicated to me. Today the police halted a taxi on the road to the collective farm, inside which were two persons travelling in a zone that is forbidden to foreigners. When questioned, they told our agents that they were on their way to the farm to write a story about it: one of them was a reporter, the other a photographer. They had heard that the collective farm was developing some original and highly interesting activities and were interested in learning more about it in their professional capacity as journalists. The taxi driver excused himself by saying that he had been unable to resist the money offered him for making the journey. But he's an old acquaintance of ours, a former camp inmate, and I fear it won't be long before he returns there again."

Dvoretsky and Dementyev nodded their heads in assent, not daring to bat an eyelid and looking straight at the general's mouth.

"Photographers and reporters beyond their permitted zone! Breaking the regulations! Who do they think they are kidding?" fumed Nedobora. "We are confronted with a colossal conspiracy, and therefore we have to act! The only way out is a sudden night raid on the collective farm: arrest everybody; search everything; search everybody! Give the necessary orders now! And spare no means to make the operation efficient—use everything we've got!"

* * * * *

The night was warm: it brought neither wind nor freshness, but was wrapped in a bluish haze that obliterated the boundary between horizon and sky. The sky was a deep blue, but clear and gave off a peaceful light; a typical Moscow June sky when darkness only hints at its presence, but never actually comes: just at that moment when sleep finally descends on the disturbed earth, its kingdom is suddenly invaded by stealthy morning, which flings open the gates to greet the day. A pale silvery moon floated in this blue-gray radiance, and scattered stars winked and shone over the woods and valleys, and over the gleaming, mirror-like waters.

An old *Moskvich* was hurrying over the roads just outside Moscow, crossing meadows and disappearing behind hills, its headlights catching and then losing the merry, cunning fireflies as they zoomed over the ground, where their mates glowed languorously in their hiding places in the grass. The *Moskvich* slowed near a lonely rise, drove extremely slowly off the road and into a field, bounced over a mound and swung behind a hill. There were two other automobiles here already. An elderly man, short and on the lean side, jumped nimbly out of the *Moskvich.*

Pulling open the other door, he bent down and helped a blindfolded woman out. When her graceful figure was standing upright and firmly balanced, the man approached her, took the blindfold from her eyes and gaily announced:

"Well, here we are, Agrafena Kupalnitsa! And now you may put on your mask."

The woman donned the white silk mask, which seemed to light up her face and her light, close-fitting, lilac dress. It was mysterious and severe in the transparency of the night, and underlined the pallor of her neck and collarbone, which were revealed by the open dress. She looked around her and saw a dense black wood about ten paces in front of her.

"We shall have to walk a little way," said the man, heading toward the trees.

The woman followed him in silence. They plunged into the wood and the silent, motionless trees surrounded them densely. The ground was carpeted with grass, moist with the night's dew. The tender light of the field remained behind them. They walked forward through the darkness of the wood. The huge fireflies did not so much light their way as confuse them with their irregular and random movements, cutting blazing trails in the air on all sides.

In this manner they walked for about half an hour. The woman caught sight of lights flickering a short distance away between the trunks and branches of the trees. The closer they came, the stronger grew the red glow, as though a big fire had been kindled in the very heart of the wood.

And so it was. Skirting some thick bushes and dead branches scattered on the ground, they came to the fire, its flames casting shadows on the people around it: men and girls. As they sat around the fire, they were sometimes illuminated by it and then seemed to recede into the darkness again, whenever the capricious light of the flames, leaping up toward the sky, suddenly blew in another direction. Off to one side were open cases full of bottles and of something else that the woman in the mask couldn't recognize.

Only when, on the heels of her escort, she reached the group around the fire did the woman notice that the girls were all wearing crowns of wild flowers. A similar crown adorned the head of a very plump, pleasant woman with dark curly hair, and the head of an extremely young, extremely tiny girl with big, gleaming, tender eyes. The flame jumped, and then she whom her escort had jokingly called Agrafena Kupalnitsa, the ancient name of the legendary figure personifying Midsummer Night, could see the girl completely, in her white, silk, embroidered dress. The girl, who was sitting beside the plump woman, turned her smiling face to look at her, showing her gleaming white teeth.

An old man in an azure robe with a silver stripe, whom the woman recognized as Matsa, rose and said:

"At last! It's late, and you, Valery, missed the birth of living fire to the glory of Yar, a mystery that old men like us shouldn't miss. We managed it all with the help of Kirill Nikitich and Fotyan Evteich here," and he pointed to two bearded peasants, whose tiny little eyes smiled back cunningly from beneath the bushy brows on their wrinkled foreheads. "Ah, Agrafena Kupalnitsa!" he said, turning to the woman in the mask, "Welcome! Sit down; let me introduce you; make yourself at home!"

The masked woman sat down next to Dunya, who knew just

as much about her as Matsa and Tarakanov, who had brought her here. Matsa and the others had arrived two hours ago, together with Timur. Timur had then gone back to Moscow to fetch some friends and at the same time was supposed to call in at Dry Ford to pick up two girls who were fully qualified to take part in the orgy, thanks to their beauty and ability to keep silent. It was past ten already and Timur was due to appear at any moment. They were waiting for him before beginning the proper ritual ceremony. Tarakanov and Dunya, who were parties to the plot involving Timur and Elena Filippovna and who had helped Matsa organize their meeting, were burning with impatience as they awaited Timur, no less than Matsa himself, who had organized everything with such extraordinary care.

Ivan and Marya
Bathed in the river:
Where Ivan bathed,
The bank caved,
Where Marya swam,
The grass began.
    She swam on Ivan's night!
    Ivan swam,
Fell into the water.
She swam on Ivan's night . . .

sang Dunya, repeating the ancient ritual song of Midsummer Night. She was accompanied by Olga Borisovna and the others. Dildor also tried to sing with them, but not understanding the sense of the words, she kept falling behind, and her little voice was always the first to die away at the ends of the lines. Before them the midsummer flame of the fire flared hotly, lighting up the daisies and forget-me-nots with which the glade was strewn.

* * * * *

Midsummer Night was taking a somewhat different course on the collective farm, Sheaves of the Future. An ordinary, run-of-the-mill midnight was approaching, leaden and threatening, like the click of steel-tipped boots, like the burnished steel of revolvers. There were no cheerful midsummer fires dedicated to the sun god, Yarila, only the winking of flashlights groping in the darkness.

Timur's *Volga* was racing over the empty night roads among copses and birch groves, among firs and pines with their reddish mastlike trunks. Timur drove in silence. Vadik, beside him, was peering at the road through slits of swollen eyes, while Gora dozed on the back seat.

Timur suddenly stiffened when he heard a helicopter overhead, four miles from Dry Ford. At that moment Gora dozed on the back seat.

"What's that?" he asked.

"A helicopter," replied Timur laconically.

"Stop the car!"

Timur extinguished his lights and the car gently drove off the road. Here, on a patch of greensward beside some currant bushes, he turned off the engine. The helicopter was coming nearer. They left the car and hid in the bushes.

The helicopter came directly overhead, described a circle and then headed north, disappearing in the distance.

"Let's walk up this hill," said Timur, "perhaps we'll be able to see Dry Ford from there."

They left Vadik to guard the car and began to scramble uphill, forcing their way through the bushes, stumbling over tree stumps, jumping ditches and making their way forward between the gloomy trunks whose foliage showed black overhead. From the top of the hill they had a view of a jumbled assortment of houses, some of them two-storied with lights in their windows, others low, squat and dark: this was Dry Ford. The whole settlement gave off a dim, diffused light.

But Timur's and Gora's experienced eyes quickly made out, in the ring of darkness surrounding the collective farm, the strange winking of constantly shifting points of light, which appeared and disappeared as they moved continually from place to place. While they were watching this, the buzz of the helicopter made itself heard again and they could see its black shadow. But it was clear that they hadn't been observed from the helicopter, either now or earlier.

"Christ!" exclaimed Timur to himself. "It's a raid! What in hell's name brought them here?" he gritted through clenched teeth.

"Best to scram out of here," suggested Gora, "before the fuzz have finished assing around. Otherwise we might bump into them on the road."

They descended the hill in silence and waited for the helicopter to fly overhead and recede into the distance. Timur started the engine and without turning his lights on, returned to the road. He avoided revving up, trying to take it slowly and avoid making too much noise. Just to be sure, he drove off the road again when the helicopter reached the spot where they had just been and from which they had traveled only a short distance.

Driving back on the road again, Timur put his foot down on the throttle, so that the automobile, with a roar, raced through the bright June night, without headlights, ready to shoot off the road at any moment if the driver saw anything suspicious in front of him. But the ring of raiders had been left behind at Dry Ford, which slept blissfully as it was enclosed in an iron ring of implacable, diligent wonder boys, acting with all the confidence bestowed on them by high-school algebra.

* * * * *

The people around the fire were totally oblivious to all this. All that worried them was Timur's lateness in arriving. They had postponed until his arrival the ancient, symbolic ceremony when a wooden splinter is ignited at the fire of the god, Yarila. It had to be held by an unsullied virgin maiden, the youthful queen of the festivity. Matsa and Marina (the former the inspirer and wizard of this ceremony, which he had reconstructed on the basis of ancient tradition, and the latter its soul and first executant) decided that it would be impossible to wait any longer, since much remained to be accomplished during the course of the night.

Marina leaned over to Dunya and whispered something in her ear. Dunya in turn whispered something in Dildor's ear.

Dildor stood up. Her slender little body showed through the embroidered white dress, with an aura of womanhood already about it, although still childlike. The dainty crown rested easily on her head, which appeared impetuous and proud. Her face was almost completely hidden by her mane of gypsyish hair, which cascaded over her shoulders and enveloped her delicate, tender neck. Her entire being was concentrated in her big, shining eyes: these, with her tender lips and the oval of her face, spoke of distant Persian origins. Anyone catching sight of her at this moment would at once have been reminded of Stenka Razin and his Persian princess.

All were silent. The brushwood crackled in the maw of the fire. Dildor approached the fire, pointing to the sky with the splinter she held in her hand. Gazing into the very heart of the fire, she waited until it blazed up before plunging the dry splinter into its depths—and was transformed into a blazing torch. Then they all cried out and began to sing: this was the birth of King Fire, bearing the life of the ancient Slavic god.

Matsa and Tarakanov stared entranced at Dildor. But at the same time they maintained the sober decorum of experienced men of the world, although they were also indulgent—a typical trait of old men who have not yet been conquered by age, and still know how to get the best out of life, having mastered all its tricks.

"Why isn't Timur here yet?" thought Marina worriedly to herself, while Elena Filippovna, whose palm had been read by Matsa and to whom no one spoke, so that there was nothing to remind her, even remotely, of the man who had captured all her feelings and then had materialized before her in his everyday guise, not as a faun or a god, but as an ordinary citizen, although king of the street—Elena Filippovna was as full of the same kind of worries as Marina, as though she were expecting something and missing someone. And Dunya was also surprised at Timur being so late.

"And now," she exclaimed, standing up, "let us all bathe in the pond, let us all swim in the cold spring water! Come on, Dildor!"

Taking the girl by the hand, she ran across the meadow with her to the moonlit water, its surface shimmering with a silver gleam. Dunya threw off her dress. Dildor followed her example.

"Look at the trees!" cried Matsa. "On this night, the trees move about and talk to one another."

He also entered the water, reverently giving himself up to its benevolent freshness. Raising his head, he gazed upward at the tops of the trees, moving in the moonlight, and at the clouds slowly drifting above them on this midsummer's night.

They splashed as they swam, made jokes and sang songs. Dunya lovingly stroked Dildor's body under the water: contact under the water was voluptuous and penetrating. Elena Filippovna floated slowly on her back, presenting her young witch's body to the moonlight. Matsa rejoiced and devoured her with his eyes. With one hand he touched his tired penis, exhausted by the struggle with age. Tarakanov snorted in the water, groping for his withered, Byzantine sister, Olga.

In the midst of this blissful intoxication, in the midst of this dreamlike vision of cold spring water, greenswards, plants and living trees there suddenly sounded a defiant brigand whistle that was like a battle summons. Everyone fell silent at once. Hearts beat loudly.

It was the whistle of the Robber Nightingale, the hero of ancient folk legend, and it was repeated two or three times. Elena Filippovna's white body sank down and disappeared beneath the water, slowly and soundlessly, and only her face came to the surface again, with its bulging, petrified eyes and trembling lips.

Then there came the sound of rustling and of snapping twigs, and the bushes beside the pond parted to reveal the insolent, fairskinned face of Timur. It was followed by his lithe, nervous body, which cut through the darkness like a blade. Behind him two more figures emerged from the darkness like guardian angels, dark and silent.

Timur came to a halt. He stood up to his full height, standing high above the water. His eyes scanned the water in search of allies. He had no way of knowing that there were other eyes there, seen once before and in a different place and now staring at him, half-frightened and half-pleased.

"Valery Borisovich," he said in a low voice, measuring his whisper to cover the distance between them, "bad news."

Tarakanov broke away from his sister and emerged from the water, dark and naked as a watersnake. Timur conferred with him in a low voice. Vadik and Gora stood motionlessly just behind him. The others continued to spash about gaily in the water. Only Elena Filippovna trembled all over and her body sank deeper into the water, with only her immobile face showing on the cold silvery surface. Her body was as dead as a withered log floating on the surface.

"Well, we'll see," said Tarakanov when he had heard Timur's story. "Not a word to the others. In any case, no one will dream of looking for us here. We are safer here than at home."

"It's almost midnight!" cried Matsa in a shrill voice from the middle of the pond. "It is time to seek the legendary fern blossom, Yarila's gift, the fiery flower of happiness. Whoever finds it will understand the language of the plants, trees and animals and will hold the key of life. Dildor will be the fern blossom and we will conquer the night, and our bodies will give birth to light in the darkness."

They all emerged from the water and scattered among the trees, bushes and tall grasses. Only Elena Filippovna remained behind in the pond, entombed in the water, and her face, as before, continued to be set in a dead mask, severe and tragic, and in this mold it shaped its last lewd smile of regret for what was slipping away from her.

Thirty yards away from her, motionless on the pond's bank and protected by the bushes and his two bodyguards, Timur then noticed this floating object in which he was able to make out at first a woman's head and then the features about which he had forgotten for the past two hours and which now came to life, hot and vital, as though by a sudden impulse. Then he simultaneously realized the cause of it and recognized Elena Filippovna.

She had seen him, but was not looking at him. Her eyes emitted no sparks, but seemed like twin fragments of mirror glass. Her whole being had been crying out for Timur and that was why she could not bear the indifference of mere recognition. But Timur pierced that face with his gaze—it was between his legs now, it was drilling into his brain, and with his penis he stroked and defiled that face. Within him kindled that cold, feverish fire that had once consumed her at the cemetery.

They were separated by a tiny distance, but it was enough to harbor a frontier: Elena Filippovna was in the legendary town of Kitezh, that invisible beautiful city that is unattainable to the unrighteous, and therefore dead for the present age both to Russia and the entire world. She was in that vanished city that can reappear only with the appearance of a new civilization, humane and just. Timur remained on this side of the frontier, despite his agonized passion for the genuine, despite the freedom he had won for himself from this planet full of simpletons and fools. He remained on this side because his ears were still filled with the buzzing of the helicopter, because, having made his way to the midsummer feast and heard the whistle of the Robber Nightingale, he had nonetheless made it his first task to consult with the lawyer; because too often his eternal restlessness conquered his better impulses.

The others returned naked and singing to the water, covered with droplets, as of dew, carrying bunches of plants and roots in their arms and bathed in moonlight. Then they crowded around the fire again and the flames lit up their gleaming bodies; which exuded lust. Then the dancing started and the couples abandoned themselves to concupiscence. Before him, like a vision, Timur saw three vessels for communing with eternity:

Marina, Dildor and Elena Filippovna. But Elena Filippovna was unattainable, she was absent, having departed by her strange death, which was like an unbreachable prison wall to Timur.

Back at the collective farm, terrified and trapped, people were thrashing about in the net that had ensnared them, seized by a grayness of uniforms and automatic pincers. The collective farm was going to the devil, it would be obliterated by the police raid. And perhaps this meant the end of the "C Business". At any rate, it was bound to suffer heavily from such an upheaval.

But this was unimportant to Timur. Behind him he could hear the cries and exclamations of those celebrating the festival echoing through the trees; in front the head stared back at him, motionless in the water. He stretched out his penis, like a wand of salvation, and she sank beneath the surface. And he felt that his gesture had been a gesture of mercy. Everything still lay before him. In this transitory world of accidence, the present was filling with the future.

19. Lord Have Mercy on Nocturnal Souls

He entered the water. Its black, immobile surface at once swallowed up his feet. As he moved forward, his erect penis shone like a sword, extending over the water's surface toward her head, as though gliding over the water, trying to reach her, expanding and lengthening to infinite dimensions like a rope transformed by an oriental fakir into a gigantic pillar, that bored into the skies in defiance of all the laws of physics.

This was exactly how it appeared to Elena Filippovna's eyes, magnified by the very light that had flared up in them, curving in an arc over the watery space that separated them, merging with Timur and becoming part of his young male body, a bridge spanning the gulf between him and her white body, throbbing with heat under the water, uniting in this way the magic instant that had brought her to life at the cemetery and the present moment, which had released her from the last few long days of non-existence, days that had succeeded one another in a meaningless tally from the moment when his magnificent male phallus had disappeared—leaving as the sole trace of its real presence a white slippery spot on a green leaf that ceased to quiver in the sun, until he himself had stepped out from the foliage in his everyday guise, with his natural gestures, recognizable but devoid of his power—until a moment ago, when he had announced his presence with a whistle in the darkness and appeared on the bank, a familiar figure in spite of the heavy armor of his ataman's and organizer's robes, whose captive he was so completely that he could not even show himself to her. But now it was quite different: he had thrown off the guise of his prosaic days and strode out, in the beauty of his male nakedness, to meet her, as on that day at the cemetery, as though transformed into a slippery penis composed of flesh and blood, of rays of sunlight and the green light of the foliage, and which now grew into something gigantic, monstrous, bearing down upon her and the entire pond, rising up out of the dark, and from the bank that she could no longer see, etched by moonlight in the darkness, filling the entire firmament, ghastly, inconceivably long, dully blue, dotted with delicate, rippling reflections from the phosphorescent, black water.

"That's not a penis, it's a . . . prick," Elena Filippovna thought once more, surprised at herself, and her body thrilled with a tremor of delight as she formulated her thought in this one word, the only possible word. At the same instant her body moved almost unconsciously under the water to meet the life-saving pole that was ready to raise her up out of the water. But from a distance the only thing visible was her head, gliding slowly over the surface with a somber gleam in its eyes, eyes that not only absorbed the light but radiated it as well, transforming everything that met their gaze. An instant later this bewitched actuality, this hyperbolic mirage that had arisen to assert the reality of the apparition, shrank, deflated, contracted into itself, thereby allowing the incarnation to come to genuine life through the contact of their two human bodies.

Timur stood before her, in close proximity, his erect penis unnaturally large and resting on the pedestal of his balls, which barely touched the water's glittering surface. He held it in his hand, and stroked it smoothly up and down, all the while coming nearer and nearer to her face, inexorable in his approach. Elena Filippovna's eyes were fixed upon it, absorbing it utterly, and she felt the mighty hulk of flesh with every cell, every nerve of her body; his penis, multiplied twofold, tenfold, seemed to be brushing against her, touching her, filling her everywhere all at once, below her belly, beneath her buttocks, between her legs, where she was hiding and protecting herself under the water. The sudden sensation almost made her lose consciousness as she gave herself up to him passively, risking partial submersion. A faint sigh escaped her lips.

Then Timur's other hand was extended towards her, disappeared under the water, found her shoulder, and grasped it firmly, supporting her and keeping her steady. She uttered a deeper sigh as Timur, continuing his masturbation, brought his monstrous penis (imperceptibly but inexorably) nearer to the white face with its motionless, burning eyes, floating on the water.

The huge, dilated organ, gleaming indigo-enamel in the moonlight, which vanished in the darkling foliage around them and slid over the impenetrable blackness of the pond's still waters, had reached the level of Elena Filippovna's mouth, the ambience of her breath, and basked in it, fed upon it, deriving new strength from it. It seemed to her that the glittering muzzle, roundish, wedge-shaped, impassive, with its single enigmatic orifice in the center, hung poised before her for an eternity, motionless, with barely perceptible, rhythmic contractions passing over its smooth, taut surface, which was so thin that it had taken on the color of the blood that pulsed within and, seemingly, would spurt out at any moment. She did not know what would happen next: did this muzzle with its enigmatic orifice contain a direful, secret threat, was it preparing to fire an arrow or a burst of deadly poison, or was it offering itself as some kind of loathsome delicacy?

Before she had managed to resolve her doubts, the muzzle approached and slapped against her lips. Timur pressed hard, his hand still holding the long, horny, quivering body of the beast with its mysterious muzzle. The controlled but insistent pressure forced Elena Filippovna to make way for it; seeking to protect herself, she was forced to admit it, to take it captive in the cavity of her mouth, to swallow and thereby destroy it. And then she clasped her hands about his tense, bending back, for she could feel her body tilting backwards as she knelt on the pond's slippery, slimy bottom.

His penis entered her throat, piercing her with a dull pain as though she had been stung from within. She recoiled. But at that instant her lips felt the tingling contact of a live, taut, pulsating body. Then she pressed her lips to it tightly, shaping them to fit it like a scabbard to a sword. His penis moved and quivered in her, giving her profound, atavistic satisfaction. Nothing like it had ever happened to Elena Filippovna before, no one had ever dared to perpetrate such an act upon her, let alone in such a crude, violent manner, and never before had she committed one with such profound carnal lust, such intense participation and such pleasure. This act had in the past meant no more to her than a game, a kiss, a cunning but always bashful tribute to the loved one. But now there were many reasons for it: perhaps the sensual passion that Timur had kindled in her even on the occasion of the first decisive appearance, the deafening siren's wail which had stirred her womanhood; or perhaps the exceptional dimensions of his penis, or her own conscious and unquestioning acceptance of that which he had silently promised her and which had become both possible and desirable; perhaps the magical, unbridled sensuality that had reigned on that evening, perhaps also the mysterious manner in which she had come to this place, or perhaps all of these things taken together—tonight for the first time Elena Filippovna took the male member into her mouth with an intense conscious pleasure, a relish and a voluptuousness, in which there mingled horror, loathing, and complicity, the desire to possess this rod, the need to dominate, and, overriding all of these, a total surrender of the self to the power of her own instincts and carnality.

Her mouth moved back and forth rhythmically, tugging and sucking, and she herself continued to clasp Timur's loins with both hands, resting her knees on the bottom of the pond. The penis filled her mouth, thick, hard, and infinitely lascivious, but she had already begun to control it, licking assiduously, absorbing a multitude of sensations, trying to take it as far as she could into her mouth and then direct it to the exit with her tongue, by touching its slippery, distended tip with the tip of her tongue. She could see its cylinder, shining with saliva, disappearing into the darkness of Timur's belly, which was thickly covered with hair, and there, beneath it, could discern the swaying mass of his balls. She could not contain herself and touched them with her hand, running her fingers over them, squeezing, caressing, and stroking those dangling, bulging appendages of brute maleness.

Under the black, impenetrable water her body was in the grip of a cold, still embrace, but Elena Filippovna felt her skin from head to toe tingling with myriad searing, stinging prickles, while between her legs, damp and more humid than the water, her sex burned soft and open. It was a sensation of painful, despairing emptiness which did not lessen but on the contrary, increased the desperate tension of that tiny, raised ridge that bloomed within the cavity. And only her certainty that what was happening was merely a prelude to what they were about to do for each other's total satisfaction transformed the preamble itself into a pleasurable act, freed of the torments of impatience.

Only then did she notice that they were not alone. Behind Timur's back and to the right gleamed naked bodies as they moved about the meadow in the darkness. There was the athletic figure of Gora, his sturdy legs planted apart, rocking to and fro, his waist gripped by Dunya's feet as she pressed her oval buttocks to his belly and swayed to the same rhythm. Her behind quivered in response to the movements and thrusts of Gora's rod, on which her female sexual organs were suspended. And although she supported herself with her hands on the ground, which helped the young buck to penetrate her with his flesh, and her to keep her balance, the woman had difficulty in keeping in one spot; she was continually moving forward like an obscene, human wheelbarrow, while Gora's strong hands supported her soft belly or squeezed her ample, pendulous breasts. Tarakanov and his sister Olga were sitting naked in each other's arms, paying no attention to the others, and enjoying the spectacle of Dildor's and Vadik's copulating. Olga's lean, withered body, enclosed in her weatherbeaten skin, was radiant with chastity and reminded one of the martyred Saint Sebastian on the canvases of old masters, his body pierced with arrows. But the arrows that tortured and pierced her were in reality rays of grace and charity, messengers of beauty and of the pure celebration of love emanating from the young couple. For Dildor had twined herself about Vadik's body and was quivering with delight in her acceptance of the man's love. She was enchanted by Vadik's beautiful voice that was tinged with melancholy, by his sincerity, his skill and his caresses that gave her such pleasure. And so she gave herself up to him, oblivious of all else.

It was only now that Elena Filippovna caught sight of them. But she could not, or did not want to see what was happening there on the dark bank, and what those figures were doing, arranged in small groups, three or four human bodies in each. She did not wish to know who they were. She was content to know that their activity was identical with hers and Timur's. But even if this had not been so, she would not have cared, because at that moment her entire world was concentrated in her body, as she knelt in the water, in Timur's penis and his powerful figure rearing above her and blocking the horizon of life around them from her view.

But if the raging lust of the surrounding couples served merely as a distant orchestra, harmonizing unobtrusively with her own music, the others, or some of them, were affected differently. Matsa, his small head bald as an egg, his mustache bristling, sat naked and gray as a lizard in the dark at the edge of the pond, between the powerful thighs of Marina. His face was turned towards Elena Filippovna and Timur, but his short-sighted eyes were unable to pierce the pale moonlight to see what they were doing. Marina, reclining on a flowery shawl spread out on the grass, her head resting on her upturned hand, was also looking at them and was describing to him what the couple was doing.

Marina's golden hair, neatly gathered into a braid as always, gleamed in the moonlight. Ripples of light ran off it over her magnificent bosom, her rounded shoulders, her belly, and the whole of her milk-white body.

"Now she's stopped sucking it and pulled it out of her mouth; she's got hold of his body with both hands, hanging on with all her weight. Look, she's above the water and her breasts are completely out. She's rubbing their pointed, upturned tips against his root; now she's put it between her two nipples and bent her head down and she's licking the tip. Timur has thrust his hands under her armpits to hold her up. Now she's freeing her own hands, taking her breasts and offering them to Timur like twin chalices, with a thick-stemmed fiery fern blossom throbbing between them . . ."

Marina's shining eyes left the couple in the pond for a moment and turned on Matsa. Her even teeth gleamed with an ardent smile: "Yarila's flower, which you helped us to find again, Gleb!"

Matsa was lying between her two fleshy pink thighs like an old tree-trunk, wizened with time and blackened by wind and rain. His clawlike, shrivelled hand lay upon Marina's hand, which rested limply on the crease between her pelvis and her leg, and gave it a slight squeeze of approval and gratitude. In his other hand he held his penis, sharp as a goat's, beneath which his extraordinarily large, bearded scrotum and balls looked distinctly incongruous. They matched his large ears and, according to popular belief, he ought to be a man of great energy who would certainly live to see a hundred.

"But Yarila's flower doesn't exist as such and never blooms, and that's why no one can find it," he sighed. "That flower really only blooms here," he added, laying his hand on Marina's pubis and her big cunt lips, "here it blooms as the flesh; here it decays like the rotting rose of life; weakened by pleasure, it decomposes and dies."

"No, it hasn't come to that yet," said Marina, taking Matsa by the wrist and pressing his hand more tightly to her sex.

"Look, Gleb, she's sucking him again. How beautiful she is! Her face of infinite purity, with that ox's penis in her mouth. And it rushes towards her, and her woman's hands reach out to welcome it, and they too are pure and beautiful, almost transparent and incorporeal next to that primitive beast, that blindly straining conglomeration of primordial cells. Her breasts are bobbing on the water, as beautiful as her hands, slightly elongated with upturned tips, more lascivious than mine. Oh, I would like to be kissing them too . . .!" Marina started at the touch of Matsa's finger on her clitoris. "Now I think he wants her to stand up, but she's resisting. He's stronger and is pulling her towards himself. His penis has slipped out of her mouth and she's trying to catch hold of it; she's moving it over her cheeks, her nose; she won't let go; she's rubbing it against her forehead, her ears, rubbing her whole face against it. Can't you see them, Gleb? He wants to lift her up, but it's just as if she's drunk; she refuses to give it back to him; she's trying to crush it to her chin, her throat; and he's all the while trying to lift her up by the armpits. Now she's had to let go of it. He's got her up, and his cock's wandering over her breasts, between them, over her belly, between her legs, along her cunt, Gleb . . . Now he's rammed it in and she's hanging on it . . . No, he's lifted her up in his arms and he's carrying her off. Do you see them, Gleb? He's taking her out of the water . . ."

Marina raised herself slightly so that she was almost in a sitting position, her gaze fixed on Timur as he disappeared in the direction of the dense foliage on the far side of the pond, with Elena Filippovna in his arms. She watched them until they had vanished and then rolled over onto the ground, spread her legs apart, pushed away Matsa's hand, and opened her large lips with her fingers as widely as she could, exposing the entire, obscene cavity of her vagina.

"Watch me," she said, her voice hoarse. "Watch what I do, feast your eyes on my indecency. I enjoy being watched. Your look exposes me, rapes me; it's worse than a penis, a rapist, more violent even than Timur's prick. Watch my fingers . . .

look at them working away . . . There, look at me spreading my legs even wider apart, I'll show you all of it . . . Come into it, come in with your cunning look . . . Try it yourself . . . Yes, I'm lewd! Try me, the unclean one, try me! I revel in masturbation; I abandon myself, give myself utterly; you can kill me if you want . . . Look at the voluptuous flower of my lubricity, my obscene flower, the flower of a pagan idol; look at my shameless cunt; see how it's started flowing, flowing, flowing . . . Your eyes are corrupting it; I know how repulsive it is now; you've done it; you're coming in to my soul . . . you're eating away my soul, Gleb, and I'm coming for you; I'm coming to you; can you feel it? Can you feel me coming? . . . Watch! Oh-oh, it's unbearable, I'm dying . . . You're stabbing me with your gaze! . . ."

Shaken by a convulsive spasm, Marina emitted a voluptuous moan, but her fingers still scrabbled frenziedly at the entrance to her distended vagina. Then she grew quiet and still, relaxing her muscles, and sank into a langourous stupor. And then Matsa, shuddering at the sacrifice that had been offered up before his eyes as an act of worship to him, Matsa, whose blood throbbed feverishly in his temples and pulsed hotly through his skull, like a brutal, destructive hammer, Matsa, trembling with arousal, positioned himself between Marina's legs, so that his face was in her perineum only a few centimeters away from her gaping, rapturous sex.

She lay staring fixedly into space, her head tossed back, her sumptuous body bathed by the moon's rays. But Matsa, sprawled between her legs, saw only one thing: the sex of a woman's young body, enlarged by proximity and swollen with voluptuousness, the softly curving contours of its flesh showing through the light brown hairs and emphasized by the play of shadows and glistening moisture. And once again Matsa was struck by the truth of an observation he had made in the past concerning the female sex organs; in his opinion they combined the properties of two contrasting spatial volumes, being at once a sheer void and a plastic construction, and achieving the maximum of possibilities in both of these: boundless receptivity as a void, and infinite flexibility of form as a plastic construction.

Tormenting his thin, goatish penis, erect and inflamed by his mental sensuality, Matsa looked his fill at those complex, elusive forms that clustered and disintegrated like bacteria under the microscope; he drank in the vision of that colony of cells, nourished, set in motion and molded by endless images, emotions, reactions, attractions, repulsions, and all the chemistry of the organism that bore them. He was trying to fathom the elusive secret of erotic arousal, which does not exist in the organ *per se*, but which occurs at certain magic moments due to the distillation of countless elements; and since neither sight nor delight could satisfy him, he resorted—as one not unfamiliar with the pleasures that forms and odors afford—to touch, to the most direct form of touch in the given instance, contact of sexual flesh with the flesh of the tongue.

His tongue brushed lightly against the lips of Marina's magnificent sex, methodically savoring to the full the sensations that accompanied this act. His tongue was so hot that these lips seemed cold to him for the first few moments. The cool of the night had already affected them in the moments following the woman's orgasm. He set about warming them with his breath and only after some seconds did he begin tenderly and unhurriedly licking her. But gradually his spinal cord, his quivering penis, his entire body—a bundle of twisted nerves—began sending powerful signals of their desire to make their pleasure a concrete one, to intensify the contact. This coincided with the desire of the woman, whose sex exuded voluptuousness: the two waves met and in uniting doubled their strength. Matsa progressed from gentle contact to lascivious tonguing, thrusting his tongue into the depths of the female organs, which were once more pulsating with pleasure.

Marina's body shuddered, as though pierced by this lovemaking, and she strained and pushed her pelvis forward, running her sex up against Matsa's mouth. He licked it a few times more with his wide, flat tongue, running it all the way along her vulva from the bottom upwards, then with the tip of his tongue he tickled her clitoris. His excitement reached white-heat: orgasm, long delayed by an effort of all his nerves, hammered in his temples, paralyzing all his limbs in spasms of tension. Only his tongue, skillful and intoxicated, continued gently prodding at Marina's clitoris; she had placed one hand on his head and was scratching away exquisitely at his skull until she drew blood. She moaned and uttered words enchantingly lewd, and her orgasm announced its imminence by the ever-increasing strength that flooded her massive legs, so smooth and feminine. They closed together little by little and Matsa's head thus became their captive. He began to have difficulty in breathing; his mouth was pressed up against Marina's vulva, his head was in the grip of Marina's nails, but his tongue still labored tirelessly, insensible to everything that did not concern the voluptuous frenzy mounting within him. She was threatening to take his whole body into herself, his entire energy; and his heart beat wildly, feeding on her blood, and his mind burst as he strove to impart to her all its wisdom. Marina's thighs were wrought of iron; like two claws they continued to close over their prey. Matsa felt himself being dragged down into a black abyss; with a desperate strength born of the instinct for self-preservation, he tried to prevent the fall, but at that same instant the sword of his orgasm struck from the head to the tip of his sexual organ, and with it a triumphant onrushing awareness of happiness, life and physical pleasure. And as he halted in his retreat, empty now of all desire, the woman, in the rapture of orgasm's inexorable onset, locked her pincer-legs together, crushing Matsa's tiny skull irrevocably between her strong round knees. He did not hear the dry, grating sound that appalled Marina, sending a thrill shooting through her and increasing her orgasm a hundredfold; he felt only a new wave of lust, melting, infinite, emanating from his brain, rippling through his body and passing out together with the life of the vital seed. His head fell limply on Marina's groin and grew stiffly cold.

Annihilated by her second, savage orgasm, Marina lapsed into oblivion. When she came around she felt something weighing heavily upon her belly and some sort of angular banging against her body and her legs. Suddenly she remembered Matsa and guessed that something irreparable had happened, and the blood froze in her veins from fear and despair. She wanted to scream, but as in a nightmare she could not utter a sound. Paralyzed with horror, she stared up at the sky, incapable of turning her head to look for friends.

Somewhere in the distance someone was strumming a guitar and quietly singing a song:

. . . While the earth still turns, while the light is still bright,
Lord, give to each man what he has not:
To the wise man a head, to the coward a horse,
To the happy man money . . .
And don't forget me . . .

The singer was Vadik; his narrowed eyes bore their usual expression and were fixed upon pretty Dildor, who was sitting opposite him. Yarila's flame was still in the blazing bonfire, casting a reddish flickering glow over Vadik's ashen face and lending the scar that disfigured his face a particularly grotesque, sinister aspect. But Dildor watched him with the rapturous eyes of one in love: for her he was a hero, because it was he she had fallen in love with as a woman; because it was she he was singing for now; and because his body was strong and silky, and she loved even his scar, because it contained the challenge and mystery of the knife.

. . . While the earth still turns, Lord, thine is the power!
Let the zealot for power hold sway to his heart's content,
Give respite to the generous, if only till eventide,
Give Cain repentance . . .
And don't forget me . . .

Vadik broke off his singing and grinned wryly—his eyes

were laughing, in contrast to the grimace that was intended for a smile. He asked Dildor:

"I take it you understand what I'm singing about, my little wild animal?" And when Dildor shook her curly head and laughed, he continued by way of a reply: "It's a song about Francois Villon, my princess. He was a great poet, but he lived among the thieves and bandits of Paris and Algiers, the rascal! Listen:

> . . . O Lord my God, greeneyed one!
> While the earth still turns and marvels herself at this,
> While she still has time and fire enough,
> Give to each man a little . . .
>   And don't forget me . . .

"There you are!" he ended and laid down his guitar. "And do you know, we've got our own Villon. Who is it? Why, Matsa, of course! The great writer-outlaw of our Russia of gendarmes and new Byrons." His eyes wandered over the meadow to the pond in search of Matsa, and suddenly he burst into sarcastic laughter: "There's he is, look, asleep between the legs of his wench, while his praises are being sung! Oh-oh-ho, Villon the unrepentant!"

"Well, well, we do have a smart, well-read chap for guitarist, not just a run-of-the-mill strummer!" Dunya teased him laughingly.

Despite her amorous games with Gora, she was in excellent form and quite fresh. Her womanly body, bursting with health, was plump and firm, and radiated the joy of living and a healthy animal sensuality. Her face was filled with laughter and her eyes sparkled so brightly that Tarakanov could not help suspecting that it must have been due to hashish. They had all smoked a bit, and it had done all of them good, including himself and his sister Olga. He was against mixing drugs with their business, but he was not at all averse to using them in private, especially on an evening like this. Dunya was high, but she was a veteran where hashish was concerned and no one doubted her energy or her ability to take it. He was more worried about Matsa, who was the same age as he, but far more battered by the winds of the times, ravaged by termites, by the terrible times Russia had lived through, by fear, disillusionment, persecution, intellectual and moral sufferings and, lastly, by the excesses to which he was always subjecting his flesh. These had continued right up to the present, and had so devastated him internally that he seemed only a shell, a husk, holding a brain and disproportionately active and avid nerves. To Matsa the use of hashish, Spanish fly or anything else that heightened his capacities, was pure routine, comparable, say, with reading a book early on a summer morning, with the contemplation of a painting, an erotic signal, or a piece of music, for the purposes of furthering his own development.

Following Vadik's and Dunya's gaze, Tarakanov glanced towards the meadow and satisfied himself again that Matsa was in the company of his trusted friend, Marina. He had been afraid that the old man would start indulging in God knows what strange perversions that he simply wasn't up to; but his apprehension had been unnecessary: she had calmed him down and there he was, blissfully asleep, like a child.

Tarakanov was silent, having set his mind at rest. Around the now smoldering bonfire of Ivan Kupala they perhaps noticed the absence of the all-wise shaman's comments on the revelry, which Matsa himself had wanted to be enriched with ancient ritual. But naturally no one thought of calling him over: the fire was dying down, emotions had been satisfied, and night was yielding to the rapidly approaching dawn of the June morning. Vadik was quietly plucking his guitar strings, while empty bottles gleamed around them.

Sunk in the inertia which usually follows intense stimulation, they were unaware that a few paces away from them, between Marina's soft legs, peaceful and childlike, there slept not the contemporary Russian Villon, but a gray, huddled corpse. Nobody knew that Marina, paralyzed and numb with shock, was trying to call them; in tranquil bliss, they were awaiting the return of Timur and Elena, which would be the signal to rise.

When Timur had borne Elena Filippovna out of the pond in his arms and disappeared with her into the dense undergrowth, all the others had been too preoccupied and in the thrall of their own voluptuousness to pay any attention to them.

And though later one or two of them, Dunya, for instance, lamented the fact that he was devoting all his time and his wonderful qualities as a thoroughbred stallion to the newcomer, deserting the company and depriving them of his presence, no one, least of all Dunya, at any point ventured to disturb the solitude that he had preferred to share with only one woman. However, Timur was no further from them than Marina and Matsa: he was simply hidden from their view by the dense shrubbery. But he could see them when he chose, and not only them, but Marina and Matsa too. And the lustful deed that he was performing with Elena Filippovna was accomplished in synchrony with acts of the other celebrants. He saw Marina's and Matsa's sympathetic and interested gaze as he bore the widow off, but he sensed that only when alone with him would she reveal what he imagined to exist within her and what, he believed, was her true nature.

He carried her in his arms, afraid that she might misunderstand his actions—she had stupidly shut her eyes and was trembling all over like a baby sparrow. He shivered with repugnance at the thought, but as if to relieve his doubts, Elena Filippovna stretched out her hand and grasped his penis, pulling the foreskin back, and began masturbating it with two fingers. Her eyes looked at him with a perverted cunning, and her half-open lips, with her tongue just visible between them, moved rhythmically and barely perceptibly, like a fish's mouth, arousing him to lascivious desire. He bent over and bit the nipple on her firm, white, conical breast. He did this with malicious intent, wanting to find out once and for all how far she was capable of revealing herself as a woman. She buried her face in his chest and gave him a love-bite that left a mark just under his collarbone. He found this pleasurable and disturbing.

When they reached a small clearing beyond the bushes, she leapt out of his arms without waiting to be set down. Now she stood with her back to him and he was able to admire her high, rounded bottom with its smooth, delicate buttocks and the narrow, but deep and well-defined cleft dividing them.

Confronted with the spectacle of this rounded bottom, so magnificently virgin, Timur could not contain himself and aimed his marbled, purple wedge at it. Again he thought that she would react inappropriately to his gesture. For if his temptation to possess her, her sex, in this way, from the rear, was a strong, almost irresistible one, she on her part could spoil everything by too premature consent. And not because she would thus underline how blindly she was following his desires, but because it could signify the absence in her of "escalation", degrees, changes in tension, of any inherent program of anticipation and response; and that would mean the absence of true sensuality. But here too Elena Filippovna remained true to the image he had formed of her: she turned quickly and this time he was really surprised when she said:

"No, let me go. Why have you been pursuing me ever since the day of my husband's funeral? What do you want of me?"

She said it as though what had happened at the cemetery had absolutely nothing to do with her, as though his exhibitionism there had not brought her to an orgasm, as though she had not sucked his cock and thrilled with lust only a few moments earlier, as though that libidinous kitten who had lain in his arms were not she. She was serious and restrained, like a party representative faced with the dissipation of the laboring masses.

"Bitch," Timur fumed, "who asked you to come? As if I asked you to lick my prick, crawling in the muck!"

Elena Filippovna did not turn a hair. Utterly aloof and indifferent, she replied:

"I was invited here by people who have nothing in common with you"—resolutely tossing her head as she uttered the last words—"I am amazed at the tone, the language you use to address a woman who is a stranger to you and whose social standing is very far above yours."

Timur would have liked to think that she was joking, or had gone out of her mind, but he was only too familiar with the guise of respectability that the finest representatives of Soviet society affect and that is their distinguishing mark, not to mention the possibility that she believed what she was saying. He had only to recall what her late husband had been like, and her own behaviour when he had stopped her outside her house . . .

The memory of this drove him into a rage. She must be a half-wit; well, so much the worse for her! . . .

Gripping her by the shoulder, he jerked her towards him and gave her a hard slap on the behind, then another, and another: he continued to beat her until her buttocks were red. Now and then his blows fell on her head, but not too hard, since he hadn't the slightest desire to break her neck. Eventually he noticed that she had burst into a fit of convulsive weeping and was cringing submissively. He wanted to stop, but the vacuum she had created in his soul after so many promises and after the inconceivable excitement he had experienced a few moments ago, made him go on automatically raining down needless blows. But here again he underestimated her. In all probability, Elena Filippovna had felt the need to be punished, to have destroyed in her everything that she no longer wanted to be, because she hurled herself to the ground, threw her arms around his feet and began frantically kissing his toes and plaintively whimpering: "No, no, don't you see, you're my master; how can you believe what I said; I've never made love to anyone before as I have to you; I've known real pleasure for the first time with you, for you, thinking about you. Touch me with your foot, can you feel me?" And sobbing, she pushed Timur's big toe into her vagina, now grown soft and moist.

He thrust his hand into her beautiful, softly waving chestnut hair, and in touching that mass of silken strands his anger spent itself, while Elena Filippovna continued feverishly to satisfy herself by means of his toes, until the tremors and sobs of desperate voluptuousness brought her to a passionate climax, and the height of her pleasure purged her of the vile poison that the counselors and the guardians of public morality had injected into her soul.

Only now, cleansed and liberated, was her cunt fit to receive the legendary, Herculean prick of Timur. At a single thrust he penetrated her, bursting with boundless fury into her vagina, tearing its walls, battering at her womb, and convulsing her whole body. Twining her tender, white arms about him, she pressed her breasts, swelling with the aching desire in their nipples, to his muscular chest, and abandoned herself to the powerful, rhythmic movements of his penis, spreading her legs wide apart, waving her small, prettily curving feet in the air in an effort to find a foothold on his back, and knotting herself around his loins. She gritted her teeth at the intense pain and the searing lust that the blows of Timur's hammer aroused in her. But in the depths of her soul she blessed, yes, blessed the sacred violence which had resurrected her and revealed the way to a salvation that she had been waiting for, without knowing it, since her early youth, discovering it for herself only at the moment of her husband's burial. But on that day the light of salvation had merely flickered momentarily before her eyes like a mirage, horrifying and tempting her; and then, finally, had wrenched her away from the rusty anchor of her past.

But to make her cast off, Timur had been forced to go on board; where she slapped the face of the bold pirate who had insulted her and dared to gaze upon the princess and annihilate all her retinue of puppets, those spurious guardians that watched over her safety and her false well-being. And only then, when the blond fugitive was her crew, did the unfettered winds of life fill her white sails and carry her off to unknown shores. And then off she went, sailing, sailing, sailing . . .

. . . to the place where Timur was now fucking her with rapacious desire, quickening his rhythmic, unceasing movements, straining with all his muscles in the act of total possession, anticipating the oncoming wave of orgasm that was about to break over him, crushing all previous waves of sensation that had foamed delightfully and pleasurably to meet him. But now the powerful wave was overtaking him from behind, breaking over his head and sucking him into its vortex. His seed spurted inside her, so utterly satisfying the whole of his being that he felt an absolute joy throughout his entire body, which pressed hard against her body and fused with it in a single spasm of all their muscles. Their skin stuck together and burned with the friction of their convulsive embrace. Their bellies were like two drums, tuned and filled with undying resonance. Her vagina, filled to the utmost with his penis, stifled it, breathed in unison with his contractions, devoured his seed as it continued its spurting, contracted in its turn and smothered it in the hot stream of her orgasm.

Then, after an eternity had passed, they stirred and rose to their feet. She stood, arching her supple, molded, provocative back, enriched that night with an inexplicable, but intensely sensual meaning, while he stood even more stalwart than before, reminding her more keenly of a young king relaxing at play, when his scepter, no longer threateningly raised, hangs loosely at rest like a huge proboscis, swollen, voluptuous, filled with blood and life, but perfectly ready to respond to any stimulation.

The princess who had come to distant India set about playing with this proboscis, and the proboscis played with her, responding to her caress, swelling with joy in her hands, and prodding blindly at her thighs and belly. Seized with curiosity, it slipped out of her hands and into the soft thicket between her legs. It was growing heavier and harder all the time, and the princess opened her legs and played, rubbing her underside with it, and her lips that burned in the thicket, and this gave her an exquisite pleasure which again stirred her to arousal.

Then she leapt at Timur and threw her arms around his neck, and clung to him; Timur guided his penis into her and clasped her buttocks with his hands, and, supporting her in this position, shuttled her back and forth on his rod, submerged in her up to the hilt, to their mutual satisfaction and pleasure.

Standing with his legs firmly planted on the ground, he told her what a beautiful pussy she had, and how he liked it, and aroused her even more strongly by tickling her tiny back passage with his finger. He glanced over past the bushes and around the meadow; his gaze flitted over the familiar figures glowing in the firelight, and rivetted on a spot to his left, which had attracted him by its cold radiance, hazy and intermittent in the feeble light of dawn. Timur's eyes searched and strained to make out that spot in the motionless heap that was Marina's and Matsa's bodies; his look became tinged with suspicion and kept returning to the spot, puzzled. And suddenly the lightning, harrowing realization of death flashed through his brain, a certainty that Matsa was dead, that Matsa was no more, that there was only the first handful of bones for their cemetery.

His throat was gripped with anguish, and he ejaculated, and a sensation of pure, keen joy swept over him. He threw Elena Filippovna to the ground immediately, was over the bush at one leap and found himself standing over Marina, between whose legs lay the withered, huddled corpse. Matsa's face was turned aside, his eyes were shut and a clot of congealed blood hung from the tip of his nose. His emaciated arms lay stretched over his stomach, and one of his palms was closed around his sharp, hard penis, with a single drop of dried semen on its tip.

All those seated around the fire rose at the sudden appearance of Timur. Timur beckoned them over and, bending over Marina, grasped her under the arms and dragged her away from the corpse. Marina stared stupidly with wide-open eyes. She was lisping inarticulately, and her body was burning hot. The first to reach her were Vadik, Dunya and Dildor, but the two quickly blocked the girl's view as she asked in a scared voice: "What's the matter with them? Are they ill?" Olga Borisovna, who had just appeared with Tarakanov, answered her affirmatively, and took her abruptly away. Dunya could not restrain her tears, but it was she who cleaned Matsa's corpse as best she could. She was aided by Timur, while the others saw to Marina.

It was decided that Timur and Vadik should stay with the dead man until the others had left, and then take him to his underground den in Moscow. They decided to let Elena Filippovna stay. Marina was driven away in her car, accompanied by Olga Borisovna, with Gora at the wheel. They were followed by Tarakanov in his vintage Moskvich, taking Dunya and Dildor. The last to leave were Timur, Vadik and Elena Filippovna with their sad cargo. They were faced with the difficult and dangerous task of driving across Moscow with the dead Matsa, who had to be smuggled into his dwelling in the very center of Moscow, where he could be safely left for a time, without anyone noticing that he was dead.

But something unexpected lay in store for them on the way. When Dunya, Dildor and Tarakanov were quite near the lawyer's dacha, where the road went through a birch grove, just by the final turn-off to the dacha, five thugs appeared, obviously the worse for drink, blocked their way and forced them to halt the car. The thugs surrounded the vehicle and one of them opened the driver's door and yelled: "Out you get, buddy!" He grabbed Tarakanov's sleeve and, as soon as Tarakanov had climbed out of the car, hit him over the head with something hard. The lawyer fell to the road without a sound. Meanwhile two of the others had dragged Dunya out of the car. Dildor, frightened to death, slipped off the back seat and down onto the floor of the car. Fortunately the bandits did not notice her, for while two of them were going through the lawyer's pockets and a third kept his eyes on the road, the ones that were dealing with Dunya had already begun pawing her, happily.

"What a swindle!" snarled one of them, evidently the ringleader, tossing aside a wallet after pulling out two or three one-hundred ruble notes. "Aha, this little ring here isn't bad, that's worth having," he exclaimed, snatching it off the lawyer's finger.

"There's a watch too," said the one standing beside him.

"A watch—huh, trash. Ah, but these cuff-links—now there's a find! OK, that's enough, boys. And what's got into you? Don't worry, I'll give it to you now," he said, turning to Dunya, who was beating off her assailants as best she could. "What's that gibberish you're yelling?"

And indeed, disguised as pitiful or indignant screams, Dunya was trying to convey to Dildor in Azerbaidzhani that she must not come out of her hiding-place.

The lawyer still lay insensible, and the two who had dealt with him left him in that state and joined the ones who were busy with Dunya.

"Not bad," pronounced the ringleader. And it was not clear if he was referring to what they had taken from Dunya and were now showing him, or to her obvious charms, which showed through her disarranged clothes. Disheveled, her dress torn, her cheeks burning from their blows and her eyes aflame with anger, she was a choice piece, a tasty bit of female flesh that promised excellent sport. It would be pure idiocy not to make the most of this. The two who had been robbing her were already considerably excited and tried not so much to beat her or hold her down as to undress and feel her. Dunya's dress was torn in front and one of her breasts hung out, huge and bare, and jiggled at every jerk, every blow they administered. Very soon Dunya realized that for the other three too, this breast and the whole of her body were the only goods they thought worth taking. Had it not been for her fury and her anxiety over the fate of Dildor and Valery Borisovich, this would not have been a problem to her. She had had time enough to judge that they were the sort who were satisfied with grabbing a few bills and having a bit of fun with a woman besides. Their own violence seemed somehow impressive to them, and they simply could not see how stupid and futile it all was. But precisely because they were novices, strong resistance could make them dangerous; they might lose their heads with rage. They were totally unaware that in a secret pocket on the sleeve of her torn, ragged dress, right in the cuff, she carried a murderous weapon: a ballpoint pen, much more compact than a pistol. An old gift, perhaps the only thing she had kept from Beria's times. But to use it now would be utterly ridiculous, at least not until . . . Resisting only as much as would make them believe in her panic-stricken terror, and in the genuineness of her resistance, she let herself be dragged by them into the bushes on the fringes of the forest that stretched on both sides of the road. Once again she shouted a few resolute words which they took for the inarticulate curses of a woman maddened with horror. But in reality, the words were a precise, laconic instruction to Dildor in Azerbaidzhani, of which Dunya had a very approximate knowledge but one quite adequate for the situation: "Run home and warn Olga!"

Already calmed by Dunya's first warning, Dildor, curled up into a ball between the car seats like a sly little fox-cub, was watching everything that happened outside through the chink of the slightly open door. When she saw Dunya disappearing towards the forest, driven on by the five men punching her and smacking their lips as they uttered choice oaths, she did not feel afraid for her. As soon as they had vanished into the darkness of the trees, Dildor slipped out of the car on the other side, scurried over to Tarakanov, her head bent low, and whispered: "Uncle, uncle, they've gone, get up quickly!" Tarakanov heard her, but was still only half-conscious and incapable of replying. Then Dildor ran off.

"So you keep your cunt for rich men only, do you, madame? We'll show you, you bitch, just what our friend means! You've got no idea what real life is, with all those spineless insects of yours!"

He was more words than deeds. That was immediately obvious, because he fell violently upon her, grasping her breast and crushing it painfully, but there was not the slightest sensuality in his grip, merely a frustrated desire for power. Meanwhile the others were unbuttoning their trousers and pulling out their penises—appendages, like noses, common to all men, and differing from one another almost like noses, each with its hallmark of individuality. But a row of noses is nothing special compared with an array of penises, which is a far more vital and real assemblage, and Dunya was excited and felt herself overcome. She looked at the boys, and the only thing that worried her was that they might notice that her gaze expressed not terror but desire. But they did not look at her face; together they ripped off her remaining garments, driven by an instinctive desire to destroy that which was seductive and exciting about her, that which they were powerless to withstand, which had to be destroyed, like timid children in need of a mother's love and her blessed sustenance. And as she pretended to resist this infantile violence, Dunya laughed at them and loved them. Ah, the sight of these erect penises protruding from their trousers, more manly and knowing than their unfortunate owners, so alive and real.

She felt like challenging them:

"Come on then, let's have it, boys! Fuck all you can: think you're going to teach me anything new!" As novices at the game, they could not fail to feel her superiority precisely where they had hoped to shame and humiliate her. Blindly they fell upon her. She was already down on the ground, stark naked. She knew that she must not say or do anything, otherwise they would feel robbed of their illusion of power and possession, that is, of everything they hoped to gain from her. She knew perfectly well that she was risking nothing, since their imaginations went no further than the ordinary act which they were inflicting one after the other on her body. Their impression of themselves as conquerors, immune from punishment, had given them strength, and therefore they believed in the pleasure that it was possible to get from a woman. Thinking themselves terrifying rapists, they were in effect merely performing Komsomol gymnastics. But that very act, and the presence of ten balls and five male bodies occupying themselves with her—although quite inanely—afforded Dunya a satisfaction which she had not experienced for a long time and which—and perhaps this explained why it came as such a novelty and a thrill

—she had never ever experienced in such an idiotic manner. Oh, what bliss to feel them pushing, thrusting forward, filling her, entirely mechanical and non-existent as men, purely tools of satisfaction that were in her power.

Somewhere deep down inside Dunya had lurked the desire, or rather the need, for a collective male assault; it was something she had long wished to experience. And she came once, twice, many times, indifferent to their voices, as brazen as a whore, incredibly aroused by the service that they were rendering her, thereby making her mistress of a situation in which she experienced real pleasure, while they, miserable toilers, labored in the name of their prestige, in order to assert their faith in themselves or at best in their own hormones. They labored, but under an illusion.

And in accordance with this logic, having thus relieved their feelings, they suddenly abandoned her and drew back, guilty and cowardly. But just at that moment, while her battered body still lay on the ground, overflowing with their vile semen, they were noisily surrounded by a patrol of wonder boys, methodically carrying out their duties according to regulations stipulated by the normal law of the land.

While driving along the highway, an armed police patrol had noticed a *Moskvich* abandoned by the roadside. It was empty, and while they were investigating it there came from the nearby wood the sound of voices and noise. Following the voices, the patrol came upon the group and was confronted with an unseemly spectacle: five men surrounding a naked woman, who lay sprawled on the ground and evidently was not objecting. The crime was still in progress and immediate arrest was called for, especially as the woman was shouting that they had attacked and raped her. Unable to make out what was going on, the policemen arrested all of them, but not without having to call out several times "Stop!" and even to threaten two of the thugs, who were attempting to make a getaway, with their weapons. Dunya, naturally, offered no resistance, playing the innocent victim, but she too was taken away for an inquiry into the facts. And unfortunately she was destined to welcome the new day in the police station, where she sat in melancholy meditation, her brain teeming with speculation as to what the fates had in store for herself and her friends.

As for Tarakanov, he recovered consciousness almost immediately after Dildor's escape, but in the darkness he was unable to find his spectacles, without which he could not drive the car. He had to abandon the vehicle and go on foot, struggling not to lose his way and following a narrow path which led through the trees to his dacha, no further than half a kilometer away.

There he found Dildor curled up fast asleep on the divan in the sitting room, worn out by all the events and hazards of the night. The girl was alone. Olga must have had to stay on and look after Marina.

What could he do for Dunya? He had to get in touch with Timur at once. But where should he start looking? Was he already in Matsa's cellar, or had he, possibly, gone off on his own business, his joyless mission accomplished? He could try ringing him. And he must not fail to telephone Olga at Marina's place. Maybe Marina would be in no condition to speak to her uncle, as arranged, and persuade him to take charge of the operation which the security organs had staged regarding the collective farm? And then he had to get Frolov moving too. How had the security group come to the collective farm? What were they after that was so special that they had had to resort to a raid on that scale? No, it was impossible! It couldn't mean the end! And poor Matsa's death . . . And this assault . . . What had happened to Dunya? Yes, the best thing was surely to go back and collect the abandoned car, to master the weariness that overpowered him to such a degree that he could barely keep his feet. And his head was splitting . . . But first, he had to find his spare pair of spectacles.

20. Epilogue: The Smile of the Prophets

On that autumn evening the crowded auditorium of the Bolshoi Theater was a blaze of sparkling lights. There was to be a performance of *Boris Godunov*, Pushkin's many-sided tragedy in which the Russian people and its constant yet ever-changing fate have for more than a century been presented with the inspired, refreshing vitality and ambiguous exactitude of genuine art. It was a real gala evening, as the presence of high-ranking guests was expected and the theater had been notified in advance.

As always, music lovers mingled with the crowd of spectators for whom the evening was a social occasion, purely a matter of prestige. There were those too, who moved in the highest circles and so had been informed that top party and government leaders would be in the government box on that evening, and had therefore taken advantage of their rare privilege as holders of tickets for seats reserved for important persons, foreigners and other illustrious citizens.

Resting upon the red velvet of one of the boxes, under the many-faceted light of the chandeliers, Olga Borisovna's slim, dry hand was glittering with the jeweled rings which adorned it. Her long, Byzantine face was motionless, frozen in an expression of austere calm. The expression was a typical one for her, and now her present surroundings required it (at least, until the lights dimmed). With her in the box, resplendent in the festive light that flooded the entire auditorium around them, sat her brother, Valery Borisovich Tarakanov, in his pince-nez; clean-shaven, with his hair combed down more neatly than usual. Also there were Marina Kerzhentseva, her shock of golden hair gathered into a braid and plaited with a black velvet ribbon, and Dunya, up from the Caucasus, smiling as gaily as ever; her ample breasts in a loose green-silk decollete attracted all the light and many stares. Dunya's face was turned upwards and she was saying something to Timur, standing at her right, elegant and polished, somehow reminiscent of Tolstoy's Dolokhov, reborn in Soviet times, attired in a dark suit that emphasized his mocking face with its frame of light brown curls. Next to Timur at the back of the box, silent and composed, sat the irresistible Elena Filippovna.

Looking at his friends, handsome, confident and even refined, entirely in harmony with the society that filled the theater, Tarakanov pronounced, with a contented, sarcastic smile: "The birthmarks of the old society."

The lights dimmed and the powerful notes of Mussorgsky's music burst upon the auditorium, drowning the hum of people, rising into the drapery of heavy velvet, filling every void, every nook and cranny, flowing through the feet of the public and soaring up to the sonorous ceiling in pillars of sound.

The stage was again peopled with the heroes of the Russian drama: Autocrat, Pretender, Boyars, Jesuits, the People—and the mouthpiece of its truth, the Fool—Vagrants, Witch, Chronicler and the palace guards. And once again that powerful Russian singing expressed with superb subtlety the essence of our great and desperate history.

The scenes at the Novodevichy monastery, where the people had been driven, alternated in rapid succession with those on the Kremlin square, where, at the beginning of the first act, the aged chronicler Pimen broods deeply on the fortunes of Russia. Tarakanov and his friends were struck by the odd resemblance of the person singing the role of Pimen to Matsa, who was not there with them today and would never more be beside them.

Meditating on this resemblance, Tarakanov completely lost the thread of the opera and instead of the words of the libretto, the words of Pushkin's own text, which had been Mussorgsky's inspiration, kept coming to mind. It had been Matsa himself who had once pointed out to him that, despite its powerful effect, the opera, even in the version performed today at the Bolshoi, has in a certain sense lost the significance and truthfulness present in the lines of Pushkin's original drama.

And so, remembering his late friend, and how he loved to read the original text in the theater, he began, unconsciously at first, repeating after the distant voice, the words which came into his head. And later, at the end of the first act, he turned to his companions in the box and recited, this time aloud, and in a clear voice:

. . . Is there any safety
In our poor life? Each day disgrace awaits us,
The dungeon or Siberia, fetters or a cowl,
And then in some deaf nook a starving death,
Or else the halter. Where are the most renowned
Of all our houses . . . Imprisoned, tortured,
In exile. Do but wait and a like fate
Will soon be thine. Think on it! Here at home,
Just as in Lithuania, we're beset
By treacherous slaves—and tongues are ever ready
For base betrayal; thieves bribed by the state . . .

At this point he broke off and smiled his usual ironic smile:

"Every detail of the diagnosis is correct! It's more than a hundred years now since Pushkin formulated it, and it was so truthful that the patient still refuses to listen to it today. It's from the scene in Shuisky's house which isn't in the opera at all."

And, continuing his sarcastic outburst, he went on declaiming:

. . . We're at the mercy of the first retainer
Whom we may have a mind to punish.
And now he's set to quash St. George's Day—
We are no longer lords of our own lands.

Don't dare dismiss an idler! Willy-nilly
You'll give him food! Don't dare coax into service
A laborer or you will find yourself
In the court's clutches . . .

"Oh," said Dunya, "it certainly isn't as bad as that! We still haven't gone that far, thanks to Frolov and company. I'm sick of all these people, and you know it perfectly well, but since we have to have protection . . . You foresaw everything, Valery Borisovich, you predicted everything right from the start. When I think what happened to me! I might still be stuck in a cell to this day, and God knows what the consequences might have been for us all! And, like a fool, I got mixed up with that major too, silly woman that I am! Timur knows," she added, observing that her last remark had not been understood, "but what can I do, it's stronger than I am: I never did speak the same language as the Black Hundreds, perhaps because I belong to the generation of people who believed in Communism . . ."

"But it wasn't Frolov who hastened to intervene on the night of the round-up at the collective farm!" Marina could not refrain from reminiscing. "It was my uncle who did it, Dunya; your memory is like a sieve! He had the entire collective farm operation halted and exposed to ridicule. The raid was staged by the over-zealous Nedobora, who imagines he sees spies everywhere. And he's been demoted, you know, and his colleagues too. They've already been moved far away from Moscow. I think they're giving their orders somewhere in the camps. Our new-style agencies don't tolerate people who make a fuss over nothing. Nobody now relishes playing the role of the mountain that gives birth to a mouse."

The curtain rose. The second act began. When it reached the dialogue between Boris and Shuisky, the tenor declaimed the words of Pushkin, included unaltered in the opera:

Certainly, my lord, your state is mighty, you
With mercy, care for others, and largesse
Have stirred a filial love in your slaves' hearts . . .

But here Tarakanov took over, as soon as the libretto departed from Pushkin's text:

> But you yourself know the insensate mob
> Is fickle, mutinous and superstitious;
> Easily given over to vain hopes,
> Obedient to momentary impulse,
> Deaf and indifferent to the real truth.
> But that same mob feedeth itself on fables;
> Shameless audacity doth enrapture it . . .

"That's for Timur!" Dunya interjected, not having the slightest respect for the glorious traditions of Russian opera, since she preferred the songs of the underworld.

As though accidentally, she moved slightly and leaned her shoulder against Timur's penis, for he was still standing at her back; and although it was at rest, it bulged under the cloth of his narrow trousers: it could be discerned despite the dark color of the cloth.

"It's not a question of boldness," Tarakanov declared, "I believe it's already quite clear to everyone that our enterprise has passed the test with flying colors and earned a well-deserved reputation. As you know, our activities are developing splendidly; we've nothing to complain about, we're making a fair profit, even if we have to take it easy for the moment with the more ambitious project for the cemetery." Then, turning to Dunya, he added: "Sweetie, how may times do I have to tell you that you shouldn't mix personal feelings and business? Frolov and his company are already has-beens. Nevertheless, they still have considerable influence. And anyway, what harm does it do to be protected by them? New people in the government, its most progressive representatives, are already well on the way toward viewing activities like ours from a not entirely negative angle. No doubt they know a thing or two, if only the little that might have leaked out from Marina's uncle or, say, Frolov himself, and still . . ."

He broke off in mid-sentence, seeing that Timur, who had

taken his seat beside Elena Filippovna, had let the tip of his penis protrude from his fly, and that her hand was already reaching to pluck the voracious mushroom that had sprouted before her very eyes.

"Don't play with fire, Timur," Tarakanov rebuked him, and, indicating the government box, added: "Today they are here and their presence is a comfort to us. Thousands of eyes are turned on them . . . and on us."

"It's all Marina's fault, it was her words: 'I love thee, thou art my treasure, thou art my master,' " Timur replied in a bantering tone, punning with a double-entendre.

But he closed his fly, and music was again the sole mistress of their box. They were all silent, and Tarakanov, annoyed at Timur's inappropriate behaviour, ceased to declaim the bitter lines from the tragedy that are omitted from the opera's libretto.

It was only midway through the fourth act that he could no longer restrain himself and supplemented the text of the dying tsar's will with the cynical advice on how to govern a people, which the poet puts into the tsar's mouth:

> Change not the flow of things. Wont is the soul
> Of states. Of late I have been forced to reinstate
> Bans, executions—these thou canst rescind;
> And they will bless thee as they blessed thy uncle,
> When he obtained the throne of the Terrible.
> As time goes on, but only bit by bit,
> Tighten the reins of government again.
> Relax them now, but keep them in your hands . . .

"You get the point! It's the whole program, from Stalin to the present day. The time has come when all these asses and buffalos need us, the busy beavers, the vixen and the cats, and the Robber Nightingales. Sheepdogs alone are no longer enough for them, so they've called in the Pied Piper of Hamelin to help. They'll stop the invasion of rats, well, and then what?

Isn't it the teaching of Boris that they follow in this country? What has Marx to do with it!"

. . . Be gracious,
Accessible to foreigners, accept
Their service trustfully. Preserve with strictness
The Church's discipline. Be taciturn;
The royal voice must never lose itself
Upon the air in emptiness, but like
A sacred bell, must sound but to announce
Some great disaster or great festival . . .

"Yes indeed, a program!" Tarakanov repeated under his breath; he loved looking for eternal truths of prophecy in famous works and associating them with phenomena of the present day. "A fine program," muttered Timur through clenched teeth. "I know better than you what young people live by nowadays. Believe it or not, fine words no longer have any effect on them, and it's not so easy to frighten them either. Everything's getting into a mess again!"

Hark! 'Tis the knell of death!

sang Boris in mortal agony, and then came his last cry, like a moan:

Wait yet a while; I still am Tsar, I still am Tsar . . .

"I've had enough of this everlasting patience!" Timur again muttered through his teeth.

He was answered by the chorus of Vagrants at Kromy:

. . . Arise!
Like a giant roused from slumber,
Valiant courage stalks abroad,
Burns with boldness of zeal, burns the Cossack blood.
Ever mounting upwards, ever spreading outwards
Russia's power has risen, like a youthful giant
Risen, exulting in his strength!
Ho! thou power of glory, thou power of freedom,

Strengthen thou our manhood, young courageous manhood!
Make them forceful, audacious, with valor to disport them,
With booty to content them, with valor to disport them,
Give them strength! . . .

"That's it," came Timur's voice.

Along the rows there passed that barely perceptible thrill which in a theater is indicative of the audience's emotional participation. The performance was reaching its close. The final chorus:

Like a giant roused from slumber,
Valiant courage stalks abroad.
Ever mounting upwards, ever spreading outwards,
Ho! thou power of glory, thou power of freedom!
Minions of Boris wander prowling,
Tormenting innocent people.
Torturing, tearing, strangling and racking
Innocent people . . .

The "insensate, fickle mob" was already hastening to greet the new pretender. In the final scene the Fool, sitting on a rock, urged Russia to lament . . .

Curtain. The lights came on, flooding the theater with bright daylight, sweeping from the stage the magical reality of art. The stage was now only an unobtrusive rectangle, but one filled with mysterious meaning, in that vast, unambiguous auditorium of glittering gold and lamps: a forest of appreciative hands and faces, curious, trustful, enthusiastic or timorous, now and then stern, turned towards the government box. Here the supreme leaders were on their feet, applauding, set in a sumptuous frame —*ancien regime* caryatids, supporting a magnificent gilded frieze which bore the emblem of the Soviet Union.

Was it by chance that those standing in the front row had fixed their gaze upon the box containing the chief representatives of the "C Business"? Or that the rest, following their glance, turned themselves to gaze in that direction? Tarakanov preferred to believe that it was not chance, and he had his own reasons for doing so. He bowed slightly and smiled, continuing to applaud. It seemed to him that he could just make out Frolov in the government box, standing behind the shoulders of the chief bigwigs. Then Tarakanov picked up his opera-glasses and this time was able clearly to distinguish Frolov's imposing figure. The latter glanced in his direction and, smiling, made some remark to the two men standing in front of him. They nodded contentedly, peering at the box holding Tarakanov and his friends.

"What a triumph!" Dunya laughed, pinching Timur. "Tarred with the same brush, eh, Timur?" and she winked at him, in an effort to underline by this audacious remark her profound contempt for the showy glitter and respectability which united all the applauders.

But Timur continued stubbornly gazing at the lowered curtain. It seemed to him that there, in gigantic print, he could see the words with which Pushkin, unlike the opera's librettist, had ended his tragedy, in capital letters:

"THE PEOPLE ARE SILENT."